A NEW SOLAMNIA

A unique leader works to forge his
nation into a powerful empire.

A new nation emerges from the
ashes of division and war.

A man who would be emperor faces the
gravest threat in his long and violent life.

He is a knight, a lord, a dictator . . . ruthless and
driven, with ambitions that trample the lives of all
who aid him. Revolutionary technology has made
him a master of war. He possesses the wife that
he needs, even as the woman he desires eludes his
grasp. But as an old enemy, mightier than ever,
rises to challenge him, new dangers emerge.

THE RISE OF SOLAMNIA

Lord of the Rose

The Crown and the Sword

The Measure and the Truth
(January 2007)

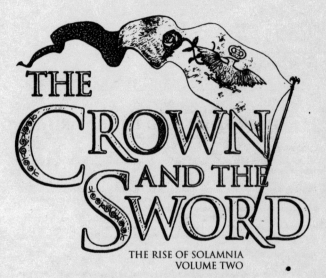

THE CROWN AND THE SWORD

THE RISE OF SOLAMNIA
VOLUME TWO

DOUGLAS NILES

The Rise of Solamnia, Volume Two

THE CROWN AND THE SWORD

©2006 Wizards of the Coast, Inc.

Cover art by J. P. Targete
First Printing: June 2006
Library of Congress Catalog Card Number: 2004116880

9 8 7 6 5 4 3 2

ISBN-10: 0-7869-3788-2
ISBN-13: 978-0-7869-3788-2
620-96885740-001-EN

U.S., CANADA,   EUROPEAN HEADQUARTERS
ASIA, PACIFIC, & LATIN AMERICA   Hasbro UK Ltd
Wizards of the Coast, Inc.   Caswell Way
P.O. Box 707   Newport, Gwent NP9 0YH
Renton, WA 98057-0707   GREAT BRITAIN
+1-800-324-6496   Save this address for your records.

Visit our web site at www.wizards.com

TO JULIETTE AND BENEDICT WEBER

CHAPTER ONE

‹-◦⊙›-◦⊙›-◦⊙❀◦⊙›-◦⊙›-◦⊙❀◦⊙›-◦⊙›-◦⊙❀◦⊙›-◦⊙›-◦⊙›-◦⊙›

THE LORD MARSHAL

‹-◦⊙›-◦⊙›-◦⊙❀◦⊙›-◦⊙›-◦⊙❀◦⊙›-◦⊙›-◦⊙❀◦⊙›-◦⊙›-◦⊙›-◦⊙›

A column of dust marked the progress of two dozen horse-men across the flat expanse of the central Vingaard Plain. They rode in a neat file of pairs, and though the men and horses were coated with a layer of grit indicating a long, hard ride, they maintained ranks with military precision. The mounts were large, long legged, and nimble, and they crossed the miles with an easy canter. Even now, as they moved into a region where the ground rose and fell, their gait remained steady, their course as true and straight as the flight of an arrow.

At the head of the column rode a single man, wearing the garb of a knight with the unusual feature that his breastplate was not adorned with any symbol—as if he belonged to none of the orders, not to the Crown, the Sword, or the Rose. His shoulders and back were draped with a woolen cape that covered the back of his saddle and flapped loosely. His horse was a nondescript roan mare, a little sloppy of gait, though her eyes flashed with intelligence.

"We approach the Narrows, Lord Marshal," commented a rider, spurring his mount as he came up on the left of the man.

The rider wore the epaulets of a knight captain, though, like the one he called Lord Marshal, he bore no insignia upon his armor.

The lead knight merely nodded, taking in the changing surroundings through narrowed, but far-seeing, eyes. Only after studying the terrain for several moments did he raise his hand and point in a direction slightly to the right of their current bearing.

"General Dayr will gather the Crown Army there. We need to reach him before nightfall."

"Aye, my lord," replied the captain.

Without breaking stride, the lord marshal tugged his reins and swerved his horse in the new direction. No word was spoken, but the rest of the company followed suit.

The horses slowed to a trot as they worked their way down the steep slope of a ravine then surged and galloped up the other side. The formation opened only slightly at the increased speed, and the close ranks held firm as they moved fleetly over increasingly broken ground.

The column of riders came upon the army encampment in the scant shelter against the wind provided by a low hill. Lookouts on top of the elevation had spotted their approach and passed word down to the troops who were making their supper preparations. Two knights, a captain and a gold-caped general, left the warmth of their cook fire to greet the new arrivals.

"My Lord Marshal, welcome! Your timing is perfect. I plan to attack Ankhar's North Wing by dawn tomorrow," reported the gold-caped general. He was a handsome knight with the flowing mustaches of a traditional Solamnic. The insignia of the white Crown was prominent upon his breastplate.

"General Dayr, Captain Franz," replied the lord marshal, nodding to the two knights as willing men-at-arms took his horse. He dismounted with the ease of a natural horseman, stretched, and for just a moment, winced at the pain of cramps in muscles that only a few years earlier would have made no complaint at the end of such a ride. Though his beard and hair were black, a trace of thin lines marked the area around his hard, cold eyes. His beard was short, neatly trimmed, and accented the outline of a strong, jutting chin.

"You made good time, my lord. We didn't expect you until late tomorrow."

"General Rankin and the Swords are advancing on the river. The enemy is in retreat in the south. Here, on his north flank, is the point of decision. I wanted to be here. And naturally, my Freemen were eager to ride."

The lord looked almost with affection at the two dozen men of his personal guard. Like himself—and unique among the three armies of Solamnia—they did not wear the insignia of a knightly order. Instead, their loyalty—and their lives—was pledged to the leader who had forged those sometimes fractious forces into one great weapon of war. Captain Powell, the leader of the guard, had been an influential knight in the hierarchy of Palanthas but had renounced that post to serve the leader who, he devoutly believed, was the only man who could restore the realm of Solamnia to its past glories.

"Very good," acknowledged the general. "Would you like a look at the position before dark?"

"Yes, right away." The lord marshal turned to the captain of the Freemen, the man who had ridden at his side when they entered the camp. Another knight, his long mustaches caked with the dust of the ride, was making a report to the captain. Both men stood erect when the lord marshal looked their way.

"Captain Powell, come with us. Sergeant Ian, see that the

men get something to eat. I want the Freemen to be well rested in the morning."

"Aye, my lord," both replied in unison.

The general and the two captains accompanied their army commander in a brisk walk up the low hill. From the crest, they could see a long distance.

The scene was dominated by a deep gorge, like a wound where a god had cleaved his sword into the flesh of the world. The Upper Narrows of the Vingaard River formed a bottleneck in that mighty flowage, a series of raging torrents and spuming cascades created as the water surged between two confining, looming walls. Even as the descending ground forced the Vingaard northward with relentless, irresistible velocity, the constricted channel compressed and accelerated the current. This was a wild place—the rocky ground around the river was inhospitable to farmers, and the water within its sheer-walled gorge too difficult for grazing animals to reach. The plains above the gorge were dry and dusty, bereft of trees and other vegetation, and subject to bitter, cold winds in winter and scorching, dry heat in summer.

It was on the west bank of this river gorge that two large military forces faced each other. The camp of the Crown Army was well situated between a pair of ridges radiating out from the round hill. With a company of infantry and another of archers on top of the hill, it was a formidable position. General Dayr had garrisoned both of the ridges flanking his camp and had an extensive picket line, with mounted outriders, guarding the main approach.

But all this was of secondary interest to the lord marshal. His attention was focused on the enemy, arrayed in a jagged, dirty smudge of fortifications backed by troops and war machines, all forming a semicircular bulge, with the gorge and the valley of the Vingaard at its right and right rear. There was a route of access—or retreat—behind the enemy camp, leading southward along this side of the river. Several paths dropped from the edge, vanishing into the depths of the canyon beside both camps.

"Is there a route through the gorge?" asked the lord marshal.

"A narrow path, my lord. We have a company defending it, and Ankhar has a similar force down there. It is a standoff—no advance for either side. And no retreat, either, considering that both paths are overlooked by the enemy."

"Good. Your men only need to stand firm down there."

"Ankhar himself is in the camp," Dayr noted. "We spotted him late yesterday afternoon."

"He knows his central and southern wings are already across the Vingaard. Here is where he has chosen to make his stand and fight," the commander remarked. "I have come here for the same reason." He turned toward Captain Powell of the Freemen, who was sitting astride his horse to the marshal's right. "Go to the baggage train and find the wagon we dispatched here. Pull out a dozen of the casks that came from the Compound."

"Very well, my lord!" Powell saluted and rode away.

If Dayr was curious about his orders, he knew better than to ask. "Would you like to review the disposition of my forces?" asked the general instead.

The lord marshal shook his head. "No, I'm sure you have prepared well. But tell me, what about the trenches?"

He indicated the fortifications around the enemy camp. Deep gashes in the ground, scored in a zigzag pattern, shielded the whole array of Ankhar's troops.

"Something novel is called for, don't you think, my lord?" Dayr turned and gestured to a young knight. The man had light golden hair, worn long, with the emblem of a crested bird on his tunic. "This is Sergeant Heath of the Order of Clerists."

DOUGLAS NILES

The commander nodded. "The priest-knights are finally arriving at the front, I see."

Sergeant Heath saluted stiffly. "I beg my lord's pardon for the delay. I assure you that it was not caused by unwillingness on the part of my company. The Council of Whitestone was slow to react, but as of this year, there are mystics and Kingfishers both sailing for your shores."

"I understand—Sir Templar has apprised me of the resistance from Lord Liam and the rest of the council. So I am doubly pleased to see you. How large is your company?"

"I have a dozen priests, my lord, and an equal number of acolytes. We pledge our swords—and our spells—to your cause."

"Very good." The lord marshal gestured at the enemy entrenchments. "Now tell me what you plan to do about those."

⚜

The camp of the Crown Army was quietly astir by an hour after midnight. Captain Powell, with his Freemen and the casks from the Compound, was already gone. Now Sergeant Heath and his Clerists slipped away from the command post and immediately melted into the full darkness that descended after moonset. Each knight-cleric wore a cloak of grayish brown and had smudges of the same color darkening the skin of their faces and hands, so they may as well have been invisible as they closed on the nearest trenches of the enemy position. Leaving their weapons and armor behind, they advanced with stealth and concealment as their only protection.

After an hour of careful advancement, the mystics were in position, only a few dozen feet short of the deep, wide trenches of Ankhar's army. Each priest-warrior was alone and knew his task; they all remained silent and in their camouflage, invisible to the enemy sentries.

Heath himself knelt before the broadest section of trench. Barely daring to breathe, he watched the shadowy figures of goblins and ogres clomping back and forth on sentry duty behind the ditch. He waited, lying flat on the ground, until he was certain the rest of his men were ready.

Night still cloaked them in utter darkness as the knight-priest rose to a kneeling position. He held a fistful of gritty clay in his hand as he murmured a prayer—and an appeal—to Kiri-Jolith. Soon he had worked the material into a hard lump. He felt the answering presence of his god, a powerful blessing of magic, and in one smooth gesture rose to his feet, shouted the climactic words to the spell, and hurled the lump of dirt into the trench.

All along the line, the Clerist knights worked the same clay magic. The sudden noise of the spellcasting alerted the brutish defenders, who rushed forward to launch spears and arrows into the darkness—even though the mysterious attackers were already falling back.

Behind them they left the results of their magic: twenty-two earthen bridges, each spanning a section of the army's trenchworks.

⚬⚬⚬⚬⚬⚬⚬⚬⚬⚬⚬

"Light!" cried General Dayr, as he heard the culminating words of the Clerists' spellcasting. "Bring out the torches!"

Flames immediately erupted from a hundred barrels, all positioned along the front of his army—directly along the lines of advance for the Crown Army's light cavalry. All three companies of the Thelgaard Lancers waited there in ranks, already mounted, prepared for the signal. These riders, lightly armored and riding very fast horses, were trained to carry long lances in the charge. But this morning, their arms would be unique.

7

Each rider carried several dry torches in one hand. As the oil-filled barrels were ignited, the horsemen started forward, their disciplined mounts filing close by the blazing containers. As the line of riders passed, each man thrust the head of his torch into the oil. The dry brands instantly ignited. Without hesitating, the riders spurred their horses into a canter. The lines of cavalry were eerily illuminated by the blazing torches bobbing and waving over each man's head, and those columns rode directly toward the enemy camp.

Where a few moments earlier Ankhar's troops had been lolling casually behind deep entrenchments, these defenders now faced the sudden reality of nearly two dozen earthen bridges, magically conjured to cross the barriers. Ogres bellowed and roared at the goblins, while the smaller fighters scrambled to take up weapons and race to the terminus of each span. A horn sounded somewhere in the rear of the camp, a lonely summons to arms.

But already the human riders were racing to confront the defenders. The Thelgaard Lancers sped across the magical bridges and charged through the chaotic soldiers trying to block their path. Shouting men drove goblins back by the simple expedient of waving burning torches to the right and left. Once they had breached the trenches, the horsemen galloped into the center of the huge enemy camp. Some threw their torches into command tents or ignited crates and barrels of supplies stacked haphazardly here and there. Other attackers continued onward, charging through the encampment toward the great war machines lined up at the rear of Ankhar's army.

A human captain barked commands, rousing a small company of men—former Dark Knights—to oppose the rush of thundering horses. In the confusion, the footmen did not have time to arm themselves properly, however; they were easily swept aside by the rampaging horsemen. More flames brightened the chilly predawn as several oil casks erupted into greasy fire, the liquid spilling along the ground, igniting as it flowed.

General Dayr, astride his steed, watched the initial onslaught with satisfaction. Even before the last of the light cavalry had crossed the bridges, he issued his next order: "Kaolyn Axers—move out!"

The doughty dwarves of this heavy infantry unit started forward to the steady beat of a deep drum. This was the First Regiment of the Axers, one of three serving in the lord marshal's army. They had come down from the Garnet Mountains for two reasons: because the ogres and goblins of Ankhar's horde were their hereditary enemies and because they would be paid well for fighting. They fought as tenaciously as any knight and with their thick plate mail shields and armor, short, muscular legs; and keen-bladed axes, they could form a veritable forward-moving wall on a battlefield.

Now the dwarves marched on the double, trotting across the bridges immediately after the last of the lancers. The black-tunicked dwarves formed a defensive semicircle around the terminus of each of the earthen spans. The mere presence of glaring dwarves and whirling axe blades was enough, for the time being, to keep the poorly disciplined goblins and ogres at bay.

At the same time, the farthest riders continued their rampage among the war machines of the enemy batteries. Some tossed their torches onto the bales of hay surrounding the position, while others dismounted to push the kindling up against the frames of the catapults, ballistae, and trebuchets. Immediately the dry wood caught fire, sending flames shooting dozens of feet into the air. Much oil, for the soaking of flaming shot when the batteries were active, was stored around the catapults. These barrels were quickly splintered and the liquid contents ignited. A wall of orange flame rose into the night.

Jaymes, the lord marshal, astride his horse very near the front of the Crown Army, watched as the enemy commander was finally spotted amidst the flaming camp.

Ankhar, the half-giant, stood head and shoulders above even the largest of the bull ogres. But it was more than size that drew attention to his presence. His voice was a roar that could drown out the sound of thunder, as he rallied shaken companies and rebuked retreating troops. Ankhar raised an arm that was like the bough of a mighty oak. His fist, an all-too-solid symbol of his army's power, punched the air over his head.

A great cheer rose from the goblins, the ogres, and the mercenary men. They gathered to counterattack, surging against the dwarves guarding the approach to the conjured bridges, rushing toward the light cavalrymen who had wreaked such havoc in the camp. Goblins howled and shrieked and threw themselves against the dwarven axes. Ogres roared, wielding huge clubs as they rushed the Kaolyn heavy infantry.

Their torches expended, the Thelgaard Lancers fought with swords; many simply flowed out of the way of the enemy troops, riding their fleet horses away from the rear of the enemy camp. Snarling warg wolves raced after them. Some of these savage canines bore goblin riders, while others simply screeched and howled, drawn by the lure of the hunting pack. But the horses were too fast, and the wolves could only follow them across the plains, away from the camp, the battle, and the decision of the day.

⊰⊙⊷⊙⊶⊙⊷⊙❋⊙⊶⊙⊷⊙⊶⊙⊷

The sun had not yet risen, but the eastern sky was now a broad swath of pale blue, brightened near the horizon by the imminent sun. The fires throughout Ankhar's camp still burned but no longer as beacons in the darkness. Instead, they spewed broad columns of dark smoke into the sky, each pyre marking the ruins of some part of the enemy army.

Jaymes turned to General Dayr, a command rising in the lord marshal's throat—but the general guiding the Crown Army was already shouting to his captains.

"White Riders, charge!"

Now the heavy knights advanced, in more concentrated columns than the Thelgaard Lancers. The White Riders formed the shock troops of the Crown Army, armored and shielded, riding huge, shaggy steeds that loomed over every other creature on the battlefield. They charged in four files, each spilling across one of the bridges near the center of the enemy camp. Trumpets brayed, marking the pace as each company accelerated.

Hearing the horns, feeling the thundering cadence of heavy hooves, the dwarves protecting those four bridges quickly wheeled to the side, allowing the knights to cross with undiminished momentum.

One company of Ankhar's human warriors tried to make a stand near the river gorge, but they were shattered by a single charge of the White Riders. Shields broke beneath crushing hooves, pikes and spear shafts snapped in two, and the little knot of defenders shrank until the last of them were ridden down.

Much of Ankhar's army streamed away, falling back around the charred outlines of the artillery park, hastening southward along the bank of the Vingaard. Three hundred ogres formed a square in the center of the melee. All around them, the troops of the horde were dropping back, sometimes with good order, in other cases in full rout.

The separated companies of the White Riders gathered. Knights lowered their visors and took up such lances as had survived the fray or drew their heavy, bloody swords. The ogres alone stood before them as the Crown Knights rolled forward in the battle's final charge. The clash of steel against steel rang out once more, mingling with the shrieks of wounded horses and the cries of bleeding ogres and dying men.

When the last of the riders finally limped away, not a single ogre remained standing.

⊱⦿⊰⦿⊰⦿⊰⦿⊰❀⊱⦿⊰⦿⊰⦿⊰⦿⊰

"We've turned the flank, my lord," General Dayr reported. He tried to maintain his detachment, but the fierce elation of battlefield success flared in his eyes, gleamed in the momentary glimpse of his teeth. "They're running for the fords to the south of here."

"Well done, General," Jaymes said, nodding toward the dust marking the enemy's retreat. "Let them go for the time being, and see to your wounded."

"The Clerists are already at work with the other healers. There remains only one stumbling block."

The lord marshal arched his eyebrow, thought for a moment, and nodded. "The company in the gorge, down at the river?"

"Yes, my lord. I have sent scouts to bring me reports on them. But it looks like they can't pull out safely; Ankhar has enough ogres left to shower them with boulders if they try to move out."

"All right. Let's have a look," the lord marshal acknowledged. He nudged his horse in the flanks and—accompanied only by the two dozen knights of the Caergoth Freemen—set out to inspect the battlefield.

CHAPTER TWO

BETRAYAL, AND BETRAYAL

The two armies, like exhausted wrestlers, had separated and now lay prostrate, gasping for breath, thirsty for cool drink. The plain around the Narrows was no longer a place for the living, but for the dead and the doomed.

To the latter end, men and monsters had done their work well. The evidence lay all around, first indicated by the sweeping shapes of the vultures and crows circling overhead. The scavengers swirled downward like dark, macabre snowflakes to settle among the lifeless forms scattered across a mile or more of the plains just to the west of the deep gorge. Here and there the shape of a great war machine, a catapult or a ballista, was discernable through the soot and ash that caked the charred timbers; this was all that remained of the lethal devices. Smoke still spiraled upward from the large fire pits where shot had been heated. In one place barrels of oil had been cracked open to soak into the dry ground. Fire burned over the very plain itself, marking the place with a thick, smudgy pillar of black smoke rising into the otherwise cloudless skies.

Nearby lay more than a hundred dead horses, a fabulous

buffet for the scavengers. Amid the slain beasts, with their torn saddles and once-grand regalia, lay a great number of goblins and more than a few ogres, proof of the charge that had, at last, broken the ranks of Ankhar's hordes. Many knights had perished here as well, but their bodies had been removed for—unlike the beasts of the half-giant's horde—the humans gathered up their slain and gave them burial or cremation.

A kind of silence had descended over the field, filled just hours before with the clashing of steel and cries of pain and exultation. Nevertheless, a listener would have heard a keen, almost mournful wailing in the wind that scoured this dusty ground. Occasionally, too, was heard the raucous protests of the birds, as crows were forced to yield to the great beaks and crushing wings of the vultures, and the ravens, in turn, were driven from their morsels by greedy crows. The black-feathered birds gave the scene a life of its own, a shifting pattern of movement overlaying the great sprawl of the dead.

Accompanied by the two dozen riders of the Caergoth Freemen, Jaymes rode across the field at an easy gait, though his sturdy roan showed signs of trepidation. She tossed her head about, veering away from a slain ogre. Her ears stood upright, quivering.

The riders made their way through the detritus of battle until they came to the rim of the precipice. They peered down into the river gorge, where the waters of the Narrows churned and plunged in the deep channel. Eyes narrowed, the lord marshal took in the situation.

Two companies of warriors were visible on a flat shelf of land beside the rapid flow, facing each other in lines ranked behind poised spears and shields. One group consisted of humans, men in leather armor and metal caps, formed around a pennant displaying the sigil of the Crown. The other was a band of goblins, ragged but fierce, with shaggy cloaks and long, wicked-looking pikes. The surface upon which both companies stood was low, barely a few feet above the water; the river beside them was deep, dark, and moving rapidly. The shelf of level ground was perhaps a quarter-mile long, but only ten yards wide. On the side away from the water, sheer cliffs swept upward hundreds of feet, leading to the rider's vantage.

The warriors in the gorge seemed evenly matched, perhaps two hundred ofn each side, and they faced each other in the center of the little swath of level ground. Even with his first quick glance, the man took in how those companies arrived at such a place. The humans had descended through a narrow ravine, a passage barely wide enough for single file, that snaked up to reach the plateau nearly a mile away from the river gorge. The goblins had marched down a narrow trail carved out of the very side of the cliff. That path twisted out of sight to the man's right, but he could clearly see the lower half and imagined that it continued up to reach the crest of the bluff some distance up the gorge.

Another company of riders appeared on the plain above the canyon, horses trotting around the pillar of smoke marking the oil fire. They numbered perhaps a dozen men, many wearing full plate armor of gleaming steel. One, a herald, held aloft a standard from which a proud banner flew—a white crown on a field of black. It matched the sigil displayed by the company down by the river, though it was a much larger and more ornate emblem—for it was the banner of General Dayr himself.

The general broke away from his entourage to ride, alone, toward the man who still sat astride his horse at the brink of the precipice. The escort of Freemen withdrew to a discreet distance, so the two commanders could speak privately.

"My Lord Marshal," Dayr said as he drew up to Jaymes. "I

hope you are satisfied with the fruits of our victory."

"Yes, General," said the marshal. "We have broken Ankhar's army in the north. I understand that, even now, he is pulling the bulk of his horde back to the east side of the river."

"True. But there is a new development. One of his men, a sergeant of the Dark Knights, has come forward under a banner of truce. He says that Ankhar himself would like to have a parley with the officer in command."

"The half-giant would so expose himself?" asked the marshal.

The general nodded. "He says he will come forward alone, to meet a lone human, on that spit of land there, above the river. There is a narrow gorge, some ten paces wide, that would divide the two leaders. Of course I am more than willing to go, Marshal Jaymes, but I thought that I should give you the option of making the parley yourself."

The rider nodded. "I'd like that. After two years of fighting this barbarian, I should like to meet with him face-to-face to take his measure with my own eyes."

"As you wish," the general replied.

"What, do you imagine, is the purpose of this parley?"

"I suspect he will bargain for mutual withdrawal of those troops you see down there by the river. The battle, of course, is over, yet the potential for slaughter remains. You see, our men—that's the Second Company of the Vingaard Arms—might make their escape through yonder ravine, but a hundred ogres have been posted upon the far rim. If our men try to withdraw, they could be crushed by the rocks dropped by the ogres from above. At the same time, Ankhar's goblins are likewise trapped. If they withdraw up the cliffside trail, our archers will be able to cut them to pieces. In either case it is likely that no more than a handful of the enemy troops will survive to escape the gorge."

"But Ankhar's army is already retreating. I presume there is a reason why we cannot simply wait him out, bring out the company when the ogres have left."

"The rains, my Lord Marshal. Up in the Garnet range it has been pouring for several days, and the river is rising by nearly a foot with every passing hour. If we don't pull the men out of there, the matter is moot; by tomorrow morning, they will all have drowned."

The marshal nodded, taking in the scene again with those sharp, penetrating eyes. The cliffs, the river, the ravine, and the trail were all as the general had described. If the men in the gorge were not soon plucked to safety, they were doomed.

"Very well," said Marshal Jaymes Markham. "Send word to Ankhar through his messenger; tell him that I will meet him and parley."

⊰⊙⊱⊙⊰⊙⊱⊙⊰❀⊱⊙⊰⊙⊱⊙⊰⊙⊱⊙⊰

The half-giant was an impressive creature, standing nearly twice as tall as the man glaring at him across the gulf of the narrow crevice. Ankhar was unarmed, as was Jaymes; this had been a fundamental condition of the parley. Still, the creature's mere fists looked capable of crushing the skull of a human soldier, and the glower on his face suggested that crushing a man's skull was a very tempting notion right now.

Jaymes studied the hulking barbarian who had been his adversary over the past two years. Ankhar's brow loomed over his eyes like the craggy outcrop of a cliff, accenting the bestial features of the ogrish face. The eyes were small in comparison to the overall size of the huge face, but they glittered with a certain cold, appraising intelligence. The man had the unsettling awareness that the half-giant was studying him with the same curiosity he himself felt.

17

"You are called the Lord of the Rose?" asked the half-giant in a voice like the growl of a bear.

"Some call me that, but I claim no such title for myself."

"You fight under the white banner, with Crown and Sword and Rose all woven together. That seems to me like you claim the sign."

The man shrugged. "You can take it any way you like. I don't see a banner over your own army, yet your troops shed blood aplenty, just the same."

The half-giant's broad mouth curled into a cruel, tusk-baring smile. "They have killed many men, in the name of the Truth. I am the Truth. They rejoice in drinking human blood, in taking human women—and miles of land!"

"Yet you have given many lands back, this last year. Three times you have faced my army and three times been defeated."

Ankhar shrugged. "The war goes on. Many more men will die. This is Truth."

"Right now, the truth is that your company and mine are trapped together on the bank of the river," Jaymes noted. "If we hold our positions, neither group can escape—each would be destroyed by troops on the heights if they try to make higher ground."

Ankhar snorted contemptuously. "Let them stay where they are."

"Was it not you who requested this parley? What, then, was your purpose?"

"Perhaps I want a face for my enemy," growled the half-giant. "You fight well . . . for a human."

"I fight when I must—and when I fight, I fight well."

"I will kill you soon enough. For now, I see you, and spit upon you!"

"You're a creature of the mountains, I am told," Jaymes replied evenly. "Do your agents tell you of the storms in the Garnet range? It has been raining, hard, for days. The creeks and streams are full, spilling down toward the plains."

The glowering brow furrowed for a moment in thought. If he was surprised by the information imparted by Jaymes, he gave no indication. "So the river rises? All our men will drown?"

"It looks that way to me," Jaymes said. "I prefer my men to die bravely, not drown ignominiously, and I am willing to let your troops live also, in fair trade."

The half-giant hawked and turning his head to the side, spit noisily. "A fair trade? So that your men can take more of my mountains? Drive my people from the plains? Kill them?" His voice had dropped to an angry snarl.

"I make no apologies. Nor will I enumerate the list of crimes committed by your 'people'—the wrongs that make it necessary for us to wage war against you."

The half-giant bellowed then almost instantly grew calm. "What do you suggest?"

"I offer to pull my archers back from the rim of the cliff, so that your company can march up the trail and rejoin your army as you cross the river. In return, your ogres will withdraw from the heights over the ravine, so that my own men can file out of the deathtrap that the gorge will soon become."

Ankhar glared, spit into the ravine again, and growled deep in his chest. Finally he nodded.

"Let us make this truce. Our warriors will live to fight another day. I agree with you. Better soldiers die in battle than drown in a thunderstorm."

"Good," Jaymes replied. He studied Ankhar's face, looking for any hint of treachery—or sincerity. "So, too, shall I agree to a truce." He looked up at the sky. "It is past noon now. The shadow of the sun will reach that white layer of stone, halfway up the cliff, in about two hours. Shall we let the truce take effect at that time?"

"Yes. To last until sunset over the plains. There will be no killing during that time."

"Very well," said the man. He nodded thoughtfully. "Your warriors fought well. It was only a fierce charge of knights that, in the end, broke your line."

"Bah. My Thorn Knights're not here. Their magic would shatter any charge—kill your tin can riders!"

"So they might have. But they did not." Jaymes shrugged as if it were a matter of no great concern. Yet he knew that the half-giant spoke the truth. The Thorn Knights had formerly served Mina and the One God in her campaign to conquer Ansalon. They were formidable wizards, devoted to the dark arts in the furtherance of their own power. In many battles their presence had proved decisive, but their numbers were few. Jaymes was well aware those potent wizards might have made a difference and was glad they were absent from this battle.

"I go now, to tell of the truce. I withdraw my company," Ankhar said. "Next time, may we shed each other's blood."

"So we may," the human replied. "I will not wish you luck in that endeavor."

The half-giant chuckled, the sound an odd mixture of cruelty and humor. "I wish you luck—to stay healthy until that day," he said. "So I may kill you myself."

"Aye—and the same to you," replied the marshal, the com-mander of all the Solamnic Armies.

Still facing each other, the two leaders backed warily away from the edge of the narrow crevice. Jaymes reached behind, took the bridle of his roan, and swung easily into the saddle. As he cantered away, he glanced back and saw that the half-giant was still watching him with those too-small, too-intelligent eyes.

⚔⚔⚔⚔⚔⚔⚔⚔⚔

The signalman caught the attention of the captain of the Second Company of the Vingaard Arms, the unit trapped on the shelf beside the river. He waved his flags at the rim of the precipice. The orders were simple: "Prepare to withdraw," followed by, "Await the command to execute the order." A simple wave of the company's Crown pennant returned the acknowledgement that the message had been received and understood.

General Dayr and Marshal Jaymes stood beside the flagman, watching the shadow that had already crept far up the canyon's wall. In another quarter of an hour or so, it would reach the strata of white rock that signaled the commencement of the agreed-upon truce. A scout rode up, and both commanders turned to regard him.

"The ogres are indeed withdrawing from the rim of the ravine," the man reported without formality. "Already they have marched more than a mile, and when I departed from the scene just moments ago, they were making steady progress away."

"Are they out of range by now?"

"Aye, my lord—the ogres are no longer able to strike at the men of the Vingaard Arms."

"It appears as though the brute is keeping his word," Dayr murmured, raising his eyebrows in a gesture of mild surprise. "I hadn't been entirely sure until now."

Jaymes shook his head very slightly. "I was sure he would pull the ogres back. But I am not yet convinced that he is keeping his word."

"And our archers are now down from the heights. They wouldn't have time to return to their firing positions if Ankhar's company makes haste."

"I'm sure they'll get out of there as fast as they can," said the army commander.

A few moments later, the sun's shadow reached the requisite position. The two men watched as the companies beside the river slowly backed away from each other, the humans moving toward the lower terminus of the narrow ravine, the goblins to the foot of the trail that twisted so precariously along the canyon's wall. When perhaps three hundred yards of distance was between them, the formations abandoned their battle lines and formed into narrow columns, each starting up its respective route of retreat.

"Now we arrive at the moment of truth," said Jaymes. "Or perhaps I should say, 'the Truth.'"

"I have heard that he calls himself this," Dayr remarked. "Even under the most severe interrogation, his warriors insist that their general is the Truth."

For several long moments, the mutual withdrawals proceeded quietly. The last of the human warriors filed into the ravine, disappearing from the sight of the two commanders, though some goblins were still visible making their way up the winding trail. The head of that column approached the first switchback and continued upward, vanishing momentarily as the trail cut under a broad overhang of rugged limestone.

"After the barbarians are across the river, do you want me to pursue them in the direction of Dargaard?" asked Dayr. He shuddered at the thought of that dark and haunted fortress.

"That will not be necessary. Ankhar's troops will not head toward Dargaard," Jaymes declared.

"Oh? What do you predict?"

"He will concentrate on the east bank of the Vingaard, to hold us at bay, while he gathers his strength against Solanthus," the marshal stated. "He has already brought his central army to the west of that fortress, while his southern force is screening the territory in the Garnet foothills."

The city of Solanthus had been besieged for two years, ever since Ankhar's horde had first rampaged across the plains—before Jaymes Markham had taken command of the Solamnic Army. Though the city had resisted the barbarian's few attempts at storming the walls, it also remained out of reach of relief columns and supplies from the rest of Solamnia.

"You think he will make another attempt to conquer Solanthus, then?" Dayr replied, moderately surprised. "Those walls have held him at bay for more than two years."

"Yes, but he has made no serious attack," Jaymes answered. "And now we have bested him in three major battles in the open field. Each time he has been forced to give up another sector of the plains, and with Solanthus to his rear, still resisting, he will see that, inevitably, we intend to break his siege, if he keeps losing ground."

"I understand that the situation is dire in that city," the general said. "It is all the clerics can do to maintain food at near starvation levels. Though I hear that the duchess has rallied the people courageously, that she eats no more than the commoners."

The lord marshal nodded. "She has a core of steel, that's clear."

Dayr agreed somewhat ruefully. "When Duke Rathskell married her, I thought she was a trite little wench, suited only for the bedroom. Now he's dead, and she is holding the city together. I am, frankly, surprised. I confess I did not give her credit for that kind of spine."

"Nobody did," Jaymes said. "Sometimes adversity seems to bring forth remarkable strength."

A trumpet blared some distance away, and both men turned quickly at the unmistakable sound of alarm. The general grimaced, while the marshal's lips tightened in anger. "Liar!" he said between clenched teeth. "So the one called the Truth is a liar after all."

"But his ogres cannot have returned to the ravine—they were too far away!" countered Dayr.

Jaymes nodded, pointing downward, where the column of goblins was halfway up the cliff, still winding along the narrow trail. Soon they would vanish from sight as they continued behind the curve of the canyon wall. But moments later, the scout came into view, lashing his horse into a froth as he galloped toward the two commanders.

"My lords!" he shouted, thundering closer and pulling up in a skidding stop. "Treachery! Ankhar's Thorn Knights—at least one of them—has appeared in the ravine. He has created a cloud of deadly gas that sinks and slithers along the trail, killing every man caught within. The survivors are fleeing back toward the river, but the cloud is moving quickly—it seems certain they are all doomed."

"The bastard!" snarled Dayr. "We should have kept the archers in position—we could pick off those goblins and show him the fruits of his treachery!"

Jaymes ignored his general, instead striding up to the nearby signalman who stood listening to the scout's report in shock, his banners neatly coiled at his feet. "Raise the red pennant—now!" snapped the marshal.

Quickly the man did as he was told. Another scout rode up, confirming that the men of the trapped company were perishing in the magically conjured gas cloud. The Thorn Knight, of course, had teleported away immediately; there was no chance of exacting vengeance upon the villain. The lord marshal displayed no reaction upon hearing this news, even as his general practically wept with frustration and rage.

The crimson banner snapped in the breeze as the flagman hoisted it upon a slender pole. He waved it back and forth in response to the marshal's curt command. Dayr and the nearby soldiers watched anxiously, knowing better than to ask Jaymes what was going on. Below, the vile gas, a greenish yellow in color, seeped from the bottom of the ravine. No man could escape that corridor of death.

The cliffs above the fleeing goblins suddenly shattered in a gout of smoke, fire, and blasted rock. The huge shelf of stone split free from the canyon wall and tumbled down toward the helpless warriors, burying some in the cloud of debris and carrying the rest to doom on the rocks a hundred feet below. Several breaths passed before the sound of the explosions—a stunning eruption of noise that bellowed and rumbled through the canyon like a violent thunderstorm—reached the watchers on top of the cliff.

"You placed charges there?" Dayr asked in astonishment. "You didn't trust the truce?"

The marshal shrugged. "Captain Powell made the arrangements. The red flag was the signal to light the fuses," he said.

Debris continued to tumble downward, an avalanche of stone and gravel and dust that swept the cliff and the winding trail clean of goblins. So great was the destruction that, in many places, the entire pathway was carved away from the cliff. A cloud of dust lingered for a long time, obscuring their view, but as it gradually settled toward the water, it became clear that not a single one of the enemy warriors had survived the blast.

General Dayr wondered aloud. "The black powder is

precious . . . and the preparations are always extensive. Had you planted the explosives in case Ankhar betrayed you? Or . . . you were planning to ignite those fuses all along?"

Jaymes looked at him, his expression cold and emotionless. "This is war," he said curtly. "And the objective is to kill the enemy. I know this, and Ankhar knows this."

And the war would go on.

CHAPTER THREE

THE ARMY OF SOLAMNIA

Jaymes ordered his army to concentrate all three wings on the west bank of the Vingaard, south of the great fork in the middle of the plains. The generals put his orders into action while he himself traveled with only the two dozen Freemen of his personal guard. Captain Powell knew his commander well enough that, for the most part, the escorting knights rode several hundred yards behind Jaymes. The party followed the meandering course of that mighty river, so the lord marshal could enjoy a few days of relative leisure before immersing himself again in the complexities of command.

At last he turned the little roan mare due south, riding with purpose now. The column tightened up. The marshal passed the first pickets of the army camp some ten miles out. These veteran scouts, in leather armor with their fleet, long-legged steeds, were not surprised to see their leader riding across the flat steppe at the head of a small company. Even before they waved him through their outposts, the scouts detached galloping riders to carry word of the lord marshal's approach to the main camp.

Soon Jaymes could make out the vast spread of his army's tent city gathered around the officers' encampment, where plain brown domes rose above the lesser dwellings. Horse corrals were small, scattered among the units so the mounts were close to their riders. A large pasture, well guarded, had been established to the rear, where hundreds of cattle—used both as cargo haulers and food—grazed.

When the dukes had ruled these troops, each noble's tent had been a huge, colorful pavilion, with attendant dwellings for retainers, courtiers, and other key members of the ducal entourage. Whole wagon trains had been devoted to luxuries such as crystal dinner services, silk tablecloths, and padded thrones. A central part of the camp would typically have been set aside for formations, parades, jousting, and other elaborate games.

But those days were gone. Now the officers, from the generals down to the platoon captains, dwelled in nondescript shelters of the same nondescript denim—larger than the tents of the enlisted troops only insofar as space was needed for map tables, rosters, and signaling equipment. Undistinguished, perhaps, but they also made it difficult for an enemy to determine where they would find the important leaders of the Solamnic Army. As an added benefit, the common men in the line understood that their officers shared their living conditions, and this boosted morale.

Lord Marshal Jaymes had appointed his officers based upon their demonstration of military ability, not because of any accident of birth. True, his three army generals—Dayr of the Crowns, Markus of the Rose, and Rankin of the Swords—had been captains under the dukes. Still, each had proved on the field that he was skilled and trustworthy; each merited the responsibility of his command.

The rank of lord marshal was new to the Solamnic military hierarchy. Jaymes had created it for himself after being awarded the united command two years earlier, when his steadfast leadership—as well as his discovery of explosive black powder—had saved Solamnia from Ankhar's horde. After the horde had been halted on the brink of attacking Caergoth, the nobles had had little choice but to reward their savior with supreme command. In the years since, Jaymes had slowly driven the invaders back, liberating Thelgaard and Garnet, finally clearing them from the entire reach west of the Vingaard.

Many of the men still referred to Jaymes as the Lord of the Rose, and he accepted this honorific when it was offered. Others called him the Lord of No Sign. For though his banner incorporated elements of all three orders of the knighthood, he was comfortable riding about in his plain woolen poncho, displaying no heraldry whatsoever.

Riding the roan at an amble, Jaymes made his way through the outer camp. These were the pikemen and archers who could form ranks in a matter of moments to defend the perimeter, while the knights with their more elaborate accoutrement armored themselves and their horses before supplying reinforcements. He was recognized by many as he approached and accepted the salutes and cheers of his men with a gracious nod to the right and left, or the raising of his hand toward a man or a company of particular note.

Many of these men had won great victories for their marshal. The Vingaard pikes, woodsmen from the mountains who wielded their long wooden pole arms with unflinching discipline, were often the first responders. Many a charge of warg-riding goblins had been broken by their iron will, and one regiment of pikemen served in each of the three armies. He rode now past the Southshore Longbows, deadly archers from across the coast of the Newsea. The dwarves of the Kaolyn Axers, not to be outdone, raised their foaming tankards aloft and roared a lusty toast to their commander, who politely declined the invitation to stop at the dwarven campfires for a friendly tankard or three.

As news of his arrival spread, men came streaming from the other encampments, adding their cheers. He came to the center of the great encampment, where the bulk of the knights were amassed. Though they were the backbone of the Solamnic Army, in actual numbers the knights formed only a small percentage of the troops. It was the pikemen who formed the battle lines, the archers who provided the covering fire, and the dwarf heavy infantry who would assemble squares to stand against any attack. Then and only then could the fleet and powerful horsemen of the knighthood fight with all their ability.

The marshal took time to greet some of the knights personally. He reached down to clasp the hands of several Caergoth Steelshields as he rode past. These were the Rose Knights who had carried the day when Jaymes had first struck north across the Garnet River, pushing Ankhar's army back from the position it had held for six months following the half-giant's initial, nearly triumphant campaign. Then there came the doughty veterans of the Newforge Regiment, Knights of the Sword who hailed from besieged Solanthus; they had pledged to lead the assault that would free their surrounded city. Just beyond them, standing at attention with their snow-pure steeds behind them, were the Crown Knights of the White Riders—the unit that had broken Ankhar's ogres so recently in the north, paving the way for this great concentration of force.

All in all, more than twelve thousand men were congregated here, and the army commander could not help but be pleased by the sight of his army. His three generals awaited him in the center of the camp. He dismounted, allowing his horse to be led away for a rubdown by several eager young squires, and stretched the kinks of his four-day ride out of his back and shoulders. He joined the generals at their small fire, taking a seat on a small stool.

"Any urgent news?" Jaymes asked.

General Rankin acted as spokesman for the trio. "No word from Palanthas, nor from the Compound, my lord."

"Regent du Chagne still prefers that his own legion guard the city, does he?" asked the marshal, shaking his head.

"Perhaps he is worried more about you than about Ankhar," suggested General Dayr.

Jaymes smiled tightly. "Probably he *should* be worried about me. But I don't have time for him now. Solanthus requires our attention, and we'll have to make plans with the assets we currently have on the field."

"That should give us plenty to work with," declared Sir Markus Haum, the general of the Rose. He was a steadfast veteran with a very impressive mustache and had rejoined the army in the winter after narrowly surviving an attempt on his life. Among the three, Jaymes regarded him as his most trusted, capable field commander. "Our forces are spread within ten miles of this very spot, ready and willing to go where you send it, my Lord Marshal."

Jaymes nodded. "What of the crossings? I presume Ankhar has them well guarded?"

"Aye, sir," Dayr confirmed rather glumly. "He has pickets posted for a hundred miles north and south of here, with strong detachments at every ford."

"We tried a probe with boats, as you ordered," General Rankin said. "We sent three hundred scouts, all of them volunteers, across the wider part of the Vingaard, a score of miles downstream from here. Ankhar's bastards waited until the boats were almost to shore, and then those damned ogres bombarded them with boulders. Most of the boats were sunk, and barely eighty men made it back to our bank alive."

"Unsurprising," Jaymes acknowledged. He had in fact expected a disastrous result with such an experiment, but he had to give the tactic a try. The loss of so many men was a steep cost, but it was a price he must pay in return for intelligence regarding his enemy's dispositions. "Has there been any word from Solanthus?"

"The last messenger to make it through the siege lines arrived more than a month ago. We've tried to send men in, but sporadic reports—by homing pigeon—indicate that none of them have made it through. There's a cloud of magic around that place, no doubt caused by the Cleft Spires. Though it blocks our scrying attempts, it is also an asset—for it certainly protects the city against the magic of Ankhar's Thorn Knights as well.

"So Solanthus is still holding out. Discipline and morale are reportedly good, my lord, but the shortage of food is becoming the worst predicament. Most of the food is going to the fighting men, of course, so the suffering is greatest among the citizenry. It will not be long before the youngest and oldest citizens will be starving to death."

"And the duchess herself?"

"She pleads for help, as soon as possible. But she also promises to hold out until we can break the siege," reported Rankin. "She's but a slip of a thing, and . . . well . . . when she married Duke Rathskell, we all made assumptions about her that have turned out to be wrong. By the gods—my men and I respect her now. We should be there with her!"

For several years Rankin had been the captain in charge of the duke's army. Following Rathskell's death, he had retained his office but had been outside the city with his mobile forces when Solanthus was surrounded. Now his eyes grew moist and his voice broke from the obvious passion of his desire to return to the city and fight for its freedom.

Jaymes himself showed little emotion in his face or voice. "The talents of the duchess obviously go far beyond the bedroom, you mean?" he asked.

Rankin nodded, flushing slightly. "I admit I made a poor judgment of a great lady, my lord."

"We all made the same judgment, I'm afraid," Dayr noted quickly, coming to Rankin's rescue. "But she's a better man than her late husband ever was."

"Indeed." The marshal nodded, reflecting privately.

"Good riddance to Rathskell, in any event," Markus huffed. Each of the generals knew that Duke Rathskell had died on Jaymes Markham's sword, but none of them saw any reason to mention the fact. Nor would they mention the fortune in gems that had vanished upon the duke's death, though they must suspect that those stones were now being used to fund the expensive, and secret, operations of the distant, mysterious Compound.

"Excuse me, my lords?"

They looked up at the approach of a young knight, a clean-shaven officer who wore a tunic of white, emblazoned with small symbols of the Crown, the Rose, and the Sword.

"Sir Templar? Please, join us," Jaymes offered.

"Thank you, my Lord Marshal. Welcome back—I am pleased to see that Kiri-Jolith has blessed you with a safe journey."

"Well, he didn't place any undue obstacles in my path, and for that I myself am grateful," Jaymes replied. "What can we do for you?"

Templar was a knight-priest, a Clerist like Sergeant Heath, one of the new breed of clerical warriors who had begun to join the ranks of the Solamnics during the later campaigns of the War of Souls. With the disappearance of Paladine, the traditional high god of the knightly orders, the Clerists had been working hard to rebuild the faith of the troops. Some of them maintained devout

worship of the merchant god Shinare, while many others, such
as Templar, were devoted followers of Kiri-Jolith, the Just.

"Well, my lord . . . it's the dwarves. We have several good,
solid priests among their ranks, and they are trying their best.
It's just that . . . well. . . ."

"Tell us—spit it out, man!" encouraged Dayr.

"Well, the dwarves are refusing to take the Oath—they
serve in the ranks of the Solamnic Army. But they won't speak
the words that pledge their commitment to all of the knightly
cause!"

"Well, they're not knights, after all," Jaymes said. "They're
not required to take the Oath. And it seems that too vigorous
efforts to bend them to that ideal might only drive them away.
I have known more than a few dwarves in my time, and every
one of them is stubborn to the core. But also quite honorable,
in their way."

"That's not the point!" protested the priest.

Dayr and Markus exchanged nervous glances—even
Jaymes's highest-ranking generals were not so quick to bluntly
contradict the army commander.

"Now, lad," said Markus sternly, clearing his throat.
"Remember your place. This is the lord marshal you're
addressing."

"I know!" said Templar dismissively. "But it's a matter that
needs to be addressed. Thus far this army has been blessed by
remarkable success—the gods have smiled upon us! But if we
don't take that obligation seriously, who knows how long this
favor will last?"

"What obligation, exactly, do you mean?" asked Jaymes
softly.

"Why, the obligation to the great legacy of Solamnia! Of
Vinas Solamnus, who forged these scattered realms into an

empire! And to the noble lords who have carried his legacy on through the ages!"

"Noble lords, such as Duke Walker of Caergoth? Who killed his own wife to further his ambitions? Who betrayed his fellow dukes and allowed hundreds, even thousands, of brave men to die because he was reluctant to spend his treasury, too lazy to leave the protection of his city walls? You mean *that* legacy?" Jaymes's voice took on an edge.

"Yes! I mean, well, no—not that part of Walker's character. Surely, he made mistakes. But he was corrupted by the Prince of Lies! It was Hiddukel who turned him from the path of righteousness!"

"But he took the Oath, did he not? In fact, he administered the Oath to countless recruits, good men who became knights."

"Yes, exactly! It was the Oath . . . I mean . . . but it's important! The Oath must be preserved and furthered as best we can. Surely you can see that."

Jaymes nodded, pausing before he replied. "Yes, the Oath is important when it is spoken by one who believes that to which he swears. And so it shall be in the Army of Solamnia. You can teach the men—and the dwarves—about the Oath and the Measure and the legacy of Vinas Solamnus. But nobody will be required to speak that oath, nor shall any soldiers in this army be criticized or harangued for failure to speak its credo."

"But—"

"Son, I think the lord marshal has made his wishes known. Thanks for bringing your concerns to us." Dayr spoke brusquely.

Templar, finally, seemed to get the hint. He looked glum as he rose, but he bowed with stiff formality and nodded to the commanders. "And thank you, my lords, for hearing me," he said before turning and shuffling off into the gathering darkness.

The lord regent's palace overlooked the city of Palanthas and the splendid, deep-water Bay of Branchala from a mountain vantage outside of the city's walls—the walls that could, in truth, no longer be said to contain the vibrant metropolis. In fact, much of this splendid city now sprawled outside the ring of ancient fortifications. These outlying districts included the splendid manors of nobles as well as the stockyards and corrals necessary for the bustling commerce that was the city's lifeblood. Markets, artisans, and manufactories lined the wide highway leading to the inner city.

Within the palace halls, on this early evening, an elegantly dressed nobleman made his way toward the regent's drawing room bearing an expression of quiet satisfaction. By the time he reached the chamber and was admitted, he was smiling broadly.

"I thank you for your intercession, my lord," said the man. "Your daughter has consented to accompany me to the Nobles Ball next month."

"Ah, Lord Frankish. Good. I knew she would," said Lord Regent Bakkard du Chagne. He was a short, pudgy man with only a thin layer of hair on his head, but his visitor—as well as most others in this city—knew that his unassuming looks were deceptive. Du Chagne was the most powerful man in Palanthas, descended from a long line of stewards who had held authority in the city since the end of the lineage of Solamnic kings. His influence, and money, was enough to intimidate other powerful persons in Solamnia—with the notable exception of the Lord Marshal Jaymes Markham.

"In fact," the regent went on, his voice dropping conspiratorially. "I encouraged her to welcome your approaches. She needs someone like you—a man of good station and impeccable loyalty—to guide her future."

Lord Frankish was also one of the wealthiest nobles in northern Ansalon, and while this, too, counted as an important factor in the lord regent's favor, neither man felt that this asset needed to be voiced aloud. In addition, Frankish was the commanding general of the Palanthian Legion. This large, well-trained, and well-equipped force had been serving as the lord regent's personal army since shortly after the fall of Mina and the Dark Knights.

Only then did Lord Frankish notice two other men present in the drawing room. One was the tall, dour priest, the Clerist Lord Inquisitor Frost; the other was Sir Russel Moorvan, a magic-user and Solamnic Kingfisher knight.

"Good sirs," said Frankish with a polite bow. Frankish was more a man of action, an accomplished swordsman and equestrian, but he understood that these two men were policy advisers who were equally important to the lord regent.

"We are discussing matters on the plains," du Chagne announced, "and would be pleased to have you join us, my lord."

The plains, Frankish knew, meant Lord Marshal Jaymes Markham. The four men were united in their firm belief that the upstart army commander—a man of common birth!—was an irritant that they could not continue to ignore. So long as his army was occupied fighting Ankhar's barbarians, it was hoped that he would stay away from this great metropolis. But as soon as that campaign was resolved, there was nothing to prevent him from marching to Palanthas and offering the city his vaunted "protection."

"His operations are very expensive," the inquisitor observed. "Can you not cut his funding?"

"I have tried," du Chagne said with a groan—and they all knew that he was a man who, insofar as it was possible, would clutch every coin in his treasury until it could be physically pried

37

out of his hands. They took him at his regretful word. "But the families of the knights stay my hand. If they feel that I am not sufficiently supporting the war effort, they make things very difficult for me—very difficult indeed."

"And how fares the campaign?" asked Moorvan, the Kingfisher.

"It is hard to tell—he shares little or no information with me," admitted the lord regent.

"Haven't we tried to place spies in his camp?" asked Frankish.

"Yes—and he willingly accepts any volunteers we send to him, but none of them is ever granted an ear at his councils. No, I suspect he rather enjoys sending my agents out on the front lines of battle."

"Then what is to be done?" asked the inquisitor.

"We must keep watching and waiting," said du Chagne. "And hope that, sooner or later, he fails miserably. Or makes a fatal mistake."

>∞⦾∞⦾∞⦿●⦿∞⦾∞⦾∞<

The lord marshal's tent was surrounded by alert pickets, who had sworn upon penalty of death to keep any intruders, potential assassins, or random nuisances from their master's domain. Even so, no one noticed the small figure that darted stealthily from the horse corral, through the armory, past the smithy tent, and up to the very base of the army commander's brown canvas shelter. Disdaining the entranceway, where two guards shifted their weight from foot to foot and stared vigilantly into the night, the figure lifted up the edge of the tent, pressed himself flat against the ground, and slipped inside.

He rose to his full height, about that of a human child, peering into the pitch darkness of the shelter's interior. He crept to the low cot where Jaymes Markham lay sleeping. Extending a hand, the intruder poked sharply into the man's face.

"Psst! Wake up!"

There was sudden movement, a flash of steel, and the marshal was awake with a dagger in his hand, the tip halting a mere fraction of an inch from the intruder's throat.

"Hey—stop it!" protested the diminutive figure, twisting away. He was stopped by the man's hand as it reached out to clamp down, hard, on a thin, small shoulder.

"State your business," hissed Jaymes, his voice as cold as the blade held so steadily in his hand.

"Let me introduce myself. I'm Moptop Bristlebrow, professional guide and pathfinder!" The intruder twisted and pulled but couldn't break the steely grip. "*She* sent me; she said it was important! Hey, let me go!"

"'She'?" The marshal sat up on his cot and blinked a few times; then his eyes narrowed. "The Lady Coryn?"

"Yes!"

"Why? Tell me what she told you, exactly."

"She needs to see you in Palanthas. Right away—as soon as you can get there."

"And you'll take me to her?"

"That's what she said—I'm supposed to go with you."

"Who are you?"

"I told you, I'm a professional guide and pathfinder. And I'm an old friend of Lady Coryn. We go way back. To before she was Lady Coryn, or a white witch, or any such thing! She trusts me even more than she trusts you. Of course, I don't know how much she trusts you. I mean, I don't want to make any presumptions—"

"The Lady Coryn is very wise," said the lord marshal, rising from his bunk. "Go to the corral; tell the squires that I order that my horse be saddled."

"Oh, all right. The corral. That's where all the horses are, right? Boy, that place really stank, you know? I rushed right past it, holding my nose. You would have thought that horses . . . well, they're so pretty, that they wouldn't smell so bad. You know what I mean?"

"Go!" said the man.

"Uh, wait—I forgot, you won't need your horse," the kender objected. He scratched his head. "I don't know if we could take it even if you wanted to," he added mysteriously.

"What do you mean?"

The kender produced two small bottles from a pouch somewhere in his tunic. "Here," he said. "We're each supposed to drink one of these, and hold hands, and—well, it's a lot faster than horses and smells better too."

CHAPTER FOUR

LORD OF THE HORDE

Ankhar, the Truth, strolled through the lines of his great army, wrestling with a sense of disquiet that loomed over him like a dark thundercloud. The half-giant's problems seemed, on an almost daily basis, to be growing more and more insoluble.

It was not the loss of his company on the canyon wall to the explosive charges placed by his duplicitous enemy—indeed, if the Marshal of Solamnia had not tried some deadly payback scheme in spite of their truce, the half-giant would have been more surprised. The violence of the landslide had been an ingenious trap; the hulking commander admitted a grudging admiration for his enemy's cold, calculating originality.

He even chuckled as he remembered the deadly cloud cast by the most able of his Thorn Knights, the wizard called Hoarst. That man was a frightening character, calm and unemotional even as he perpetrated mass murder. The poisonous cloud had been silent and utterly lethal, and it came as a complete surprise to the enemy. Hoarst and his companions had proven invaluable to Ankhar during the first years of his war against

the Solamnics. The dark magic-user and his friends possessed
many useful talents.

But there was one other adviser who was closer to Ankhar's
ear, and to his heart. Now it was to her, to Laka, the hobgoblin
shaman who had rescued him as a babe from a cabin in the
mountains, that the half-giant made his way. She would be
in her tent, the shelter that had evolved into a kind of mobile
temple during the course of the past two years. Two burly ogres
stood guard outside the door, and they snapped to a semblance
of attention, holding their great halberds upright as the army
commander approached.

"*Est Sudanus oth Nikkas*," said one, chanting the army
motto.

"Aye. My power is my Truth," the half-giant echoed,
pleased.

"You are the Truth, lord," pledged the other ogre.

Ankhar acknowledged the honorifics with a grunt. He was
pleased to have his troops stand at "attention" and to offer him
salutes. These innovations had been introduced to the horde by
one of his most capable officers, Captain Blackgaard, formerly
of Mina's Dark Knights. Such civilized ideals of obedience and
discipline could only make his fierce fighters more effective in
battle.

Stepping through the open flap of the temple-tent, the
half-giant blinked and allowed his eyes to adjust to the gloom.
He was keenly aware of the smells—Laka's smells, including
the acrid stink of perspiration, the sweet musk of the oil she
smeared through her hair, the perfumes and incense that she
used in the myriad of confusing rites she performed, all of which
were devoted to the greater glory of Hiddukel, Prince of Lies.
Cinnamon and cloves sweetened the air, while in the background
lurked an essence of something hinting at very old cheese.

Her voice, a cackling rasp, emerged from the shadows and as always, brought him comfort and hope.

"Ankhar, my bold son, you come to me with troubles weighing upon your shoulders."

"Aye, Mother." He could see inside the gloomy tent now and made out the twin green specks of fire that marked the eyes of Laka's most potent talisman. She raised it high, a ghastly human skull set upon a shaft of ivory, and when she shook it, the luminous emeralds rattled around in their sockets, tumbling and blinking with power. The death's-head was a trophy of Ankhar's first great victory; it had formerly housed the brain of a captain of Garnet, the first city sacked by the half-giant's war on Solamnia.

Gradually, the rest of the shaman came into view as she shuffled forward. Her skin was wrinkled and brown as old leather, a dark contrast to the gold chains that ringed her narrow throat and clinked noisily across her skinny chest. She wore the same ragged shirt of fur that had kept her warm through the snowy winters of the Garnet range, though the baubles of pearl and ruby on her fingers were proof that her circumstances had improved from those days as a scavenging nomadic barbarian. Two gold teeth sparkled brightly from her lower jaw, an ornamental touch that gave her great pride, but nevertheless struck in Ankhar a small note of unease every time he saw them.

"Tell me the cause of your worry," she urged him, laying a clawlike hand upon his wrist. She squeezed with a grip like iron.

"It stands on the plains east of here; it taunts me with thick walls and high towers."

"It is the city that the humans call Solanthus," she replied evenly. "And it vexes you like a thorn in the paw of a mighty lion. It cripples you, so that you cannot march away from here, and yet it is shelled like a turtle so you cannot reach the soft meat within."

Ankhar had not thought about it in exactly those terms, but he nodded in agreement. "Now the knights reclaim lands west of the river. My army needs a great victory, a triumph to give my warriors hope and show to the humans my power—my Truth."

"Yes! You must take the city—destroy those walls, and slay all the humans who cower within. This is the victory you deserve. It is inevitable."

"But—how?" he asked. "Every one of our attacks have been driven back. We cannot strike at men inside parapets. My warriors die by the hundreds in trying."

"This is the question I will put forth in my dream," Laka declared in a tone that bolstered Ankhar's confidence considerably. "You go forth now, and make your army ready for a great battle. I will consult Hiddukel, and the Prince of Lies will show me the Truth."

⊱⊰⊱⊰⊱⊰❀⊱⊰⊱⊰⊱⊰

"We have captured three deserters. I suggest you summon the rest of your troops to witness their executions. It will be a valuable lesson to other cowardly souls." The speaker wore dark armor and a metal helm of the same color, with a breastplate that barely showed the faded outline of a black rose. He spoke to the half-giant with supreme confidence.

Captain Blackgaard, as usual, was making a lot of sense. Ankhar thought about the proposed executions for just a moment and nodded. "Do this. Are these deserters goblins?"

"Two are gobs. I regret to inform you that one is a human, a former Dark Knight who has disgraced the legacy of his company and his officers. All of my men will be punished for his

44

transgression. And I request, my lord, that the manner of these executions be such that it will create a vivid impression in the minds of those who view the punishment."

"Yes, they should leave an impression," the half-giant admitted. "How will you kill them?"

"I would like to have each deserter, in turn, rent by four powerful ogres, one pulling upon each of the wretch's limbs. The victim will be crippled beyond recovery and then will be left to lie in the sun until he succumbs to his shame . . . and his pain."

Blackgaard and Ankhar were meeting on a low hill that lay on the outer fringe of the horde's vast encampment. From here they could see a column of troops marching toward them from the north, the last detachment of the ogre brigade that had guarded the crossings of the Vingaard on the northern plains. They had been two hundred miles away when Ankhar gave the orders for the grand assembly, and thus, it had taken them nearly a week to reach the main force.

The half-giant commander stood on the hilltop, holding his mighty spear in one hand. With the butt resting on the ground, the spearhead rose as high as his head, and it cast a light that, in shadow or darkness, could be seen for miles around. The tip of Ankhar's spear was not steel, nor any other metal. Instead, it was a massive emerald, chiseled to a razor sharp edge on both sides, and enchanted with the mystical power of Hiddukel, Prince of Lies. When he held it thus, and it caught the sun, the spearhead cast a brilliant iridescent light visible for vast distances. Whenever his warriors saw that enchanted light, they took heart from it, and roared their approval of their mighty commander.

"We have warg riders posted in a picket line some fifty miles away," Blackgaard explained, confirming that the half-giant's orders had been carried out. "If the Solamnics make any move in our direction, we shall be certain to hear of it long before they become a threat. The river is defended for more than a hundred miles to the north and south. The bridges and fords are fortified; the Solamnics won't easily cross the Vingaard."

"Good." Ankhar turned from the empty plains to the west, casting his eyes upon the great square block that rose from the foothills to the east. The city, a massif of stone, high walls, parapets, towers, and gates, filled the horizon. At this distance, Solanthus seemed like a range of mountains—only with spiked towers and flat stretches of wall.

Ankhar was a trifle unsettled when Hoarst, the Thorn Knight, materialized several dozen paces away from him and came walking up to join the human and half-giant on the hillside. The man's teleportation magic was admirable, but Ankhar had taught him long ago not to blink himself into existence too close to his easily startled commander.

The trio stood in silence for a time, each gazing at Solanthus, each considering in his own way the problems of taking that great bastion. The entire place was surrounded by a lofty stone wall, more than thirty feet thick at the base. Numerous battle towers jutted above the main parapets; the humans could shower attackers with arrows, great rocks, and burning oil from these lofty vantages. Three massive gatehouses, each the size of a castle, provided access to the city at the west, north, and eastern walls.

To the south, Solanthus merged into the craggy foothills of the Garnet Mountains and was protected by an outcrop of rock that was separated from the rest of the range by a deep, almost impassable canyon. One road descended the north wall and climbed the southern face of this canyon, but it was easily covered by archers from the city's parapets—any attacking force trying to advance in that direction would likely be decimated before it could reach within a half mile of the small south gate.

Inside the city walls could be glimpsed a double pillar of rock, the Cleft Spires. It stood as though it were a monolith of bedrock left over from some long-petrified and colossal forest and as though, at some point, a god had taken a great, immortal axe and cloven the thing in two. Now the two slabs of rock stood side by side with a narrow gap between them. Aligned to the east and west, the sun was channeled refulgently through the gap during the spring and fall equinoxes. It was rumored that any tasks performed under the light of this narrow sunbeam, between the massive shadows of the opposing spires, was destined to draw the attention of the gods. Of course, this attention could be manifested as good or ill, such caprice being ever the purview of the deities.

Now the spring equinox was past, of course, and the long, hot summer loomed. If the city could not be taken during the upcoming season, Ankhar feared that the Solamnics would finally catch up to him, their great forces breaking the death grip of his army and relieving the starving city from its long siege.

"Do you see weakness there?" the half-giant asked. He had formed his own opinion—favoring the West Gate—but he was interested in what these humans thought.

"The gate to the west of the walls is where we should muster our main attack," Blackgaard declared. "See how it juts forth from the nearest angles of the main walls. It is not protected as thoroughly as the gates to the north and east. A large attack, with diversions to draw the attention away from the main effort, stands a fair chance of success."

"I agree," Hoarst said, "though it will be costly, in any event. Those gates are ancient, hewn from Vallenwood trunks that date back to the Age of Dreams. Even my most potent spells will be feeble against them; your army will have to storm the place with brute force, and there will be much shedding of blood."

"I have seen the way you and your Thorns flit about with this teleport magic. Can you not magick yourself into the city and work some mischief there? Perhaps even assassinate this duchess who has rallied her people so well?"

Hoarst shrugged noncommittally. "You have asked me that before. If I could do so, I would not hesitate. But there remains an aura around the place—I believe it is keyed somehow to the godly power in those two great spires. For some reason, teleport magic—my teleport magic, in any event—cannot penetrate that barrier. My men and I have tried this many times, and always the spell is cast to no effect; that is, the caster remains outside the walls. We cannot use magic spells to penetrate the defenses."

"Then it becomes a matter of smashing down a gate, probably the gate in the west," Ankhar said, trying to sound hopeful. But in truth he did not feel very optimistic. Somehow the plan lacked imagination, flair.

"Do not despair, my son." Laka spoke to Ankhar quietly, having shuffled up to the hilltop while the attention of the others was directed toward the city walls.

"Do you bring a message of hope?" he asked eagerly.

"I have lain with the Prince of Lies in my sleep, and he has given me a dream," she said. "You cannot breach those walls by yourself, but with the aid of an unusual ally, the attack has a better chance of succeeding."

"And what ally is this?" Ankhar inquired skeptically.

Laka grinned, and chanted in a sing-song voice.

"Flaming fist—ablaze of gaze,
Lord of fire, these walls will raze!"

Hoarst and Blackgaard exchanged a look.

"What does that mean?" pressed the half-giant, unfamiliar with the murky phrases.

"We must seek him on a quest—you and me, and the wizard should come too. It will not be easy, but if we succeed, you will gain the means to win this fight."

"But how do you know that this mysterious ally will join forces with my horde?"

Laka produced a pair of metal rings from her pouch. They were steel bracelets, small enough to encircle her wrists, too small even to be worn by a normal-sized man such as Hoarst. To Ankhar, they would have made loose rings on his largest fingers.

"These will bind him to your service. They have been blessed by the Prince of Lies, and the magic-user will make them especially potent with a spell of mastery. When we put them on this being that we seek, the being will become your slave."

"I know such a spell of mastery," Hoarst said, his voice low. "But these bracers are so small—how can one who wears them be an ally of such incredible power?"

"Leave that to me . . . and to the Prince," Laka said. "Cast your spell, and then we go seeking."

"I'll need to make some preparations. But I can begin tonight, and I might be finished in eight or ten hours."

"Very well," agreed the half-giant. "So let us start this quest in the morning."

꘡ⵔⵔⵔ꘡ⵔⵔⵔ꘡

Ankhar's optimism waned considerably as his mother led the trio on an arduous climb up a rocky ravine, ascending into the wilds of the Garnet range. Finally she halted, gesturing in triumph toward a shadowy cleft in the precipitous wall rising before them.

49

The mouth of the cave looked too small to accommodate Ankhar's bulk, and he growled his disappointment. "This is the way we must go?" he asked.

"This is the cave that was shown to me in my dream," Laka confirmed.

"Who or what is this ally?" he demanded to know, not for the first time.

Laka shook her head. "You will see when you see. Now come; we must make haste."

"But how will I fit inside?" demanded Ankhar, leaning forward to peer into the cleft. The interior was lost in shadow.

"You will fit. But the wizard should go first," Laka replied.

Hoarst stood beside the half-giant, his expression unreadable. He had consented to join the commander and the witch doctor on this quest—of course, he really had had no choice—though he had his doubts. Now he merely shrugged and started into the dark, stone-walled passage. He drew his rapier and murmured a word of magic, causing a glare of bright light to burst from the blade. Holding this metallic glow over his head, he led the way forward.

"You go next," Laka said. "I'll follow."

Mutely, Ankhar lowered his head—not quite enough because almost immediately he bumped his noggin against a sharp stalactite—and followed. He had to edge sideways to move his bulky form through the tight passageway, and with a subsequent turn to the side, the pale daylight of the cave's mouth was utterly screened from his view. But then the cavern widened, and the ceiling arched to a more comfortable height overhead. Hoarst and the light were moving a few paces in front of him, and the half-giant hurried unconsciously, reluctant to find himself isolated in the encompassing darkness. Laka, her dark eyes gleaming like sparks, traipsed after him with her short, nimble steps. She held her death's-head talisman aloft, and the emerald stones glinted wickedly.

The green glow added to the light from Hoarst's blade, and gradually Ankhar's eyes adjusted to the darkness.

The cavern floor descended through a series of winding turns, not unlike the creek bed in a narrow canyon. Indeed, there were stones and boulders jumbled together as if they had been washed here by torrents of water. The half-giant shivered as he pictured a subterranean flood, a deluge sweeping through here that could drown him in the eternal depths of the world.

But the stones on the floor seemed dry, and any flood of old seemed long gone. The trio made their way deeper and deeper below the surface of Krynn. For a long time they walked. Ankhar had a hard time estimating the hours they had been underground. Nevertheless, he felt certain that they had walked many miles and gradually became convinced that those hours had stretched through the night and into the following day.

Of course, there was no way to tell by the absent sun. The chill of the subterranean shadow land penetrated his clothes and his skin, made his sweat clammy and acrid. The place was utterly soundless except for the faint sounds of their passage: the scuff of the Thorn Knight's leather moccasins on the rocks, the clinking crunch of Ankhar's hobnails. Laka's breaths came from behind, sharp pants that indicated her exertion or perhaps her taut excitement.

The half-giant grunted as he pulled his bulky frame around a large boulder. He cursed under his breath every time his head knocked into an unseen overhead obstacle.

"Hold that damned light higher!" he hissed, irritated at the panic in his voice. Hoarst seemed to be pulling farther away from him. The magic-user obligingly halted and held his blade so the path at Ankhar's feet was clearly revealed. The cavern floor continued to descend, growing steeper with every footstep until they were almost skidding down a narrow chute.

Abruptly Hoarst halted and raised a cautioning hand. Ankhar came up slowly behind him, straining to see. He saw exactly *nothing,* only a void of cold air. The magic-user waved his illuminated sword around, revealing that the cavern walls to the right, the left, and above them all abruptly terminated; so did the floor.

They appeared to stand at the edge of a vault of space.

"I saw this place in the dream!" Laka declared excitedly, her breath hot at Ankhar's side. Her flashing eyes fixed upon the magic-user. "We must leave this cliff and get down to the bottom!"

Hoarst's eyes narrowed, but he bit his tongue.

"How?" demanded Ankhar.

"You tell us!" Laka cackled, still staring at the Thorn Knight. "*You* must get us down from here. To the bottom! And then our quest will go on."

CHAPTER FIVE

THE WHITE WITCH

'Hey, I thought we were going right to Coryn's!" Moptop protested as the two travelers materialized on the highway about a mile south of the great city of Palanthas. The towers, walls, gates, and palaces of the place stood outlined by the morning sun, gleaming against a clear blue sky. "I'm the pathfinder, remember? What did you do to screw up my path?"

"We'll be there in an hour or two," Jaymes replied, starting forward with measured strides. "But first I'd like the people in the city to know that I've arrived."

Ignoring the dozen additional questions and objections lodged by the kender, the lord marshal turned into a reputable livery stable. He purchased a fine white gelding with a saddle and tack to match the splendid animal. Thus mounted, he proceeded toward the city gate with the sulking kender perched on the saddle before him.

Palanthas sprawled along the southern shore of the Bay of Branchala, white and glittering and prosperous looking. The whole of the place was visible from the mountain road, and Jaymes

53

found the sight both energizing and oddly sinister. He liked the commerce of the great city, the throngs of people, the wealth of goods and services unmatched anywhere else on Ansalon. But he distrusted the lords and nobles who ruled here, who jealously amassed then guarded their fortunes with such miserly greed.

The richest, and probably most miserly, of these was the lord regent of the city, Bakkard du Chagne. His palace was clearly visible from the road, for it stood not within the city walls, but upon the slopes of one of the mountains that rose over Palanthas. The Golden Spire, the regent's lofty tower where his great treasure of gold was secured, rose from the midst of his residential compound, the highest point for miles around. It was a fitting location, Jaymes reflected, for Bakkard du Chagne to live, as the lord regent considered himself not of this place, but above it in all ways. He had cheated, stolen, deceived and—though only a few knew this—committed murder to achieve his station.

Jaymes was one who knew the full extent of the regent's crimes. It was quite possible that he could have brought the arrogant nobleman tumbling down from his high pedestal by publicizing all that he knew. But such a destructive act would not serve any useful purpose, Jaymes had decided some time ago. So instead he had bit his tongue, taking some comfort from the fact that the regent knew he knew . . . and hated and feared him.

But Jaymes had not teleported to Palanthas to visit Bakkard du Chagne. He had other things in mind.

Moptop Bristlebrow brightened as the prancing gelding moved down the wide highway toward the city's main gate. "Let's go to the docks, first, all right?" the kender suggested, pointing excitedly. "They were bringing some huge crabs in from the north shore just before I left. Maybe there's still a few claws left. They were giving them away!"

"Giving them away?" Jaymes mused. "I thought they were

a delicacy—a few claws can pay the wages of a fisher for two tendays."

"Well, they were giving them away to me," Moptop declared offhandedly. "I guess other people might have to pay."

"No doubt," said the marshal. "But I don't have time for crab claws just now. If you want to go to the waterfront, I'll happily drop you off right here. It sounded like Lady Coryn's summons was rather urgent, though, so I think I'd best check in with her."

"Well, yeah. She did kind of indicate that it was important. So maybe I'll go with you for now. And later on we can visit the docks, right?"

"Who rides there?" called a liveried sergeant at arms, wearing the tunic of the Palanthian Legion. He stepped into the roadway and raised his hand, while several comrades, armed with halberds or longbows, emerged from the shadows below the tower to stand beside him.

"The Lord Marshal of the Army of Solamnia," Jaymes replied.

"Make way!" added the kender, unnecessarily it turned out, for the guards, recognizing the human rider, hastily had cleared out of the way.

"Welcome to Palanthas, my lord!" offered the sergeant, saluting smartly.

Jaymes nodded as he guided the horse through the open gate and along the main avenue leading to the heart of the city. People pointed and whispered, and several ladies tittered as he glanced in their direction. Boys went running down the streets, calling out the news of his arrival.

When he turned toward Nobles Hill, the lads shouted the news to the gathering citizens: "He's going to the wizard's house!"

Coryn lived in one of the great manors in that auspicious neighborhood, a house that was owned by the Mistress of the Red Robes, Jenna. The Head of the Orders of Magic, nowadays Jenna resided in the Tower of High Sorcery in Wayreth Forest, and had willingly ceded the use of her house to the powerful white-robed enchantress.

The Lady Coryn—the White Witch to some—was a fascinating figure to all of Solamnia. She was beautiful and mysterious, a wielder of immense power, a friend to the weak and downtrodden, and a ceaseless worker toward the future of a realm that was just, strong, and eternal. To Jaymes Markham she was all this . . . and much, much more.

Jaymes kicked his new horse in the flanks, and the gelding agreeably broke into a jaunty trot. Jaymes scanned the streets, eager for his first glimpse of Coryn.

"Hey, you're whistling!" noted the kender in delight. "I didn't take you for a whistler! It's like you're suddenly happy or something. Are you?"

The Lord Marshal of the Solamnic Army frowned, shaking his head in surprise. "It's been a long time," he admitted. "I'm looking forward to seeing her again."

"Well, there it is—that's Coryn's house, right there."

"I know," Jaymes said. If the sight brought back a whirl of memories—and it did—his face betrayed no hint of his emotions. Yet he kneed his horse's flanks so hard that the steed tossed his head, bucking a little as they trotted into the wide courtyard.

The house was a splendid villa, dominating a shoulder of Nobles Hill. The yard was sprinkled with fountains, elaborate statuary spouting geysers that were magically sustained all day, every day. The original fountains had been created by Jenna, but Coryn enjoyed them enough to maintain them, and indeed, the splashing rivulets that babbled and gurgled in their basins added a soothing element to the enchanted environment.

"Hey—I see goldfish! Let me off here!" insisted Moptop as they rode past a deep pool lined with lily pads, home to a dozen or more huge, brilliantly hued carp. Jaymes obliged quickly, lowering the kender by one arm while barely slowing his horse.

He reined in as he drew up before great carved doors atop broad marble steps leading to a portico. A lad with a broad grin stepped down to take the reins of his horse.

"Hi, Donny," Jaymes greeted him. "How did you know I was coming?"

"Well, Lady Coryn told me to keep an eye out; she thought you'd be here today. I'll take care of your horse for you, my lord."

"Thanks," Jaymes replied, handing over the reins. "He deserves a good rubdown—but go easy on the oats until he's rested a bit."

"Will do, sir!" Donny led the gelding away, toward the stables on the far side of the courtyard, while Jaymes sauntered up the broad steps. The front doors opened before he reached them, and he nodded at Rupert's welcoming smile.

"Good day, my lord," said the faithful attendant. The man was butler, watchman, and all around helpmate to the enchantress. He had worked in Jenna's service for years, and had smoothly switched to serving Coryn. "I hope you had a pleasant journey."

"It went by very quickly," replied the marshal. "And it's over now. The lady?"

"She is up in her laboratory, sir, expecting you, I should think. She ordered that, when you arrived, you were to be guided directly into her presence."

"Thanks, Rupert. You're looking well, and Donny seems to be turning into a fine young man."

"Thank you, my lord. He does have a good head on his shoulders, it seems to me. And a warm welcome to you."

Jaymes well knew the way. He took the steps three at a time up the grand circling stairway that climbed from the main hall. The upper floor of the villa was divided into two wings, one where the bedrooms, guest suites, and other inhabitable rooms were located, and another that housed the wizard's laboratory. Jaymes turned in that direction, inhaling the familiar musty scents of incense and soot. There were stoves and even a miniature forge here, as well as storage rooms containing a myriad of exotic ingredients. But the main chamber was a long workroom with wide windows arranged to catch the maximum amount of sunlight and a veranda that offered a chance to pace and reflect or simply a splendid view of the Old City and the harbor beyond.

"Coryn!" Jaymes said, striding into the laboratory through the open door. She was standing with her back to him, her black hair fanned out across her shoulders, falling almost to her waist. Her white robe was, of course, immaculate—even when she worked with sooty components, shaping objects in clay and mud, blasting gouts of high heat through burners, she never seemed to get so much as a speck of debris on that robe.

Jaymes started across the room toward her and reached for her shoulder, but something in her still, rigid posture held his hand. He stopped, letting his arms fall to his sides.

"Coryn? The kender brought a summons . . . from you, he said."

"Yes," she replied, turning slowly to regard him. Coryn was a very beautiful woman—one of the two most beautiful women Jaymes had ever seen—but now her eyes were cold, her gorgeous cheekbones as white as though etched from ivory. "I did send for you. What took you so long to get here? We should have started working at dawn."

His face didn't betray how much her cold gaze unsettled him. "I rode through the city," he explained. "It's been a long time since the people of Palanthas have seen their lord marshal. But I came here directly. What's the urgency?"

"I need your blood. Sit, there," Coryn said, directing him to a chair beside a long wooden table.

He obeyed, watching her through narrowed eyes. "My blood? All of it or just a few drops?"

For the first time, her icy facade cracked with a flicker of emotion that made him think that she would rather enjoy taking all of his blood. But she merely shrugged and picked up a large glass vial. "I need to fill this up. You'll find yourself a bit tired afterward, but with some rest and food, you'll be back on your feet soon enough."

Footsteps pounded down the hallway, and Moptop burst into the laboratory as Jaymes was taking a seat in the chair.

"I brought him right here, Lady! Just like you ordered. He wanted to go down to the wharf and look for crabs, but I told him he shouldn't dilly-dally."

"Well, thank you very much, Moptop. You are a very professional guide."

"I myself brought Coryn here, all the way from the Icereach," the kender said to Jaymes proudly, "back when she was a girl. I'm pretty good at guiding folks."

"Now why don't you guide your own way down to the docks. Have Rupert give you some coins so that you can buy some crab claws for dinner."

"*Buy* them? But they give them away! At least, I think they do!"

"Well, do me a personal favor and pay for them this time, all right?" Coryn urged, gently insistent.

"Well, all right." The kender seemed more puzzled than disappointed, but he nevertheless rushed off to find Rupert.

Jaymes had been thinking. "All this fuss about my blood," he mused. "It means that you've figured out a way to make the potion. The elixir you told me was impossible to make."

She glared at him, and he began to see the reason for her attitude. "I thought it *was* impossible. But there were certain clues in some of Jenna's oldest books. It's a dark spell, and if I didn't see the need, I would never attempt it. This is more like a job for Dalamar than for one who wears white robes—and I don't like it!"

"But we both know how important it is for the future—if Solamnia is ever to be a kingdom, an empire, again. You know as well as I do why it is necessary!"

"Yes." She stared at him. "But I rather hoped such a potion was impossible. After all, the princess is not my enemy! However, I agree with you that this may be a way to unite the plains states with the city of Palanthas."

In fact, the city-states on the plains had been in terrible disarray until recently. Their dukes had been weak and petty and spent an inordinate amount of time feuding with each other. Ankhar's invasion had weakened the realm beyond repair, and Jaymes Markham had usurped the dukes, one by one. With Ankhar on the brink of ultimate victory, Jaymes had united the armies under his command and driven the invaders from the environs of Caergoth, then he had liberated Thelgaard and Garnet. Some three-quarters of the lands of the ancient Solamnic kingdom were now under the protection of the lord marshal. Only besieged Solanthus remained behind the enemy lines.

Palanthas, the most important of all Solamnic cities, remained under du Chagne's iron control, however. Furthermore, du Chagne administered the wealth that financed Jaymes's armies. As long as Jaymes was successful, the lord regent grudgingly accepted the cost. But he kept his own substantial army, the Palanthian Legion, safe at home. Now Jaymes needed that army, and du Chagne's wealth, to carry the campaign to its conclusion.

"So my blood is a key ingredient."

"Yes." The white wizard had picked up a short, thin dagger and nimbly whetted the blade on a small stone she held in her left hand. The *scritch . . . scritch . . . scritch* of metal against rock seemed to echo her mood. "You're a real bastard, you know that?" she said.

He flinched. "I'm merely doing what needs to be done for Solamnia. You and I both know that."

"*I'm* doing what needs to be done for Solamnia. *You're* doing what you want to do . . . for yourself. You treat the princess like just another of your pawns—like you treat me!"

"You know that's not true," he replied. "Let's get it over with."

"Bastard!"

He shrugged. "Maybe this job needs to be done by a bastard. Solamnia needs a strong ruler!"

"Hold out your hand." She set down the whetstone and touched the dagger with the edge of her thumb. "Put it down, here." Coryn moved the glass vial to a small stool next to the chair and arranged Jaymes's arm so his hand was hanging down, with his fingers just above the top of the container.

With one smooth gesture, the wizard sliced the blade through Jaymes's forearm. He grimaced; the pain was sharp, intense, and burning. Immediately blood began to flow, a crimson stream running down the skin of his wrist, over his palm, and down his fingers. He watched as a steady trickle of the precious liquid flowed into the large vessel.

By the time the vial was filled, Jaymes was beginning to feel light-headed.

"All right, lift your arm." She deftly wrapped a cloth bandage over the wound, spinning the material around his arm three or four times, pulling it tight, and cinching it with a quick knot. "Can you stand up?"

"I think so." Jaymes swayed as he took his feet, but Coryn supported him, and he leaned on her gratefully as she steered him toward the door of the lab. They went out into the hall. The wizard guided him through an open door and to the edge of a small bed where he sat down gratefully.

"Rest here for as long as you need to. I'm going back to work."

"Thanks. Coryn?"

"Yes?" She stopped at the door.

"How long will it take? The potion?"

"Don't worry about that for now. The most important thing will be for you to get back to your army and break the siege. Matters in Solanthus are dire, and the suffering there grows greater every day. I'll preserve the potion until you get back."

He leaned across the small bed, resting his back against the wall, fighting dizziness. But he met her steely gaze. "No, I want the potion before I leave the city. I intend to use it right away."

Her eyes narrowed. Her scorn—and hurt—was palpable. "There is no battle more important, nowhere else where the fates of light and darkness are so tautly drawn. Win that battle, Jaymes—let light prevail!"

"Yes, Solanthus is important," the marshal acknowledged. "But so is that potion, important to me. I'm in Palanthas, and that's where I need to use it. So you will give it to me when it is done. After I've used it, I'll go back to my army. And then we'll break the siege."

She stared at him. Despite the powerful magic she could wield at the snap of her fingers, she looked for the moment more like a girl than a woman. Coryn blinked, but if there were tears brimming in her eyes, she held them back. Setting her jaw, she shook her head. "No."

"This is not negotiable," Jaymes said flatly. "I tell you I need that potion—as soon as it's ready. You will give it to me, or there will be trouble between us. Agreed?"

She sighed, her shoulders slumping, seeming to shrink, becoming smaller, almost frail.

"It will be done tomorrow," she said, closing the door behind her.

⊰⊙⊱⊰⊙⊱⊰⊙⊱✿⊰⊙⊱⊰⊙⊱⊰⊙⊱

Jaymes woke sometime in the afternoon, feeling refreshed. He joined Moptop, Rupert, and Donny for a dinner of steamed crab claws and melted butter. Coryn remained at work in her laboratory, and after a few hours of restless pacing—and several curt rejections when he made so bold as to knock on her door—he retired for the night. A downy mattress and soft pillow were his bed, preferable to the woolen bedroll spread on the ground that was his usual resting place.

Or maybe it was the loss of blood that caused the lord marshal to sleep more soundly than he had in a very long time. When he awoke, he could hardly believe that the sun was streaming through his window and that dawn had passed—unnoticed by him—several hours before.

He rose and dressed hurriedly, irritated with himself for sleeping late. He headed immediately for the laboratory. This time, after his peremptory knock, Coryn beckoned him to enter.

He was vaguely aware that she had been crying, but his eyes went immediately to the small, clear container the white wizard held gingerly in her slender fingers.

"That's it?" he said. The container was barely larger than a thimble, and the contents—a potion of liquid as red as his blood—would barely have filled a teaspoon.

"That's it," she said coldly. "You should add it to some wine . . . red wine, of course. It is tasteless, has no smell. When she drinks, the . . . the potion will take effect. And you don't have to worry if you drink some; since it is made from your blood, it will have no effect on you."

Jaymes reached for the small vial. It was hard to imagine this small amount of liquid had the power to solve his problems.

He looked at Coryn and saw that she was blinking rapidly; her eyes were still moist. He nodded, slowly, and opened his mouth to speak.

"Don't say anything!" she said.

He shrugged, turned away, and departed. The laboratory door slammed behind him so hard and so loudly that he almost dropped the vial.

CHAPTER SIX

THE LORD REGENT

The lord regent's palace guards knew the lord marshal by sight. Though he was not welcome in this place, they also knew better than to try and delay him at the gate. Instead, the sergeant made a great ceremony of greeting the lone rider, ostentatiously ordering the great drawbridge to be lowered while, at the same time, dispatching a runner to warn his master of the impending arrival of the visitor from the plains.

Jaymes barely acknowledged the reception, instead guiding his gelding at a walk into the deep courtyard below the lofty palace walls. Handlers emerged from the stable, and he dismounted before the great doors to the regency residence. He was already striding up the steps before the horse was led away.

Those massive doors swung open at his approach, a pair of guards snapping to attention while an officious, bewigged courtier hastened down the great interior hall.

"My Lord Marshal!" cried Baron Dekage, the regent's aide-de-camp. "What a splendid—and unexpected—surprise! We had a report that you were in the city but could only hope that you would find the time to pay an official visit to his lordship.

65

He is expecting you, of course. Can I show you the way to his office?"

"I remember how to get there," Jaymes said brusquely, sweeping past the flustered nobleman. He took another few steps then halted, turning to regard Dekage with a raised eyebrow. "But can you tell me: is Lady Selinda in?"

"Why, er, yes. Yes she is."

"Could you send word to her? I'd like to drop in and say hello to her after I've finished my business with her father."

"Why, yes, my lord. Of course—I'll let her know immediately." The aide started away.

The lord marshal looked up to see Lord Frankish, the captain of the Palanthian Legion, coming up the corridor. The big man walked smoothly, like a great cat. His long arms swung at his sides, and his black mustache shined as if it had just been oiled.

"Excuse me, my lord," the captain said. "I couldn't help but overhear."

"And?" The lord marshal's tone was bored.

"And"—Frankish, a Lord of the Order of the Rose, stiffened— "I am afraid I must insist that you tell me why you would like to meet with the Princess Selinda."

"Ask her yourself . . . after I'm finished," Jaymes replied. "If she wants you to know, she'll tell you."

"Do you understand, my lord, that my interest in the matter is more than casual?" The lord's tone was as oily as his mustache. But he was a warrior, and it seemed to take a real effort of will for him not to strike out at the lord marshal.

"I don't really care what your interest is. I'm not discussing my affairs with you. Good evening."

Jaymes stalked away. Lord Frankish stood in place for a long time, his fingers clenching and unclenching as he watched the departing figure of the lord marshal.

Lord Regent Bakkard du Chagne was standing at his desk, staring impassively at the door that an attendant opened to admit Jaymes. "Hello, Lord Marshal," du Chagne said warily. "How fares the campaign against the horde?"

Jaymes shrugged. "As you know, it would be going better if I had use of the Palanthian Legion. Two thousand more knights, with infantry, would probably be enough to turn the tide."

Du Chagne shook his head. "I've told you before—it's out of the question. They're my only remaining reserve, and if I send them to the plains, I'll leave this great city all but undefended." He offered a reptilian smile. "I will speak to Lord Frankish, to see if he can spare a few companies, however."

"Don't bother. I can guess where he stands."

The lord marshal sat in one of the regent's comfortable armchairs and helped himself to a cigar from the humidor on the table by the fireplace. He leaned forward and lit the cigar off of an ember from the fading fire. Du Chagne took the adjacent chair, helping himself to a cigar as well. For a moment the two men sat in silence, a cloud of smoke surrounding them until it gradually began to be drawn up the chimney.

"I could make the same arguments that I've been making for a year," Jaymes said with forced casualness. "That the only threat to this city is Ankhar's army, the force that I'm facing on the plains. That your knights are growing fat and lazy here and need some battle time to remind them who they are and why they exist. But I won't make those arguments. Not tonight."

"I'm pleased that you have started to see the matter through my eyes," du Chagne noted, smiling. "After all, you have three armies under your command already. And it's simply not wise to put all of our troops too far away from the base of our power . . . which is here, of course, in Palanthas. And you know, as to funding, of course I will continue to meet your payroll needs. Here in the city we're all grateful for the job you and your men are doing—truly we are. But it's—"

"I'm not making those arguments tonight because I didn't come here to see you," Jaymes interrupted sharply. "I knew that would have been a waste of time."

Du Chagne's eyes narrowed. "Why did you come here, then?"

"I came to see your daughter. I just stopped in your office for appearance's sake. We both know that there's no point in going over the same ground we've been debating for the last year."

"My daughter?" The lord regent was nonplussed. He stood up, puffing his cigar until a furious coal glowed at the end then paced over toward his desk. He paused and turned to face his visitor. "Listen to me, Jaymes. I want you to stay away from her!"

Jaymes stood up. "I'm happy to hear it. Because I also came here to give you a message regarding your daughter: Your wishes are of no concern to me," he said.

Du Chagne's eyes suddenly flicked to the door, and the lord marshal turned to see Lord Frankish and a lord knight dressed in a white tunic with the Kingfisher emblem. Jaymes recognized the magic-user by reputation, though the two men had never met. The two strode into the office unannounced but clearly welcomed by the lord regent.

"Ah, my lords!" declared du Chagne, obviously relieved. "Welcome. Lord Marshal, this is Sir Russel Moorvan of the Kingfishers." The regent waved absently at the white-clad lord, who regarded Jaymes with an odd smile of curved lips.

"Your reputation precedes you, Lord Marshal," said the magic-using knight.

"I see that you arrived safely from Sancrist," Jaymes said wryly. Moorvan flushed—the placid waters from Sancrist to Palanthas offered one of the most secure sea routes of Ansalon.

"Several of my companies are arriving shortly. I intend to have one of them join your units in the field," the mage declared icily. "If they would be welcome."

Jaymes nodded, his eyebrows raised. "I can use men who can fight—whether with swords or sorcery."

"*Magic.* Sorcery is the purview of those who do not honor the three moons," Moorvan clarified. His hands danced before him, fingers entwining and untangling as if making a subtle demonstration. His eyes, cold and aloof, never left Jaymes's face.

"In any event, by all means, send them to the front as soon as you can."

"I believe, my Lord Marshal, that you were about to report to the lord regent about the state of affairs in the field. I should like to hear," the wizard said softly. His eyes were warm now, even friendly, and Jaymes blinked, trying to assess the situation.

Then, with a shrug, he nodded and with a wave of his cigar, began to outline the situation: His three armies were gathering on the Vingaard, ready to strike a combined blow eastward in an attempt the break the siege of Solanthus. He described the placements of his forces and those of the enemy, as far as was known. He deliberately refrained from inviting their suggestions as to strategy.

In fact, the lord regent and his companions asked several perfunctory questions before surprising Jaymes by pronouncing themselves pleased with matters. Jaymes struggled to focus on their words, feeling that he was missing something—but what?

"Thank you," du Chagne said. He stood, bowed, and gestured the lord marshal to the door. "Now if you will excuse us?"

Jaymes nodded, happy to leave. He departed the hall, collected his white horse from the stable, mounted the animal, and rode back toward Coryn's house. His mind was strangely vacant; it was as though he were riding in a dream, unaware of his surroundings.

It wasn't until he talked to Coryn later that he figured out what had happened.

⌖⊶⊷⊶⊷⊶⊷⊶⊷⊶⌖

The lord regent retreated to his private drawing room, lamplight gleaming from the windows of a single large room high up in the sprawling palace. This was the sanctuary du Chagne used to retreat from the myriad pressures, concerns, and complications of his office. The room was stoutly barred and when he was not present, securely locked. Whenever he was here, two burly axemen—lifelong veterans of the Palanthian Legion, sworn to serve du Chagne—stood on guard outside the door.

Inside the room were three other men. The temperature in the drawing room was stifling, for the day had been hot and the flames of the many oil lamps added warmth to the chamber. Nevertheless, the lord steadfastly refused to open the windows, and his guests, each a trusted subordinate, had long ago learned not to ask.

"They spy upon me whenever they can!" said du Chagne. "The White Witch seeks to know my every plan and intention, and the marshal has agents everywhere in the city—I'm sure of it! This is why I had you inspect, by magic, every inch of this room!"

"Of course, Excellency," Sir Moorvan replied in a soothing voice. "And there are no threats now."

Du Chagne nodded, not entirely convinced. "Even so, we will open no window, allow no gap that will ease their espionage by a single whit!"

The other three men exchanged glances. Sometimes du Chagne's excessive caution verged on the absurd. On this night, however, he had good cause for his paranoia.

"The lord marshal arrived in the palace this evening, hours ago." The chubby, balding regent continued to fume, pacing back and forth before one of the lofty windows. He was staring at the third man, the high priest of the Knight Clerists, for the other two in attendance had been privy to Jaymes Markham's presence in the palace.

Du Chagne stared out the window, his soft hands curling into fists. His city sprawled below him, mostly dark but brightened by the street lamps in the wealthier districts and by torches and other fires that glittered from tavern windows and from the guildhalls that were common gathering places. These were mere flickers in the vast, inky darkness.

A bell, probably on the temple of Shinare, dolefully tolled the eleventh hour.

"I must say he was insolent, contemptuous as usual. And he left only under persuasion—magical persuasion—from our Kingfisher here."

Moorvan shrugged modestly. "I merely clouded his thoughts for a little while, causing him to forget why he had come here."

"You cast a spell on him?" Inquisitor Frost, the Knight Clerist, expressed mingled surprise and admiration, but his expression was scolding. "Surely he will not let this insult go unchallenged!"

"Bah—I have greater things to worry about than insults to the lord marshal's dignity," the lord regent interjected snappishly. "He announced his intentions to see my daughter, and as soon as he comes out of his mental fog, he is bound to return!"

"My lord!" Lord Frankish leaped to his feet in unseemly agitation. "I must protest! He cannot be allowed to sully the reputation of the Princess Selinda!"

"No, I agree, Frankish. He certainly cannot. Who can guess his plans? He could at this moment be scheming to send some kind of secret message to my daughter. I admit she has had a soft spot for him, ever since he was acquitted of his crimes."

"If you wish, my lord," offered the Kingfisher. Sir Russell Moorvan was late of the order of White-Robed Mages but recently had been appointed as the new master of the order of Solamnic Auxiliary Mages—the Kingfishers. "It would be a simple matter to cast an enchantment such that we will be able to observe the princess in her chambers, here in the palace. If you could but provide me with a mirror, or even a bowl filled with clean water—"

"That's enough!" squawked du Chagne. "Spying, spying! Too much spying. I will not have you spying on my daughter!"

"Very well. I apologize, my lord," said Moorvan with a gracious bow.

"But we have to do something!" declared Lord Frankish peevishly. "The lord marshal grows too bold; he is a rogue and an upstart. Today he menaces your daughter. Tomorrow he may menace all of us. How do we know that he won't bring his army over the mountains and lay siege to *us* after he has finished with Ankhar and Solanthus."

"We don't. And that is precisely why I have called you here tonight," the lord regent said. "He must be stopped!"

"There are several ways we could proceed," Moorvan began, choosing his words carefully. "Of course, public perception must be taken into consideration. And timing. But I suggest that while have an opportunity to, we act now, while he is here in Palanthas."

"Can't you just order him arrested?" asked Frankish. "He does represent the Army of Solamnia, after all, and as such, should be expected to hold to the traditions of the knighthood. Everyone knows he blatantly ignores the tenets of the Oath and the Measure. We could challenge him on his disgrace to the knighthood."

"No," du Chagne answered curtly, shaking his head. "Nothing would be more certain to inflame the people to support him."

"Perhaps a more direct approach, then?" said the Kingfisher. "Some of my agents have, of necessity, established contacts with some of the more unsavory elements of our fair city—those who lurk in the darker sections of the waterfront. It has been reported to me, for example, that there is even a fledgling Assassin's Guild taking shape. . . ."

Again, du Chagne shook his head. "He is alert to treachery. I am familiar with a case—one of the late dukes was to blame, of course—where an assassin tried to waylay him. Even though Jaymes Markham was chained and a prisoner of the knighthood at the time, he succeeded in vanquishing the killer and making his escape. All around it was an embarrassment to those"—he coughed nervously—"involved."

"Er, yes, I had heard something of that as well," said the magic-using Kingfisher. "At the time, he was suspected of being the Assassin of Lorimar, was he not? He's a slippery one, that's for sure." He chuckled almost admiringly.

"Don't you have anything to suggest, mage?" demanded Frankish.

"I suggest we continue to cast the lord marshal in an unfavorable light so that public opinion gradually turns against him. Your speech at the recent harvest festival, Excellency, did a nice job of laying the groundwork. The people grow weary from the long war; certainly, they are tired of *paying* for that war. And it is well known that the lord marshal rose to his current position without birthright, without noble entitlement."

"No—unfortunately it was a matter of acclamation by the knights, after he had saved the army from Duke Walker's ineptitude," the Clerist said. "Really, it was a simple matter of momentary popularity. And he is certainly popular."

"Unfortunately," du Chagne said, "his popularity shows no signs of waning."

"All the more reason why we should not delay. If he returns to the front, benefits from some good fortune on the part of his troops, some signal victory, the marshal will be the people's darling." Moorvan stood and paced. "That cannot be allowed. We must arrange to have him removed, at least from his position of power, and possibly more."

"We decided that assassination is out of the question," the priest noted dryly. "At least, this was His Excellency's firm position!"

"Yes!" du Chagne said. "The risks—to us—are too great!"

The thin-faced magic-user gazed pensively at Lord Frankish. "You, my lord, are among those who would court the fair daughter of our regent, are you not?"

"The fact is well known! But what does that have to do with anything?"

"It's just that . . . if anything should impugn the honor of the princess . . . well, it seems to me that she might need a loyal and accomplished champion to defend her honor. That might supply an honorable solution to this whole predicament."

"You mean, take on Jaymes Markham in a duel?" demanded Frankish. He stood and paced toward the door. Dueling was rare in Palanthas, but it had a long tradition in Solamnic culture. It was structured around ritualized combat and frequently

74

resulted in the death—or at least crippling—of the loser. It was a testament to the lord's courage—and to the fervor of his interest in the Princess Selinda—that he did not immediately discount the idea.

"Do you think I could defeat him?" the Rose lord asked.

"You're an accomplished swordsman, certainly." It was the Kingfisher who spoke for the group. "Given matching weapons, a fair fight, you would have a very good chance."

"But *only* a chance!" the Clerist protested.

Frankish stretched to his full height—he was a big man, broad shouldered and formidable—and addressed the lord regent. "I am not afraid of the marshal," he said. "If it is your wish, my lord, that I issue this challenge—"

"I can't afford to lose you!" snapped du Chagne.

"No, indeed, we—none of us—could afford to lose our esteemed General Frankish." The Kingfisher spoke soothingly. His eyes narrowed as he scratched his chin, staring at Lord Frost. "My dear Clerist—would it be possible for you to research this matter in the temple archives? The last duel under the knighthood's rule was many decades ago, but it would be useful to learn the nuances. You could clarify the rules and the risks."

"Certainly, if it is my lord's wish."

"Please," du Chagne said. "I would consider it a personal favor if you would investigate this matter at once."

"Of course, my lord. It is my pleasure to serve." The priest rose from his chair, bowed, and left the room. The lord regent spoke again as soon as the door closed behind him.

"Think, now! A duel is too dangerous. We need a better plan, something more assured of success."

"Begging the lord regent's pardon," the Kingfisher said quietly. "I had not finished outlining my plan. But I don't think we need bother the lord Clerist with the details."

"Hmm, I see." Du Chagne was intrigued. "Go on."

"I think our Rose Lord Frankish could be furnished with the means to win this duel in a way that will remain undetected. As you know, part of the dueling ritual requires that opponents be armed with identical weapons, and that an impartial judge and at least two wizards are present to ensure that neither party makes use of any magical device."

"Yes, I know all that," the regent said impatiently.

The Kingfisher refused to be hurried. "I suggest that I cast upon our lord here a spell of haste, before the fight. If he is reasonably subtle in its employment, such that he limits himself to slight improvements in his normal reflexes, attack speeds, parries, and so forth, no one ought to notice the enchantment. But it will provide him with enough of an advantage that he could block every blow directed at him and—eventually, after putting on a convincing show for the judge—enable him to make the killing thrust. I didn't feel the Clerist would care for my little subterfuge and thought it best to send him on a little errand while we discussed things."

"Hmm, but what about the other wizard? The White Witch will surely be alert for any treachery."

"A spell is not like a magical device. There is no detection she will be able to conjure that will indicate Lord Frankish is the beneficiary of a haste spell. It will depend upon your discretion, of course," the Kingfisher noted, turning his attention to the lord. "If you move about in a blur, she will suspect—so, as I said, subtlety will be the key."

"Can you do that?" asked the lord regent.

"Yes, of course!" replied Frankish. He stood and paced around the room, punching his fist into the palm of his hand. He whirled, shuffled his feet, almost as if he were mentally choreographing his movements in the duel. "I shall challenge him at the first opportunity."

"Who will be the judge?" asked du Chagne.

"I do believe our colleague, the Clerist lord inquisitor, would serve well in that role," declared Moorvan slyly.

The three men were silent for a long time, each lost in thought.

"The White Witch remains a danger to us," said the lord regent, breaking the silence. "She will undoubtedly attend and be on the lookout for mischief."

"I will seek her out after the challenge and suggest we attend together," Sir Moorvan replied. "I can make sure that she finds no opportunity to cast spells of her own. She will neither detect the haste spell, nor influence the fight by magic. And by my invitation to attend, she will perhaps have her suspicions lulled."

"Very well," declared the regent firmly. "The matter is decided. Now, how do we initiate the plan?"

"There, too," said the Kingfisher with a thin smile, "I have an idea. . . ."

❧◦❀◦❀◦❀◦❀◦❀◦❀◦❀◦❧

"From the look on your face, I will judge that your mission was unsuccessful," Coryn said curtly. She had been seated behind her desk when the lord marshal returned to her laboratory, and after a curious look at Jaymes, she returned her attention to the thick tome she had been reading.

He merely shrugged and crossed the office to the cabinet where she kept several bottles of wine as well as a corked bottle of fine brandy. After a cursory inspection of the wines, he poured himself a generous draught of the dark liquor. Taking a sip, he turned to regard Coryn and saw that she had set her book aside and was looking at him speculatively.

"The wizard confounded me," he admitted at last. "I never even noticed him casting his spell. But I departed without seeing the princess—without even remembering why I was there, in fact!"

"Sir Moorvan is capable of skullduggery, no doubt. But this is not too surprising. Will you return to your army now?" Coryn asked without a great deal of hope.

Jaymes glared at her. "No. This was a temporary diversion. I will go back there tomorrow, and if the magic-user tries to bewitch me again, I will run him through."

"That would be taking matters to the extreme," said the white wizard disapprovingly. She stood and closed her book, returning it to the shelf. "Right now," she said with a sigh of resignation, "we need to get some rest. You can use the same room you slept in last night."

"We?" Jaymes asked warily.

She nodded. "Tomorrow, when you go to call on the lord regent and his daughter, I'm going with you."

CHAPTER SEVEN

ARMY OF DARKNESS

"We must get off this cliff—down there into dark," insisted Laka, gesturing with her death's-head totem. She glared at Ankhar and Hoarst when neither of her companions made any move to fling themselves into the apparently bottomless space.

The chasm was vast and eerie, utterly lightless yet somehow strangely alive. Every whisper they made, every scuff of feet or clink of a buckle, was amplified by the gulf of darkness. Ankhar felt the hair at the nape of his neck prickle, and could not suppress a growl. The half-giant clenched his great spear in both fists, brandishing the emerald head.

"Do you know what's down there?" asked the Thorn Knight skeptically. "Or even how far it is to the bottom?"

"It doesn't matter," the shaman replied. "This is the way we must go. It is one reason you needed to come."

"There is another reason as well, I presume?" the wizard wondered.

"Yes, but that is for later. First, you must get us down to the bottom of this great space."

The Thorn Knight looked as though he were inclined to argue, but after a moment he nodded curtly. "I can do this," Hoarst replied, addressing Ankhar. "But it will take courage. I must cast a spell upon you, my lord. You will need to trust in the magic, and to step off the edge of this precipice. The spell will guarantee that you float gently, like a feather, down to the bottom."

"And my mother?" asked Ankhar.

The wizard shrugged, and there was just a glint of cruel merriment in his eye as he explained. "I have but the one spell. You will have to hold her in your arms and carry her with you."

"I do this," agreed the half-giant, though his heart was in his throat and his chest was constricting with terror at the thought of himself and his precious shaman plunging through the black void. "You, too, will come down to the bottom?"

"Yes—I have another spell that I shall cast upon myself. I will be able to fly for a short time, and thus I can follow you down to where you will land."

"Very well." Ankhar was suddenly anxious to get this adventure over with, perhaps because he knew that if he hesitated for very long, he would begin to reflect on the dangers and back out. "Cast your spells," he ordered gruffly.

Hoarst removed a small pinch of fluff, like a bit of goose down, from one of the pockets of his robe. He held it up to the half-giant's face—his chin, actually, since that was as high as he could reach—and muttered a series of harsh-sounding words. Such strange words did not even sound as if they could be articulated by a human.

After waiting patiently for a few moments, Ankhar didn't feel any different. "How do I know spell is working?" he growled.

"Trust me," Hoarst answered coolly. "And remind yourself that I am as anxious for us to succeed with this quest—and get out of this forbidding place—as you are."

"Carry me!" Laka insisted, tugging on the half-giant's burly hand. Reluctantly, he released his two-fisted grip on his spear, clutching the weapon in one hand as he picked Laka up with the other, cradling her bony form like a baby against his broad chest. Hoarst helpfully lifted his sword so its light clearly revealed the edge of the precipice and the whole vast nothingness beyond.

Ankhar could think of a whole host of reasons this suddenly seemed like a very bad idea, but he could not shame himself in front of his mother or the powerful wizard who was his underling. So he closed his eyes, unconsciously holding his breath, as he took the first great step out into the void. He grunted in surprise as he felt himself toppling forward. Despite her professed confidence, Laka gasped in fright, and her fingers dug like talons into the half-giant's arms. She clutched her talisman, and the green light from the ghastly sockets bobbed and swept through the vast darkness. They were off the ledge now and tumbling into the chasm.

But they were falling, as Hoarst had promised, very, very slowly. As the wizard with his glowing sword took to the air above them, flying around them in a lazy circle, Ankhar could see the dark wall of the chasm sliding past. He could have reached out to touch it, but he dared not relax his grip on the trembling hob-wench who clutched him in such palpable panic. Instead, he simply clung to Laka and waited, half amazed and half terrified, as they slowly descended farther and farther below the surface of the world.

Ankhar tried to estimate how long they fell, how much distance they traveled down past that smooth, dark opposite wall. Once he scuffed against an outcrop of extremely cold stone, but the impact was soft and the force of the bump pushed him away from the surface. In the end he gave up trying to guess how deep they had plunged—surely they were farther underground than he had ever imagined possible. All the while Hoarst fluttered nearby, made visible to him and Laka by the glowing sword that he carried, which was the only light in this whole dark vault of space.

At long last the magic-user dived below them, circled a few times, and came to rest on a stone floor. Ankhar could make out a surprisingly smooth surface, sloping gently downward away from the wall. As he drew near, he cradled the still-trembling Laka, flexed his knees, and came to a soft landing on the solid ground. His first thought was, how would they ever get out of this place, would Hoarst's magic just as easily permit them to float up? But he bit his tongue. Instead, he set Laka gently on the ground, and as they both stood in the circle of light cast by Hoarst's magically illuminated sword, he asked, "Where are we? And where do we go from here?"

"Good questions," replied the human magic-user. "Not easily answered, though. This feels like a killing ground; there was death here at one time—lots of it."

"Look." Laka raised her talisman, green light spilling from its ghastly sockets, brighter even than the glow from the magic-user's sword. The green brilliance illuminated many objects on the broad, sloping floor. Ankhar saw a broken shield, several sharpened points that looked like spearheads, a cracked helm, a part of a breastplate . . . and bones. What had appeared to be a series of regular, rounded boulders he could now see were skulls, hundreds of them, scattered haphazardly. They were ancient and dusty, and at first glance he could not tell if they had belonged to humans, goblins, dwarves, or some other creatures. The eyeless sockets seemed to stare at him in reproach . . . or warning.

"This was once a battlefield," Hoarst surmised.

Hoarst kicked at one of the spear points, which was heavily corroded. A dusty, dry stench filled the air. Then the human picked up the spear point and used it to scrape away the crust that had developed over a crude, heavy sword blade. "Bronze," he mused. "Or copper. These warriors fought a long time ago, even before the advent of iron."

"A great host fought here and many died," Laka observed, holding her talisman higher. The green light spread far, bathing the rough outlines of battlements, shadowing the scar of a trench and the skeletal remnants of chariots and wagons. The wheels had long crumbled, but the outlines of the vehicles remained, layered in dust but still mostly intact.

"But how could a great army ever get down to these depths? Or *two* great armies?" wondered the half-giant. "What kind of battlefield is this?"

"Perhaps it was not always under the ground," speculated Hoarst. "It is said that in the early days of the world, the land was very different than it is now. Perhaps this was a plain at the foot of a mountain, back in the Age of Dreams. But some time after the killing, the battlefield itself sank beneath the ground, to be preserved in this great vault for all time."

"Maybe," Ankhar acknowledged, frowning. In fact, he couldn't think of another explanation. "It's certainly been here a long, long time—on the surface these bones, those relics, would rot away into nothing." The half-giant was beginning to feel very uncomfortable about the place. "We should get away from here."

"Hsst! Look, there!" Laka declared. "Something moves!"

It looked like a wisp of smoke, at first, but Ankhar knew nothing could be burning down here. Was it fog or some sort of mist? In his heart, which began to pound like a smith hammering on a metal band, he knew it was neither. It was like tangible frost—it *looked* cold—and he took a step back, his hands tightening around the haft of his spear.

There were several of the smoke shapes, ghostly forms rising from the skulls, the scattered and broken weaponry, the other debris on the ancient battlefield. They stood like pillars, perhaps the height of a man or a little taller, and they seemed to be rooted to the ground, while freely waving back and forth—though there was not even the hint of a breeze here in the deep underground. Whenever Ankhar turned his head, the smoke shapes seemed to waver, almost to disappear, but when he peered intensely at the figures, he could discern features—not faces, exactly, but holes where eyes ought to be, apertures that gaped soundlessly as though they were mouths giving vent to silent screams.

The half-giant felt a stab of fear. Helplessly, he looked at his stepmother and saw that Laka was glaring at these apparitions. Her teeth were bared, her eyes flashing with fury.

"Stay back!" Ankhar growled, waving his weapon.

"No—they will come," the hob-wench hissed.

Indeed, the spires of mist acted as one, slowly, soundlessly moving toward the three intruders who huddled together. No dust was stirred by their passage; they floated as if propelled by a wind. The green light from Laka's skull totem surged into greater brilliance, and this only magnified the horror, for now Ankhar could see that many more of the spectral images—dozens, scores, even hundreds of the smoke shapes—were rising from the ancient killing ground. The many mist figures writhed in the air with unspeakable hungers and desires, advancing upon the half-giant and his two companions.

Tall, slender wands of vapor waved above some of the shapes, as if spectral spears were held aloft. Here and there Ankhar saw round disks, like primitive shields, also raised in the air. Wispy blades waved back and forth in the grasp of some of the smoke shapes, and all the intangible weaponry was arrayed toward the three surface dwellers who had dared to trespass on this ancient, long-forgotten killing ground.

"Destroy them! Blast them with magic!" Ankhar barked to Hoarst, his voice, suddenly loud and startling, a violation of the eerie silence.

"These beings would not be vulnerable to the kind of magic I possess," Hoarst croaked, the usually imperturbable magic-user sounding, to Ankhar's ears, deeply shaken. Testing his own doubts, Hoarst raised a trembling finger and shouted a magical word of command. Arrows hissed and sparked outward from his accusing digit, magic missiles streaking into the darkness, piercing one then another of the ghostly, advancing smoke shapes. The arcane projectiles continued on until they faded and vanished, but the specters advanced unchecked, unhampered by the magical fusillade.

They were close now, and Ankhar thought he detected faces in the grotesque mist figures—visages locked into expressions of eternal torment. Mouths flexed, and though they made no sound, the half-giant felt the blast of cold breath against his skin. It was colder than a winter gale in the high mountains. The mighty warrior, commander of a horde of thousands, slayer of a hundred enemies, felt his knees weaken, and he staggered backward. A grievous moaning reached his ears, but he was only vaguely aware that it emerged from his own, slack-jawed mouth. He stared into hundreds of empty eye sockets, his bowels churning at the looks of hatred and hunger he perceived there.

"Courage!" snapped Laka. "See how they feed upon your fear!"

It was the truth: as Ankhar's terror weakened him, the spectral warriors grew stronger, lunging for their victims now, stabbing with their vaporous spears. One ghostly tip touched the half-giant's knee, and he felt a sharp pain. The contact was icy and quickly spread numbingly up and down his leg. He stumbled, grasping his spear and using the stout haft as a crutch. There was no thought of using the weapon to fight these things; he understood instinctively that certainly no blade on Krynn could damage them.

"Back to the wall," Hoarst whispered. His voice broke, and it terrified Ankhar further to realize that even the redoubtable wizard was frightened.

Slowly the trio retreated, but there was no real escape. The spectral images came at them from three sides, stopping just a few paces away, filling ranks into a solid mass. The black wall rose behind the trio, an impassable barrier. They were surrounded.

"What are these things?" Ankhar said in a low voice.

"They are ghosts of the slain," Laka declared with surprisingly calmness. "They have been here for ages, thousands of years, longing for the feel of warmth, the touch of the sun—or of blood."

"How do you know this?" demanded Hoarst incredulously.

"They were part of my dream," replied the old hob-wench. Her left hand cradled some of the baubles on her necklace while her eyes darted back and forth across the ranks of spectral warriors.

"You *knew* about these things?" Ankhar was aghast, resisting an impulse to bash his stepmother senseless. But fear was a greater impulse, and the half-giant understood that only Laka could rescue them from this horror.

Her bony fingers continued to caress the beads on her necklace while her right hand still clutched the haft of her totem. Apparently she located the right combination of stones, for she abruptly raised the death's-head with its green gems fixed like eyeballs on the encroaching spirits.

"Fear the Prince of Lies!" she crowed exultantly. "Truth shall be his sword!

"Kneel before Lord Ankhar! Hail him as your lord!"

Green light pulsed from the skull's face, a brilliant wash shooting through the vast battlefield. Ankhar saw ridges outlined in the distance, gaps in the rough ground, and hundreds, even thousands, of the ghostly warriors amassed before the trio. The beams of emerald illumination seemed to transfix them, however, for suddenly they all halted, trembling and shivering in a grotesque caricature of awe, terror, or wonder.

"Hold, warriors of the ages!" Laka cried again, louder. "For you are in the presence of a mighty lord! Kneel, all of you!"

Ankhar heard a faint sound, barely, at first, like a slight breeze keening through a forest of leafless trees. It swelled very slowly, becoming a moan, then a cry, and finally building into a howl. The shrieking erupted from all around, and the half-giant had to resist the urge to clap his hands over his ears. But he stood tall and held his hands at his sides, knowing he needed to project an aura not just of fearlessness, but of command and power. One by one, the ghostly forms slumped, a semblance of humans dropping to their knees. The eerie genuflection rippled outward through the vast, silent ranks.

"Are these ghosts my new ally?" Ankhar asked Laka wonderingly. "They could terrify the humans, surely."

"No," the shaman replied curtly. "They would perish under the sky, as soon as they felt the kiss of the sun. They are condemned to remain here, to guard the legacy of their defeat and death, though their time, the Age of Dreams, is long past."

"Then, why?" demanded the commander of the horde. "Why are we here, risking our own deaths?"

"The answer is simple. They are merely one obstacle—another obstacle, like the cliff we just floated down—on the path to our destination. Behold, now: the power of Hiddukel will hold them at bay. But do not let them detect your fear—the blessing of the Prince will only benefit those who have the courage of victors."

"Lead, then," grunted Ankhar. "And we show our courage."

Laka started forward, her totem held high, the green light sweeping back and forth across the faces of the ghostly warriors. Their intangible spears still waved in the air, and their grotesque mouths gaped and flexed hungrily. But as the half-giant and the wizard followed the old hobgoblin, the crowded ranks of spirits parted to let them pass.

The shaman went first. Ankhar strode after Laka with Hoarst trailing behind. The gaping faces glared, the eerie sockets and mouths twitched and quivered, but the half-giant was determined to maintain his fiercest expression and his steady pace.

If any of the spirit beings so much as started to ease into their path, the ancient hobgoblin spat a curse and shook her beads to warn them out of the way. Laka glared to the right and left, brandishing her totem as if it were a mighty weapon.

It seemed to take forever, though Ankhar would later reflect that they passed through the silent ranks of ghost shapes in a matter of moments. Their destination was a gap that gradually materialized in the far wall of the underground canyon, a passage that wound out of sight, descending ever deeper into the sunless world beneath Krynn.

Behind them, the silent army stood waiting, watching . . . hungering for warmth and blood.

CHAPTER EIGHT

TWO CHALLENGES

Coryn hired a company of drummers, all dressed in red satin tunics with shiny leather boots. The leader of each section—bass, kettle, and snare—wore a hat with lofty plumes. They gathered before her manor with great fanfare and made a splendid procession as they led the lord marshal and the wizard, both mounted on white horses, through the heart of the city and up toward the gates of the lord regent's palace.

The procession attracted a great deal of attention. Goodwives hoisted their babes onto their shoulders so they could see the famous man and the beautiful wizard ride past. Soldiers and merchants cheered, and even the sergeants of the Palanthian Legion saluted smartly as the procession passed through the city gates. On they went, climbing the winding road toward the lord regent's palace, advancing directly through the open gates and leaving the swelling crowd behind.

Once they entered the courtyard of the imposing structure, the drummers and the Lady Coryn continued toward the front door of the keep. The white gelding pranced proudly beside her, and the aura of magic on the big horse's saddle made it seem as though Jaymes Markham rode there as well. Certainly the servants, attendants, and courtiers all believed they saw him astride the white gelding until the horse came to a halt and closer inspection revealed the saddle to be empty.

By that time, the lord marshal was already slipping through the stable, entering the keep through the kitchen door. The drummers, the horses, and the wizard made, for form's sake, one last promenade around the huge courtyard.

"My Lord Marshal," said Selinda du Chagne as she greeted her visitor in the anteroom to her private apartments. "This is a surprise. To what do I owe the pleasure?"

"It is been a long time since we talked," Jaymes replied, settling himself into one of the comfortable chairs as she pulled a rope to summon a servant. "I very much wanted to see you again."

"Why?" she asked bluntly. "I tricked you into being captured, tried to arrange for you to come back here for trial—and execution. I should think you'd want to stay as far away as possible from the likes of me!" She laughed nervously, pacing about the room, avoiding the chairs to either side of Jaymes. He couldn't help but notice her stunning beauty. She twirled a lock of her golden hair in the fingers of her right hand, sidestepping at the window, looking at him with her large eyes narrowed in curiosity.

"I should have thought that little misunderstanding would be forgotten by now," he said, chuckling. "It is by me; you also helped to save my life in Caergoth, when Duke Crawford would have had me killed."

"That wretched man!" she exclaimed. "He was a disgrace to the knighthood, to the whole history of Solamnia! The realm is better off without him."

"I couldn't agree with you more," Jaymes said, easing back and resting his foot on a stool.

"You've made some progress since that time in Caergoth. Has it been two years? It seems so long ago. Bringing the army north across the Garnet River, driving the barbarians out of Garnet. . . . You've had great success. Tell me, was that city horribly razed?"

"The damage was bad, yes. But much of the population has moved back, and the rebuilding is coming along very well."

."And you've driven the barbarians from all the western plains? This half-giant, Ankhar, he just holds on to the area around Solanthus?"

Jaymes nodded. "And soon he won't even have that."

"Yes, you've come a long way from the outlaw I discovered hiding in a shadowed cellar on the plains," she remarked wryly.

"My life has taken a few unexpected turns," he admitted.

A maid entered and curtsied. "Would you care for something to drink?" asked the princess. Her manner had warmed a little.

"What will you have? Red wine, perhaps?" he asked.

"Yes, actually. That sounds good. Marie, will you bring us a bottle of that Nordmar Rose—some of the vintage from two years ago?"

"Yes, my lady. At once."

The servant departed, and Selinda turned back to the lord marshal. Her eyes were narrow, appraising. After studying him for a few breaths, she spoke. "I think you are still a very dangerous man."

"Sometimes the world needs dangerous men," he replied with a shrug. "Ankhar's horde isn't about to be defeated by a group of perfumed gentlemen or pompous nobles."

She looked at him archly. "Do you think I'm a pompous noble?" she asked accusingly.

"When you found me hiding in that dark cellar, and you came in there to talk to me . . . that was about as far from pompous as a person can get." He paused for a moment. "I'm still amazed by what you did. Did you think I was a dangerous man then?"

"I knew it, immediately."

"But you weren't afraid?"

"Oh, I suppose I was terrified."

"Why? What is so frightening, so 'dangerous' about me?"

She frowned and was spared from answering by Marie, returning with a decanter of red wine and two crystal glasses. "Shall I pour?" asked the servant, setting her tray on a nearby buffet.

"Allow me?" Jaymes asked, rising smoothly to his feet.

"Be my guest," Selinda replied. "That will be all, Marie." The princess took a seat in the chair next to where Jaymes had been sitting.

Jaymes crossed to the buffet as the servant girl departed, closing the door behind her. The marshal spoke over his shoulder to the princess. "So—you were going to tell me why you think I'm dangerous," he prodded.

The tiny vial was in his hand, screened by his body from Selinda's view. He lifted the decanter and swirled it gently, allowing the dark liquid to circle within the goblet. He looked as though he were admiring the exquisite cut of the crystal as he smoothly poured the potion into one of the two glasses. Then he carefully added the wine, filling first her glass, then his own about three-quarters of the way to the top.

"I guess. . . ." Selinda was preoccupied, struggling to reply to his question. "I guess it's because you don't wait for things to happen; you make them happen. You *take* whatever it is that you want, and to the Abyss with the consequences."

He turned around and walked slowly back to her, extending one of the glasses. She took the wine and he sat beside her. Then he raised his glass. "Perhaps I could offer a toast to a new beginning? One that doesn't start in the dingy cellar of a burned-out house?"

"I'll agree to that," she said lightly. They clinked their glasses gently, and each took a sip of wine. It was indeed a rare vintage, smooth and rich without a hint of bitterness. Jaymes nodded approvingly, watching her as he took another sip.

"But I'd like to get this one thing straight," Selinda continued. "I find you a dangerous man but an interesting one. I recognize that you are good for the future of Solamnia. If our nation is ever to be united and grow powerful again, we need to have a strong army and a strong commander of that army. But I hope that you're not here to court me, as my father has warned me because I'm *not* interested in that."

"Fair enough," Jaymes replied, staring at her as she took another sip. "May I ask—are you not interested in being courted by me or in being courted, period?"

"Both, I should say." Selinda leaned back in her chair, swirled the wine in her glass, and looked at him over its rim. "My indifference to courtship may seem foreign to you. But there are lots of men, the most powerful nobles in all Solamnia, who seem to view me as some kind of prize, like the trophy that might be claimed at a royal joust. Lord Frankish practically drools over me. And I hate that feeling; I absolutely *hate* it."

"I think I can understand," he allowed.

"My father knows how I feel. As soon as I reached my majority, which was just two years ago, I made him agree that I would marry whomever I choose, whenever I choose. I'm under no pressures from him. There will be no political match in this house!"

"And how did the lord regent react to that?" Jaymes inquired, raising his eyebrows. "I should tell you—Bakkard du Chagne seems to me like another man who takes what he wants, rather than just sitting around and waiting for it to be offered."

She giggled involuntarily then clasped her fingers over her mouth in surprise. "I can't believe you said that. I've never heard anybody speak about my father like that!"

"That's because he's a dangerous man too," the marshal replied bluntly. He was still leaning back in his chair, gently swirling the wine in his glass. After another sip he continued. "Are you frightened of him?"

"No," she said with a firm shake of her head. She met his stare with a confident look, amusement twinkling in her eyes. "Of course not. He's my father. And I just realized something: I'm not frightened of you either."

"I'm glad," replied the man. He set his glass on a table and leaned forward to study her. Most women would have fidgeted, looked away under that intense scrutiny, but not the princess of Palanthas. Instead, she giggled again.

"I wish . . . I wish I had a big brother like you."

He blinked, sitting back in surprise. "A . . . *brother?*"

"Yes. Oh, not that you're not a handsome man. Do you know, I think the Lady Coryn is in love with you? And Dara Lorimar certainly thought she was!"

She looked surprised at herself after she uttered the last statement, and her eyes clouded with painful memories.

"Dara Lorimar was but a girl. A lovely girl, to be sure. However, she didn't live long enough to learn the meaning of love." His tone was harsh.

"I know that she died too soon! But I told you before, we were friends, had been since we were little girls. And she talked about you when she came to Palanthas that last winter, when you worked for her father, protecting him, his house, his family."

"Some protector," snapped Jaymes. He made no effort to keep the bitterness out of his voice. His memories were also painful. "She died trying to keep the assassins away from her father, and I failed them both. I didn't even realize they were in danger!"

"But when you found out, you honorably avenged them . . . and gained a whole army in the process," Selinda said. "And didn't you love Dara, just a little?"

"I told you, she was a young girl—a mere child!"

"She was a year older than me!"

"Well, that was a long time ago," he countered flatly. His wine glass sat on the table beside him, forgotten. She had nearly finished hers, he noted with interest. Abruptly he tossed back the contents of his glass, rose, and crossed the room. He came back with the decanter. Selinda mutely emptied her own glass and extended it so he could pour another. This time he set the decanter between them as he once again took his seat.

"What about Lady Coryn?" Selinda asked coyly.

"What about her?" he asked sharply.

She didn't flinch. "I . . . I mean . . . do you love her?"

"She's a good friend, a powerful ally. She helps me, and I help her. But she wears the white robes—she loves virtues, ideals, truths that I can never wholeheartedly embrace."

"What do you embrace?" Selinda asked. Her eyes were moist, her tone almost pleading. "Why did you take up the banner of the Lord of the Rose? Why do you lead the Army of Solamnia against the horde, when you could go any place, do anything you want? I confess you are a vexing mystery to me."

He rose and paced around the room. He flexed his hands unconsciously, his fingers curling into fists until he forced himself to stretch them out again. For a long time he was silent, seemingly unaware that she was watching him, waiting for his answer.

"Solamnia could be the greatest country on Krynn," he said at last. "But none of the leaders born to their roles—including your father!—have the will or the strength to forge its greatness. Coryn, because she is good, envisions a Solamnia such as once existed, defended by knights who are pure of heart, noble of deed.

"But I know that history has come too far for a realm like that to exist, except in storybooks. The world is a new place, changing more every day. It is filled with dangerous men. The greatest of the old gods are gone, and even magic is giving way to new technologies, knowledge that places power in the hands of industrial strength. . . ."

"Technologies such as the substance that everyone talks about, your black powder?" she asked. She was staring at him, rapt.

"Yes. With that black powder, when I learn how to channel it properly, and with an army made up of natural leaders and courageous, motivated soldiers, I think that Solamnia can reach heights of greatness she has never before attained."

"What about Solanthus?" she asked, surprising him. "Those poor people there, starving, surrounded. Do you think you will be able to free them without disaster?"

"I am going to do everything in my power to free Solanthus." He went back to the chair and sat down, looking at her earnestly.

"I believe you are!" she exclaimed. She leaned toward him, placed her hand on his knee as she stared into his eyes. Powerful emotions shone in her look, feelings that brought a flush to her cheeks. "I do believe you are the only one who can do what you say! I don't know why it took me so long .... but it's so clear to me, now. You are the man who might succeed where others failed . . . I could *help* you. I *want* to help you. I want. . . ."

Her voice trailed off. She was breathing hard now as she looked at him, her lips parted. Nervously she moistened those lips with her tongue.

He stood up. She rose as well. Her body moved as if of its own will until she was pressed against him. She reached up to his shoulders, her eyes staring into his. Her eyes glowed with warmth and something else . . . Hope? She tilted her head back.

Jaymes Markham took the princess of Palanthas in his arms, and he kissed her. She was willing and kissed him back with a fury that took him by surprise. Her hands went around his back and down to his waist as she pulled him close, trying to merge her body with his.

And he made no move to push her away.

×◦◦-◦◦-◦◦-◦◦-◦◦×

An hour later Jaymes was making his way through the vacant hall of the regent's palatial residence. He headed for the stable, having already sent a servant to saddle his horse. It was late, and the great building was quiet and dark.

He stiffened abruptly as he approached the door. A man, armored in a rose breastplate and wearing a long red cloak, appeared from the shadows to block his path. Jaymes recognized Lord Frankish, the commander of the Palanthian Legion.

The lord marshal stopped. He was unarmed, except for a small dagger, not that he feared attack. Nevertheless he was taken aback when the other man, without warning, raised his hand, and sharply slapped a leather gauntlet across Jaymes's face.

"You are a scoundrel, sir!" snapped Frankish. "All the palace is aware of your outrageous conduct behind closed doors with the princess. I warned you, and her father warned you. You have no business with her!"

"Do you think *you* have business with her?" Jaymes growled, raising a hand to rub his cheek. "Or is your true business with me?"

"Think what you will—you are a wretched fellow. I demand satisfaction!"

Jaymes snorted. "You're challenging me to a *duel?* I urge you to think again. You would be out of your depth."

"Your impertinence is astounding," replied the lord.

"Then, sir," Jaymes said, more irritably than angrily, "I will match you. How long will the arrangements take?"

"I have already notified my second, the wizard Sir Moorvan. He will be ready momentarily. I assume that your own wizard—"

"The Lady Coryn?"

"I know that she is within these walls, as we speak. Perhaps you would care to speak with her?"

"I'll leave it to you to make all the arrangements, then," Jaymes said, pushing past the man roughly enough that he knocked him off stride. In two steps the lord marshal was out the door, standing alone in the quiet of the night. Then, with a sound that was a cross between a snort of amusement and snarl of anger, he turned back to the palace.

Once again, he would slip in through the kitchen door.

≈◦⊙◦⟨⊙◦⟨⊙◦❀◦⊙◦⟩⊙◦⟩◦⊙◦≈

Baron Dekage apologized for interrupting Coryn in the palace library. "It's Sir Moorvan, the Kingfisher," the baron explained. "He begs your pardon for disturbing you but insists he must see you on a matter of urgent and grave importance."

A few moments later, dressed in her immaculate white robe with her black hair combed loosely back from her face, the wizard greeted the mage knight as he entered and bowed.

The Kingfisher wore the expression of a man burdened with ill tidings. "I was thinking that, perhaps, you had not heard the news," he suggested to the white wizard.

"And what news would that be?" Coryn retorted, rather disagreeably. She knew Moorvan, and in fact they had worked together when the Solamnics had reclaimed Palanthas from the Dark Knights. She knew that he was a schemer and that his primary interests lay not with magic and justice, but with the ambitions of Lord Regent du Chagne.

"There is to be a duel shortly after midnight, in the palace courtyard. Between Lord Marshal Jaymes and the Rose Lord Frankish. Ah, I see, you had *not* heard."

"No," Coryn said, her face betraying her shock. She turned away from him, staring across the room, the darkly elegant study chamber in the regent's palace. The Kingfisher waited for her to say something, but turning back, she merely glared at him.

"I am sure you agree that it is imperative that such a match occurs without interference from interested parties," the wizard-knight ventured as politely as possible.

"Yes. Yes, of course," Coryn agreed, thinking furiously. A duel? How could Jaymes have been so stupid?

"To that end, I was hoping that you and I could second the match, together. We will keep an eye on, uh, matters. Is that acceptable to you?"

She frowned. She needed time—time to consult her auguries, to consider her options, simply to think. "When did you say this duel is to occur?" she asked numbly.

"At one bell. Three hours from now."

There was little else to say, then, and virtually no time for any preparations. "Very well," she said. "I will meet you in the courtyard and bear judgment."

⤖⋘⊰⊱⋙⤕

"You're going to fight Lord Frankish? No! You can't! You mustn't! You might be injured, even killed!" Selinda sobbed as she threw herself into Jaymes's arms, clenching him so tightly that he had to unclasp her arms just to draw a breath.

"Are you so sure I'm going to lose?" he asked with a very slight smile, holding his arms around her, looking down at her tear-filled eyes.

"You don't know very much about Lord Frankish, do you? He'll do anything to win—anything! You can't trust him! He's killed many men already! Oh, this is all my fault!" She broke away and turned to stomp across the anteroom of her chambers. The duel was an hour or two away. Selinda whirled angrily. "I'll bet my father put him up to this—I'm certain of it! But I'm not going to allow it! Do you hear me? I won't allow it!"

"I hear you," Jaymes said, striding over to her, again pulling her close. Willingly, she melted against his chest. "But this is not something you can, or cannot, allow. I've given my word. It's something that's going to happen. And"—he pulled back to look into her eyes—"don't worry. I don't intend to lose."

"But—why?" she cried. "Why are you doing this?"

"More or less because Lord Frankish forced me into it," he conceded abashedly. "It was not my idea. But I believe I can turn this to my—to *our*—advantage."

"He's only doing this because he's jealous—he knows how much I care for you. He thinks he can commit legal murder this way. He intends to kill you!"

"He won't. And I told you, this will work out in our favor."

100

She shivered, wiping her eyes with the back of her hand. "How could it possibly work in our favor?"

"That hasn't been entirely settled yet. I needed to talk to you first, and afterward I will pay a visit to your father. That's why I came here before going to the combat field. I needed to ask you something."

"What? What is it? What did you want to ask me?"

He stared into her eyes, placed his strong hands on her trembling shoulders. "In the event of my victory in this fight, I mean to ask, with humility and affection, if you will consent to be my wife. Will you marry me?"

Her eyes grew wide. She gasped for breath. In the next instant she pulled him close, nearly strangling him again.

"Yes!" she cried, her voice a mixture of sobs and laughter. She would always remember what had happened this night, before and after the duel, she thought.

"Yes," she repeated through the laughter and tears. "Yes, I will!"

CHAPTER NINE

THE KING OF THE UNDERWORLD

Ankhar gradually noticed the warmth, which struck him as unnatural in this dark, sunless place. For timeless miles and uncounted days, the trio had trudged through chilly blackness, cloaks wrapped tight against the penetrating cold. Deep into the world they went, far away from the sun, and still they descended. Ankhar shivered when he slept, longed for the comfort of a campfire. But there was no fuel, no light beyond what their little party carried.

Until, one day—or was it night?—the half-giant felt a sheen of sweat on his forehead and unconsciously loosened his woolen cloak. Curious, he reached out and touched a nearby outcrop of stone and found it warm to the touch. The air felt thick and moist, with a hint of acrid smoke. Within a few moments, they all had removed their outer garb, and suddenly the cavern seemed like such a sweltering place, he began to wonder if he was taking leave of his senses.

"We are very far below the surface," Hoarst declared, mopping his brow with a soft cloth. "We must be drawing near to the fires in the very belly of the world." The wizard still carried his glowing blade, but now with its point slanting downward at his side. The once-bright light had faded to a pearly glow. Even so, that faint illumination was enough to show the path before the trio's increasingly sensitive eyes.

"How long we been on this dark path?" grumbled Ankhar. "I lose track of miles . . . and of sleeps."

"The sun has come and gone six times since we entered the cave," Laka declared. "It is now dawn on the world of the surface."

Ankhar found himself longing for a look at the world above, even just a glimpse of the bright sun that he had taken for granted throughout his life. He tried to imagine how dwarves and even some goblins could spend so many of their days underground, shielded from that blessed warmth, that refulgent brilliance. He shuddered at the very idea.

Hoarst knelt to sip from one of the pools of clear water that were common in these caves. When he did, the flap of his cloak briefly covered the blade of his sword, yet Ankhar realized that he could see quite well without its illumination. The dark was fading!

The half-giant squinted ahead, noticing a faintly reddish cast to the cavern walls in front of them. It was as though they traveled through a canyon after sunset, and the fading glow of daylight lingered in their surroundings. Like some sunsets, this one glowed a faint orange color, which marked the high walls to either side of them, even casting shadows from the stalactites on the arched ceiling so high over their heads.

As they came around another bend in the still-descending cavern, they saw that the horizon was limned in fire, a strange, hellish light that forced the half-giant to raise his hand in a futile effort to shield his face from its infernal glare and heat.

"We are drawing near now," Laka said, "for this is another place that was revealed to me in my dream."

"Good," Ankhar said. Now that they were actually close to encountering the mysterious, powerful ally Laka had been searching for, he felt more bluster than courage. He thought a growl might be impressive and made a sound that rumbled deep in his chest.

The brightness continued to build as the subterranean canyon twisted through a few more turns, until finally they came to a ledge, where a series of shattered rocky outcrops formed a descending stairway. For the moment they halted, all three of them staring wordlessly at this remarkable place.

The trio stood high above a cavern that was as vast as a deep valley in a large mountain range—except that the rocky faces above them soared upward to merge into an upside-down version of a chasm that twisted and curved through a central, vaulted ceiling. The depths of the upper gorge were lost in shadow, but the rest of this great cavern was outlined in the brilliant fires that surged and crackled everywhere.

Most striking was the river of liquid fire, glowing orange and red, which appeared to emerge from a channel on the opposite wall of the great valley, spilling downward like a garish, mighty waterfall. The spume tumbled hundreds of feet from its lofty origin, burning the whole way, splashing explosively at the base of the wall. There the liquid fire bubbled and churned amidst a great lake of crimson-orange. Dark outcrops of rock jutted like islands above the surface, while currents eddied and surged along the inhospitable shores.

Other lakes and ponds—some fiery lava, others dark and sludgy as oil, or lightless water—dotted the broad valley floor. Far to the right the wall of the massive cavern was obscured by mist, as water from some unseen source made contact with the scalding rock and sizzled into steam. The cloud seethed and shimmered like a living curtain, and as they watched, it expanded to fill the whole end of the cavern. A few moments later, it dissipated, dissolving into a shower of rain that spattered and hissed on the hot rock, instantaneously evaporating, then thickening into fog, as the process started over again.

A thunderous blast rent the air, shaking the bedrock beneath Ankhar's boots. To the left a geyser of liquid fire erupted, shooting a spume of burning rock hundreds of feet into the air. Several massive pieces of stone broke free from the walls and ceiling, jarred by the force of the blast. They tumbled and rolled down the slopes, most coming to rest in tangled piles, while a few plopped into the viscous lake of fire to be quickly swallowed up.

"Do we cross this place?" Ankhar asked skeptically. "Did dream show you that?"

"No. We must go down there." Laka pointed to the vast lake situated in the middle of the cavern. "That is where we will find our ally."

"Huh! Then let's go find this ally," the half-giant grunted, though he was hardly eager to visit the lake of fire.

"Be ready with your spear," the ancient shaman hissed before turning to Hoarst. "And prepare to use your spells. There will be enemies here, and we must vanquish them or die."

Ankhar drew his great weapon off his shoulder, taking comfort in the feel of the smooth, familiar haft. He looked around for something to stab, mildly disappointed to discover the absence of any foe. He started down the rocky slope, his long strides easily taking him from shelf to shelf of the natural staircase. With his spear in one hand, he helped Laka over the ledges, some of them set at precipitous intervals. All the while, he kept alert, his eyes scanning the cavern, looking for the enemies his mother had warned of.

The first such enemy abruptly rose into view close to them as they neared the cavern floor—it had crouched among the rocks, indistinguishable from the boulders strewn everywhere, until its sudden movement. The thing reared now, a giant-sized being made of stone, with rippling sinews of rock outlined in two legs, two arms, a torso, and a great crude block of a head. A pair of dark hollows gaped beneath a clifflike brow.

Despite being startled, the half-giant struck at once, thrusting his great spear against the stone fist punching toward his face. The emerald head of his weapon, enchanted with the blessing of the Prince of Lies, shattered the stone fist, and the elemental creature of stone and dirt staggered back. The creature was larger than Ankhar but less nimble, and the half-giant followed his first thrust with a series of fierce stabs, chipping pieces away from the grotesque being. Finally Ankhar thrust his weapon straight into the stony torso, a blow that knocked the beast backward off its perch. Tumbling to deeper bedrock, the elemental shattered into so many crumbs of gravel.

Before Ankhar resumed a more cautious descent, he saw Laka reach down, paw through the shards remaining from the elemental, and select a piece that was small enough to hold easily in her palm. Nodding in satisfaction, she tucked the stone away in one of her many pouches and curtly gestured to the half-giant to continue his pace.

They proceeded downward, alert and careful, toward the cavern floor. They came to a broad ledge, perhaps halfway down from the vantage where they had entered the chamber. Ankhar took a step onto what he thought was a solid shelf of rock, but stumbled as his foot sank into soft, oozing mud. He toppled and lurched forward, maintaining his balance only by plunging his second foot into the mire. In a matter of a breath he had sunk to his knees and felt the warm goo steadily rising up toward his thighs.

"Hsst—beware!" cried Laka, raising her totem. The green light outlined a shape rising from the mire just a few paces beyond Ankhar. This was another elemental, forged from the muddy water much as their first opponent had been crafted from rock. The half-giant stabbed with his spear, but his balance was poor and the blade made only a small gash in one of the elemental's limbs. The water swiftly flowed back to close the wound, and the magical creature continued to rise from the pond, drawing the liquid from the pool to collect itself into a gigantic foe more than twice the height of the half-giant.

"Drop down—duck!" said Hoarst, and Ankhar instantly squatted. So much earth had been drawn into the creature's body that the half-giant could fling away mud and hurl himself to the side as the wizard behind him snarled out the words to a spell.

The eruption of magic was soundless and lightless, but the great power of it penetrated to the half-giant's core. The savage blast of cold passed just over Ankhar's body, leaving an icy chill skittering across his skin as it swept outward in an expanding cone of lethal frost. The spell struck the mud-giant full across its body, covering it with an instantaneous layer of frost, then freezing the creature hard in its posture of mid-attack. One leg still twitched, but the rest of the body twisted rigidly, awkward and frozen.

"Now—strike it with your spear!" cried the Thorn Knight.

Ankhar stabbed with all of his strength, again holding his weapon with both hands, driving the chiseled emerald head into the frozen water elemental's midsection. The monster shattered like a statue made from ice, blocks of frozen water tumbling to the ground, slowly melting back into the residual muck of the ground. As with the stone elemental, Laka paused to reach down, collected a piece of the creature's remains, and placed it safely in one of her pouches before giving Ankhar the signal to continue.

"We must hurry," Ankhar urged, lifting Laka by one arm and swinging her to the far side of the pit before striding after her. Hoarst, moving quickly, skirted the bowl-shaped depression to join them on the far side. The half-giant glanced back warily, wondering if the pieces of the water-monster would show signs of reassembling into life. But the blocks of ice remained inert, even as they melted into little puddles of muddy water.

Strangely, the ancient shaman seemed gratified by their encounter. "These are the servants of the one we shall enslave," she said proudly. "And to judge by his retainers, he is mighty, indeed."

Next to materialize were guardians made of fire, a trio of flaming giants spewing up out of the liquid rock. Waving crazily, uttering roars like the fiery blasts of a furnace, they emerged from the lake of lava to block the travelers' path. Casting sparks, dripping flames, they surged up the slope toward the mortal intruders. Ankhar pierced one with blows of his enchanted spear, though not before their flames singed both his fists. Laka doused the other pair when she brandished her skull totem and somehow conjured forth a rainstorm that spilled torrents of water over the fiery shapes. They hissed and sizzled and eventually, washed out of existence. Before they completely faded, she gingerly picked up the glowing ember of one fire guardian and hastily dropped it into a chain-mesh pocket.

As they drew near to the edge of the fire lake, the searing heat practically baked their skin. Sweat flowed in rivulets down Ankhar's face, and he had to blink repeatedly to clear his eyesight. Shielding his eyes, he felt something surprisingly pleasurable —something cool. A breeze wafted over his skin, evaporating his sweat and easing the infernal heat. The only trouble was that the growing breeze came from another attacker.

This attacker was a guardian drawn from the very air. Now it swirled like a tornado, sucking at them with winds so powerful, they were almost forced off the ledge and into the bubbling, churning lake. Rising taller than any of the other elementals, this air guardian screamed like a tortured goblin, wailing all around them, leaning in close.

Ankhar's strength saved them, for he planted his feet, crouched low, and wrapped a brawny arm around the shoulders of each of his two companions. The gale whipped and pulsed and whirled. Like the other elementals, the creature of air had taken a physical shape, and it appeared like a tornado with whirling tendrils that reached out, tried to suck and pull the mortals apart from each other, drag them forward into the lethal, bubbling magma.

Hoarst pulled some kind of powder from his pocket, blinking at the dust that flew up and stung his eyes. The wizard gritted his teeth and spat out the words to the spell, finally spreading his hands wide and stepping forward into the very heart of the cyclone's suction. The air elemental almost lifted him up and away—only Ankhar's strong hands held him in place—until, at last, Hoarst's magic sparked into being. The bright flash of light utterly dispelled the enchanted creature, leaving only a series of random gusts swirling across the lava lake, churning up smoke, blowing futilely at the tiny rivulets of fire.

Laka produced a small suede sack, supple and empty and very tightly sewed. She waved it about with both hands, capturing one of the errant gusts and trapping it inside so it puffed out the bag like a balloon. She quickly drew a string around the mouth of the sack, closing it tightly shut, then lashed it to her belt where it bobbed lightly.

"Now we must go over there, to that island," Laka declared, pointing.

"How?" demanded Ankhar, gazing at the dangerous crimson liquid that seemed to surround the pinnacle of dark rock indicated by his stepmother. "Swim?"

"There seems to be a path," Hoarst said.

The half-giant blinked, shaking his head skeptically. Nevertheless, he could see the snaking path of black rock, like the ridged back of a stony crocodile, that jutted above the surface of the lava. They might be able to walk across it without coming into direct contact with the liquid rock. And if they soaked their cloaks in water and wrapped them tightly as protection, they *might* be able to withstand the baking heat.

"Are you sure?" the half-giant asked, his jaw jutting belligerently. "Why can't slave, er, ally come to us?"

"Because this is the path showed to me in my vision," Laka replied calmly. "It is the Truth."

There was no argument against that. Grudgingly, Ankhar stepped in front of his two companions, leading the way to the terminus of the narrow, steep-sided isthmus of rock. The heat felt searing against his face, burning his skin wherever it peeked out; he had pulled his cape over his shoulders and head, tightening it into a narrow chute around his eyes and nose.

The ridge was narrow, capped with loose and blistered rock, and each footstep kicked some of the rubble free to tumble down the steep sides and into the lake. Wherever they struck, flames erupted from the liquid. To Ankhar these snaky tendrils of flames seemed like hungry lampreys, mouths lunging upward, seeking their flesh.

The heat became a smothering blanket, wrapping him in a cocoon of pain. He could barely see through the tears that streamed from his eyes, the sweat that poured from his brow.

Each breath was like a blast of fire sucked into his lungs, more pain that sustenance, and he staggered along, fearing any misstep that would send him plunging into that bubbling cauldron— promising an instant death that began to seem like a mercy.

Stumbling on loose rock, he dropped to one knee, burning his gloved hands when arresting his fall. Grimly, almost unconsciously, he pushed himself to his feet. He almost sobbed in relief as, finally, he stepped onto the solid ground of the black island. He crawled and scrambled upward, climbing away from that horrible, killing lava.

Only when he reached the summit of the hill on that conical island did he remember his stepmother and the magic-user. He spun, somewhat surprised and ashamed to see that she was gamely hobbling after him. Sweat glistened in the creases of her wrinkled face, but her eyes gleamed with a triumphant glare that could only make the half-giant feel guilty about his momentary cowardice. He extended a hand, helped her up the last steps of the incline—and was grateful for the touch of her strong, wiry fingers, the encouraging squeeze she administered as she arrived to stand behind him.

Hoarst came last. Ankhar was amazed at the Thorn Knight's calm, even arrogant appearance. He calmly brushed his dark hair back, and looked around through narrowed eyes—as if already relegating the unpleasant ordeal of the crossing to memory.

Ankhar was busy gasping for breath, wiping the sweat and tears from his eyes, and thanking the Prince of Lies and all the other gods for his survival. Then he noticed that the clearing upon which they stood, which was only about twenty feet in diameter, had been leveled by some purposeful force—it was as smooth as the marble floor of a nobleman's great hall. In fact, the coal-black bedrock had been polished to such a sheen that the surrounding fires were reflected in it everywhere he looked.

There were four curious features in the floor, each carved from the same black stone as the floor, and when Ankhar stepped over to look at one, he saw that it held a smooth bowl, a semi-circular depression that had been chiseled out of the pedestal's flat top. A quick glance confirmed that there were three other pedestals of similar design.

Hoarst inspected the stone pillars, touching them, looking closely at the surface around each bowl, and finally nodding as if they were exactly what he had expected.

"Fire and water, stone and air," he explained, indicating the bizarre hieroglyphics that Ankhar had noticed etched into the stonework around the rim of the shallow bowls. Each pedestal was devoted to a different one of the earth elements.

"Here, take this," Laka said, handing a piece of stone to Ankhar. He recognized it as one of the shards of the rock elemental that he had shattered with his spear. The shaman looked at the wizard expectantly. "I cannot read the signs—tell me which is which."

"That is the bowl for the stone," Hoarst said, pointing to the pedestal nearest to the half-giant. "And these others," he gestured to each in turn, "are for water, fire, and air."

"Good." Laka took out the three sacks holding the scraps of the other elements. She set each beside the appropriate bowl then glanced solemnly at the Thorn Knight. "Now you must be ready with those bracers. You will have only a short time to clasp them onto our slave."

"What if there isn't enough time?" Ankhar asked.

"Then we will all be killed, and our bones will be devoured by the fires in the belly of the world," Laka said with a shrug.

"Be ready!" the half-giant ordered Hoarst unnecessarily as the dark wizard bore a very serious mien as he took out the manacles and held them in his hands, watching Laka warily.

"Now follow these instructions," the shaman continued. If she was as worried as her companions, she was giving no outward sign. "Place the stone in that bowl. Good. Now the water." Ankhar spilled the muddy contents of the pouch into the depression on the second pedestal. He glared at it expectantly, but nothing much seemed to be happening.

Laka herself rolled the glowing remnant of the fire elemental into the third bowl. Ankhar's hand nervously clutched the haft of his spear as she readied the fourth sack, the puffy balloon of air. Hoarst's eyes followed the shaman's every move.

The ancient shaman held the sack of air over the fourth bowl and abruptly compressed the bag, forcing the little gust into the depression. Immediately Ankhar sensed a new, ominous presence. That was the only change, except perhaps for the ember of the fire elemental, which flared brightly, as if it had been fanned by a bellows. The half-giant spun on his heel, looking to the right and left, hardly realizing that he had raised his spear before his chest and was holding it at the ready in both of his big hands.

Then he heard a fresh sound, a faint roaring, like a distant gale that gradually swelled in volume and power. The lump of stone quivered, and the little puddle of dirty water shimmered and shook. It seemed as though the ground under his feet were vibrating. The shaking caused several large pieces of the cavern's ceiling to break free. These shattered on the rocky wastes or splashed into the lava lake, raising great spumes of liquid fire into the air. Debris rained down, barely missing the three intruders.

But this random bombardment was all but forgotten when the tangible presence of something massive, magical, and monstrous took shape on the little clearing atop the island. Ankhar lifted the spear, but there was nothing to strike, no tangible foe.

Yet, undeniably, something was there.

Amid the noise that howled around them like a hurricane, Ankhar felt a faint tickle of something, like a breath of wind, caressing the back of his neck. He spun around, stabbing with his spear, then felt the same eerie touch behind him. The sensation raced down his arms and along his spine, and he imagined invisible ants crawling all over his skin. He glared at his companions, wondering if they felt the same disturbing sensations. Laka's eyes were aglow, her thin lips drawn back, revealing her irregular yellow fangs in a grotesque caricature of a smile. She threw back her head and crowed exultantly, a ululating cry that was almost overwhelmed by the cacophony swelling in the air.

Hoarst stood still, the slender metal bracelets in his hand. Ankhar wanted to curse the Thorn Knight for an inept fool—how could he think those little trinkets could contain even a fraction of the palpable, fundamental force that was drawing in on them like a cloak, a noose.

A physical presence pushed against him, shoving Ankhar almost to the lip of the steep slope. He pushed back, and though he couldn't see anything, he felt resistance, as solid and palpable as a rock. The half-giant pushed as hard as he could, but it was like trying to push away a mountain; not only did the unseen presence fail to budge, it barely responded to his exertion.

Ankhar saw that Laka and Hoarst, likewise, had been pushed to the perimeter of the small clearing by the new threat that was taking shape. Although he raised his spear, the half-giant realized it would be futile to strike a blow, and instead he gaped upward, wondering how the three of them could possibly hope to survive this creation of a god.

A pair of burning eyes glared down at the three intruders, like spots of fire in the heart of a blast furnace. A mouth took shape amidst the vague semblance of a face, and when that mouth opened, the bellow that emerged shook the very air with a pure power that superseded the hurricane roar surrounding them, rattled the ground, and roiled Ankhar's guts, almost compelling him to drop to his knees and beg for mercy.

Only his unwillingness to shame himself in front of his companions kept him on his feet. Laka was glaring upward with her usual fierce, exultant grin, while Hoarst looked remarkably calm as he shifted the pair of manacles he held in his hands.

But as yet, there was nothing to shackle. Between the fiery eyes and cyclonic breath and the rock-solid pillars of legs, there was an intangible middle, only a wispy outline that churned and billowed like a storm cloud. The wisps parted for a moment, and Ankhar briefly spotted a heart of pure water, pulsing and surging like a living organ, shooting gouts of fire and water and air throughout the condensing, gigantic form.

Abruptly, two arms took shape, each as large around as Ankhar's waist. They were capped by fists of black rock, attached to the huge torso by seething tendrils of black cloud. The half-giant almost laughed aloud at the absurdity of trying to subdue those great limbs with the tiny manacles, toylike, that Hoarst was now raising in the air.

"It is time!" cried Laka, her shrill voice somehow piercing the thunderous commotion—almost as if she had spoken directly into the minds of Ankhar and Hoarst.

The magic-user shouted out some arcane phrase that was immediately swallowed by the din. He held aloft the two measly rings of metal. But the manacles glowed brightly and caught the attention of the fire-eyed giant. Its mouth gaped, a cavernous maw that sucked in air like a vortex, sweeping Ankhar off his feet and sending Hoarst, clutching his manacles, lurching forward toward that ravenous orifice.

The mighty creature's two fists swung together, down toward the Thorn Knight, a blow that would inevitably crush the magic-user to jelly. Ankhar felt awe at the human's courage, to face such a fate without quailing. He himself was ready to turn and run, uncaring of the steep hillside or the burning lake at ground level. The half-giant was doomed, for certain, and the only choice he had was to select the manner of his death.

Instead of fleeing, however, he continued to stare, rapt and horrified, as the creature's mighty fists swept toward the Thorn Knight. As they did, the glowing bracelets changed, surprisingly; they were still shooting beams of golden light, but they had grown huge all of a sudden and were great hoops outstretched in the magic-user's hands. Then, in a flash too quick for Ankhar's eye to follow, the manacles were gone from Hoarst's grasp, magically transported to clap themselves around the arcane giant's wrists.

In that same instant the great gale of noise fell away, utterly vanquished by the power of Hoarst's spell. The monstrous creature still stood before them, but its mouth was closed, its blazing eyes banked. The thing raised its two great fists, staring in stupefaction at the golden rings that encircled its arms and compelled its obedience.

A groan sounded in the stillness. The Thorn Knight, pale and trembling, was swaying on unsteady legs, and Ankhar quickly stepped to his side, grabbing him before he collapsed.

Laka, overjoyed by their success, launched into a frenzied, primitive dance, gyrating around the shackled monster and calling out praises in the name of the Prince of Lies.

Ankhar lowered the unconscious Hoarst to the ground and looked up at their new slave, the king of the elementals, a mighty recruit for his surely now-invincible horde.

Laka grinned triumphantly at her son, making a dismissive gesture toward the Thorn Knight, stretched on the ground. The magic-user would recover soon enough.

She produced a small box, studded with bright rubies, and opened the lid. She hurried to each of the four pedestals to collect a bit of residue from each, scraping it into her box. She placed that box between the mighty feet of the elemental king, and it slowly began to shrink, as if the entirety of that massive form was being sucked into the little container. In just a few breaths, indeed, the monstrous being had disappeared, and all that was visible, when Ankhar peered down into the box, were the two metal rings, circlets again small enough that they would have looked comfortably sized around his stepmother's thin, bony wrists. She lifted the sparkling red box and handed it to the half-giant.

He gazed upon it in wonder. Ankhar muttered in pleasure, "The walls of Solanthus will not stand for long."

CHAPTER TEN

THE DUEL

The lord marshal left Selinda in her chambers. The princess was still distraught but at the same time overwhelmed by her new pledge of troth. She had wavered between weeping and pleading, and he had been forced to physically pry her arms from around him.

Gently but firmly Jaymes told her it was time for him to go and defend himself. He asked her not to come and witness the duel, but had little doubt she would do as she pleased.

The contest was to take place in an area called the Dog Run, which was actually a small courtyard to the rear of du Chagne's massive palace. Jaymes was making his way there, alone through the empty hall, when he spied a white shape among the shadows. Coryn stepped into view from between two pillars where she had been waiting for him.

"Hello," he said lightly. "I imagine you've heard the news. Came for the spectacle, did you?"

"I came to *warn* you," she snapped. "Du Chagne is up to something. This whole match smells of his doing, and he's not enough of a gambler to take chances with such a game. They must have something rigged, some kind of treachery."

"I don't doubt that for a moment," he agreed. After a pause, he added, "Thanks for the warning, though. I'll be careful. I had hoped . . . that is, would you second for me?"

She nodded curtly. "Yes, Kingfisher Moorvan and I have agreed to keep an eye on things. The Clerist inquisitor will be the judge of the event. He's du Chagne's man, but I think he still has a conscience—unlike some of the rest of that circle."

"If you say so," Jaymes replied. He did not appear overly concerned about the matter.

"Listen. You have to understand, I won't be able to do anything to help you," Coryn warned.

"I realize that. Don't worry; I can take care of myself."

"Can you? It was only two nights ago that the Kingfisher distracted you with a spell, so much so that you completely forgot your purpose in coming here. If it wasn't for that misadventure, we wouldn't be in this mess today."

He glared at her. "Well, I will count on you to guard against any further magical treachery. As for Frankish's steel, I shall meet that threat on my own terms."

She drew a harsh breath. "What were you thinking, letting him goad you into a match like this? He's the most accomplished swordsman in Palanthas; he kills for sport. While you—you have far more important things to do, like winning the war against Ankhar! Instead, you're risking your life in a duel over a woman!"

"Believe it or not, winning this duel might aid the war campaign more than anything else I could be doing right now. This duel is not over just any woman, remember. And I told you: I didn't instigate the challenge, Frankish did. But now that I have agreed to a duel, I think I can turn the situation to my advantage."

"How?" she demanded.

"You'll have to wait, but you'll see, just like everyone else. Meanwhile, you might be interested to know that your potion seems to be very effective."

"Dammit, why do you have to be so difficult?" she cried, tension cracking her voice. Angrily she clamped her mouth shut, her lips set in a thin line. "Just try not to get your head lopped off!" she snapped before turning and stalking away into the darkness.

"I will try," he said, too quietly for her to hear, before he followed her to the gate leading to the Dog Run.

⭗⊶⊙⊷⊙⊶⊙⊷⊙⊰🏵⊱⊙⊶⊙⊷⊙⊶⊙⊷⭗

Coryn and the Kingfisher were standing side by side at the opposite end of the Dog Run. The two mages wore solemn expressions. The lord regent, together with his aide-de-camp, the Baron Dekage, stood to their left. The Clerist Knight Inquisitor Frost stood in the traditional judge's position, halfway around the right side of the oval floor.

The courtyard was relatively small, with high walls on all sides enclosing the interior. Jaymes came through the barred door at one end to see that someone had installed burning torches in sconces around the wall. The run was lit up almost as bright as day. In a way that was a disadvantage to the lord marshal, who had keen night vision.

Just then Selinda arrived, accompanied only by her servant, Marie. Both young women were breathless and pale, with Marie trailing the agitated princess.

"My dear! This is no place for you!" the lord regent insisted as soon as his daughter came through the gate.

"Actually, Father, this is the *only* place for me!" she replied coldly.

"But, my princess—" Lord Frankish began to object.

She whirled upon him, eyes flashing, spitting her words. "How *dare* you presume to speak to me . . . or for me! If you think you will win my heart by slaying anyone who stands in your path, you know me very poorly, my lord. It will be my pleasure to watch your blood spill onto the ground!"

Frankish drew himself up stiffly. "If you have so little care for your honor, at least take heart from the fact there are others who will watch out for you. Whatever bewitchment this wretch has—"

"You're a bully and killer!" she interrupted. "And I care not a whit for your protection."

With a visible effort she composed herself, stood tall—and she was an unusually tall woman—and glared first at Lord Frankish then at her father. Her next words were spoken carefully and with quiet dignity.

"You both should know that I have pledged my hand to Lord Marshal Jaymes Markham this night. There is nothing either of you can do to change that fact. So put aside your foolish notions of honor, all of you. Leave here and go to bed. This is a fight over nothing."

Du Chagne's face paled, while Frankish displayed an opposite effect: a flush of bright crimson slowly crept upward from his neck, through his cheeks, and over his forehead. His eyes were furiously fixed upon Jaymes.

"I don't know what treachery, what villainy, you have managed to work," Frankish addressed Jaymes. "But for those very words uttered by this gracious lady, for that alone, you must die and face an eternity of torment in the Abyss."

Jaymes stoically ignored the taunt, glancing at Coryn, who was glaring at him with a fury that matched Frankish's. He looked away, rather than meet her jealous gaze.

The Princess Selinda du Chagne stalked away from her father and went to stand at the opposite side of the courtyard. Selinda stared at the lord marshal with almost hypnotic intensity, her hands pressed to her mouth as the torches sputtered and smoked over her head. Her eyes were shining and her skin was taut; she looked as proud as she was terrified.

Lord Frankish came over to stand beside Jaymes, though neither man further acknowledged the other. The lord inquisitor came forward and placed a small table before the pair of combatants, upon which he set a long case. Frost opened the case to reveal two long, slender rapiers of impeccable craftsmanship, made of fine dwarven steel, with lethal, needle-sharp tips.

"Lord Frankish has issued the challenge. It falls to the lord marshal to select his weapon first," the Clerist declared.

Jaymes merely chose the closer of the two swords, swishing it through the air a few times, admiring its balance. He took the tip in his left hand and bent the blade, impressed by the supple strength of the steel.

"This will do," he said as Frankish grabbed the other blade and pronounced himself similarly satisfied. Immediately the table and the empty box were whisked away. The judge returned and swiftly patted down the two warriors, checking to see that neither concealed any extra weapons. The lord inquisitor declared the contestants suitably armed.

Next the two wizards circled the Dog Run slowly, methodically. Each cast a magic detection spell upon the two duelists, ensuring that neither wore a ring or other magical device. They examined the walls, the gates, and even the torch sconces for anything untoward. Sir Moorvan and finally Lady Coryn pronounced the arena free of magic.

"Take your positions," Lord Inquisitor Frost ordered, guiding Jaymes to the left and Frankish to the right. "Ten steps away."

The Clerist knight stood at attention, clearing his throat. Lord Frankish looked at Jaymes with undiluted hatred, while Lord Regent du Chagne's face was a mask.

Lord Marshal Jaymes Markham bristled at all the rigmarole. It was time to get on with it, by all the gods!

Selinda blew him a kiss, even as her eyes were bright with tears.

And Coryn the White still glared at him through slit eyes.

"The Solamnic duel is a challenge of great import and tradition," the inquisitor intoned, speaking to both combatants directly. "From the times of antiquity, the knighthood has placed full faith in the tenets of the Oath and Measure, and nowhere else are those tenets so clearly on display."

That was patently illogical, thought Jaymes, but he betrayed no emotion as the Clerist lord continued to speak.

"This is a test of arms . . . and of skill . . . and of courage. Know that there is no shame in defeat, should a knight give his best effort in the attempt. At any time either combatant may surrender to spare bloodshed—simply by throwing down his weapon and calling for mercy. The foe is honor bound to obey such a plea and will be regarded as the winner of the duel, though the loser remains alive."

"A waste of words, priest," Frankish sneered. "This cur will never submit, and I will have no need for mercy."

"Nevertheless," Frost admonished sternly. "The disengagement is ingrained in the tradition of the duel. It *will* be observed."

The two duelists eyed each other carefully. Jaymes fingered his blade. Though the rapier was not his weapon of choice, he was skilled in its use and confident in his speed and quickness.

He was not afraid.

"Now—let the combat commence," the inquisitor pronounced after a long pause.

Lord Frankish approached swiftly, his weapon poised, feet gliding across the dusty floor of the Dog Run. Jaymes shifted slightly, anticipating his opponent's first strike, and made ready to sidestep. But Frankish launched a whirling attack, and the lord's sword moved faster than Jaymes's eyes could follow. He raised his own weapon in the planned parry, but felt a slash on his arm before his blade could make its block.

The lord marshal retreated a few steps, and Frankish came on furiously and aggressively. Jaymes suddenly realized his opponent was expert, and he was fighting for his life. He slid to the side with his enemy charging undaunted. When he tried to fake to the left, Frankish drove at him from the right, lunging forward and plucking at Jaymes's hip, carving a nasty scrape before the lord marshal could whirl away.

As nimble as he was, his enemy was impressive in his attack. When Jaymes blocked high, his foe's blade came in low. When he retreated, Frankish advanced. And when the lord marshal offered a modest counterattack, he was belabored by such a succession of blows he could only fall back, almost stumbling as he hastily backed away.

His enemy's blade slid under his defenses with terrifying speed. Jaymes fell to the rear again, barely knocking the blows away, but before he could catch his balance, another slash came in from the right. He twisted to the left, lunging to escape a wickedly fast strike, but could not evade before the blade tore through his sleeve near the wrist.

Across the Dog Run, the Princess Selinda screamed.

Blood coursed over his hand, dripping from his fingers, and the lord marshal fumbled as he retreated. All too soon, he felt the cold stones of the courtyard wall against his back. Frankish's eyes lit up with a cruel gleam of triumph as he closed in. Jaymes feinted, lunged, and parried, but he felt as if he were anchored in thick mud.

━━━━━━━━━━━━━

He's not that good!

Coryn realized almost immediately that, somehow, the Rose Lord had enhanced his abilities—without using a magic device, which she certainly would have detected. Frankish moved in a blur, dancing around the eminently skilled—yet clearly outclassed—lord marshal. Jaymes's parries looked sluggish; Frankish struck at will.

Again and again Frankish dashed in close to Jaymes, flicking with his rapier—leaving bloody scratches—and dancing away before the lord marshal could respond.

Coryn looked at Sir Moorvan, who was staring at the Rose Lord with undisguised irritation, even animosity. The Kingfisher's hands twitched at his sides, as if he wished he could reach out and strangle the man. But why should the Kingfisher be upset, the wizard wondered—when Sir Moorvan surely *wanted* Frankish to win!

And suddenly she understood.

"You cast a spell of haste on him, didn't you?" she hissed furiously.

He looked at her in astonishment, guilt flitting across his features, and in that instant she knew. "He was supposed to be discreet about it, wasn't he? But he has failed his subterfuge. He is being too obvious!"

"Don't be ridic—"

"You will dispel the magic—now!" she insisted angrily. "Or I will cast the same spell for Jaymes—and make a mockery of this whole duel! And then I will reveal your perfidy, and the lord regent's, making it known to everyone concerned, from Palanthas to the Council of Whitestone and even the Grand Master himself!"

With a pained look, the Kingfisher squirmed in his seat. "But I can't—"

"Do it—right now!" demanded Coryn.

Grimacing, Moorvan waved his hand at the Rose Lord, dispelling the magic, and almost immediately, the lord marshal scored his first wound of the match.

✕─◉◈◦◈◦◈◦◈◦◈ ✿ ◈◦◈◦◈◦◈◦◈─✕

Jaymes advanced steadily now. He saw the fear growing in his opponent's widening eyes, the sweat that increasingly sheened his forehead. Now it was the lord marshal's turn to thrust aggressively. He shuffled his feet forward, thrust again and again, repeating the maneuvers with smooth precision. Poised on the balls of his feet, knees bent, balance distributed evenly, Jaymes advanced and drove his opponent back.

Frankish reacted weakly to the increasing tempo of Jaymes's attacks, blocking and parrying with mounting desperation, with little suggestion of his formerly blinding speed. The lord's reflexes had slowed considerably, and now his skills were sorely tested. All the while the lord marshal pushed at his opponent mercilessly, steadily backing him across the floor. Frankish's best efforts could do little except hold him at bay.

When the Rose Lord tried to circle away, Jaymes gracefully cut him off with a slide to the left. When his enemy made a desperate lunge, slashing and swiping almost frantically, Jaymes stood his ground, parrying and blocking. Their blades met with increasing fury, a *clash, clash, clash* that melded into a steady hiss and clangor.

126

The lord marshal yielded not an inch, and inevitably, Frankish fell back, sweating heavily and gasping for breath. Again Jaymes took up the advance, making slow, methodical progress across the courtyard, moving no more than eight or ten inches with each gliding step. His enemy continued to retreat, nearly stumbling, until backed up against the wall, directly before Lord Regent du Chagne. Frankish was flailing now, frantically slashing against Jaymes's blade and leaving himself wide open to thrusts.

Jaymes was toying with Frankish now, and he backed off slightly, glancing at the pale face of Lord Regent du Chagne. Smiling coldly, fixing his eyes again on his opponent's face, Jaymes swung hard, bashing the other man's sword to the side.

Suddenly, startling him, Lord Frankish let go of his sword. "Mercy!" he cried, dropping to one knee. "I beg mercy, upon the Oath and the—"

But Jaymes stabbed Frankish before he could finish his plea, driving the tip of his sword through his opponent's chest and deep into the man's heart. Even as Frankish died, the lord marshal's eyes were fixed coldly upon the other man, the noble who stared back at him with shock, fear, and fury written plainly across his face.

"Sorry, I didn't hear him in time," Jaymes said, yanking his blade free from the other man's chest. Frankish slumped to the ground, and the lord marshal tossed the bloody weapon onto his opponent's corpse.

CHAPTER ELEVEN

SECRET COMPOUNDS

Jaymes took his time riding away from Palanthas. For four days he traveled by horseback over the High Clerist's Pass, along the foothills of the Vingaard range, and up to the thriving village he had founded two years earlier—the place called, simply, the Compound. He had reasons for going there, and he needed time to clear his head.

After the duel, Coryn, naturally, had wanted to teleport him directly back to his army so he could launch a plan to save Solanthus. She had made a reasonable explanation: the bridging equipment for which he had contracted in Palanthas would not reach the army for several weeks, and operations at the front would have to wait until then. He reminded her that the Vingaard was a deep, wide barrier; the river crossing was challenging, and the outcome of the campaign would depend on it. That was the truth.

But another truth he held more privately. As much as Coryn had helped him, he could not allow himself to fall completely under her influence. Though he was saddle sore by the second day of riding, though rain and wind lashed him through the high pass, he relished the discomfort. He would do things in his own time; Coryn be damned.

The parting from Selinda had been an easier test of his will, though it had involved high drama. The princess had wept and pleaded with him, clearly terrified that he would come to harm in warfare—or perhaps, that his desire to marry her would wane with time and distance. He had assured her, quite honestly, that his ardor would remain as passionate as ever, awkwardly disengaging himself from her arms and riding away.

The white gelding he rode previously had been splendid for show, but with a mountain road before him, he had left the animal in Donny's keeping and purchased a sturdy black mare. She had proven a fast and tireless mount and seemed to share his restlessness as she climbed into the fragrant pine forests of the Vingaard foothills. Jaymes gave the mare her head, and the horse shivered with delight in the cool shade. The air was moist, and the fragrance of evergreens made a rich and soothing perfume. The rider allowed their pace to ease a little as the land rose; his customary urgency was tempered by a rare pleasure in his surroundings. This valley, his destination, might not have been home to him, but it was as close to a home as any place else in the world.

The trail climbed steadily, but the weary horse only picked up speed, as if she sensed the nearness of their destination. She trotted up a series of inclines, following the winding trail beneath the overhanging limbs of the pines, then broke into a trot as the path leveled off and the trees ended abruptly at the mouth of a wide, flat-bottomed valley.

Here the scent of pines was replaced by the acidic stink of smoke and ash. A cloud of smoke hung in the air, like a permanent stratus cloud roofing the valley, enclosing this secret place and shielding it from unwelcome eyes—as if to say "not even the gods may look here!" But to Jaymes Markham, all was as it should be in this place.

The Compound had changed a great deal over the past year. Where once a clearing had formed but a small gap in the vast forest, now the trees had been harvested not only from the valley floor, but also from the slopes of both of the adjacent ridges. The barren ground was brown, streaked with gullies and ravines where erosion had begun. Great piles of logs were stacked to the right and left, the timber drying in the air. Dwarven laborers, well paid and hard working, were busy lashing teams of horses as they hauled skids of logs, bringing more lumber down from the mountains. Others chopped and split the logs or pounded hammers into spikes as they worked at assembling buildings.

Instead of the rudimentary shacks of the original log buildings, there were long, timbered structures containing the factories, as well as a series of barracks where the workers—now numbering in the hundreds—lived and ate. The sounds of industry echoed through the whole valley, from the steady cadence of axes, the hammering of smiths, the roaring of forges, and the cacophony of overseers and foremen shouting their commands.

The arrival of the lone rider attracted notice, and messengers raced to inform their foremen and bring news to the great house in the center of the Compound. But work continued as Jaymes rode into the corral before the largest house in the entire place. It was a great, sprawling manor with two wings and a tall, colonnaded facade. Two young handlers, both human lads, came out of the stable to take charge of his horse, and as he made his way up the steps before the house, a bearded dwarf hastened across the yard, wiping his hands on his apron and meeting the marshal with a scowl just outside the front door.

"I thought you weren't coming until three days from now!" Dram Feldspar complained crossly. "I have the test planned for then!"

"Events are moving quickly," the marshal replied. "And I wanted to come up here now; I need to be back with the army within a week, for the next campaign."

"Well, it's too bad. And Sally will be disappointed; we were going to butcher a prize hog and spend a day roasting the thing, so we could celebrate in style."

"Your simple country fare will be fine, I'm sure." For the first time, the man cracked a thin smile, pointing toward his old friend's bulging gut. "It looks to me as if you've been feasting plenty."

"Aye," Dram agreed without a hint of embarrassment. "I'll tell you, married life agrees with me."

"You don't say? Sally hasn't tossed you out on your ear, then?"

"Not a chance. Though I confess, I get a bit of the longing for the trail, and a warm campfire, now and then. And the sound of a good battle—now, that's something that would get my blood pounding again."

"Be careful what you wish for," Jaymes cautioned.

Dram brightened immediately. "Are you here to call me back to arms? My axe is sharp—I keep the blade oiled, you know. I can be ready in—"

"No, no," the lord marshal countered, raising a hand. "You know better. I need you more here."

"Bah. I mighta figured. Rubbing shoulders with hill dwarves and gnomes all day!"

"Speaking of hill dwarves, how's Sally's father? Still tolerating you?"

The mountain dwarf snorted. "Swig Frostmead would tolerate anyone who brings him as much profit as I do. As to Sally, let's just say that she and I make each other very happy. As a matter of fact, our family seems to be growing—she's expecting a little forge-master before the first frost." He blushed, his pride beaming through the redness that tinged his rugged face.

"Well, congratulations. Even if it turns out to be a forge-mistress."

"Bite your tongue!" grunted the dwarf. But he halted, and scratched his beard in thought, as if the idea had never occurred to him before. "Do ya think . . . ? Huh! Well, come on in and make yourself comfortable. I sent a message to Swig as soon as the lookouts reported you were coming. No doubt he'll be over in time for supper."

"Good."

"Can you stay for longer than a few days?" He cleared his throat, trying to sound gruff. "I've missed . . . that is, there's a lot to show you."

"No, this will have to be a quick visit. The army is concentrating on the west bank of the Vingaard, and I need to meet them in camp as soon as possible. How long will it take to put together the demonstration?"

"Well, I'd prefer more time to prepare, but there's no real reason why we couldn't do it first thing in the morning—that is, if you really have to get going." He looked rather crestfallen, but his expression brightened at the sound of a female voice from the next room.

"Jaymes!" Sally Feldspar came running, or more accurately waddling, into view. The dwarf maid's rosy cheeks crinkled into a broad smile, and she turned half sideways so that her bulging belly allowed her to clasp the visitor in a powerful hug.

"You're looking mighty healthy, Sally. Dram told me your good news, or I never would have guessed."

"Oh, you're a smooth one, Jaymes Markham. That you are. And I bet a thirsty one, too. That husband of mine doesn't have the manners to offer an old friend a drink?"

"Darn it, woman!" barked the dwarf, who even then was filling a pair of large tankards from the keg that rested to one side of the entry hall. It was a permanent fixture of the room. "He only just came through the door!"

"Well, let me help the cook get the fire started," Sally declared cheerfully. "I'm sure you two have a lot to talk about. Get the boring stuff out of the way, won't you? At dinner, I'll be joining the conversation and by then I hope you'll have got around to something *interesting*."

"Ah, she's a nag, and she bosses me around," Dram said affectionately as his wife disappeared into the back of the house. "I don't know how I ever lived without her."

"It's a long way from sleeping on the ground next to a fire, wondering if goblins are sneaking around, getting ready to attack our camp. Do you really miss that life?"

"You know?" Dram reflected. "Sometimes I feel like I do. But when I think about it other times, I don't." Still, the dwarf's eyes did not turn back to the kitchen or pantry, or his wife. Almost unconsciously, his gaze shifted to the open window, to the mountain horizon, and the blue sky beyond. He passed a beer to Jaymes, and both sat down, sipping their refreshment and saying nothing further for several moments.

Swig Frostmead arrived shortly. He came into the parlor where Dram and Jaymes were having their beers and enthusiastically pumped the lord marshal's hand. Jaymes opened his belt pouch and took out a small leather sack. The beaming hill dwarf, Dram's father-in-law, hefted the sack, feeling its weight, and as he did so, his grin grew even wider. "Hope you don't mind if I have a little peek?" he asked with a wink.

"Not at all," said the human.

The hill dwarf chieftain dumped the contents of the bag into his palm, and his eyes glittered as brightly as the pile of gems was revealed. "Diamonds, rubies—and a few of them emeralds I like so much!" he crowed. He looked up at Jaymes and smiled even more broadly. "It's a pleasure doing business with you, my good man!" he said. "And this time I'm not even going to ask where you keep finding these lovely little baubles!"

"You keep your dwarves busy working in my compound—and keep strangers away from here—and I'll make sure you keep getting paid," declared the man.

Swig's appearance had changed quite a bit since Jaymes had last seen him, before the winter. Where the hill dwarf chieftain had once been content to wear buckskin clothes and soft moccasins, he now sported a silk shirt, tailored trousers, and shiny black leather boots. Platinum chains encircled his neck, and the marshal estimated their weight to be no less than twenty pounds of precious metal. The dwarf's fingers were studded with rings, and a diamond earring was set into the lobe of his left ear. The formerly bushy beard was now neatly braided, and his long hair combed and oiled, bound with a silken ribbon into a tail that draped most of the way down his back.

Dram might not have had time to roast the hog he had planned to butcher, but the household cook—with considerable help from Sally—managed to lay out quite a feast. They started with crusty bread and creamy butter followed by a soup rich and thick with bacon, potatoes, and onions. The main course was a fat turkey, one of the plump and tasty birds that roamed so freely through the foothills of the Vingaard Mountains. It was stuffed with a mix of mushrooms and herbs, and served in a pool of savory gravy. For dessert there was a tort made from flaky pastry, cream, and fresh strawberries harvested from the bogs that dotted the lowlands at the very fringe of the mountains.

Not surprisingly, Dram had asked about the progress of the war, and now Jaymes filled him in on the latest developments, including how the Crown Knights and foot soldiers of General Dayr's wing had broken Ankhar's northern force and driven them, finally, east of the Vingaard River.

"Ah, the thrill of battle! The chaos, the sounds, the danger," Dram said, taking a deep draught from his tankard. He wiped the foam from his whiskers and shook his head with melancholy. "You know, I miss them times! The best times of my life!"

"You can't be serious!" Sally snorted, her eyebrows raised scornfully. "The killing, the pain, the suffering? All those things you tell me you've tried to forget!"

"Er, yes," Dram mumbled sheepishly. "Maybe I did a better job of forgetting than I thought. But still, I feel like I should be there with my friend here, should be helping somehow."

"You are helping, in case you've forgotten that too," Jaymes noted pointedly. "The black powder you're making here in the Compound is going to be a decisive factor in our strategy; I'm sure of it. First, we need to learn how to use it in battle."

"That's what the demonstration is for, tomorrow. The gnomes are supervising the preparations right now. Knowing Sulfie and Pete, they'll be up all night working and tinkering, making sure we're good to go after breakfast."

After an evening of companionable drinking—Jaymes merely sipping, while the hill and mountain dwarves tried to outdo each other, as usual—the visiting marshal slept comfortably in his host's guest suite. After a hearty breakfast, and some grousing from Swig Frostmead about the early hour, the three followed a stone-paved road through the heart of the Compound, toward the testing range at the far end of the valley.

As they passed the many buildings, Jaymes took note of the improvements made over the winter. There was a large charcoal factory that had been recently completed and vast yards where hardwood imported over the mountains—the oak, hickory, and maple of the coastal forests—was stored. The heavy, tough timber had proved more suitable than the local pines for the charring process. In the sulfur yards, mountainous piles of the yellow rock excavated by Swig's miners lined both sides of the road.

An entire section of the Compound was given over to the purifying of the black power. This was the brilliant contribution of the gnome, Salty Pete. The purifying buildings were sided with planks instead of logs and roofed with actual slate shingles. The whole area looked more like a quaint mountain village than an industrial center.

"Those are the mixers, down near the creek and the pond," Dram explained proudly, pointing to several iron casks that were each the size of a small barn. From within these came the sounds of grinding and churning. The three crucial ingredients of the secret formula were being ground into fine powder and mixed in carefully measured proportions.

Despite the early hour, activity churned across the compound. Most of the factories were staffed with hill dwarves of Meadstone, Swig Frostmead's village, though there were a few gnomes and humans who had been drawn to the hard work here by the promise of good pay. The marshal could hear forge doors slamming, smiths pounding on iron and steel, and furnaces roaring everywhere. Passing the open doors of one foundry, he could feel the blast of heat against his skin.

Dram pointed inside. "Those foundry-feeders are the dwarves who really earn their pay," he said. "For them, it's like working in the deserts of Neraka without the benefit of shade."

"Aye, they're a hearty breed, those dwarves of Meadstone," Swig remarked proudly.

Beyond the manufacturing area, a series of stone-walled structures, half buried in the ground, dotted a field as large as a parade ground. Wide spaces of grass separated these warehouses, and each was surrounded by moats filled with still, murky water.

"These are the storage centers—twelve of them now, with eight more to go up this summer."

"Good. I'm glad to see you have them dispersed. So even if there's an accident in one warehouse, we should be able to protect the rest of the powder stockpiles."

"Yep. Don't want to have a repeat of the yule disaster," Dram agreed heartily. Jaymes hadn't witnessed that calamity, but the results had been recounted in a grim letter the dwarf had scribed the previous winter: Someone had sparked a fire in the main storage house, and the entire stockpile of powder had vanished in a tremendous explosion. Some dozen workers had perished, and all the nearby buildings had suffered damage. Following that tragedy, Dram had immediately instituted safety precautions. Now some facilities were underground, others spaced apart; and tanks or trenches of water were interspersed throughout the camp. There had not been a repeat of that incident.

Finally they reached the end of the developed part of the Compound. The lord marshal spotted an intriguing device a half mile away, across the remaining field. There lay a massive tube, like a huge tree trunk that had been trimmed of all branches and bark. As they drew closer, Jaymes noticed a series of stout metal bands wrapped the tube.

"We've made this test barrel out of ironwood," Dram explained. "After the oak we had been using got shattered in every previous test."

"And the projectiles?" Jaymes asked.

"We've got some boulders, chiseled to fit the exact diameter of the tube. That's one thing we learned—if the ball is too small, there's not enough pressure to shoot it out. Too large, of course, and it gets jammed in the pipe. Then we just end up blowing up the whole thing."

"Oh, hi, Boss. Better stand back if you don't want to get blowed up."

The speaker who popped up from behind the huge tree trunk was a gnome female with frizzy hair and a slightly irritated expression. She wore a pair of spectacles—new since the last time Jaymes had seen her—perched on her tiny nose. The lenses were so smudged, the marshal found it hard to imagine they could be any help with seeing.

She blinked up at Jaymes and went back to her work, which involved scrutinizing figures she had written down on a scroll of parchment then comparing the amounts to the black powder being poured into three different casks. Each was about the size of a small beer barrel.

"Thanks for the advice, Sulfie," Jaymes replied. He watched as the diminutive technician, one of three siblings who were attempting to perfect the black powder for warfare, went back to work. Her brother, Salty Pete, wore a stiff leather apron as he bustled from keg to keg, double-checking the amount of powder in each. If he in any way noticed Jaymes's arrival, he didn't let on.

"The kegs are the same size, as you can see," Dram continued smoothly. "But we're putting different amounts of the powder in each. We'll start with the smallest—just three pounds. This will repeat the measure that we tried with our last test, the one that burst the seams of the barrel. This tube we've made at nearly twice the strength specifications, however, so we have a greater expectation of success."

"Test away," said the marshal. "I'd like to see it in action."

Jaymes, Dram, and Swig watched as two hill dwarves gently eased the first keg into the mouth of the tube. A third hill dwarf with a long plunger carefully pushed it until it was lodged in the terminus of the shaft, which was about twelve feet long.

"We run a fuse through the little hole here," Dram indicated as Salty Pete knelt behind the barrel and fed a stiff piece of rope through a small aperture. "We've been working on that little problem, too. We use a weaving of string with some of the powder added, so the fire moves down the line at a controlled speed. 'Course, it's still not too exact; sometimes the danged thing goes out, and other times it races along like you won't believe."

"Fuse is ready. Let's load her up," Pete declared brusquely.

Two burly hill dwarves hoisted a boulder that, as Dram had described, looked to be the exact diameter to fill the tube. They placed it in the mouth of the shaft then helped the dwarf with the plunger to shove the heavy sphere all the way in, until it was lodged against the keg of powder set in the deepest end of the tube.

"Now's the time where we should all back up about a hundred paces," the mountain dwarf said pointedly. Sulfie, Swig, Dram, Jaymes, and all of the hill dwarves withdrew to a safe distance. Only Salty Pete lingered behind. The gnome held a flint and a match up in the air, keeping his eyes on Dram.

"Ready?" asked Dram, his eyes sweeping around.

"Whenever you give the word is fine with me," Jaymes replied.

"Fire away!" hollered Dram. "Best cover your ears," he added for the benefit of the novices.

Salty Pete struck a flame and extended the match to the end of the snaking fuse. As soon as the rope began to fizz and crackle, the gnome turned and sprinted for the others, arriving just as the fire advanced to the terminus of the tube. Then it hissed out of sight, and there was a moment of torturous suspense, when nothing seemed to happen. Even the wind seemed to falter, waiting, hesitant and fearful.

The explosion was sudden, incredibly loud, and impressively violent. A *boom* of sound pulsated in the air, and a cloud of fiery smoke billowed from the mouth of the tube. The round boulder emerged from that cloud, flying lazily for about a hundred paces before it plummeted to the ground, rolled another few dozen feet, and came to a rest.

"Hmm. So far so good," Dram declared.

"In principle," Jaymes agreed noncommittally. "But not much use on the battlefield—a good longbowman can fire an arrow three times that distance."

"Well, that was just for starters, just a warm-up of course," the mountain dwarf huffed. "Now we'll try it with some real pop and bang."

The crew of hill dwarves scurried back to work. First they swabbed out the tube with a wet rag. "We learned the hard way not to put in a keg back in there while there are still glowing sparks inside," explained the mountain dwarf.

Then they eased the second cask into place, one containing twelve pounds of black powder. "Four times as much blast," the dwarf noted proudly. "More than we've ever used before—but the barrel is four times stronger than any we've tried, also. So keep your fingers crossed or say a prayer if you're the religious type."

They watched as Pete knelt down and rigged another section of fuse, leaving a generous amount outside the base of the barrel. Finally the dwarves loaded a second stone ball and rolled it into place in the base of the tube. The workers hurried away.

"This blast is going to be louder," warned Dram.

Jaymes nodded and put his hands over his ears, as did the other observers. Salty Pete waited for the signal from Dram then struck a match, touching the burning end to the fuse. Immediately the fire took hold, racing and sputtering along the line so quickly that, by the time the gnome had hopped to his feet and spun around, it had advanced halfway to the breech.

"Run!" cried Sulfie.

"Damn—it's a speed burn!" Dram grunted.

By the time Pete had taken two steps, the fire had reached the base of the bombard and vanished into the hole. The explosion was much louder this time, but immediately Jaymes realized that something had gone terribly wrong. Instead of a gout of flame and smoke bursting from the mouth of the tube, the entire structure seemed to swell and redden with heat, then the whole device was obliterated in a blast of shocking violence.

The tube, the mount, and the gnome were gone in a single, massive flash.

"My brother!" cried Sulfie, starting forward.

Dram grabbed her by the scruff of her tunic and pulled her back. "Wait!" demanded the dwarf, ignoring the protests of the struggling, weeping gnome. In a few breaths there was a second flash, followed by a steady rumble as the kegs of powder behind the revetment, showered by sparks from the first blast, also began to explode.

After a few more moments of explosions and fire and light, there was nothing left but stink and smoke.

CHAPTER TWELVE

THE ELEMENTS UNLEASHED

Even now, with the dome of sparkling stars above him, the moons of red and white both visible at differing ends of the sky, Ankhar could not dispel the appalling sense of isolation and entombment that had pressed so heavily upon him during the sunless quest. He had never expected to miss so much of the world he had always known. Never one to wax poetic over the song of a bird or the fragrance of a lush forest, he had nevertheless found those sensory memories tormenting his dreams, jolting him awake and near despair as he recognized the stone and dark and cold of his subterranean surroundings.

Furthermore, the miserable journey back to the surface seemed to take twice as long as the descent, an exhausting climb back through the underground labyrinth. His muscles ached from weariness; his hands were blistered by the work of lifting himself over rough rock. Often he had to hoist Laka over challenging, steep stretches of the climb. At one point the return trip was eased by the levitation spell Hoarst had cast so, once again with his stepmother cradled in his arms, the half-giant had been able to rise up the miles-long precipice he had magically descended a lifetime earlier.

At least it seemed like another life. Only the thrilling—and terrifying—success of their mission had given him the strength to persevere, trudging blindly through the long caverns leading, he desperately hoped, back to the surface. Laka's spirits had never flagged, however, nor had she displayed any doubts as to the correctness of their path. As usual, her wisdom was proved sound.

By the time the weary trio had approached the mouth of the cave, squinting against the blinding daylight even though it was just past sunset, the commander of the horde had somehow straightened himself. He had even attained a measure of swagger by the time he and his two companions returned to the camp. There they learned that nearly twenty days had passed during their sojourn. The army's positions hadn't changed in that time, but Ankhar learned the knights were massing across the Vingaard, so it was with a sense of growing urgency that the half-giant ordered immediate preparations for the attack on Solanthus.

His most important captains were summoned to arrive at the rendezvous point by midnight. Bloodgutter reported that his brigade, which was to lead the assault once the city wall had been breached, was on the march, and would be in position below the West Gate before dawn. Captain Blackgaard rode up on his midnight-blue charger, the animal snorting and pawing the ground as if it sensed—and thrilled at—the nearness of battle. Rib Chewer Wargmaster was also here; though his lupine cavalry would not be involved in storming the walls, Ankhar wanted his most trusted commander to hear all the plans and view the new power of the Truth. The goblin chief settled beside the fire, wrapped his cloak around himself, and promptly fell asleep.

As the hours ticked by, the half-giant paced worriedly. All these captains, all of their fierce and veteran warriors, would not be enough to win the battle he intended to wage. Finally he pulled his stepmother aside and spoke in a hoarse whisper. "Where is he? What keeps the Thorn Knight?"

"Sir Hoarst has much work to do," Laka reminded him. "If he makes a mistake in the creation of his device, it will be difficult—maybe impossible—to control the king once we open the box."

Ankhar shivered. The memory of the king of the elementals, shackled and restrained, was terrifying. The thought of him running amok was completely unacceptable.

Dawn was already streaking the eastern sky, silhouetting the lofty battlements, spires, and ramparts of the West Gate, before the wizard made his appearance. He carried a slender wand, a stick no longer than the span between the tip of the thumb and little finger on the half-giant's splayed hand.

"That?" Ankhar asked skeptically.

The wizard looked haggard; he had dark circles around his eyes and a pallid cast to his skin, his paleness accentuated by the long period under the ground. He had not rested since they had returned to the camp, and now he fixed the commander with a glare that caused Ankhar to immediately regret his tone.

"This wand is the product of a great deal of research, spell-casting, and careful carving," Hoarst snapped. "If its appearance is not suitably impressive, I suggest you find someone else to control the creature!"

"No! It will do—it must!"

By this time the ogres had arrived, nearly a thousand of the brutish creatures assembled in five battle columns, each ten abreast and twenty deep. The sheer mass and crushing momentum of such a formation would overpower any normal army, and if the elemental king could but smash through the gatehouse, Ankhar was confident that his ogres would be able to strike deep into the city's defenses. They would be followed by thousands upon thousands of goblins, hobgoblins, and Blackgaard's mercenaries.

The half-giant could almost taste the coming victory! But there were still many questions to be answered. He sat with Hoarst and Laka beneath the army headquarters banner and tried to hammer out the details. The ruby box rested on the ground at his feet.

"The box is the ultimate means of control," the Thorn Knight explained. He had gone over this before, but if he was impatient now, repeating himself, he didn't betray the fact. "As long as the king wears the shackles when he is out, he will be compelled to return to the box when it is opened."

"Thus it was in my vision, the image of the Truth," Laka confirmed. She nodded at the slender wand. "And your twig?"

Hoarst shrugged. "It is a means of focusing the creature's attention on a target. I must wield the wand—it requires a spell-caster to effect its function. When we open the box, the king will emerge, and he will be consumed with rage by his entrapment. But the shackles bind him to our will, so he will not attack the one who holds the box or any nearby.

"With the wand I shall steer him to the gate, and his innate fury will drive him forward in a destructive frenzy. I hope, and expect, that the wand will function as a powerful prod, that I will be able to guide him from a distance of several miles away."

"But if he gets too far away, he could break the spell?" This seemed to Ankhar to be a rather important point. "Could he turn on us?"

"If we begin to lose control of him through the wand, Laka must open the box. He will be drawn back to us and be compelled to enter his prison."

"Very well," decided the army commander. The sky in the east was already pale blue, and sunrise was less than an hour away. He summoned Bloodgutter with a wave. "Make ready," he ordered. Then he turned to his stepmother.

"Time to open the box."

━━━━━◆━━━━━

Sir Cedric Keflar looked in on his children, all three sleeping in the single narrow bunk. Violet, the oldest, was nearly as long as the bed, but she curled her slim frame against the wall so her younger brothers could nestle in the softer, central part of the crude straw mattress. The knight leaned down and kissed each child's smooth cheek, his heart breaking at the gauntness of those precious faces, proof of the hunger that had sunk once bright eyes so deeply into their sockets. He was grateful they didn't awaken; Violet only sighed quietly and shifted a little in her sleep.

Barely a foot away in the tiny room, Kiera, Cedric's wife of twenty years, lay shivering on her own pallet. He touched a hand to her forehead and felt the fever that was burning her up. He took the time to moisten a rag and place it over her clammy skin. Then he leaned down to kiss her, grateful for the flutter of eyelids that was as much acknowledgement as she could offer.

Dawn was coming, and with dawn came duty. The sun would wait for no man, and Cedric Keflar, Captain of Swords, was determined to be as reliable as that cosmic orb when it came to his duty. He eased out of the tiny bedroom and buckled on his great sword, the weapon that had belonged to his father's father's fathers for as far back as any of the Keflars could reckon. Silently he closed the door to the apartment, trying to keep his armor from clanking as he made his way past the sleeping families crowded into the other rooms, and clustered on the balconies and landings of the rickety building's stairways.

This was the way of life in crowded, besieged Solanthus. Cedric's rank would have entitled him to a house for his family alone, but only if such houses were available. The entire human population for a hundred miles in every direction—at least those humans who had survived the horde's initial invasion—had come to seek shelter behind the city's high, impregnable walls. They subsisted on starvation rations and during the last winter, had burned every stick of wood within Solanthus. Clerics labored to create food, and while their efforts kept many people alive, there was never enough.

Cedric had to step over several people sleeping on the front steps of his building, and more were huddled against the curb, in each alley, sometimes tumbling into the roadway. Moving through the darkness, the knight captain walked carefully. Here and there a pair of bright eyes watched him from the darkness, and he did his best to look calm and capable as he marched toward another day at his post.

As he turned down the gate street, he glanced over his shoulder, toward the heart of his city. The Cleft Spires loomed to the left, but the lofty, graceful outline of the Ducal Palace dominated the view. Flanked by slender towers, with an arched roof that looked more like a cathedral than a castle, it was a view that never failed to inspire Sir Cedric. It reminded him of so many of things they were fighting for.

"Bless you, my lady," he whispered, thinking gratefully of the woman who dwelled there, the duchess who moved among her people with such serenity that the citizenry couldn't help but take hope from her example.

As Cedric moved closer to the West Gate, he passed through a broad marketplace, now dark and silent except for the snores of sleeping refugees. Beyond, the steep walls of the gatehouse rose before him. He paused in the plaza before entering the building. Outlined by the growing light of dawn, the Cleft Spires stood out against the rosy sky. Silhouetted against the setting of the white moon rose the gatehouse and the formidable walls to the west. That was where Cedric headed this morning . . . and every morning. As Commandant of the West Gate, he was responsible for one of the key components of the city's defense.

"How fares it, lads?" he asked the men of the night watch, who snapped to attention as their captain climbed the stairs to the First Tower, the rampart directly over the thick, iron-banded gates.

"Bit of a rumpus out there in the wee hours, sir," replied the sergeant major who ruled the post during the hours of darkness. "Seems to be some ogres moving up to within a mile of the gate."

"Well, Mapes, we'll have to hope the blokes creep a bit closer," Cedric replied cheerfully. "And our archers can turn a few of 'em into pincushions!"

"Aye, Captain!" Mapes said with equal cheer. The men of the ranks, a dozen or more of them standing within earshot, looked at each other and nodded. Already whispered reports of the exchange, verbatim, were being passed along the lines on the wall tops, through the interior bastions, and down into the central courtyard. With confident leaders like these, the men trusted they were invincible.

The West Gate was more than just a gatehouse; it was a sturdy castle in its own right. The gate was wide enough, when opened, for two freight wagons to roll through or ten fully armored knights to ride abreast. The approach crossed a drawbridge some forty feet long, over a moat that was nearly as deep. The bottom of the moat was a muddy morass of sewage, brackish water, and mud deep enough to swallow a tall man up to his neck. When the drawbridge was raised, it formed the first barrier of the gates. Immediately within was a massive portcullis of iron bars—the second line of defense.

An attacker who penetrated the portcullis would find himself in a constricted corridor, blocked by another portcullis forty feet inside. Overhead was a slotted ceiling—whose slots were murder holes, designed for hot oil to be poured down the openings or arrows to be loosed at the heads of any encroaching foes. If the assaulting force broke through the second portcullis, its soldiers then would have to cross a courtyard a hundred feet wide, surrounded on all sides by high ramparts and towers. From those elevations a devastating fire could be directed at the hopelessly exposed invaders. Then, across the courtyard, the whole process of the double portcullis corridor had to be repeated before the enemy actually broke through to the city streets of Solanthus.

Sir Cedric had a garrison of more than five hundred men to hold just this one gatehouse. Though the troops, like everyone else in the city, were hungry and discouraged, they were brave fighters and if given the chance, they would certainly acquit themselves in a manner worthy of the Knights of Solamnia. Indeed, the greatest enemy that they faced—besides hunger—was the long period of inactivity that had worn away at their readiness over more than thirteen months of siege. To combat this forced lassitude, Cedric and Mapes had organized countless drills and driven the men through numerous training regimens scheduled in the deep central courtyard. But the nearing prospect of battle, the chance to strike back at the ever-present, but thus far unreachable, horde, was to the captain's thinking the best medicine he could ask for his men.

Still, Cedric could not quell a sense of disquiet as he gazed over the wall, spying the great blocks of the ogre columns increasingly visible as dawn turned to daylight. The ogres were organized in tight file formations—that is, one file directly behind the other—such that they would assault the gate almost as one. Their drums, in a measured basso thumping, were marking a slow, almost dirge-like tempo, he noted. Ogres were tough brutes, Cedric well knew, but even if they held great shields over their heads, the devastating fire of arrows, rocks, and burning oil from the heights would surely decimate a great number of them before they could crawl through the mud of the moat. So the captain doubted they would attack in a mass and suspected they must have some other plan.

The first clue to their strategy came now, when a hulking shape, accompanied by a more normal-sized retinue of soldiers, appeared at the fore of the first ogre company.

"Why, that's the half-giant himself," Mapes exclaimed, "or I'm the son of a gully dwarf!"

Cedric, who had a spyglass, raised it to his eye and stared. "No, Mapes, your bloodlines can reasonably be assumed to have flowed through humans," the captain confirmed.

As the bestial, tusked face of the horde's commander glared back at him, the knight felt his first shiver of apprehension. "That bastard is up to something today," he said warily.

He scanned around, examining Ankhar's party. Next to the half-giant, he saw a man in the armored breastplate and ash-gray cloak typical of a Thorn Knight. On the other side stood a short, stooped creature with bestial features, apparently some kind of witch doctor, clutching a grotesque talisman that looked to be a human skull mounted on some kind of short stick.

The latter, a gnarled female, placed a small box on the ground before Ankhar as the first rays of the sun streamed over the battlements and brightened the ground. Something as red as blood, rubies no doubt, glittered brightly on that container, as the witch doctor pulled back the lid.

Cedric continued to stare, betraying no emotion, as a pair of sparkling embers rocketed out of the box, climbing, spiraling around each other, circling into the air. They soared to a height above the heads of the strange trio, then floated unsteadily, bobbing and weaving, occasionally intermingling or floating past each other. Now his eyes returned to the box, which was spewing smoke, a dark cloud of vapor that billowed upward into an impermeable column, masking the half-giant and his two companions. The black vapor shot up to the height of the circling embers then halted its rise, though more smoke continued to pour from the box, filling out the pillar, thickening it, giving it an almost tangible solidity.

The captain could hear wary mutters and whispers from the men on the ramparts. "Steady, fellows," he counseled. "Mapes, get a couple of the Kingfishers up here right away."

The sergeant major hurried to fetch a couple of the Solamnic Auxiliary Mages, new to the ranks of the ancient order. These men, universally young and keenly intelligent, devoted their time to the study of spells and wizardry rather than the customary use of the sword and shield. As their symbol was the kingfisher, many of the veteran knights had taken to calling them by that name. Cedric had a feeling the Kingfishers might be of some use against this new, as yet unknown mystery. Already the vaporous form was taking a shape, vaguely humanoid, with arms and legs and a broad torso. The entire huge body was an image in midnight black, except for the glowing coals, and a pair of large silver rings that seemed to encompass each of the monster's wrists.

The twin embers had settled into the face where eyes ought to be, and the knight captain, vanquisher of many horrible foes, felt a shiver run down his spine as those flaring, evil orbs seemed to flicker before focusing directly upon him. With a muttered curse, Cedric lowered the spyglass and drew a breath. He could see the vapor monster well enough with his naked eye: the conjured being seemed to be standing upon stony legs, while fire surged and flickered all across its torso, arms, and face.

"Look sharp there, men!" he ordered. "Archers, make ready. Torch the oil pots. Get the reserves back from the ramparts. But all of you, stand by."

By the time he had finished his commands, the giant creature was already striding forward, heavy feet pounding the ground with steps that reverberated all the way to the top of the high rampart. This was no smoke monster, he saw now; clearly, it had become a solid mass of rock or metallic weight. Cedric thought of the thick, iron-banded gate below his feet, and with a twinge wondered if it could stand against this foe.

The drums, massive kettles pounded by ogre drummers, picked up the cadence to a marching tempo. The first column of ogres swung toward the gate, trailing the giant by several hundred paces. But the monstrous creation led the charge . . . all alone.

Not that it looked like it would need much help.

Closer and closer the monster came, seeming to grow and loom larger with each thunderous step. Its growth was an illusion, Cedric realized—by the time it was two hundred yards away, the thing loomed as tall as the great drawbridge that, naturally, had been raised into blocking position. At one hundred yards, the distance previously marked by white posts on the ground before the gatehouse, the captain uttered a sharp command:

"Archers: mark the range! Volley fire!"

A cloud of arrows rose into the air, the missiles launched by more than two hundred longbowmen of the gatehouse garrison.

The missiles converged in the air at the apex of their flight, glittering in the dawn's light for a moment before plunging down to shower the conjured giant and the ground around him. Cedric stared, his hands clenched into fists as he muttered a prayer to Kiri-Jolith—a prayer that went conspicuously unanswered as the shower of missiles seemed to disintegrate upon striking the monster's enchanted flesh. Some of the missiles missed their target altogether, of course, and they hit the ground, leaving a grotesquely elongated outline of the gigantic shape tattooed onto the dirty plain.

Cedric glanced over his shoulder as two young mages, beardless, clad in white tunics emblazoned with the colorful bird, joined him on the platform. They were looking, aghast, at the massive apparition.

"Kingfishers! Make ready!" commanded the captain. With trembling limbs, they raised their hands, chanting their spells. Several magical missiles blazed outward from the first mage's fingers, the crackling bolts vanishing as they made contact with the fire-eyed giant. The second tried to cast a more complicated spell, but terror apparently drove the words from his memory—he mumbled an inarticulate sound, gesturing wildly, but nothing happened.

The creature lumbered on with no appreciable change in speed, drawing closer and closer with each passing breath. Cedric ordered a second and third volley of arrows released, but they had the same inconsequential effect. The ogres in the column behind the conjured giant roared a hoarse challenge, exultant as they sensed the power of their new ally.

"Ready the oil! Shower the bastard when it crosses the moat!" cried the captain. To both sides heavy caldrons were rolled to the very brink of the rampart, levered upward, and balanced between the jutting balustrades. The giant strode on, one foot plunging into the muck of the moat while the other crossed the wide obstacle in a single stride. The mired foot came free with no visible effort; then the monster was, literally, at the gate.

"Now—dump oil! Toss the torches!" Cedric's voice strained not with fear, but with volume; he would betray none of the terror he felt. He gripped the sword of his father, silently daring the creature to come within the weapon's reach.

But first would be the trial by fire. Cedric watched as the hot oil shimmered as it fell through the air, splattering across the creature's head and torso, outlining the black body in a slick, dense layer. Its flesh, closer up, looked more like rock than iron, the captain decided, fully conscious that neither substance was especially vulnerable to fire.

Dozens of burning torches tumbled downward, tossed by courageous men waiting upon the battlements. They smoked and sputtered through the air, and when they contacted the oily form of the monster, they ignited the liquid fuel almost instantly. A huge wall of flame roared up into the air, driving the soldiers back momentarily.

Within mere moments the gigantic form was engulfed in flame, but if it felt any discomfort from the intense heat that burned the faces of the Solamnics, it gave not the slightest indication. Instead, the monster cocked one mighty fist and delivered a crushing blow to the heavy planks of the drawbridge. Cedric heard boards splintering and felt the groaning collapse of that massive barrier as the tower itself swayed under his feet.

"Rocks! Drop them—now!" cried the captain, despair growing.

Immediately the huge baskets that had been poised on the rampart toppled forward, spilling their heavy loads downward. Large boulders struck the monster's head, torso, and arms—but even the heaviest of these simply bounced away without causing any visible harm.

Even under this barrage, the monster continued his pummeling, smashing the raised barrier again and again. Soon pieces of timbers, then whole beams, broke free to burst or tumble out of the way. The creature reached through the gap to seize the heavy portcullis, the second barrier to the gateway, and yanked at it. With a single, massive effort, the monster ripped that barrier aside; the iron grid, which weighed tons, was simply jerked off its mounting brackets. The monster tossed the heavy portcullis aside as though it were a toy. It fell across the moat where it would serve as a bridge for the following ogre troops.

Now the way into the gatehouse was clear. Men gathered above the murder holes, ready to stab downward with long pikes in a valiant effort to pierce the monster from above. But instead of advancing, as Cedric and the other defenders expected, the beast paused, turning its attention to the stone wall to the right of the open gate. With a series of heavy blows of those great fists, it shattered the masonry and crumbled the wall.

The captain sprang to the side as he felt the ground start to give way under his feet. Other men were not so lucky; at least a dozen soldiers toppled downward as the creature hewed a gap right through the outer wall. Cedric heard their pathetic screams as they fell directly on top of the creature—sounds of panic that were quickly silenced by death. The elemental giant crushed the defenders with swatting blows of its hands and feet, shot fiery blasts at them out of its eyes, roared flames out of its gaping mouth.

Still, the giant clawed at the wall, pulling down another great section, rubble and stone spilling into the moat, filling it, piling onto the plains beyond and also tumbling into the deep courtyard.

More bridges were created across the moat. More of the rampart fell. Both Kingfishers—among many other warriors—fell to their doom, Cedric saw. The veteran captain fell back to safety just as another section of the wall flew away.

Only after the elemental giant had hacked apart a gap more than a hundred feet wide did the monster enter the courtyard of the gatehouse. It kicked through a company of archers—those few men who had survived the shower of rock from collapsing walls—and Cedric realized that it would shortly decimate those men, cross to the far wall, and smash down that barrier as well. With that, the route into Solanthus would be open.

Now, however, the creature appeared to hesitate, whirling back to peer at the only fragment of the outer wall still standing. Sir Cedric and a few brave survivors were standing there, waiting. The captain dutifully raised his blade, the sword that was the legacy of his father's fathers' fathers. He felt the heat of those coal-ember eyes as their inhuman gaze fastened upon him, and the monster drew back a boulder-sized fist.

"By the Oath and the Measure—you shall not pass!" cried the Captain of the West Gate.

He hurled himself from the parapet, his sword extended. The blade struck the monster's face . . . and shattered in a fiery burst.

Sir Cedric himself met exactly the same fate.

⚔⚔⚔⚔⚔

The gatehouse was now a ruin—a great fan of rubble spilling out from the shattered wall, filling the moat, and making a passable, if rugged, path for the first company of ogres. Ankhar felt a sense of admiration and awe, mingled with no small measure of terror, as he witnessed the great destruction wrought by the elemental king.

Already events were moving beyond the half-giant's control. After smashing the outer wall, the drawbridge, and two of the tall towers flanking the West Gate, the elemental king had advanced out of sight. Ankhar hastened forward, keeping pace with Hoarst and Bloodgutter, just to the rear of the first company of ogres. The drums were booming now, and the commander unconsciously matched his own gait to their increased cadence. He saw rocks flying through the gap in the wall, and watched in wonder as the top of another formidable tower began to sway. It eased to the left then tilted back to the right. When it swayed again, it just kept going, plunging from Ankhar's view. A few breaths later, a great cloud of dust billowed into the air, rising far above the height of the wall.

There were some humans remaining on the flanks of the breach, he noted. Their counterattacks started with desultory arrow volleys, a few longbowmen recovering their wits and courage enough to snipe at the block of ogres, while the packed warriors struggled over the broken ground within the gap. Even this light fire was effective, as the steel-headed missiles inevitably struck home among the close ranks, the heavy shafts striking with enough force to drive their razor-edged tips through shields, armor, and bone.

With startling speed, the archers reorganized, and as the ogres put their heads down and surged toward the breach, concentrated volleys of arrows began to shower the front of the formation. Ogres fell, crippled, writhing, or stone dead, and the next attackers stumbled and dispersed as they veered around the obstacles formed by fallen comrades. The attack slowed as the ogres raised shields in a vain attempt to halt the lethal shower. Half of the first company had dropped, and more were dying with each relentless volley. The survivors hesitated, some glancing back toward the safety of their own lines.

Where was the monster, the elemental king? Ankhar wondered, trying in vain to catch a glimpse of the creature amidst the melee.

"Charge, you miserable cowards!" roared Bloodgutter. "Carry this place by storm—or die trying!"

He lunged ahead, ready to personally lead the assault, but Ankhar laid a restraining hand on the ogre's shoulder. "I need you alive," the commander told his captain, who looked at him furiously.

The situation was equally maddening to Ankhar. He could see the gap, the huge breach in the wall leading right into the city! But how many warriors would he have to sacrifice in that breach? The carnage would be horrific.

And still there was no sign of the elemental king. From the broken, rocky ground rose a din of ogres howling in pain, bellowing commands and challenges, while the humans on the wall shouted and cheered. Behind it all, the drummers kept steady cadence. Ankhar turned to Hoarst, who had come up beside him and was now looking at his commander questioningly.

"Call him back!"

The Thorn Knight shook his head and looked at the wand. "The wand will allow me to direct him away from us, but it won't summon him."

"Where did he go all of a sudden?"

"He could be slaying ogres now, for all we know. He is gone from my sight, too."

Hoarst's insolent tone, under other circumstances, would have sorely tried the half-giant's patience. As it was, he glowered at his lieutenant then snorted in exasperation.

"Laka!" he bellowed, looking around anxiously in the smoky, dusty chaos. "Where are you?"

"I am here, my son." He was surprised to see that the old hob-wench was, in fact, right behind him. "What is your command?"

"The king has moved too far away from us. Open the box; bring him back."

"As you wish." Laka immediately knelt and gently placed the ruby box on the ground before her. Slowly she lifted the lid, and as she did so Ankhar felt a chill penetrate his skin—like a wind from the Icereach that had wafted all the way to central Solamnia. It was the glacial sensation of someone opening the door to a long-cold tomb.

Beyond the ruined gatehouse, Ankhar saw that the murky air was churning, the smoke and dust was gathering like a tornado, rising into a dark funnel that stretched to loom over nearly all the city, challenging even the granite massif of the Cleft Spires in its grandeur. The sound that accompanied the churning air was that of a howling gale, the kind that drowns all speech, uproots the trees, and drives men and beasts to seek shelter.

But Ankhar stood firm, planting his fists on his hips, leaning forward slightly to brace himself against the building force of the funnel. He blinked, wiped a hand across his tearing eyes, and tried to peer through the murk. Bits of debris pelted him, stinging his skin, and his great cape flapped behind him. Laka nearly tumbled backward, but he put his big hand on her back and held her firmly, all the while staring into that gusting gale.

There it was, finally: a hellish glow of fire billowing and brightening within the interior of the cloud, drawing closer and growing more intensely hot as it neared. The half-giant could feel the fire against his skin now, and at last he could make out the returning shape of the elemental king, which towered high above the army commander. It slashed back and forth in obvious fury as it fought the confinement of its magical bonds.

Hoarst also stood fast, raising his wand to admonish the king before they were immolated. Laka laughed shrilly, a cackle of pure pleasure, as she held the lid of the box open. Slowly, thrashing in palpable frustration and fury, the immense column of stone and flame writhed and condensed and contracted, sucking slowly downward until, with an abruptness that left them gasping for breath, it vanished into the stone-covered box.

In the abrupt silence, Ankhar shook his head, trying to clear his mind. Laka showed no hesitation, however; she slammed the lid.

The king of the elementals was back in his prison, and the outer walls of Solanthus were breached.

CHAPTER THIRTEEN

EMERGENT DANGERS

The manor in Palanthas was dark again, except for the enchanted glow in the central room, the alcove off of the wizard's laboratory. Here Coryn stared into the white porcelain bowl, studying the surface of slightly bubbling white wine. The bowl glowed with its usual pearly incandescence, but now there was a green tint to the light in the shadowed room, a viridescent light that emanated from the small emerald the wizard held between the thumb and index finger of her right hand.

That stone was poised above the liquid, and the viridescent light served to illuminate the murky figure revealed. Even as though seen from a great height, the broad shoulders and looming size of Ankhar the half-giant were recognizable. Beside him stood his two most dangerous allies: the Thorn Knight who had served Mina during the War of Souls, and the hobgoblin who was never far away from the hulking army commander.

Coryn had spent much of the last year observing Jaymes's adversaries, ever since she had finally discovered that emerald was the element most inclined to reveal Ankhar to the magic of her scrying spell. She had watched him in his camp and on the

161

field, studied his mannerisms and relationships. She had watched his captains too. Gradually Coryn had discerned that the Thorn Knight served Ankhar because he was greedy. The half-giant had claimed much booty from the sacking and plundering of Garnet, Thelgaard, and smaller towns, and he shared generously with the powerful magic-user. Hoarst had taken his treasures and teleported them away to some as yet undetected trove.

The hob-wench, with her feathers, tattered cape, and hideous talisman, was a different matter. There appeared a deep bond between the withered old crone and the huge half-giant, but Coryn had yet to figure out what that connection was based on. Of the pair, the wizard was inclined to think the witch-doctor was the more dangerous because her motives were more obscure and in some way, she seemed to act out of love. Greed could be thwarted and diverted, possibly even outbid, Coryn knew, while love had a way of holding to its course.

For nearly an hour, the white wizard had stared in horror, using her scrying spell to watch as the fire giant tore through the West Gate of Solanthus and into the city beyond. She had seen hundreds of brave fighters die, all in vain, trying to stop the horrific creature. She had watched as the monster ignored arrows, rocks, flaming oil, and plunging spears, striding through each attack while barely taking notice of the humans' exertions.

The destruction within the walls of the city was terrible. The stone structures inside the gatehouse had been smashed to rubble. When it reached the first block of wooden domiciles, flames exploded from the monster's mouth, and tongues of fire spewed forth to ignite the buildings instantly, rising to an inferno within a few breaths. People had streamed from the crowded structures in abject terror, while others—too many to enumerate—had perished in the conflagration. The monster had continued its rampage through a market, where precious few sellers were still at work. Even so, the stalls had erupted, and small stockpiles of wool, timber, and oil in casks had swiftly burned to ash.

Beyond the market stretched another neighborhood of crowded wooden buildings, blocks and blocks filled with people. Coryn pressed her hand to her mouth in horror as she watched the creature approach these dwellings. Then, unaccountably, it halted. She noted the resistance, the manlike limbs flailing as the beast struggled to press forward, but instead it was dragged almost physically backward, through the still-blazing wreckage and the shattered gatehouse, where Ankhar's ogres hastily withdrew before it.

Finally it vanished into a mere box, a ruby prison that apparently could contain a magical creature that was far bigger than the box's obviously small confines.

"An elemental," she whispered to herself. "Somehow he has gained control over an elemental."

But this was not just any elemental, she understood. She had dabbled with the magic used to control those extraplanar creatures, had felt the searing heat of a fire elemental and known the willful taunts of one spun from air. She knew the flooding power of pure animated water and the crushing strength inherent in the bedrock of the land itself. But she had never beheld a creature of such power, such size—one that embodied all four of the mighty elements. It was as if Ankhar had captured the lord of all elementals and was now wielding it as a weapon at the behest of his army.

She stared again into the clear white wine. The bubbles had mostly dissipated and the outline was gray, but in its center she could see the ogres advancing now to claim area around the smashed gatehouse. The brutes tossed boulders into piles, formed a makeshift barricade, erected a wall of planks as protection from the defenders' arrows, and clearly established a strong front within the very walls of Solanthus. Once that makeshift fortress was secure, Ankhar would be able to move more of his force into the breach, and she could guess what was next: a fresh attack with the elemental king in the lead.

There was no time to waste.

Coryn set down the stone and stood up. When she opened the door to the alcove, the glowing bowl immediately grew dark. Emerging into her laboratory, she pulled down a thick tome from the shelf above her desk and started thumbing through it with one hand. With the other, she rang a small bell.

She found the spell she was seeking just as Rupert knocked quietly on the door. Marking the space with the tip of one of her slender fingers, she looked up. "Come in."

"Yes, my lady. How can I help?" asked her servant and loyal friend.

"I need to go away for a few days. Have Donny collect my cloak and boots. I'd like to have a little food—not much. Oh, and you can empty the wine in the scrying bowl."

"Of course," Rupert said, advancing quickly toward the alcove. He paused, looking at her questioningly. "Is everything all right, my lady? That is, you seem rather upset."

Coryn grimaced. "Everything is not all right. The war has taken a turn for the worse. Unless I can get Jaymes and the army of knights on the move immediately, I am afraid Solanthus is doomed."

"I am sure you will meet with success, my lady," Rupert declared smoothly. "And I trust that you will be back in time for the lord regent's ball?"

"Ball? Oh, damn, I forgot about that. When is it, again?" She was annoyed to be reminded, but knew it was imperative she attend the gala function. Lord Regent Bakkard du Chagne was capable of many surprises, often unpleasant ones, and an occasion where the eyes of all Palanthas, including the city's considerable diplomatic community, were upon du Chagne, was just the kind of opportunity where he needed to be monitored. Coryn wanted to be there to make sure he didn't announce any new policies certain to harm the war effort.

"Yes, I'll be there," she snapped, realizing she had to hurry. "But that means I'll have to get out of here in the next few hours. So we all have work to do."

"Of course, lady," Rupert agreed, bowing slightly before he entered the alcove. By the time he came out carrying the porcelain bowl, Coryn was so engrossed in reading her spell that she didn't note his departure.

⋊⊙⋋⊙⋌⊙⋋⊙⋌⊙⋋⊙⋌⊙⋌

Dawn broke over the Compound. A thick gray mist hung in the air, grimly mingling with the cloud of smoke that lingered from the blast that killed Salty Pete. Jaymes awakened shortly after first light. He dressed quickly and made his way through the nearly silent manor. Sally, red eyed and grief stricken, tried to intercept him with tea, but he merely shook his head and strode out of the house into the cool day.

The scent of soot and brimstone coated every breath, and the stench only grew stronger as he made his way across the muddy compound toward the scene of the previous evening's disastrous experiment. He found Dram and Sulfie already there. The pair was poking listlessly through the scattered debris, lifting the charred timbers that had forged the long tube of the bombard. Here and there were bits of the iron straps that had held those boards together.

"Pete wore a ring—it was on a chain around his neck," Sulfie said, choking back tears as she stared at the tall lord marshal. "Our Pap gave it to him, and he always wore it. But it wasn't on his body—it must have gotten blown off when he was killed."

165

"I . . . I offered to help her look for the ring, first thing this morning," Dram admitted. "But it don't seem to be around here anywhere."

Jaymes shook his head understandingly. "Not much chance of finding it, I suppose. But why don't you have a work crew come up and comb the place, at least for the rest of the day. Maybe it'll turn up before we have to get back to work."

"Yeah, I was kind of hoping you'd want to do that, soon as possible," Dram said. He regarded Jaymes cautiously, his eyes hooded and the expression on his face further concealed by his bristling beard. "Anyway, I already ordered them to come up."

The marshal nodded, leaning down to pick up one of the broken brackets. "Perhaps we should use stronger steel?" he asked, turning the shard over and over in his hand.

"*More* of it, certainly," Dram said. "Thicker bands and twice as many. But that's Kaolyn alloy—you won't find a stronger metal anywhere on Krynn. And the lumber we used came from ironwoods, so that can't be improved on."

"The only solution is to make it bigger, then?"

"Bigger and heavier, aye," the dwarf acknowledged. "This one weighed a bloody three tons, so Reorx only knows how big the next one will have to be to avoid"—his eyes took in Sulfie, still sifting through the wreckage—"accidents."

"Maybe we—" Jaymes stopped suddenly and spun on his heels. His eyes narrowed as he studied the shadowy doorway to the long warehouse where the logs were stored.

"What is it?" Dram asked. He followed the direction of the marshal's gaze and huffed as brightness flashed within the dark shadows. "Humpf! I mighta guessed," the dwarf said sourly, addressing Jaymes. "But how did *you* know she was going to pop into sight all of a sudden?"

"I got a feeling," the lord marshal said with a shrug.

A mist of sparks whirled momentarily in the shadows of the doorway, and the White Witch was standing there. Her alabaster robe reflected the dim light with the purity and luminance of a sunlit glacier. Her long dark hair was unbound, flowing around her shoulders, the dark strands still a little brittle from the lingering effects of her teleport magic. Her lips, usually so full and warm against the gentle oval of her face, were drawn into a tight line of concern.

She stalked toward them. The hem of her robe occasionally brushed the scorched, sooty ground, but somehow the white material stayed perfectly clean. Sulfie was gaping at the wizard in awe, her troubles momentarily forgotten, while Dram edged forward to stand next to Jaymes. Coryn was still twenty paces away when she began speaking angrily.

"You must get back to your army right away," she declared. "There has been a development."

In blunt terms she described the attack of the monstrous elemental king, the damage wrought, and the danger created by the breach in the city's defenses. "I fear that if you don't counterattack at once, it will be too late. Even with all haste, I am afraid."

If Jaymes was dismayed or upset by the news, his voice showed no emotion other than agreement and determination. "I presume you have the means to move me swiftly, without a horse, sparing me a four-day ride across the plains?"

She nodded.

"Very well." The marshal motioned to the dwarf, who grabbed his arm as he turned to go.

"I'm coming too," Dram said. "I mean, take me with you! You need me!"

Jaymes turned back to Dram and Sulfie. "No. I badly need you, it's true, but not on the battlefield. There is no time now.

167

You are going to have to move the Compound. I want you to pack up the workers, the raw materials, everything. Buy every wagon you have to—that probably means every wagon in the west of Solamnia. Head east. I want to set up operations in the shadow of the Garnet Range, as near to Solanthus as possible."

"But . . . we . . . we can't just move the whole Compound!" Dram spluttered. "Everybody lives here! All the dwarves of Meadstone are here. And the logging—"

"Dwarves can move, the same as buildings. Remind your workers they're being well paid and will continue to be well paid. As to the logging, you can set up lumber camps in the Garnet Mountains just as easily as the Vingaard range. And you were telling me the steel comes from Kaolyn. This will put you that much closer to the alloy."

"No, it's crazy," Dram persisted, shaking his head. "I don't see how it can be done. And there's Sally, and Swig. I mean, they'll have objections—"

"I want this done," Jaymes said coldly. "I want it done without delay. Sally and Swig can come along, or they can stay here and wait for you to return. But I need you and your operations, I need the black powder, and I need the Compound to be closer to the action. Now, I want your promise to get going on this—right away!"

"All right, all right." Dram's voice was an angry growl, and his eyes all but flashed sparks as they shifted from the marshal to Coryn.

Sulfie had watched the exchange, her eyes wide, still moist with tears. Now she spoke hesitantly. "But . . . what about . . . what about Pete's ring? It's out there somewhere!" She sniffled plaintively as she swept her hand across the blackened circle of soot, the wide scars from the previous day's explosion.

Coryn looked at the black swath as if seeing it for the first time then turned toward Jaymes and raised her eyebrows reprovingly.

"An experiment that failed," he said curtly.

"And we *will* take the time to comb the wreckage," Dram said bluntly. He rested a hand on Sulfie's shoulder. "We'll find your brother's ring. And we'll give him a hero's wake." The dwarf lifted his head and looked at Jaymes with a challenging glare. "That's the least we can do here. And after that, *then* we'll get ready to pick up and move."

The warrior regarded his old friend for a moment then nodded. "I'm sorry about your brother," he said to Sulfie with unusual feeling before turning back to Coryn.

"Take me back to the army," he said.

⊷⊶⊷⊶⊷⊶◉⊷⊶⊷⊶⊷

"We're going to force the river crossing at every ford, first thing tomorrow morning," Jaymes informed his generals after startling them at their breakfast with his teleported arrival. Coryn had appeared with him, but—knowing her presence made the knight commanders uneasy—she swiftly withdrew to a small tent to "tidy up." The marshal wasted no time in issuing his orders and putting his generals on alert.

"It will mean an all-night march to get the men in position," Markus warned. "At least, if you want to cover more than ten or twelve miles of river. And then we'll be attacking with exhausted troops."

"There's nothing that can be done about that. And I do mean to cover much of the river, stretching Ankhar so thin he can't hope to hold us everywhere. I want an attack at every crossing spreading over twenty-five miles in two directions—in effect, a fifty-mile front. General Dayr, you take the north flank. You'll have to cross by boat, since there are no suitable fords there. It's

169

imperative you get started under the cover of darkness—that means I'd like to see you get moving less than twenty-four hours from now."

"Yes, my lord," Dayr replied grimly. "Should I get the boat companies on the march immediately?"

"Yes, do so." As the general of the Crown Knights hastened to give the necessary orders to his subordinates, Jaymes turned to the other two wing commanders. "Have any of the bridging companies arrived from Palanthas?"

"The first came in just this afternoon," Markus replied. "I understand there are two more on the way, but they still must be several days out."

Jaymes nodded, thinking. "General Rankin, you will command the middle. There are three fords that should be passable. Make simultaneous attacks at each, and try to force a bridgehead on the east bank.

"And Markus, you will take the south wing. There is one ford I believe you can use, but I want you to supervise the bridging company as well—post it north of the ford, where they won't be expecting us to cross." The first bridging company was a unit of the lord marshal's own invention, a wagon train of pontoon boats and plank sections. They had practiced extending a temporary span across a wide river and had met with considerable success, but the tactic had never before been attempted in a combat situation. "Make your attack at the ford first, and see if you can take them by surprise with your bridge. I will see if I can get you some kind of concealment for your activity."

"Very good, my lord," Markus said. He sent a runner to get the bridging company on the march.

General Dayr returned, and Jaymes spent another hour making specific dispositions, speaking with the quartermasters to make sure the wagon trains of food, fuel, and arrows were dispatched with all haste. He spoke to the captains of two score companies, impressing upon them the urgency of the relief mission. He described the appearance of Ankhar's new, powerful ally, and the desperate straits in Solanthus. By the time he was finished, the camp had become a frenzy of activity, with tents being struck, corrals dismantled, horses and oxen haltered and prepared for the march.

Only then did Jaymes return to Coryn, who was waiting patiently beside the muddy patch of ground that had, a quarter of an hour earlier, been the command compound in the midst of neatly arrayed tents. "Once you make up your mind, things happen pretty fast," the wizard noted wryly as a column of Crown Knights thundered past them, and three files of pikemen formed up for a rapid march to the north.

"By evening tomorrow too many of these good men will be dead," Jaymes said. "They know it—we all do—but no one hesitates when battle is necessary."

"You're the only man who could bring all these knights, these soldiers, together," Coryn said. "And I know the crossing will be dangerous. But it has to be done."

An advance team of boatmen trundled past, a caravan of five horse-drawn wagons. They, and others like them, would ride toward the major crossings, carrying bundles of canvas and strips of supple wood. Under the cover of darkness they would assemble hundreds of boats in a single night.

The heavy bridging company also got under way, rolling south in a separate wagon train, carrying long pontoons and sections of planking. Their goal would be to establish a usable span across the river in the next twenty hours.

"Send for Sir Templar," Jaymes barked to a nearby courier. In a few moments the cleric-knight appeared, out of breath and red faced, before the army commander.

"Yes, my lord!" he cried, extending a salute and standing rigidly at attention. "I await your orders!"

"At ease," Jaymes said. "I want you and your apprentices to go with General Markus—to the south. Stay with the bridging company. When they start to put their pontoons in the water, do whatever you can to help conceal their work—whether it be fog or darkness or some kind of invisibility spell. Many lives will depend on those bridging sections reaching far across the river before the enemy takes note of them."

"But. . . ." Templar looked stricken, then immediately stiffened again. "Yes, my lord! As you wish! We will do whatever lies in our power."

"I'm sure you will. And understand, there is no time to waste."

"Certainly, my lord! Yes, of course!" Templar stood still for another beat then seemed to realize he had been dismissed. With a salute, the Clerist spun about and hurried away.

"Do you think they'll be able to help?" asked Coryn.

"We'll know better tomorrow. But they've been riding along with the army since we moved north from Caergoth, eating our food, preaching the creed of Kiri-Jolith to whoever happens to be within earshot. It's time to find out if these cleric-knights can be any kind of real asset to this army."

The white wizard's face went pale and her eyes moist as she watched another company, mostly young swordsmen from the northern plains, march past. They were singing a battle song, though several of the soldiers—mere boys, really—looked almost faint with fear.

"War is such a terrible business," Coryn said, a catch in her voice.

"Yes. We'll lose a lot of men," Jaymes said. "But by hitting them in so many places at once, I expect we'll find a chink in

Ankhar's defenses somewhere. Once we find that chink, the knights will pour through."

"But Solanthus is still nearly fifty miles away," the wizard pointed out.

"We'll march as fast as we can. One column, a steel fist that will smash any of Ankhar's defenders out of the way."

"Even so, it will be costly," she said quietly.

"What would you have me do?" he demanded, his tone growing sharp. "We're bound by certain restrictions—and the speed an army can march is one of them!"

"Dammit!" she snapped back. Her dark eyes bored into his for a moment until she sighed and looked away, turning toward the east. "Yes, you're right. I'm angry at myself—all this bloodshed."

"It's a fact we must deal with it and move on." He grimaced and shook his head. "I do wish we knew more about this monster, this king of the elementals. If I could see it, observe it, I would have a better grasp on how we might make war against it."

"There is one thing we can try," Coryn said. She sounded strangely hesitant, and when she looked at the marshal, her eyes had softened. There was fear, there, but it wasn't fear of danger or death.

"What's that?" Jaymes looked away, studying the troops as a company of horse archers trotted passed.

She bit her lip nervously then spoke. "I could try to teleport you into the city. You would have a chance to do something there that no one else can do because no one else possesses your courage . . . or your sword."

"Are you suggesting Giantsmiter could slay this elemental king?"

"No, not slay it. I doubt that anything can slay it—it would be like trying to kill the very essence of the world. But I have been reading a great deal of history. The gist of it is that your sword was created by Vinas Solamnus, but he had the help of a mighty wizard. It might just help you to learn something crucial about the elemental, to discern some weakness, some way we might banish it back to its lower plane.

"By pointing your sword at the being and staring into its eyes, you might be able to read its mind. It's a dangerous strategy—reading the thoughts of other beings is a frightening experience under the best of circumstances. But if you can stand before the elemental and study it while you point your sword at it, it is possible you could perceive some weakness, some frustration of the beast that you might be able to exploit."

"If it doesn't kill me first," he noted.

"If it doesn't kill you first, right," Coryn agreed.

"And how do I go about this?"

"You must stand before the creature. And try to get a look at its eyes, drawing the monster to look at you. If you concentrate, listen carefully, you'll get a sense of its intentions, its fears."

"I'll try," he said without hesitation. "My generals can command their wings and win this battle. I myself will go to Solanthus and find the elemental," he said. "Can you send me?

"It's not quite that simple," she demurred. "You know about the Cleft Spires, of course?"

"The big split mountain, in the middle of Solanthus? Sure."

"Well, it is a rock with powerful magical properties. Ever since the siege began, the wizards of the city have used it to block teleportation magic. This is to prevent Ankhar's Thorn Knights from sneaking into the city or sending assassins, saboteurs, and the like into its midst. Their magic makes it more complicated to send you there."

"Is there any way around their magic?"

"I think I can circumvent it, when the white moon is high. Solinari is full tonight, so I will send you when he reaches his zenith in the skies. Perhaps you want to get some sleep first."

"My troops aren't sleeping tonight; I won't either. But that will give me time to write out orders, send detailed plans to the generals."

"Very well," Coryn said. "I'll prepare the spell. And I'll enchant your ring, the one I gave you years ago. You will have one teleport spell, so you can get out of the city when you've accomplished your mission."

"I thought you said teleportation doesn't work in Solanthus?"

She shook her head, like a tutor impatient with a slow-learning pupil. "The barrier keeps people from teleporting in. There is no restriction on leaving—in fact, I have been visited by wizards who have come from the city. It's one way I'm able to keep aware of what's happening there."

"All right. Let's do as you say, then."

‹◦◦◦◦◦◦◦◦◦◦◦›

Twelve hours later, all but the last remnants of the army had abandoned the camp on the west bank of the Vingaard. The troops were advancing toward their planned crossings under the milky light of a full white moon. Jaymes stood alone in that same moonlight, and Coryn calculated the passage of time.

Finally, she cast the spell. Magic swirled around Jaymes Markham. He felt the pull of the magic, a world whooshing past. He saw the walls of Solanthus and recognized the Cleft Spires outlined in the cold moonlight. Disorienting sensations surrounded him, surging through his gut, dizzying him so much that he could barely see. He sensed the nearness of his obstacle and wanted to reach out and bring himself to ground in the city.

But there was a barrier! Strong magic reared before him, pushed him back, and screened the city from his sight, his reach. Finally the spell sizzled away, and he found himself standing on uneven, rocky ground. There was no source of light to illuminate the utter darkness, so for a few breaths he didn't move. He groped with his other senses.

The air was cool, still, and very damp. It penetrated his sweaty tunic and chilled him to the bone. Somewhere nearby water dripped, a musical plink-plink amplified by the lack of any other noise, save for his own increasingly ragged breathing.

No wind. One eternal sound . . . and that penetrating cold. He knew at once:

Coryn had teleported him some place under the ground.

CHAPTER FOURTEEN

A PATH, FOUND

Everywhere around him was pitch darkness, a cold and lightless void that utterly engulfed the lord marshal. Jaymes heard a terrible hissing in his ears and only vaguely realized it was the pulsation of his own blood, impelled by the heightened hammering of his heart. A sudden wave of vertigo swept over him, and he staggered, trying to regain his balance, but his foot stumbled over a jutting rock, and he fell to his hands and knees.

His fingers felt rough rocks, some of them loose and crumbling, as small as gravel, and others that seemed to be part of the bedrock of what was obviously some kind of cavern. His right knee throbbed where it had landed on a jagged stone, and he clutched the ground like a drowning man clinging to a raft. Bile surged in his throat, but the warrior forced it back down and clenched his jaws, forcing his breathing to slow.

"Where am I?" he demanded of the darkness, the words a bare whisper of sound passing through his parched lips.

"*I'm* somewhere under the Garnet range," a voice said. "The question is, how did *you* get here?"

The voice came from behind him and though the tone was friendly, the mere presence of the speaker was enough to startle Jaymes. He whirled around, pushed himself into a crouch, straining to see some sign—any sign—of the other person. Unfortunately, the rough ground proved his undoing again, and his feet slipped out from under him, dropping him unceremoniously onto his rump.

"Who's there?"

This time the reply was only a sharp, scraping sound, followed immediately by a flaring light. The brightness was a searingly painful sensation, blinding him every bit as effectively as had the previous darkness. Jaymes closed his eyes against a yellow brilliance that was like staring right into the sun. He raised his hand to screen his face.

But he quickly realized that there was no sensation of heat upon his skin, nothing to suggest that sunlight was actually spilling into this forsaken pit. Almost immediately he recalled the harsh sound that had accompanied that flash: it was merely the scraping of a match upon tinder! Opening his eyes again, keeping one hand raised to shade the spot of fire from his direct gaze, he began to discern more about his surroundings.

The match-holder's feet were plainly visible; he was clad in moccasins that—like the voice—were strangely familiar. When those feet advanced closer, not in a stride, nor a charge, but with an almost childish skip, the warrior understood.

"Moptop?" he asked in amazement. It was the first time in his life that he was able to derive even a modicum of pleasure from the presence of a kender. "Is that you?"

"Sure is. This is the most amazing place! You should see it! Well, I guess you will see it, now that you're here—unless you rush away as fast as you arrived. But tell me, confidentially of course, how did you *do* that? Get here so fast, I mean?"

"Wait. Let me collect my thoughts." Jaymes turned his back to the light and inspected his surroundings. He found himself in a cave, an area that was very constricted. A cracked and broken wall loomed no more than four or five paces away, and—though the overhead ceiling was lost in shadow for the most part—he could see the tips of fanglike stalactites jutting down from above in all directions.

The floor was even rougher than he had imagined. A glance around showed that he would have been in for a nasty fall if he took more than a single step in any direction. It seemed the teleport spell had brought him to the top of some kind of square-edged boulder in the middle of a small cavern. The kender was standing on another rock nearby, and as Jaymes's eyes adjusted, he perceived the opposite wall was not very far beyond his diminutive companion.

"Where did you say we are?" asked the warrior. "Under the Garnet range?"

"Yep. I just happen to be exploring through here. You know, working on my maps. I was thinking there might be a way to Solanthus through here. I wanted to go there and see that place—I've never been inside of a siege before! But the goblins wouldn't let me walk through their camp when I tried to go the regular way. So I came down here. That's what I was doing when I heard you come along. But you never told me how you—wait a moment! *She* sent you, didn't she? The White Lady has magicked you here! Wow, that's great! She must have figured I'd be needing a partner! Can't have too many partners when you're exploring. Real mind reader, the White Lady."

"Hmm, it's damned disorienting," Jaymes retorted. "And confusing. I don't think she was trying to send me here—we both thought I would arrive in Solanthus!"

"Oh, but you can't go there by magic. Everyone knows that.

There's a spell that prevents such a thing. I'm surprised she didn't know that. I should probably write her a note or something and advise her accordingly. You don't happen to have a piece of paper on you?"

"No! And she does know about the magic barrier. She thought she had found a way to defeat it."

The kender laughed merrily, the sound grating on the man's nerves like a squeaking axle. "Well, she was wrong!" Moptop's voice dropped to a conspiratorial whisper. "It's annoying how, sometimes, she acts like she knows everything!"

"Yeah, annoying," growled Jaymes. He checked over his gear, trying to think, to plan. His great sword, Giantsmiter, was secure upon his back, and his pair of small crossbows remained in their holsters at his waist. Fortunately the sensitive weapons were not loaded—he might easily have shot himself while stumbling around in the darkness here. He was wearing his ring, the little circlet of metal Coryn had imbued with one additional teleport spell. He briefly considered using that to escape this place but shook the idea away. No, Coryn must have some reason for sending him here with the kender. And it would be bitterly disappointing to simply return, without having accomplished anything.

"Ow, hey—that burns!" snapped the kender, dropping the consumed match and most likely popping his singed fingertips into his mouth as darkness surrounded them again.

"Do you have another one of those? Or maybe a torch?" asked Jaymes. He thought of Giantsmiter's blade, the steely edge that could hiss with its own bright, bluish flame, but he was reluctant to use the legendary weapon for anything so mundane when he would soon need all its powers. He was also loathe to advertise the existence of the weapon, with all its ancient and potent magic, in a place he knew so little about. And it wouldn't do, he reminded himself, to tell the kender anything he preferred to keep secret.

Fortunately, Moptop did indeed have a supply of dry, lightweight torches, and he quickly ignited one of them and handed it to the man. "I don't *really* need the fire to see down here," he explained. "We kender can see pretty well in the dark. But sometimes a torch is good for details. I like to put in a lot of details when I'm making my maps."

"Now tell me again: What are you doing here?" Jaymes asked. "Looking for a way into Solanthus?"

"Well, I'm making a map, seeking the best path of course. Did I tell you I'm a professional guide and pathfinder extraordinaire? It's kind of what I do."

"Yes, you mentioned that. But isn't it a little different, taking me to the Lady Coryn's house in Palanthas, and poking around through some lightless cave under the ground?"

Moptop shrugged. Clearly, no difference was apparent to him. "A path is a path. Some places have better maps, is all."

"So you know a path out of here?"

"Well, no. I never said that, did I?"

"How did you get here in the first place?"

"Well, I did come down the path that leads *into* here, of course."

Jaymes drew a breath. The torch quivered slightly as his fingers clenched around the wooden length. "All right. Think about it this way. Couldn't we walk out of here on the same path that you walked in on? And wouldn't that make it a path *out* of here?"

"Well, for you maybe. But that's not the way I'm heading. Plus that would simply take me back the way I came, when what I really want to do is find a path to Solanthus. Didn't you say that the White Lady was trying to magic you into the city? This must be her way of telling you that you might have to go about it the old-fashioned way."

"And this cavern, you think, will take us to Solanthus?" Jaymes asked warily.

"Well, I sure hope it does, otherwise this whole thing has just been a big waste of time. Not entirely, of course. Lots to see down here." Moptop pulled out a piece of parchment from one of his innumerable pouches. From another he found a short stick of charcoal with one end sharpened to a point. He gestured to the torch. "Here, I'll show you. Hold that up a bit, will you?"

Jaymes obliged as the kender slid down off of his boulder to stand on flat space between the two rocks. The man dropped down beside him, holding the light up, and studying the kender's map as Moptop added a few notes with the smudgy black stick.

Unfortunately, to the human the sketch was simply a confusing mess of scrawled lines and shapes, often intersecting or curving around each other. In some places, crude notations were marked: "No!" "Rong turn" "Watch owt—sinkhole!" and "Oops" were among the few he could decipher. Now the pathfinder was laboriously adding "Find Guy," next to a big black **X**. Abruptly, he looked up to see Jaymes observing him.

"I know you're not just a 'guy,' " Moptop exclaimed hastily. "But I couldn't fit Lord Marshal Jaymes and all that into this little space."

" 'Guy' is fine," the warrior said curtly. "But what about Solanthus?"

"Oh, that's where the really interesting part comes in. . . ."

◄◑◒◓◒◐◉◐◒◓◒◑►

An uncountable number of hours later, Jaymes was starting to understand exactly what "the interesting part" entailed. It

182

meant numerous smashes of his head against low-hanging rocks, long stretches of spelunking where he had to crouch down on his hands and knees and crawl along over dust and grime and irregularities in the floor that scraped against his shins or, on more than one occasion, sent him sprawling onto his face.

The farther they continued along, the more he was convinced that Moptop Bristlebrow was simply poking around down here, that he didn't have any real idea of where they were going, or, more important, how they would ever get there—that is, to Solanthus—through this nightmare world of darkness and stone. By the same token, he despaired of the kender's ability to retrace his steps, so he was forced to conclude that his best hope was to simply press on and take his chances with the professional guide and pathfinder extraordinaire.

Even so, more than one time, Jaymes caught himself fingering his ring. He considered activating its one precious teleport spell. He merely needed to twist it on his finger and envision a destination, and he would be out of here in an instant—an increasingly attractive option, the more time he squandered on his quest with the kender.

"Here we are!" Moptop finally announced brightly.

"What's that?" Jaymes held the torch up as they stumbled into a small, circular chamber. He spotted at least four dark passageways shooting off in different directions.

"Well, here." The kender helpfully raised his map and indicated a splotch on his parchment. The man couldn't help but notice that the sheet had grown increasingly smudged and illegible as they had ventured deeper into the labyrinthine caverns. "It's very clear. This is where we are, and we've been through here three times already. Well, *I* have; you've only been with me twice now. But that means there's only one more of those caves leading out of here to check out. So we're narrowing things down, which is good."

"You mean—we've been spinning in *circles?*" The marshal's voice was very low and threatening.

"Not really." Moptop shook his head, dismissing the idea as inane. He brandished his map as proof positive. "It's more like a zig-zaggy square pattern. We were going north by northeast for a while, but then here we zigged straight west, and there we zagged west by southwest—or south by west-west, or something—and then we came back to north-north-east, and like I say, here we are."

"In the same place we were before!" Jaymes's voice rose a notch.

"Well, yeah. But now we've ruled out that way, and that way, and that way—and that way too—so we know that *this* way is probably the best way to go!"

"Probably! What makes you think that *any* of these damned passages leads to Solanthus?" demanded Jaymes.

Moptop looked at him in amazement, an amazement that suggested he had never been subjected to such a stupid question before. "Why, where *else* is left?" he asked. He plunged into the—presumably—unexplored tunnel before Jaymes could come up with a reply.

Surprisingly, this cavern seemed more passable than the others they had traversed. Right from the start the floor was smooth and relatively free from obstruction, though the occasional chunk of stone or rock had to be stepped around. Often they could discern, in the torchlight, where these obstructions had broken off the walls or ceiling. In combination, these facts suggested this place had once seen a lot of use, but it had been centuries, perhaps many centuries, since anyone had taken the trouble to clear the floor.

But there were other signs of onetime habitation as well. The narrow bottlenecks that had constricted so much of the rest of the cave network had been expanded in this cavern, even carved into regular arches and frames. The stonework was so flawless it looked almost like a natural extension of the bedrock.

"Do you suppose dwarves hollowed this out?" Jaymes asked as they passed along a section where both walls had been smoothly widened, so the warrior could easily walk without bumping his head or shoulders against the confining stone.

"Nope," Moptop replied with certainly. "With dwarves you at least see some chisel marks. And they're masons, for the most part, not carvers. They build with stones and bricks—those arches would have keystones, for sure, if dwarves made 'em. These look like they're just the regular stone of the underground, but *shaped* somehow."

The marshal had to agree with his guide. He was just about to say as much when the kender stopped so abruptly that Jaymes nearly bumped into him.

"Uh-oh," said Moptop.

There are few phrases that arouse more alarm in a listener than when those very words are uttered by a member of the almost suicidally fearless kender race.

"What?" hissed Jaymes, holding the torch high, trying to peer into the shadowy distance. His free hand drifted to the hilt of his sword.

The narrow corridor opened abruptly into what looked like an underground hall that appeared to be lined with stone pillars placed at regular intervals on the right and left sides. The torchlight was inadequate to reveal the extent of the hall or to penetrate the galleries that yawned, dark and shadowy, behind the parallel rows of pillars. But the regular lines and careful right angles were clearly the work of some intelligent design.

Jaymes waved the torch and the resulting flare of light did little to illuminate the farther distance. It did, however, bring the nearer stone pillars into crisp focus. The warrior recognized that they were not columns at all, but statues—statues of warriors dressed in ancient garb and standing at rigid attention along both sides of this long hall.

They wore skirtlike kilts that looked to be carved models of originals that had been formed of metal strips, perhaps bronze. Their helmets were tall, with stiff plumes extending like cocks' combs from brow to nape. Each warrior's left hand gripped a small round shield to his breast, while the right held the shaft of a spear planted on the floor, with the stone tip rising slightly higher than the crest of the warrior's helm. The stone spear shafts were slender and held close to the bodies but intact and unbroken despite their apparent fragility. At each statue's belt was a short sword with a broad, crude-looking blade. This weapon, like the armor, was suggestive of an era before the blacksmithing of steel, and possibly even iron. The faces of the statues were impressively realistic, down to creases in cheeks and brows and the wrinkled skin of knuckles. Several were bearded, and the unremembered carvers had gone to the trouble to etch individual hairs in place. But, equally obvious, the faces were of stone, cold and lifeless and eternally immobile.

"I think maybe we should go back," Moptop said quietly.

"Go back? To where?" growled Jaymes. "No, this is the way to Solanthus. You said so yourself, and I think were right. I can feel it now. We've got to continue on!"

"Do you think these guys really *want* us here?" the kender pressed.

"They're statues. They don't want anything!"

"All right!" the kender agreed. "If you say so. I just didn't want the wizardress blaming me if something happens.

186

Because you *know* something is going to happen."

Again, Jaymes had to agree with the kender. There was an eerie sense of vitality about these very lifelike statues. He wondered how many of them there were, how long this hall could be. Jaymes raised the torch and waved it back and forth to fan the flames into brightness. There were easily eight or ten visible on each side; the existence of many more was suggested by his flickering, unsteady light. Their presence was distinctly uninviting.

"Here, hold this." Jaymes handed the brand to Moptop, who took it without comment, watching as the warrior pulled the great sword from its scabbard on his back. Holding the hilt in both hands, Jaymes extended the weapon upward and held it poised behind his right shoulder. With a twist of his hands, he ignited the blade, bringing to life the blue flames that flickered silently but brightly along both edges of the weapon.

"Hey, I like that!" Moptop declared. "Can you do different colors?"

Jaymes ignored the kender. In the enhanced illumination, he saw the hall extended a very long way indeed—the terminus was still beyond his sight—and, as far as he could see, the two ranks of silent guardians stood at attention, facing each other across an open aisle perhaps a dozen feet wide extending down the middle of the hall. The shadows were inky, the cool light casting an azure hue over the stony faces. The ceiling was lost in shadow.

"Let's go," Jaymes replied.

Together they started down the hall, stepping cautiously but quickly, casting glances back and forth. The stone statues remained immobile, carved images yet seemed to threaten at any moment to step down from their pedestals and do battle. Steadily the two companions advanced past the silent guardians, the light from Giantsmiter's blade showing the way. Jaymes had the sense of an immense room. How big *was* this hall?

He glided a little to the right, holding his sword high, letting the light spill between two of the statues. He spotted, illuminated by the surging flames, another row of stone guardians, apparently identical to the front rank and standing several dozen feet behind them. Though the light was insufficient to show anything else, he had no difficulty imagining a third row behind the second, and an unknown number more extending into the darkness beyond. The echoes of their steps suggested a very large space.

"It's like a whole army!" Moptop said. "But frozen!"

"Let's just hope they stay that way," Jaymes acknowledged. "Move along, now—hurry."

They picked up the pace. The cavern mouth from which they had emerged was swallowed by the shadows closing behind them, yet they still couldn't see an end to the hall of stone statues. Jaymes turned and retraced a few steps, warily scrutinizing the motionless shapes. He had seen a hundred or more already and had stopped counting.

The threat, when it first came, was not seen, but heard—a simple sound, at first, like the scraping of one piece of stone against another. It rasped from the unseen darkness behind them and off to the side and almost immediately was augmented by similar sounds. Hoarse and sibilant at the same time, the noise swelled to encompass them. With a chill, Jaymes pictured a host of massive snakes, scratching and slithering along the stone floor.

He wished it were snakes, but the truth, he felt certain, was going to be something even stranger and nastier. He strained to see something, hardly reassured by the fact all the statues within his view remained utterly still. Finally he detected the source of the sounds, his worst imagining ever since they had entered this place. Almost imperceptibly, one of the guardians at the far limit of his vision behind them turned and slowly, stiffly, stepped down off the low disk of rock that had been its post for the gods only knew how long. The one right beside this guardian, closer to the two intruders, then did the same. Then the next and the next, and soon enough a whole rank of them had stepped down in echelon, joining together in a rippling march that moved closer to the two intruders.

"I don't think they want us here," Moptop noted.

"Then let's get out of here—run!" barked Jaymes.

"Which way?" yelped the kender.

The man's answer was to sprint down the hall, with Moptop racing right beside him. The two ran past more statutes, boots scuffing along the floor, shadows dancing and flaring around them as the torch and the sword burned fitfully from the speed of their gait. The stone warriors didn't pick up the pace of their measured march, but they continued steadily. And with every step through the hall more of them sprang to life.

"There's the far end!" Jaymes called, finally discerning a high, smooth wall rising up in front of them. He looked at the base of that wall, desperately hoping to see a continuation of the cavern there, a passage that would lead them out of this place.

Then he saw it: a looming black hole high enough for a giant to march through. But before he could even register this hopeful development, a phalanx of stone guardians swung around to block their path. The ancient warriors were standing shoulder to shoulder, the stony points of their weapons extended, shields held aggressively forward.

"Well," Moptop admitted, skidding to a halt before he impaled himself on the spear tips lowered to block their path. "Looks like we might be trapped."

"We'll have to fight our way through!" Jaymes declared. Flames sparkled and surged along Giantsmiter's blade as he lifted the great sword over his head. "This will cut them down to size! Stand back—but follow me as soon as I break through their midst."

"Wait!" yelped Moptop. "Maybe we should try talking to them or something. I mean, there are lots of them, and only one of you. I'm sure you could smash them up pretty good with your sword and all. Maybe break ten or twenty or, gosh, a hundred of them. But still—"

Jaymes hesitated, eyes narrowed. His aggressive advance had provoked no response. The spears remained pointed, rank after rank of them, at least a dozen deep standing before them. But once again, the guardians had stopped moving.

"Try talking, then," the marshal growled. "See what happens."

"Hey!" Moptop said cheerfully, stepping in front of one swordsman, fixing a beaming smile upon the stony countenances of the warriors. He spun on his heel, cheerfully making eye contact around the whole ring of them, those in front and those who had closed in from behind. "You guys must be really patient. I mean, to stand here all this time waiting for something. Were you really waiting for us? Because we didn't even know we were coming here, ourselves, really. Of course, I am a professional guide and pathfinder extraordinaire, but—here's a little secret—I was just a teensy bit lost, myself."

He glanced sheepishly over his shoulder at Jaymes, who held his sword at the ready but made no move to attack. In his own way, the man was as impassive and unreadable as the rocky guardians. The kender seemed to feel the burden of being the only truly animated person in this place, and he resumed his pleasant chatter with a gesture that conspiratorially encompassed all the surrounding guardians.

"Well, geez. Can you guys back there even hear me? I mean, maybe you could back up just a little bit. Someone is going to get hurt on those pointy spears." He touched one of the weapons and gingerly tried to push it aside. There was no movement.

With a sigh, Moptop looked around again, his shoulders slumping. Finally he turned back to Jaymes. "I give up. They don't seem to want to talk. Makes me wonder what they're thinking, looking at those rock faces. Are they afraid? Do they want to kill us? They were moving and marching just a little while ago, and now they might as well be statues again."

"Could they be afraid?" Jaymes had been only vaguely paying attention to the kender's prattle, but that phrase tickled his mind, wiggling around and churning up another conversation. "You'll at least get a sense of its intentions, its fears." Coryn had said to him, explaining the power of his sword, the power of mind reading!

Slowly, gradually, he raised Giantsmiter and pointed the blade, aligning the weapon with the face—with the blank, stony eyes—of one of the statue legion.

The first sensation was a warmth that was not uncomfortable, but almost immediately Jaymes began to hear murmurs. They were strange and muted, like hearing a crowd of people conversing some distance away—too far to make out individual words. The kender's chirping background presence was also there, curious and bubbling. As if sensing the intrusion, Moptop glanced over his shoulder, his eyes meeting Jaymes's for a moment—and the kender's thoughts were suddenly articulated in the marshal's mind.

. . . Goofy sword . . . kinda funny looking, even . . . but these guys aren't the humorous sort . . . sort of thought he might try to do something useful instead. . . .

Jaymes looked back at the statues and mercifully, the kender's blathering ceased. The man looked directly into the face of the nearest statue, focusing on the stony warrior's blank eyes. And as he did so, he heard a swelling of sound, and felt another creature's feelings twisting around inside his own skin. He strained to make out the noises and couldn't suppress a shiver as a powerful, raw emotion swept through him.

Fear!

He was sensing the thoughts and emotions of these guardians, Jaymes knew, and they were afraid—indeed, terrified of the menace that had woke them from their centuries-long slumber.

"Why do you fear us?" he said softly. "We mean you no harm."

The answer did not come in words, but in pictures inside his mind. He experienced a torrent of images, felt a sense of horror and mystery. He perceived the image of a great, fiery giant and sensed that the guardians were most afraid of that extraordinary being. Feeling their terror, Jaymes wanted to look away but forced himself to hold firm, to continue to learn, to understand. He felt the statues accuse him, felt a swelling compulsion to harm him and the kender, a hostility coming from all directions.

They blamed Jaymes and Moptop for something, but for what?

He suddenly felt a strong sense of self within one of the statue creatures; this one spoke for the others. *Adamites.* The word came to him, whispered in his mind.

"They're called adamites," he said. Then he felt the accusation and understood the fear.

"They think that it is we who have freed the elemental king!" the marshal exclaimed. "They're his jailers, and they failed to keep him secure. They blame us."

"Hey, it wasn't us that let him loose!" Moptop proclaimed in a wounded tone. "Why, we're trying to stop him. Jaymes here—that is, my friend the Lord Marshal—is going to person-ally kill him, or put out his fire, or something."

More jumbles of pictures swirled through the swordsman's mind, and he realized that the creatures had actually understood the kender's speech. Now their thoughts were questioning, demanding.

"The king was taken by my enemy," Jaymes explained. "I am on a quest to stop him. I only seek to reach Solanthus. That's where he's gone—where he's proving a danger to the whole world."

Now a vivid image appeared in his mind, the Cleft Spires— the rocky landmark that dominated the besieged city. "Yes!" he cried. "That's the place—that is where we are going, where we must go to find the elemental king."

There came a shifting, a rattling of movement as the circle of warriors opened, several of them raising their spears and stepping away to open up a path. The route led toward the exit, the tall gap at the far end of the hall that had been Jaymes's destination. The other guardians stood expectantly, weapons still poised, but made no move to attack.

"I think they want us to go that way," Moptop said, starting toward the gap in the ring. He waved his torch, lighting the way. Jaymes didn't hesitate to follow, for now sheathing his sword. It wouldn't have mattered if they preferred a different route. The warriors formed twin ranks to either side that pretty much limited them to the one course.

The stone warriors channeled the two into a wide, high tunnel, a file of the guardians shuffling along beside them on both the right and the left sides. For more than a mile, the human the kender walked in this strange fashion, moving forward as quickly as they could, climbing a winding ramp between the silent, shifting ranks of stone warriors.

Finally they came to a flat stone wall, an apparently solid surface that blocked all further progress. Here the columns of warriors stood shoulder to shoulder on both sides of the pair, leading up to and merging against the wall. There was no other way forward.

Once more the marshal felt the tickle in his brain, and a picture that formed there showed him that the wall of stone was tenuous, more a gauzy curtain than a solid barrier. "Keep going," he ordered the kender, and for once Moptop didn't balk at his orders. The kender took another step, raised his hand as though to touch the stone, and yelped in surprise as the rock wall yielded to his push. His hand, his wrist, his whole arm sank out of sight, and with a delighted skip the kender sprang forward and vanished.

Jaymes, following more slowly, stepped behind, and also passed through the wall as if it didn't exist. Then the cave was behind them, and a backward glance showed only a stone wall. He touched the gray surface and felt it was as hard as any granite face.

The next thing the lord marshal noticed was the sunlight, a crack of blue sky gleaming high above him, shining down between two sheer, smooth cliffs. To the right and the left, the floor between the cliffs was smooth, and some distance ahead he could spot the walls of a building and the spire of a temple.

"I know where we are!" the kender cried. "These are the Cleft Spires—we're come out of there standing right between them! Hey, am I a great pathfinder or what?"

"True enough," Jaymes grunted, feeling generous. "It looks like we've arrived in the middle of Solanthus." He slipped his sword into its scabbard, slung it once again over his shoulder, and started along the narrow gap toward the light, the open air, and the besieged city.

CHAPTER FIFTEEN

CROSSING THE VINGAARD

General Dayr stood on the west bank of the great river. The land on the opposite side was concealed by a dewy mist that hung low across the placid water, but over that cloudy vapor, the first rays of the sun already poked from beyond the eastern horizon. For now, the fog provided valuable cover for his gathering army, but it wouldn't last long in the face of warming sunlight. To take advantage of the obscuring mist, he needed to launch his attack now, get his army most of the way across the river before they could be discovered by Ankhar's troops—troops that were firmly dug in, and poised to meet an attack.

Unfortunately, the Crown Army was not yet ready. Dayr could only watch and wait in frustration as the boatmen labored to finish assembling their flimsy craft, and as the columns of infantry—divested of much of their armor in order to reduce weight—gathered impatiently on the riverbank. One by one the boats were slid into position on the bank, but by first light there were still only a few dozen of them.

The general knew that ranting and railing at his men would only undermine their spirits. The men could see the mist as

195

well as he could, and they understood the dangers they faced in this risky assault. So Dayr bit his tongue and simply paced back and forth.

By the time the mist burned off, after an hour or so, there were fifty boats in position, but that was only enough to launch a small fraction of Dayr's force. Now the far bank was revealed to all, and he could only curse and pace in agitation, knowing the attack would be far bloodier than it needed to be.

And, indeed, the enemy looked prepared to fight. On the opposite bank stood rank after rank of goblin archers. Between the blocks of bowmen, lines of brutish cavalry—more goblins on their savage wolf mounts—waited. Their lines extended up and down the bank, as far as Dayr could see, and his scouts reported there were more enemy troops beyond his sight in both directions.

General Dayr had no choice but to proceed with the attack. Two other wings of the Solamnic Army would be driving forward at the same time, and the coordinated triple prongs of the offensive would be mutually supporting. Even if his army didn't get across, the theory went, the enemy would be forced to commit vital reserves in the defense.

It was nearly noon before Dayr had the four hundred boats he deemed necessary. There were other craft still gathering, but they would help form the second wave.

"Commence the attack!" he shouted. The Crown pennant fluttered in the breeze over his head, and all along the line, signalmen hoisted similar flags, so flags communicated the command along nearly seven miles of river frontage. Immediately the boatmen slid their canvas-skinned craft into the water, where they splashed and bobbed lightly beside the bank. While the launchers held them against the current, the lightly armored infantry and archers climbed in. Six men in each craft took up paddles, and the boatmen began to stroke the water, pulling for the middle of the river.

More boats remained on the bank, with others still being assembled. Reserve troops advanced to nearby positions. Dayr was unwilling to crowd the river with too many boats at once. So the second wave would set out only after the first group had almost landed.

"General—Father! I beg you—please allow the knights to go as well!"

The speaker was Captain Franz, leader of the Crown Knights, a veteran of every one of Dayr's—and Jaymes's—battles in the campaign of liberation. And he was the general's only son. Franz had risen through the ranks to become an eminent leader in his own right. He and his armored warriors, the White Riders, were not part of the river crossing force, a fact that had caused him considerable frustration during the day of planning.

"My son, we've been over this—the boats are too small."

"But, Father, if we establish a foothold on the far bank, you will need us to drive back the counterattack that is bound to ensue. You'll *need* us there! We could go in the reserve boats—at least two horses can fit into each boat!"

"I wish I could honor your request, my son," said Dayr, not unsympathetically, "but each boat can hold twenty footmen, as compared to two knights and their horses. If we secure the bridgehead on the far bank, we'll swiftly send across your regiment, and you'll have plenty to do, taking the lead role in breaking away from the bank."

It was also true, Dayr through grimly, that a heavily armored knight, in a sinking boat, was doomed to drown, while lighter infantrymen would have a chance to swim to safety.

"But, Father"—the knight's tone was almost frantic—"it's not fair to shield us from the risk!"

"I've made my decision, Captain. Your regiment would be of little use in the landing. Now stand ready to move when you are needed," the general ordered.

The knight captain stood beside his father, both watching the progress of the boats. The line of fragile little craft was more than halfway across the river by now, paddles still churning. The current bore the boats slightly downstream, but this effect had been factored into the launching. To Dayr, it looked like they were on course.

As the first boats drew closer to the far shore, volleys of goblin arrows arced through the air, soaring high above the water then plunging down to hiss into the river, with more than a few of them slicing into the boats and their human cargo.

Dayr heard the screams of the wounded, and each cry was like a cut in his own flesh. He knew the men were all but defenseless in those watercraft. The water churned as the troops redoubled their paddling efforts. They knew their only chance was to reach the opposite bank as quickly as possible. Even as the boats moved faster, however, ranks of goblins advanced toward the riverbank. And more arrows, volley after volley, filled the skies, showering down on the water and striking the Solamnics.

"Launch the second wave!" General Dayr commanded. He and several of his officers, as well as a half dozen couriers and aides, climbed into a boat bobbing in the shallows. They started across with the next group of vessels, churning toward the far bank with agonizing slowness despite the frantic paddlers. Burly young men stroked at the water, but the liquid seemed to resist fiendishly, slowing their progress to a crawl.

The first boat was nearly ashore, however. The general could see countless others boats drifting aimlessly, crews slain to the last man. Some careened and wobbled, propelled by only one or two unwounded oarsmen. Dayr saw two boats capsize within a dozen paces of the far bank. Men scrambled into the shallow water, stumbling across the muddy riverbed, flailing as they tried to scramble up the muddy slope into the very teeth of the goblin resistance.

Still the arrows fell, and now the boats of the second wave had become the target. Dayr's aide-de-camp fell silently into the hull, pierced by an instantly fatal arrow that had plunged almost straight downward into his skull. A boatman in the stern was bailing constantly—the frail craft tended to be leaky—and when he went down with an arrow in his back, the water began to accumulate.

The battle on the bank raged, a bloody tangle of goblins and men. Swords clashed against shields, and spears stabbed right and left. Howls of triumph mingled with cries of pain—a ghastly cacophony. Men tumbled backward, bleeding and dying, to slump in the shallow water, too weak or injured to pull themselves to safety. Their companions, locked in the desperate battle for survival, dared not pause to offer aid.

Finally the watercraft of Dayr's command mingled with the surviving boats of the first wave, pressing against the shore. The general tumbled out, drawing his sword, bellowing commands and encouragement to the men battling for their lives on the muddy riverbank. He took note of the piercing cry of a horn and knew his enemy was issuing some new command but was unsure what it was.

There came a gap in the surging line, and he saw: the goblin cavalry, on their fearsome warg wolves, was advancing at a trot, ready to commence a lethal charge.

❧⊰⊛⊰⊛⊰⊛⊰❦⊱⊛⊱⊛⊱⊛⊱❧

General Rankin ignored the water that filled his boots, the chill liquid that sloshed over his saddle as he whipped his charger through the center of the great river. His army was crossing one of the best fords on the upper Vingaard: nearly a quarter mile in length but relatively shallow across the entire span. Furthermore, the gravel bottom, packed down by centuries of wagon wheels, formed a solid bed underfoot. The liability of the ford, of course, was that the enemy knew about its virtues as well as the Solamnics; they had a company permanently posted there on guard, and had already summoned reinforcements when dawn had revealed the Sword Army on the far bank.

The general rode just behind the vanguard, three companies of the Spireshadow Swords, with their shields and long blades, who were wading the river that, in places, came up to their chests. The solid footing in the ford made a path perhaps a hundred yards wide, and this was crowded with a column of brave soldiers from the Sword Army.

As they approached the far bank, the men raised their shields over their heads. They were approaching a mixed group of enemy troops, goblins and humans mingled together. The humans formed a shield wall near the bank, while the goblins launched volley after volley of arrows from their stout, curved bows. The missiles showered the men, many *thunking* into the upraised shields, but others finding gaps, piercing shoulders and arms and torsos. Still, the Solamnics moved forward, keeping discipline.

Rankin rode past the body of a footman who floated motionless, facedown with an arrow through his throat. The bloodletting was increasingly staining the water red. Another arrow scored a deep gash along the withers of the general's horse, and the big gelding bucked in sudden fear, almost dumping the wing commander into the water.

"Steady, steady!" Rankin urged, clinging to his seat as he stroked his animal's neck. After a moment the charger put its big head down and plunged forward.

More arrows swished past, and Rankin repressed the urge to duck or flinch. He wouldn't display any sign of weakness. He carried no shield, and with his gleaming breastplate—emblazoned with the image of the Sword—and his silver helm, he made a conspicuous target. But it was important to him that the men see their commander's courage and take heart from his example, so he remained erect and continued to press forward, even amid the hailstorm of deadly missiles. Perhaps Kiri-Jolith had protected him with an immortal shield, for even as his aides and escorting knights were struck down, the general himself remained unscratched as his horse finally plunged through the shallows, churning through water as it heaved toward the gentle, graveled bank.

The edge of the river here was dry and firm, unlike so many other stretches where the banks were muddy and choked with reeds. Now, along with Rankin, the first rank of his troops struggled out of the river, swords drawn.

Hoarse cheers erupted from the men as they made a ragged charge into the waiting defenders.

"Solanthus!"

"For the Swords!"

"By the Oath and the Measure!"

These men, many of whom called that besieged city their home, hurled themselves at the enemy with a vengeance.

A whole row of human fighters, formerly pledged to Mina's army, met them with their own steel unsheathed. Within moments a tremendous melee raged along the river's edge. More and more of Rankin's men surged forward, and the defenders' line slowly yielded. Grotesque leers, growling determination, and frantic slashing and stabbing rippled along the ranks. In places the Dark Knights fell back, stabbed and bleeding, but in other parts of the line, the Solamnics faltered, with many of the dead and wounded rolling right back into the river.

Even so, the fury of the attack was carrying Rankin's men forward. He sensed the weakness in the defending line and steered his men to exploit the gaps.

"Knights of the Sword—form ranks, multiple lines abreast! Charge!" cried the general.

The armored knights of the Newforge Regiment, on heavy chargers, came hard behind the footmen. The infantry was well drilled, and the line separated in many places, the swordsmen forming tight squares with the waves of knights charging between them.

Relieved to be on dry ground, Rankin yelled exultantly. His sword raised, he led a contingent of knights right through the enemy line. The general himself cleaved a man from forehead to sternum with one blow. Overwhelmed by the armored riders, the defenders stumbled back. Many were trampled under the heavy hooves, while others were cut down from behind as they tried, with utter futility, to outrun the horses.

But now there were more humans joining the enemy line. Rankin saw the long shafts, tipped with gleaming steel heads and razor-sharp blades, and his heart fell. He grimaced in dismay, but there was nothing else to do, no choice but to continue.

There was only one infantry formation that could stop a charge of knights, and that was a disciplined formation of pikemen. The enemy captain had prepared a three-rank line of pikemen some three hundred yards long. The men in front knelt, those in the second line crouched, and those in the rear stood. All of them held their long-shafted weapons securely braced against the ground, with the heads of the pikes forming a lethal hedgerow of deadly steel. The pikemen blocked the army's path onto the plain.

"Ride them down!" cried Rankin, hoisting his sword and steering his horse with his knees. Hundreds of knights joined him in shouting as they thundered forward.

There was really no alternative. Retreat, back into the river, through the hail of arrows, would be ignominy. To General Rankin, it was the pikemen or certain death.

"Form on me!" he cried as his own signalman raised his horn and brayed a call that echoed up and down the line. "Men of Solanthus—those wretches stand between us and our city! Ride them down!"

It seemed as though the wind itself ceased to blow, holding its breath for the results of the clash, as the line of knighthood plunged toward the immovable array of pikes.

✦⊰⊹⊰⊹⊰⊹●⊹⊰⊹⊰⊹⊰✦

General Markus watched his Rose Wing column as they crossed at the south ford, meeting fierce resistance. Then the commander's attention was drawn elsewhere.

He called Sir Templar over.

"The bridging company is in position. Do what you can to give them cover," he ordered. "And do it quickly."

"Yes, General!" replied the young Clerist. "I believe I have something that will work. I have posted my apprentices along the shore, and if I can just summon—"

"Don't tell me about it; show me," Markus barked.

"Yes, of course, sir! Right away!"

The cleric-knight hastened away. The general turned to watch his attacking troops as they battled at the far side of the ford, making little headway. This spearhead was only a small fraction of the Rose Wing force and did not include any of his armored knights; the bulk of his troops would be hurled across the bridge once it was in place. How long that would take was anybody's guess, for a bridge had never been tried on a river this large.

Only a few moments later, Markus noticed a hazy mist gathering along the reedy bank north of the ford. The massive

203

pontoons of the bridge sections were hidden in those reeds, he knew, and he felt hopeful as he watched the haze thicken into a genuine, obscuring fog. Whatever the cleric and his men were doing, it seemed to be working. From his position a quarter mile away, he couldn't see even the riverbank any longer, much less the activity going on there.

Markus mounted and rode quickly to Captain Perrin, the chief of the bridging company. "Look sharp, lads," he called, with avuncular firmness. "Go there. Now bring in the next one. Now, another, and then the next. Hurry up, fellows!"

One by one, the sections were floated out from the shore. The tubes of the pontoons were aligned perpendicular to the river's flow, allowing the current to slip past without exerting a lot of pressure on the bridge. After six of them had been put in place, Captain Perrin himself supervised the dropping of a heavy anchor into the silty mud. Another was placed after twelve pontoons were extended. As the sections extended farther out from the shore, these anchors would help to ensure that the span remained in position, as the bridge steadily progressed toward the opposite bank.

Simultaneously, as each new pair of pontoons were arranged, additional troops maneuvered planks across the pieces of lumber and hastily lashed them together. The boards were long and thick, necessarily heavy because the bridge was designed to allow the crossing of mounted knights. Moment by moment the bridge grew across the wide but placid flowage.

The fog remained thick and obscuring, spilling farther and farther across the river as the bridge building continued. As the span passed the halfway point, the general rode out on the bobbing but secure construction and approved the work. When he saw daylight penetrating the fog past the middle of the river, he ordered Templar to come forward, and as the construction proceeded, the cleric remained near the steadily advancing end of the bridge, maintaining the magical fog as more and more sections were laid.

Meanwhile, the troops crossing at the ford continued to suffer heavy casualties. A messenger came back across, asking permission to retreat, but with a heavy heart the general ordered them to remain steadfast. Their sacrifice, he desperately hoped, would not be in vain. Each life lost distracted their foe from the unnatural fog, and the encroaching bridge, ensuring that the enemy remained fixed upon the fording troops.

Markus rode back to the west bank, galloped down to the ford, and sent yet another company into that lethal stretch of water. As they departed, determined to sell their lives at a high cost, he saw his bridging officer approaching at a gallop.

"The bridge is ready, sir!" Captain Perrin reported finally.

"Knights of the Rose—here is your road to victory! Charge!" ordered General Markus, standing aside to watch his armored riders start across. The plank road bobbed and shifted under the hooves of the heavy horses, but the bridge held, and the knights thundered across the river, toward the east bank, the enemy lines, and the besieged city beyond.

❦❧❦❧❦❧❦❧❦

"Fall back!" General Dayr's heart broke. He gagged on the bile raised by the bitterness of defeat. How many boats had been lost? How many men had drowned or been slain by the rain of arrows? The survivors of his wing were trapped on a small section of the riverbank, fighting for their lives against the continual attacks of the goblin cavalry on their savage, lupine mounts. The snarling jaws of the wolves snapped and drooled practically in his face, and he cut down yet another of the brutes with a chopping blow of his sword. Shaggy and fierce, the size of small ponies, the savage wolves were fleet and fearless and even more deadly than their goblin riders.

Moment by moment more men fell, trying to hold their tenuous position on the bank. For most of the afternoon his brave troops had stood firm, but the small section of dry ground they held shrank with each vicious attack. Several hundred boats were clustered along the bank just in the rear of the battle line, and it seemed the only alternative to annihilation was to load them up with his surviving troops and begin to retreat, back across the river toward the safety of their starting positions.

It galled the proud General of Crowns, but thousands of painted, beastly warriors, crowing and howling in exultation, pressed them from all sides, and Dayr knew it was better to bring some of his men back alive than to lose them all in a hopeless cause.

"Into the boats!" he ordered. "We're going to retreat."

The withdrawal was chaotic, swords clashing against goblin shields in the muddy—and bloody—waters at the edge of the river. Men scrambled into the boats so hastily that some of them foundered, and it was only by shouting themselves hoarse that the sergeants and captains were able to bring a semblance of order. Finally the last of the little craft pushed away from the bank, the men paddling through waters they had crossed at cost, while the whole east bank of the river was lined with jeering, hooting goblins.

"They may have used up most of their arrows," suggested Captain Johns, one of Dayr's few surviving commanders. Indeed, the barrage that had blanketed them on their initial approach was a desultory shower now. But that was the only thing Dayr could be thankful for. He was leaving behind more than a thousand brave men, and as the last boat pushed away, he had not gained even a single foot of ground to show for those lives.

"Stand firm, there! Raise those shields! Here they come again!"

General Rankin issued his orders from his charger, the weary, bloodied horse still trotting smartly as it carried him back and forth behind the lines of his companies, the men who had fought their way across the great central ford. They had gained the far bank, but his units had progressed no more than a hundred yards from the river's edge. With a line barely a quarter mile long, he knew that his army was in a desperate circumstance.

The cause of their frustration, he knew, was that wall of pikemen. Hundreds of his knights and their horses had fallen there, pierced by the keen steel tips. The veteran human warriors who gripped those shafts were schooled in Mina's armies. Rankin's riders had assaulted them many times, desperate to break through the lines, to shatter the enemy army and race onto the plains.

But the enemy's determination was strong. Rankin himself had led several charges, had tried to fight his way toward the enemy commander—a former Knight of Neraka he recognized as a man named Blackgaard. Each time, the pikes had drawn tight, an impermeable barrier that cut down any brave riders who dared to come close.

In the end, the Army of the Sword had been forced back to the riverbank. Here they held, exacting a bloody toll on the enemy whenever Blackgaard sent forward a contingent in an effort to drive them into the water. But all they could do was hold their ground, try to stay alive, and pray for relief from one of the other wings of the Solamnic Army.

Without a breakthrough somewhere, it seemed the whole Army of Solamnia was doomed.

"Charge!" cried General Markus. "Caergoth Steelshields, carry the day!"

The planks of the bridge thrummed and vibrated underfoot as the column of armored knights, charging only six abreast because of the narrow span, thundered toward the east bank of the great river. They burst out of the mist, galloping from the edge of the bridge onto dry land.

A small company of goblins, apparently designated to investigate the mysterious fog, stood at the edge of the bridge, but they were smashed without even slowing the momentum of the charge. Warhorses pounded on, cutting down the terrified defenders in their path. The few panicked goblins who turned to flee fared miserably as they were chopped down by swords before they could take more than a couple of steps.

Sir Templar, exhausted, collapsed at the side of the bridge but raised a hoarse cheer as the file of riders continued to thunder past. Others of his Clerist company filed onto the bridge to come and join him, all of them cheering as the knights galloped across.

Ashore, Markus bade his mounted men to form companies. The first three of these he directed southward, to ride to the aid of the beleaguered troops trapped at the eastern end of the ford. The others, as they came across, he dispatched across the plains, or northward to link up with the forces of General Rankin, commanding the center of the great attack.

"General! They're sending fire ships!"

The alarm was brought to him by a breathless messenger. Markus looked onto the river and saw several massive barrages, ablaze, drifting along with the current. In another few moments they would come into contact with the wooden—flammable—bridge.

Once again it was Sir Templar and his knight-priests who came to the rescue. The young cleric roused himself and started to weave another spell. Within moments a cloud took shape in the air, dark and glowering, that hovered directly over the blazing barges. Soon a light drizzle started to fall from that cloud, and the rain quickly became a soaking shower. Soon the fire rafts merely sizzled, steaming heaps of ash, drifting harmlessly, utterly doused. Carried by the current, they eventually nudged against the pontoons, but presented no threat to the bridge or the attacking Rose Army.

The Rose Knights were all across now, and the columns of infantry came behind. They, too, spread across the plain. Hundreds of men rode toward the horizon, unimpeded by defenders.

An officer rode up from the south, and Markus recognized one of his captains, a man whose company had been attacking at the ford.

"How fares the crossing?"

"The knights who came across the bridge made a flank attack, General, and carried away the defenders at the edge of the ford. Our men are advancing to the east even as we speak."

Only then did Markus relax. He eased himself from his saddle, for the first time noticing the aches and weariness of a long day's battle. But the fight had been worth it.

The Army of Solamnia was across the Vingaard.

CHAPTER SIXTEEN

THE DUCHESS

'Use that whip, dammit!" barked Dram Feldspar, as the heavy freight wagon struggled through the last leg of the ford over the Vingaard River.

The hill dwarf teamster in the driver's seat, already lashing his team of six oxen for everything he was worth, didn't bother to reply to the mountain dwarf. Instead, he roared at the beasts, hauled on the reins, and called the laboring animals every manner of vile name. The massive bovines responded by lowering their heads, straining in their harness, and hauling the massive wagon up the bank and out of the water. Rivulets streaming from the cargo bed, the wagon rumbled and skidded into the ruts on the muddy road.

"Now you, there—move!" shouted Dram, turning to the next—and last—in the long line of wagons. He reached up to grasp the bridle of the massive draft horse leading the team and tugged until his face turned an alarming beet red, as if by dint of his own strength he could pull the animal and heavy wagon where he wanted it to go.

Whatever small contribution he made, it worked. The four big

210

horses pulling this last wagon surged and strained, and finally pulled free of the river. The broad, hair-skirted hooves of the team churned through mud, and the wagon rocked and jolted through the ruts worn by the wheels of previous vehicles, finally rumbling onto the plains road.

Dram's legs were about ready to give out. Sweat ran in his eyes, and his left shoulder throbbed where he had been kicked early on in the fording process. But finally the entirety of the huge wagon train was across the Vingaard and rolling toward the distant heights of the Garnet Mountains. The big vehicles carried everything needed to rebuild the Compound on its new site, including all of the raw materials, equipment, and personnel to resume operations. Fortunately, as they moved away from the river, the roadway hardened and the dry, solid ground allowed the laboring beasts to pick up speed.

Wearily Dram returned to his horse, where it was being held by a young hill dwarf. Normally he detested traveling by horseback, but now he was honestly grateful to pull himself up into the saddle and to let the animal carry him along. He rode a stocky, short-legged gelding—little more than a pony, actually—but the gruff mountain dwarf had become rather fond of the steed during the long days of riding across the plains.

Now he spurred the gelding into a trot, conscious of the fact he looked far from graceful as he clutched the reins with one hand and the bridle with the other. The saddle jarred and shifted beneath him, and it was all he could do to keep his balance. But it was important he catch up with the head of the column, already several miles away across the plain.

He jounced and bounced past dozens of large wagons. Many were hauled by teams of draft horses. These contained the household supplies as well as food and other sustenance (thirteen wagons hauled thirty-two casks of beer, each) for the whole community that lived and worked in the Compound. The even larger freight wagons, hauled by teams of oxen, carried the vast stockpiles of precious black powder, as well as the charcoal, saltpeter, and sulfur that were the raw materials of Dram's work.

Other oxen dragged massive timbers of ironwood, hewn from the coastal forests and first hauled up and over the Vingaard range, now drawn hundreds of miles to the east, following Jaymes's orders to reestablish the Compound in the Garnet Mountains. The Compound had been closed down and packed up in a little more than week, and by that time Dram's agents had returned after purchasing every wagon within a hundred miles.

It had taken the long wagon train five days to reach the Vingaard River and two more to get all the wagons across. It was fully a week after the fording that the massive column finally drew near to the lofty, snow-peaked mountains of the Garnet Mountains. Dram had sent a scout party, led by his wife, ahead of the main body. As the mountains took shape on the horizon, Sally returned to the caravan to inform him they had located a valley with the requisite characteristics: flat ground in the bottom, plenty of water, and hardwood forests nearby.

"It's right up there, through that notch in the foothills," she explained, pointing. Though she had been apart from him for a week, she avoided meeting Dram's eyes.

"Good," he replied. He cleared his throat awkwardly. "Look, I know this is hard on you—leaving the Vingaards and all. I just want you to know that I'm grateful; I'm glad you're here."

"I am here," was her reply. She left unspoken the truth they both understood: she was a dutiful wife and would follow her husband wherever he needed to go.

"All right!" Dram shouted, urging on the lead wagons. "We've got a destination. Let's roll on up there so we can get to work!"

~⊙~⊙~⊙~⊙~◉~⊙~⊙~⊙~⊙~

As befitting Solanthus's status as a stoutly fortified city, the ducal palace was more like a castle than a grand manor. Situated near the center of the city, it was easy to find, and as the kender and lord marshal emerged from between the Cleft Spires, they made their way directly to the grand structure. Four tall towers rose, one each at the corners of the walled compound, which occupied an entire city block.

The streets themselves were nearly abandoned. The swordsman drew minimal interest from the few passersby, though the citizenry inevitably gave the kender a look of horror and clutched whatever purses and valuables they carried tightly to themselves as they hurried past.

Moptop ran ahead of Jaymes as the two approached the massive gate at the front of the palace. Immediately a pair of guards scrambled from a little hut beside the gate, one taking each of the kender's arms and lifting him right off the ground.

"Hold it right there, you rascal!" one declared, shaking the little fellow rather more than was strictly necessary.

"Hey! Ow! That hurts!" cried Moptop, squirming fruitlessly in the double clasp.

"He's with me," Jaymes said, striding forward. "Let him go."

"And who in the name of the Abyss are you?" asked the second guard, his hand on the hilt of his sword. When the marshal didn't slow his approach, the man released the kender and drew his weapon, extending it aggressively.

213

"Hold it there, stranger," he said in warning then addressed his companion without shifting his gaze. "Lew, better call out the sergeant major."

"Do that," Jaymes replied. "But let the kender go."

"Who are you, sir?" huffed the mustachioed knight who emerged from the guardhouse a moment later. "What's the meaning of all this?"

"I'm Lord Marshal Jaymes Markham, commander of the Army of Solamnia. I'm here to see the Duchess Brianna, and this kender is my guide. I ordered him released, and if your man doesn't comply, I'll see that he's not fit to hold so much as a chicken leg when dinner comes around!"

"There, there," soothed the older guard. "Lew, release the kender. Max, go tell the majordomo that the duchess has a visitor—give him a good description. In the meantime, why don't we all just calm down and get this sorted out?" He fixed Jaymes with a wary look. "Though, if you'd been around here for a while, you'd know that none of us has had so much as a glimpse of a chicken leg in quite some time."

Moptop made a great show of wounded dignity in adjusting his topknot and tunic, making sure all his pouches were in order. He stalked back to Jaymes with the air of one who had endured a great insult, but the dignified effect was somewhat ruined when he stuck his tongue out at the scowling Lew.

"You're the lord marshal, eh?" said the sergeant major, making an elaborate show of spitting a stream of tobacco off to the side. "Don't have much of a uniform. I suppose that would have been a bit of a distraction, when you rode through the enemy lines, eh? You and your kender guide."

"I'll tell my story to the duchess," Jaymes said easily. He stood a dozen paces away from the guard post, watching as more men appeared atop the palace wall. A door opened off to the side and still more guards hastened out, quickly circling outward to form a ring around the two visitors.

"So did you get a look at the half-giant when you slipped past his tent?" continued the sergeant major, swaggering forward. He had an increasingly skeptical look on his face. "Maybe share a cup o' tea with him?"

The guards numbered more than a dozen, and all of them regarded the visitors with blatant hostility. Their faces were gaunt and unshaven, and their sunken eyes gleamed with suspicion. The effects of hunger were clearly visible in every face.

"Psst—I don't think they're very glad to see you," Moptop whispered loudly, tugging on the lord marshal's sleeve. "Maybe we should go back to the Cleft Spires."

"We'll stay here until we have a chance to talk to the duchess," Jaymes replied calmly.

"Maybe she's got some more important business than talking to a spy," the guard sneered.

"He's not a spy! He's the lord marshal of the whole army, and I'm his professional guide and pathfinder extraordinaire!" the kender declared, bristling. "And we didn't come through Ankhar's army—we found a new way to get here! And you just better—hey!"

Moptop squawked in alarm and ducked behind his companion's legs as a shadow suddenly flashed above them. A large net, a circular web with heavy weights around the fringe, soared from the wall, having been flung at them by a pair of guards. It spun itself taut and dropped toward the two travelers standing outside the palace gates.

In the same instant, Jaymes reached over his shoulder and pulled Giantsmiter from its sheath. Blue flames flashed in the sunlight as he swept the weapon in an arc over his head, neatly slicing the strands of the net as it plummeted. The weights carried the fringes to the ground, but the swordsman and the kender stood, unencumbered, in the middle of the ruined net.

For the first time, the sergeant major's eyes showed the shadow of respect. He scowled darkly, while several of his men whispered among themselves. "That's the sword of Lorimar, all right," one of them said quite audibly. "Mebbe he is who he says."

Further debate was prevented by the arrival of a woman, a very young woman of striking beauty, dressed in a supple leather skirt that reached to her feet. Hair of coppery red spilled across her shoulders, curling and full. Her face was pale except for the dark circles surrounding her sunken eyes. Her cheeks, neck, and arms had the same slightly gaunt look that was characteristic of everyone in the besieged city, but they were also alight with a glow of warmth, greeting, and something else—hope, perhaps.

"My Lord Marshal," she said, stepping through the ring of guards to approach and holding out her hand in greeting. Jaymes took it and bowed. "How nice it is to see you here."

"The honor is mine, Your Grace," he replied.

"Sergeant Major Higgins," she said, turning and regarding her guard with slight disapproval. "Perhaps you could help our visitor disentangle himself from the net?"

"But . . . Your Grace! So you do know this man?" Higgins sputtered. "He's not from the city—and yet, how could he come through the siege lines?"

"I have never met him—but he looks exactly as Dara Lorimar described. Those eyes! They look like they could stab you from ten paces away. The beard is a nice touch, my lord. It gives a weight of maturity to your countenance." She turned to the sergeant major, the hint of a smile playing about her lips. "And from what Dara told me about him, years back, I should think that if Jaymes Markham wanted to pass through the lines of a siege, he would be able to figure out a way to do that."

"I showed him the way!" Moptop proclaimed.

"How very nice of you," the duchess said with a dazzling smile. "You must be a splendid guide."

Moptop beamed in return, and seemed to grow a good two inches.

✦❀✧❀✦❀✦❀✦❀✧❀✦❀✦

The city of Solanthus was still intact, Jaymes could see as the duchess led him through the streets toward the western quarter. The buildings were mostly made of stone, and many of them loomed two or three stories high. Their facades were undamaged, their stonework and outer staircases clean and neat. But upon close inspection he saw that many structures had an unfinished look, and this was because wooden porches had been pulled down. Benches were gone, and even unnecessary doors had been removed.

"We burned almost all of our wood during the last winter," Brianna explained. "Even so, we lost a thousand people—mostly the very old and the very young—to the cold."

"Your brave stand has been remarkable," Jaymes acknowledged. "The whole of Solamnia is heartened by your example." Even to his own ears, the words sounded hollow. How could anyone who was not here understand what these people had been going through?

He noticed, as they passed corrals and stables and small barns, that there were no animals about. They, like the wood, had undoubtedly been consumed during the nearly two years of siege.

"We were faced by a new attack just a few days ago," Brianna explained as they walked, without ceremony, through the city streets. "It was a being of magic, gigantic in size, terrible in its destructive force."

"I received word of that," the lord marshal replied. "A wizard told me—she described the creature as an elemental, a magical composite of fire and water, earth and air."

"Oh! Did she tell you how we might kill this magical foe?" the duchess asked.

"Not in so many words," Jaymes said, shaking his head. "That's one of the reasons I came here; I am helping her search for the answer."

"Come this way, and I will show you some of the damage it wreaked."

They passed several knots of defenders, all of whom stood at attention when they saw it was the duchess approaching. The men of her garrison obviously regarded her with affection bordering on awe. They hastened to clear a path for her, lunging to kick pieces of rubble out of her way, following her reverently with their eyes as she walked past them. Despite her beauty, there was nothing of lust in their expressions—rather, they reflected more the adoration a young boy might show for his mother.

Jaymes noted the duchess's eyes were filled with sorrow, however, as she guided him and Moptop through the city, escorted only by a quartet of palace spearmen who materialized an unobtrusive distance behind them. Word spread, seemingly through the cobblestones themselves, announcing her approach. The people turned out along the whole way, leaning from upper windows, lining the walks beside the narrow streets. They did not cheer, but quietly nodded, bowed, and curtsied as the duchess passed.

These same people regarded Jaymes with frank curiosity and an occasional scowl of apparent hostility.

"They remember the promises of Caergoth and Thelgaard," Brianna explained apologetically, "and the knights who never appeared here. Very little is known about you, of course, though we have word that your army came north across the Garnet River. But they have had so little cause for hope in this last year."

"As of now, my army should be crossing the Vingaard. Relieving your city is our objective, but even so it will take days for my armies to close in upon the enemy camp."

"Until then, of course, we must continue to survive," said the princess coolly. They came around a corner and saw a whole block of devastated buildings. "Come this way. We'll climb the wall, and you'll be able to get a good look."

They made their way up a narrow stone stairway, quickly ascending to the top of a city wall. The duchess climbed the steps with easy grace. At the top, she gestured to an adjacent area that looked like the desolate ruin of some long-past civilization.

"Just a week ago this was a complete, fortified castle," Duchess Brianna remarked sadly. "But the fire-giant did all of this damage in less than an hour. More than a hundred men died."

Jaymes nodded his head. He had seen Garnet after it was sacked and burned by Ankhar's horde, but this devastation was worse. The rubble contained jutting pieces of broken stone and shattered timbers, but the wreckage was so thorough, he found it hard to imagine that the materials he could identify had once been part of an actual building.

He eyed the duchess, whose faraway look was full of unspoken heartbreak. She was so very young, a year or two past twenty at the most, but she carried herself with impressive dignity and purposefulness. Her leadership, the marshal knew, had inspired the long and stubborn resistance that Solanthus had offered to the besieging army.

"Why did you come?" asked the duchess, turning to him suddenly. "It cannot have been easy to get here—I know about the magic shield raised by the Cleft Spires. And couldn't you do more to help us by being with your army, and riding at its head?"

Taken aback, Jaymes pondered before replying. "Whatever did this to your city, it's a force that alters the balance of this war. This battle will be decisive. I needed to see this creature for myself, to formulate some kind of strategy to fight it."

"What can you, one individual, do?" she demanded then shook her head. "I'm sorry. I know how important it is to keep up hope; it's the only thing that keeps us going. But how can we muster any optimism in the face of *this?*"

She indicated the gap where the gatehouse had been, where the enemy was busy within Jaymes's view. Under a screen of heavy shields rolled in on carts, dozens of ogres were hauling rocks away. They were building tall, wide barriers to either side, clearly clearing a path for an attack that would smash through the city streets at some point in the near future.

"We showered them with arrows on the first day," Brianna explained with an edge of bitterness. "But we have only so many arrowheads, though the armorers' smithies are working day and night to produce all that is necessary. We've been melting down pots and pans, shovels and plows. But we can't maintain a constant barrage."

"They're very methodical about it, aren't they?" Jaymes watched a team of ogres maneuver a shield forward, while a dozen others advanced, picked up the rocks strewn everywhere, and started to heave them to the sides. The rock barrier, as it rose continually higher, gave protection to the ogres, while funneling an attack into the city.

"I suppose this is just one of several routes of advance that are being prepared," said Jaymes quietly, "and when they are ready, then he will once again release his elemental."

"And what will happen to us then?"

"I have with me a tool, a magical tool. The wizard thinks it might allow me to understand something vital about this conjured giant. In any event, I think our goal must be to strike at those controlling the elemental. It will be waste of time to attack the elemental itself."

"A waste of time," murmured Brianna, frowning.

"But there *is* cause for hope. Imagine a vicious dog, restrained by chain and collar, clubbed by a brutish master. When freed, that dog can be counted on to turn on its master. Perhaps we can free the elemental to turn on its controllers."

"My Lord Marshal," the duchess said, smiling suddenly. As she took his arm her excitement was palpable. "You must tell me more about this vicious-dog strategy. And I'm certain you're famished and tired. Please, let's return to my palace—I will provide you and your companion with guest apartments and then ask you to join me for dinner."

⊱⊷⊶⊷⊶❀⊷⊶⊷⊶⊷⊰

Moptop and Jaymes were shown to private rooms in the palace. The dinner invitation, it seemed clear, did not extend to the kender, and Moptop would have felt slighted if he didn't feel the tug of more interesting temptations.

"You go ahead and have a boring dinner," he told Jaymes cheerfully. "I've never been in a palace under siege before, and I'm going to have a look around this place."

"Try to stay out of trouble," the lord marshal counseled, not very optimistically. He took the time to wash some of the dust out of his hair and beard; then he surprised himself by deciding to shave, trimming his whiskers to some semblance of neatness. By the time he was finished, a servant girl had come to escort him to the dining room.

221

There were several other guests, including two noblemen, Lords Harbor and Martin, and Lord Martin's son, Sir Maxwell, who was a Solamnic Auxiliary Mage—a Kingfisher. An empty chair had been placed at the table, in memoriam to a brave captain named Cedric Keflar. He had led the valiant but futile defense of the West Gate, paying with his life.

"He left behind three children and a wife who is terribly sick," Brianna explained sadly. "And yet he did his duty by us all on that terrible day."

"The Oath and the Measure compelled him, Your Grace," said Sir Maxwell. "He was an inspiration to all of us who served under him."

"Tell me," Jaymes said, turning to the Kingfisher. "Have you found much use for your spells in withstanding this siege?"

The young man nodded seriously. "Not yet. But I have been marshalling my resources, and I have ideas for what may be helpful in the future, my lord."

"Sir Maxwell has proved an excellent spy," Brianna said. "He masks himself in all manner of sorcery and has become thoroughly familiar with Ankhar's camp."

"That is good," acknowledged the lord marshal.

"Why is it taking so long for your army to come to our relief?" asked Lord Harbor. "We hear of victory after victory, yet these triumphs are remote to us, and so far as I know, your troops are still on the far side of the Vingaard."

"Perhaps you don't know as much as you think you do," Jaymes replied.

Over a meager meal of bread, dry cheese, and thin soup—all of which was presented on elegant china and eaten with silver utensils—Jaymes shared information about the campaign to date. He outlined the ongoing plan for crossing the Vingaard.

"The three armies were to have launched this attack yesterday morning. By now the issue should have been resolved," he declared, feeling a twinge of annoyance that he couldn't claim to know what his army had accomplished during his absence.

"We will pray for the best, of course, and know that, if courage and ingenuity can prevail, your army will have crossed successfully," said Sir Martin, offering a toast.

"I have seen the barricades and breastworks in the street," Jaymes noted, awkwardly changing the subject. "How well are you prepared to stand against another attack?"

The duchess nodded at Lord Martin, who wore the tunic of a Sword Knight with the golden epaulets of a high-ranking officer. "Bartholomew, can you summarize our situation?" she prompted.

"Most of the wall, and the other two gatehouses, are still intact. But the destruction at the west gate has created a tremendous vulnerability, as you no doubt saw today. We have established command posts at inns, stables, and warehouses within the area of devastation and committed most of our reserves to holding those streets. But if the fire giant comes like before, I don't know how we can expect to hold anywhere."

That bleak assessment, all too realistic, cast a pall over the rest of the meal and conversation. But finally the food was eaten and the other guests departed. The duchess rose and indicated two soft chairs near the large, currently chilly, hearth.

"Please understand that your visit here has boosted morale," she began, taking one of the chairs and gesturing him toward the other. "*My* morale, in any event. I'm pleased you have risked coming. And I am intrigued about this magical tool you speak of possessing. What more can you tell me about it? I pray it gives us a fighting chance."

He shook his head ruefully. "It is not a weapon. At best, it will allow me only to learn certain things about this creature. I have to believe that this knowledge, this intelligence, will lead to a winning tactic. I can't promise any more than that."

The serving girl returned to the room, bringing a fresh bottle of red wine—a rare vintage that, Jaymes suspected, the duchess had been saving for a very long time.

"That will be all, Darcy," the duchess said after the last plates of dinner had been carried away. "But you may leave the bottle."

"Yes, Your Grace," said the maid, curtsying politely then closing the door behind herself as she departed.

"So you were a friend of Dara Lorimar's?" Jaymes asked, settling into the chair beside her.

"Yes, and of Selinda du Chagne's. I come from Palanthas but spent summers on the plains. Lord Lorimar's estate was a favorite refuge of mine, and I do remember seeing you back then, when you worked for the lord as his guard captain. Dara was a little bit in love with you, I think. I'm beginning to understand why."

"She was only a girl," he said. His tone was cold, cutting off further inquiry. "And she died too soon to know anything about love."

"You are a strange man," Brianna rebuked him sharply. "Cold and frightening, but frightened in your own way, as well." Then she smiled almost coyly. "Don't you think I know that you killed my husband? That you stole the Jewels of Garnet from his wagon?"

He blinked, momentarily taken aback, before shrugging. "I didn't come here to apologize. He deserved to die. And I needed the jewels—for Solamnia," he replied.

"Yes," she said tersely, "you are right. The duke did deserve to die. He was a coward, venal and greedy at heart. And he abandoned his city when his people needed him the most. I'm glad he's dead."

"Of all the possible reactions, that is not what I expected to hear from you," Jaymes allowed softly. "To be honest with you, I must tell you the rest of the story—the whole story. I killed your husband to punish him for a terrible crime. But, as it turns out, he didn't commit that crime. Someone else did. Someone who remains free."

"You killed him because you thought he killed Lord Lorimar?" asked Brianna, smiling thinly. "Yes, I heard that. But I know he didn't have the courage for such a deed."

"He had a reputation as a splendid swordsman; he'd faced men in duels to the death and always won. Except that last time, of course."

"But he fought you because you challenged him; usually he was very careful to arrange his duels so that he couldn't possibly lose." She shrugged. "So he died for something he didn't do, when there were many things he did do for which he deserved punishment. But enough of this talk—I don't want to reminisce about my late husband."

Jaymes looked at her with fresh, wondering eyes. She was indeed a rare woman.

The duchess leaned forward with the decanter and filled his glass with wine, rich and full and almost the color of blood. Then she added enough to her own so it, too, was full. She raised it to him, and he followed suit.

"You, my dear Lord Marshal, are just what this nation needs—if it's ever going to be a nation again. You don't lose your head in battle, and men seem to follow you, even die for you. *Lots* of men." She smiled again. "And some women, too, I would dare to venture."

He shrugged. "For the most part, I do things by myself. I act alone."

"Tonight," she said, sliding into his willing arms. "You will not be alone."

CHAPTER SEVENTEEN

BATTLES ANEW

"The Solamnics have crossed the river at the south ford—using a bridge made of pontoon boats—and have established a strong position on the east bank," Captain Blackgaard reported. He was still covered with dust from his long ride but had wasted no time in reporting to Ankhar when he reached the army's position outside Solanthus.

"Can they be pushed back into the river?" growled the army commander.

"Doubtful, my lord. Very doubtful," reported the veteran officer and former Dark Knight. "At best, the goblins might be able to hold them for a few days. And Rib Chewer's warg riders will harass them well as they advance. But there are now at least a thousand knights on this side of the river. They can go where they will, and I suspect they soon will be coming here."

"This bridge—how did they build it so quickly?"

Blackgaard described the pontoon and plank operation, and Ankhar frowned, shaking his head. "Ingenious, I admit. And this 'bridge' was sturdy enough for armored knights to cross?"

"Indeed, lord. And they used magical concealment, a conjured fog, to slip it across without our men detecting their activity."

"Huh! But it is clear they are acting with desperation," the half-giant reflected. "They must have heard about our pet and the attack that has left Solanthus vulnerable. I wonder how they are able to obtain such information so soon. Well, no doubt about it, the elemental king has captured the full attention of the knighthood."

"You are right, lord—they are desperate. The marshal threw his whole army at us in three great attacks. The Solamnics suffered heavy losses, but they seem determined to forge ahead."

"All the more reason why we must smash the city now," the half-giant concluded. He addressed several goblin runners who were standing by, waiting for orders. "Summon Bloodgutter, and that hob Spleenripper. Also Eaglebeak Archer. Bring the Thorn Knight and my mother to me as well. I will go to await them at my watchtower."

Within a few moments, Ankhar's key lieutenants had joined him on an observation hillock just out of bowshot range of the former West Gate. The half-giant stood on the earthen rampart, high above the level of the plain, his fists braced on his hips. He glared across the gap created by the elemental's swath of destruction and studied the still-standing walls of Solanthus. The Cleft Spires rose from the center of the city, the twin monoliths outlined clearly as the morning sun rose from the horizon beyond the city.

The captain of the Lemish Ogres arrived, having followed a covered trench back from the ruins of the West Gate. "Have the attack paths been cleared?" Ankhar asked Bloodgutter, one of his most trusted captains, a cunning and savage warrior.

"Three routes are ready," the captain replied. "Two more will be open by tomorrow."

"We can't wait until tomorrow. We attack today."

"Yes, my lord," the ogre replied, snorting aggressively. "We're ready to kill."

"I know that. Here is the plan. You will send a third of your troops up each attack route. Push past the human defenses and seize the buildings immediately inside the walls and the towers to either side." He turned to another subcommander, one who had been part of his great horde ever since they had first descended from the Garnet Mountains some three years earlier. "Spleenripper, I want you to send a thousand hobs and gobs after each group of ogres. When you get into the city, spread out and drive the humans before you."

Spleenripper cackled, gesturing to the ranks of brutish warriors already gathered behind the hillock. "We are already in position. Give the word, lord, and we will move!"

Ankhar nodded, turning to the captain of his goblin archers. "Eaglebeak, your companies must shower the humans on both sides of the gap with arrows. Shoot as fast as you can—don't worry about using all your arrows. By tonight, we will be able to pick them up from the streets of Solanthus!" That worthy warrior, too, pledged his obedience.

Finally the half-giant turned to Laka and Hoarst. The Thorn Knight in his ash-gray cape stood there, listening stoically, while the old shaman, for her part, hopped back and forth on her feet. She barked with mirth as her stepson asked to see the small, delicate box. The rubies lining the cover and sides sparkled brightly in the midday sun.

"The king is ready, my lord—my son!" she crowed. "I will release him upon your command."

"Good." Ankhar looked at Hoarst, who nodded and pulled

his cape back, just enough to reveal that he gripped the slender wand, the tool that barred the elemental from attacking them, ready in his right hand. The half-giant nodded, satisfied.

"Eaglebeak, assemble your archers. As soon as they launch the first volley, my mother will open the ruby box."

⊱⊹⊱⊹⊱⊹⊛⊹⊱⊹⊱⊹⊰

The morning light heightened Brianna's gaunt features, and as she blinked herself awake, Jaymes couldn't help but see she was close to starvation. But she smiled at him, and warmth in her eyes softened her thin face and seemed to give life to her cheeks, her eyes, her lips. He had been propped up on an elbow, preparing to rise, but now he lay still, regarding her.

"You're an admirable woman," he said, shaking his head slightly. "You didn't deserve to suffer a man like Rathskell, and yet now you're doing his job far better than he ever did. The people of Solanthus are fortunate."

"I . . . I'm not usually like this," she said, sitting up and demurely holding the blanket to conceal her nakedness. "But . . . I needed—"

"I needed something too," the man replied, touching her cheek. "I understand and I'm glad that it happened."

"So am I," she said before abruptly popping out of bed with the blanket draped, toga style, around her. "Now you have to get out of here." She glided to the wall and pushed on a panel, revealing a dark passage behind a door he had not noticed before. "This will take you back to your room—hurry," she said.

Jaymes returned to his bedroom along the secret hallway. It was already past dawn, and he could hear the sounds of footsteps and dishes rattling in the kitchen, all proof that the ducal palace was astir. He dressed quickly and was slinging Giantsmiter in

230

its heavy scabbard over his shoulder when someone knocked, rather insistently, at the door.

"Come in," he barked, picking up one of his miniature crossbows, making sure the spring was cocked, ready to receive one of the lethal bolts into the firing groove.

A courier in golden epaulets, one of the officers who had been at dinner the previous evening, opened the door and bowed his head briefly. "Forgive the intrusion, my Lord Marshal, but there is activity in the enemy camp. The duchess has been informed as well. She suggests we observe from the tower nearest to the ruin, atop the city wall."

"I'll be right with you." The lord marshal prepared his other crossbow and settled both of them in the straps at his belt. "Take me straight to the wall," he said.

They proceeded at a trot past many of the defensive breastworks that had been set up in streets, at intersections. Jaymes glimpsed archers assembled atop flat-roofed buildings and a walled courtyard where a small company of armored knights had gathered, holding the reins of their horses. They arrived at the base of the city wall, where four Sword Knights stood guarding a small door. The four knights stepped aside to let the two men pass so they could head up the interior stairs.

A few moments later, Jaymes climbed, slightly breathless, onto the top of the tower nearest to the ruined gatehouse. He was rather surprised to find the duchess already there. Brianna looked at him in welcome, though he saw no trace of the soft familiarity that had been in her eyes when he left her. She gestured to the plain beyond the city.

"They will be coming very soon now," she said in a tone of icy calm.

She was right, Jaymes saw immediately. Huge columns of ogres, three thick formations, had moved to within a few hundred yards of the city, remaining just beyond longbow range. To either flank, even larger formations of goblins advanced, but where the ogres held to their massive columns, the gobs formed a series of long lines ranked parallel to the city wall. These were archers, and their bows were strung.

Inside the area where the West Gate had stood, Jaymes could see several wide, smooth paths through the rubble, each of them protected by steep, high walls of rocks to either side. Those attack routes emerged into the plaza that had once been directly inside the gate. In that open square, the city's defenders had erected a series of wooden barricades and stone breastworks. The line was manned by able warriors, their spears and swords bristling, but they were a paltry substitute for the fortress wall that no longer existed.

"I need to go down there among the defenders," Jaymes said. "I must get ready to meet and face this monster, in close quarters, when it comes."

"But you won't be able to see through all the chaos," Brianna countered. "Shouldn't you stay up here until it materializes and then take up your position?"

"No, it will attack there," he said, pointing at the manned barricade across the plaza, utterly confident in his ideas. "And I need to be blocking its path, right in front of it."

"Go, then, and may the gods grant you protection and success," she said, putting a hand on his arm. For just a moment her eyes softened, and he saw the warmth, even a hint of the need for intimacy that had filled her face last night.

"Thanks," he said, nodding and holding still for her touch. Finally Jaymes turned and started down the tower's interior stairway. A moment later he emerged at the base and proceeded to follow the street just inside the city wall until he came to the plaza.

Looking around the plaza, which was busy with defenders rushing back and forth, he loosened the flap on the pouch holding the helm. But as yet he didn't put on the helm.

"You look like an able-bodied bloke; take up a place here on the left flank," said a Sword Knight, apparently the captain of this section of the line. "Can you use that big blade you're carrying?" the knight asked skeptically.

"Yes. But I want to be in the middle of the line," Jaymes said.

"Suit yourself," the man replied, eyes narrowing slightly. "Hey, are you the lor—"

"I'm a warrior and a swordsman, and I'm here to do my job like everyone else." Striding past the officer, the lord marshal made his way to the center of the long breastwork. The barrier consisted mainly of overturned wagons and carts all nailed together with long sections of planking. Here and there, large square stones had been stacked together to make a more solid barrier. The men who were holding this line were gaunt and sallow soldiers, with some citizens mixed in. All wore determined faces.

The battle began as a faint stirring of noise that first came from sections of the city wall to either side of the plaza. Jaymes watched as a shower of arrows materialized, high in the sky. The missiles clattered along the parapets, many of them skipping off the stones to plummet into the city streets. He hoped the duchess had ducked inside; the tower where he left her was the target of a particularly dense volley.

Arrows flew outward as well, launched by the defenders lining the walls, but the volley was meager compared with the shower of missiles that flew from the goblins. At the same time, a steady drumming became audible; the ogres were on the march. The sound rattled the very ground Jaymes stood on, swelling in volume with the tempo.

"They're comin' at a goodly clip," one gray-haired veteran declared sagely, to the nods of the men and boys around him. "Be here real soon, that's my guess."

But they had even less time than that before a monstrous shape appeared, towering over the piles of rubble that marked the site of the gatehouse. The king of the elementals was as tall as the city walls, Jaymes realized. The creature bore closer with a steady, ominous gait. Its two eyes burned outward from a massive face that resembled nothing so much as a craggy cliff.

Several of the defenders, boys too young to shave probably, began to cry softly as the monster neared. "Reminds me of Mina's red dragons at Sanction," the old veteran said conversationally, taking the time to spit on the ground. "Lotsa noise and fuss—they was really something to see, I tell you. But they're just critters like the rest of us. Critters what can kill, but critters what can be killed too."

The boys listened, wide eyed, and the man's words seemed to calm some of their fears. Jaymes didn't feel any need to dispute the fellow's claim, though the king of the elementals seemed different than any "critter" he had ever witnessed.

Its torso looked to be solid rock. Its arms lashed about, supple as tentacles, translucent in color—and clearly powerful, as one reached out to smash at a chimney that had somehow survived the ruin of the gatehouse. Smacked by that limb, it crumbled like a toy.

Finally the whole of the monster could be observed as it stepped right into the plaza. Jaymes saw that it was balanced upon twin, whirling cyclones—black tornadoes of swirling, tumultuous air. The sight was terrifying and violent as its mere presence stirred up geysers of wind, spattered dust and rock across the ground, and rattled the heavy boards of the barricade. By all the gods—how was it even possible to stop something like that?

The lord marshal raised his sword and stared along the blade, seeking to make contact with the creature's hellish eyes. When he did meet them, he staggered backward from the physical impact of the elemental's raw emotion. Jaymes's knees buckled and he went down, bracing himself with one hand on the breastwork, veering dizzily.

But he did not lower his eyes. He forced himself to stare into that monstrous visage, holding his sword aimed straight at the creature's eyes, allowing the magic of the ancient artifact to find and grab the creature.

The elemental king's gaze seemed like liquid fire being poured directly into Jaymes's skull.

Fury.

He had never imagined such rage, such a thirst for destruction, vengeance, retribution. The violence of the elemental king's emotions made him sick to his stomach, but still he would not look away. Jaws clenched, he stared, unaware that his own fingers were curling into fists. Staggering, he pushed himself up to a standing position, still leaning against the barricade, his knees bending as if in preparation for a charge.

Hate.

The elemental directed its anger to the very sky, and the sun that burned so loftily above. It hated the whole city of humankind, the thousands of souls that flickered and survived here, living and dying quickly in a way that this monster could never understand. The elemental king despised all living creatures, and it craved to end life. Deeper, Jaymes probed that hateful consciousness, seeking to penetrate its monstrous core.

Wrath.

Anger was fundamental to this seething creature. The elemental hated not just the humans, but it hated its own army. In particular, Jaymes perceived an image of the half-giant,

Ankhar the Truth. There flashed another image of a man in a gray cloak—the Thorn Knight—and the withered, hideous visage of the hobgoblin shaman. Those were the beings, the marshal understood, for which the monster reserved its worst malice.

Fury . . . Hatred . . . Wrath.

All these emotions were focused, most forcefully, against those three beings, its own allies.

Why did the creature attack Solanthus, then? The answer seemed obvious: because it could not strike at the ones it hated the most. Jaymes perceived this basic truth amidst the elemental's many churning emotions. The monster was restrained from attacking its most hated foes, so it inflicted utter annihilation on anyone within reach.

✖◦✦◦✦◦✦◦✦◦●◦✦◦✦◦✦◦✦◦✖

Moptop Bristlebrow poked around another corner and looked to the right then the left. The shadows of these dingy confines were broken here and there by a few shafts of sunlight. He stood ankle deep in water, not even noticing yet another of the many stagnant puddles that littered the city sewer system of Solanthus.

Which was, beyond any doubt, the most fabulous city sewer system the kender had ever seen. A beam of sunlight, grid-patterned because of the iron grate over the manhole above, offered him a chance to consult his map. Moptop made a scratch mark with his charcoal pencil then started along the left-hand tunnel, the passage that, he guessed, led either due west, or on some angling vector toward the north and east.

Altogether these tunnels formed a truly intricate maze, which he was having a splendid time exploring. He had been down here all morning, traipsing around, exploring, adding crucial details and highlights to his maps. And there was still a lot more to see.

This was even better than poking through the ducal palace, which had occupied most of the previous night. He had almost been thwarted in that endeavor, since he had quickly discovered someone had accidentally locked the door to his guest bedroom so he couldn't get out. Strangely, though he could hear servants walking past, and though he had pounded and yelled for quite a while, no one had noticed the commotion and come to unlock the door. Fortunately, a drainpipe extended near his fourth-floor window, and it had been a simple matter to scamper up to the roof and climb down one of the chimneys.

Of course, the ducal palace was a fascinating place in its own right. He had enjoyed making the rounds during the night, investigating several bedrooms. There were lots of guards patrolling the halls, and though Moptop had frequently been tempted to introduce himself to one or two of them, they always looked so serious that he guessed they were very busy with guard stuff. So he had simply melted into the shadows and let them pass.

He had even found a secret passage! When he went over to Jaymes's room to see how the lord marshal was sleeping, he had been surprised to find him missing. Then he had discovered a panel of the room's wall that slid silently out of the way, and when Moptop had been poking around that particular passage Jaymes himself had emerged from another secret door, this one connecting to the room of the duchess. Here, too, Moptop had been tempted to say "hi," but the lord marshal had looked so preoccupied that the kender had allowed him to walk right past without announcing his presence.

But after six or eight hours, Moptop had seen just about as much of the palace as he wanted to. In the cellar he discovered a drain, which someone had gone to the trouble of securing with a grate, which was practically tailor-made for a kender's egress. He had slipped through then slid down a bumpy chute of slick, mossy stones—a fun ride, that!—soon finding himself in this far vaster network of places to explore.

He was just starting to skip westward—or north by eastward—when something shook the floor under his feet. Debris fell from the top of the sewer tunnel, bits of gravel and dust spattering onto the kender's topknot. He saw concentric ripples in the puddles that had, up until now, been lying there perfectly still. A moment later he felt the shake again . . . then again, at a regular tempo. It reminded him of being in a house where somebody large and heavy was walking around on the roof or in a room right over his head.

"That's what it is; somebody's walking around up there!" he remarked, certain of his explanation.

Then his eyes widened: it had to be somebody very huge. After all, there were people and even horses tromping all over in this city, and he hadn't heard so much as a single little whisper from any of them. This was someone thumping the ground hard with each step.

Moptop looked up and down the tunnel. There was still so much to see down here—miles and miles of sewer remained unmapped, at least as far as he knew—but curiosity about what was going on up above got the best of him. He hurried back to where the beam of sunlight arrowed through the sewer grate and scrambled up the rusty metal ladder on the side of the pipe. At the top he was able to poke his head between the bars, though they were too close together for him to slip out.

And—drat his luck!—the giant walker had just gone past! He saw a glimpse of a rocky shoulder and great, dark head looming high above the ground, but they vanished behind a pile of stone rubble almost immediately. Well, it sure was huge! Huger than anything he had ever seen, and he almost wept in despair at the thought that he missed his chance to get a really good look at the elemental king monster.

Fortunately, Moptop's climb to the grate was not entirely wasted; he was thrilled to notice heavy hobnailed boots approaching at a clomp. Lots of boots! Ogres! A whole army of them! At least, that's what it seemed like as they came marching along, tromping right past where he hid down in the grate. The kender was almost ready to wave a cheerful greeting but, as he lifted his hand, his foot slipped off the slick metal ladder's rung and he dropped a foot, out of sight from above. By the time he climbed back up, they were marching past, and he thought it best not to disturb them.

Next he saw a pair of boots that were even bigger than ogre boots. Beside them strode a set of legs as skinny as toothpicks, with oversized feet wrapped in old leather sandals. Moptop lifted himself up, and realized that he was looking at the half-giant, Ankhar the Truth, himself! He was accompanied by an old hobgoblin wench, a gray-robed warrior, and a couple of swaggering Dark Knights that looked like bodyguards.

"Where is the king?" Ankhar demanded. "Don't let him get too far!" He sounded kind of upset, even worried, to the kender.

"If you listen, you will hear. He is crushing the humans in the plaza. But he has not moved into the city yet," came the reply from the man who wore the long, gray cape. "We still drive him before us!"

"Then I must find a place to see—a place where I can watch this city die," crowed the half-giant.

Suddenly the sewer wasn't so interesting anymore. The kender looked around, recalling another grate a little ways back that might be big enough to let him get out.

It seemed like maybe he better go and find the lord marshal.

"Move up—charge there, forward, and to the left!" Ankhar was advancing at a run, chasing the ogres that had spilled into the city's plaza and swiftly overrun the pitiful remnants of the human defenders. This time, Truth willing, he was not going to let the elemental king advance out of his sight.

"Where is Eaglebeak?" he roared. "I need him and his damned archers up here now!"

Surprisingly enough, the hobgoblin captain appeared at his side only a moment later. Eaglebeak's feathered headdress was askew, his ruddy cheeks flushed with the excitement of battle. "What are your commands, lord?"

"Bring your archers up as soon as Spleenripper's columns have passed. I want a shower of arrows to bracket our advance, sweeping like a hailstorm on each flank."

"It shall be done, lord," declared the hobgoblin turning smartly and loping away to put the commands in motion.

Ankhar strode out of the avenue of cleared ground and entered the great plaza. The elemental king remained in view, having kicked through the feeble breastwork that the humans had erected.

Already the ogres were charging, bellowing in fury, heavy boots shaking the ground as they swept across the flagstones. Hobgoblins and gobs spilled after them. Spleenripper's troops paused to gut, scalp, and otherwise mutilate the bodies of the humans who had fallen. But their captain was diligent and vicious, and freely wielded his whip to prod them on.

Within a few more moments, the attackers were spilling into the streets of Solanthus, racing this way and that with no coherent defense standing in their path.

His head throbbed. Dry, gritty dust filled his mouth. Jaymes spit—or tried to spit, but found he had no saliva—and struggled to remember where he was.

The smell of smoke was his first clue. As the ringing in his ears subsided, he heard men groaning in pain. Somewhere nearby a child was sobbing, utterly distraught. The marshal was lying on hard paving stones, facedown. The fingers of his outstretched hand touched something wet and his first thought was a keen longing: water! But almost immediately he realized the texture was all wrong—this was a sticky, viscous liquid, warmer than the ground and the air.

Blood.

Then the memories returned. The elemental king had closed on the barricade in three steps, kicked it aside in one more. The planks had burst into flame and the old gray-haired veteran in the middle had been easily crushed when a massive, windswept foot had smashed down upon him. It was his blood, a smear on the plaza, Jaymes was touching.

He pushed himself upright, shaking his head and ignoring the ringing pain at the sudden movement. A weeping boy was nearby, huddled over the corpse of his brother. Drumming filled the air, and a glance beyond the smoking, smoldering barricade showed a whole rank of ogres advancing down the street. Their bloodlust raging, they roared in exultation as they poured through the shattered defenses, their drums' rolling thunder urging them on.

"Come on!" Jaymes said roughly, staggering to his feet, lifting the boy by his shaking shoulder. "Run!"

The lad's eyes widened as he caught sight of the lumbering ogres. When Jaymes started away, the boy followed, and the two raced together out of the plaza and into one of the many side streets connecting to the wide-open space.

Jaymes and the boy came upon the Sword Knight who had tried to recruit the lord marshal for the left flank of the wooden barricade position. The entire rampart was wrecked and burning, with many defenders dead, and the mustachioed warrior was wounded. He was sitting up, leaning back against a block of granite, wiping at a bloody gash on his head. A few other men, most of them bleeding, were picking themselves up and trying to reorganize.

The ogres were spilling through the gap in the middle of the wreckage, but none diverted from the main charge to come after these few limping survivors on the fringe of the battle.

"Get these men out of here," Jaymes said, assisting the wounded knight to stand. "Find a bottleneck in one of these side streets and try to make a stand there."

"Yes, my lord," the man replied. "By the Oath and the Measure, they will not pass!"

"Good," said the lord marshal, clapping the man on the shoulder. In a few steps they came to a side street, finding a dozen men-at-arms standing there, looking wildly from the lord marshal to the ogres, who lumbered down the avenue toward them barely a stone's throw away. When he looked across the plaza, the lord marshal saw the elemental king had passed this way, smashing a crude swath through several rows of sturdy stone houses.

"You stay here; help these men fight the ogres," Jaymes ordered the boy, who nodded seriously. "And for the sake of all the gods, form a line!" he barked at the men who were still staring, aghast, at the scene in the plaza. "Rouse yourselves! Hold this street!"

"You heard him! Line up!" snapped the Sword Knight, suddenly finding his voice.

"Yeah! Line up!" shouted the boy.

242

Jaymes reached over his shoulder and drew Giantsmiter. With the blade extended, he started away at a sprint, heading for the ruins that spoke of the elemental king's passage.

He hadn't gone halfway when he was startled by a familiar voice and out of the corner of his eye he spied a small figure, waving to him from beneath one of the city's ubiquitous sewer grates.

"Jaymes—hey, Lord Marshal! Yoo-hoo!"

The voice, quite unmistakably, belonged to Moptop Bristlebrow, professional guide and pathfinder extraordinaire.

"What are you doing down there?" he demanded.

"Looking for you!" cried the kender. "And you won't *believe* what I just heard. . . ."

CHAPTER EIGHTEEN

A SMALL ATTACK

Jaymes, with Moptop in tow, accosted a Captain of Swords who stood with a small band of men at a barricade on the Duke's Avenue. "I need to find the duchess!" the lord marshal announced. "Where is she?"

"She was commanding the left flank," the knight offered. "I saw her come down from the tower before the giant stormed through. The garrison has a strong point at the Black Tiger Inn— the big stone house, there—and I think that's where she went."

Nodding his thanks, Jaymes took off at a sprint, skirting the plaza—still crawling with ogres—and heading through a narrow alley. The kender, unusually somber, trotted along, keeping up. They reached the Black Tiger a moment later and were both quickly passed through the gate into a large courtyard.

They halted to make way for a company of archers, all of them young men, scrambling up a ladder to take positions on the roof. A messenger came racing in the same door the swordsman and the kender had entered, shouting a plea toward the stables. "Ogres are flanking the Duke's Avenue—a dozen or more, heading through the Silver District!" he called.

Four knights quickly mounted their horses and put spurs to the steeds, racing across the courtyard as a pair of men swung open the main gate. The riders clattered into the street, and the barrier was swung shut before they reached the first corner.

"The duchess has to be in there," Moptop said, pointing toward the inn's main hall, a large stone building on the other side of the courtyard.

Men in armor were coming and going through the open door to that hall, and the pair crossed over to it quickly. Jaymes entered the building and squinted as his eyes adjusted to the semidarkness. Moptop followed, sticking close by his side.

The duchess was speaking to some of her captains at a table. Lord Harbor was pacing nervously behind her. Brianna's face was ashen, and she had a scrape on her cheek, but she was poised, her words commanding. He could see at a glance that her presence had a calming effect on the agitated men-at-arms who had gathered around the table.

"My Lord Marshal," she said, looking up at his approach. "I'm glad to see you; we all feared you perished when the giant crossed the plaza."

"Many did," he said. "I was fortunate."

"But what can we do now?" she asked, a hint of despair in her voice. "The elemental has destroyed blocks of buildings and roams unchecked through the city. At the same time, ogres and goblins are spilling through the gatehouse. I'm afraid. . . ."

Her voice trailed off, but he could see the fear in her eyes. Her city and her people were doomed.

"The situation is bad, but we may have some options," Jaymes declared, striding to the table. The knight captains made room for him at the side of the duchess and even allowed Moptop to push his way into the midst of armored men. "It's true, we can't fight the elemental. I don't know what on Krynn *could* fight that thing. But we might be able to stop it another way. We might be able to affect those who are controlling it."

"Tell me!" she said, her eyes suddenly bright. "What have you learned?"

Moptop spoke up, looking surprisingly subdued as he addressed the duchess and her captains. "Well, Ankhar has that creepy witch-doctor with him, and also a Thorn Knight—you know, one of the Gray Robes. They are all moving around together and making all the decisions about this army, and this monster—Ankhar called it 'the king.' "

"The king? Of what?" one of the knights spoke up.

"I'm not sure," Jaymes replied. "But I think it springs from far underneath the ground. It embodies many of the fundamental elements, and seems to be a kind of king of elementals."

"A king? How can we fight a king of elementals?" Brianna asked.

"These three leaders of the enemy army are the controllers of the elemental. They are the key. They are moving about recklessly and are not themselves very well protected. They have a small bodyguard, according to the kender, and have remained well to the rear of the front line. But if we could get close enough to them . . . " Jaymes said. "I propose we try to strike them down. Their deaths cannot help but throw the enemy army into disarray, and I believe it may disrupt their control over the monster."

"Assassinate them!" exclaimed Lord Harbor, frowning. "It is dishonorable!"

Jaymes quickly glared the man into silence.

"How could you get to them?" asked Brianna.

"The same way I found them—underground!" Moptop retorted.

"How do you know this?" demanded Lord Harbor. "And why should we trust the word of a kender?"

"*I* trust him," Brianna said sternly. Her tone softened as she looked at Moptop, her smile briefly flickering. "Still, I, too, would like to know how you came by this information, little one, and how you think you might be able to find these three behind enemy lines"

"I found them before—through the sewers! I was mapping the sewers—that's what I do, usually. I'm a pathfinder extraordinaire. The White Wizard calls me that! And I was going along under the city, and I saw the giant go by, and then the ogres, and then came Ankhar and his friends. So I just listened real hard while they were talking. Kind of like a spy. A very brave spy who laughs in the face of danger. Ha!"

"I believe you are a brave spy," the duchess said. "And I believe you are very good at finding things. I'm impressed with your boldness and would like to try your plan."

The kender glowed, nodding his head and looking around at the other men in the room, daring them to contradict the duchess. Most of them, unfortunately, were looking at their feet.

The duchess raised her eyes, looking at Jaymes speculatively. "How do you suggest we proceed?"

"First, your forces must stand firm against the enemy army; any success against the giant will mean nothing if Ankhar's troops are running amok in the city. The inn here is a strong point, and there are others around the periphery of the plaza. The first column of ogres is already heading down the avenue toward the palace, but there's a good captain rallying some knights. They'll try to hold them at bay. I just saw a small party of knights ride out to hold a side street. You need to keep up that kind of pressure on the enemy army while we try something to take away their chief threat—this elemental king."

Jaymes turned back to the kender. "I want you to lead a small party through those sewers. We might be able to take Ankhar and his entourage by surprise if we can come up out of the ground, behind his lines, without warning. I'll strike down the Thorn Knight first, he's a magic-user and needs to be dealt with. Then let's go after the half-giant and the witch-doctor, they'll be trickier. It's likely we will be able to disrupt their leadership and disperse the attack, and it's even possible that we can turn back the elemental king."

"How do you propose to do that—oh, never mind," Brianna replied, nodding decisively. "I agree. Time is short, and the risk is worth taking." She turned to one of her officers. "Sir Michael, what's the latest word on the whereabouts of the elemental?"

"North of the Duke's Avenue, the report came just moments ago. It's wrecking the manors of many of the mercantile nobles, after going through a block of laborers' houses."

"And moving east from there, Your Grace," added a young knight—it was Sir Maxwell, the only one present clad in the garb of the Kingfisher instead of the Sword. He held up a small disk that looked like a compass. "I was able to place an enchantment upon him. It has limited value, I'm afraid, allowing me to track his position with this."

"That might prove very useful. Now it's time to go," Brianna declared. She picked up a pair of gauntlets and slid her delicate hands into the metal gloves. She looked at Jaymes with a glint of challenge in her eye. "I'm coming with you."

"But, Your Grace!" objected Sir Michael. "I won't allow it! The risks are far too great!" His words were swiftly echoed by the other knights who were gathered around the table.

"Do not forget, sir, I command here!" she replied tersely.

"I won't allow it either," Jaymes said. "You're needed here."

Brianna's cheeks flushed, but her tone was icy. "You presume to—"

"I presume to understand how important you are to this city. The people need you. They need to see you, rally around you. If we can strike down the commanders of this army, we will have a chance to win! It would be foolish for you to risk your life with us—"

"On a wild-ass, insane gamble that has a miniscule chance of success!" Sir Michael completed. He glared at Brianna then shifted his attention to Jaymes. "However, I must insist on coming along with you, my lord," he said in a more level tone.

"Naturally," Jaymes agreed, nodding his head and almost cracking a smile.

"I acquiesce," the duchess snapped. "Let all who are here understand that I do so, unwillingly and reluctantly. But, please Jaymes, take a few more men with you."

"I'd like to come," said the Kingfisher eagerly. His eyes were wide, but his voice was confident.

"Good. We could use a wizard to hunt a wizard," Jaymes agreed.

A chorus of others, virtually all the men in the hall, quickly offered their services to the risky mission. Sir Michael quickly pointed to the Kingfisher and two other burly swordsmen. "That makes five men . . . and er, a kender," he appended, as Moptop tugged anxiously on his sleeve. "Is that enough?"

Jaymes nodded. "It'll have to be. Where do you suggest we start from?"

"My temple is just this side of the palace. We can climb the steeple there and try to get our bearings. From there we should be able to spot these three leaders," said Maxwell.

"Lead the way," said the duchess. She stared challengingly

at Jaymes and Michael. "I daresay you won't forbid me to come along that far, will you?" she challenged.

With a shrug, the lord marshal started for the door, and the rest quickly followed him.

⚜

"I can have a ton of it here by tomorrow morning, if the price is right," said Rogard Smashfinger, master forger of Kaolyn. He stroked his blunt fingers through his gray beard, and waited for Dram Feldspar to reply, his expression guarded

The pair were meeting at a table in a clearing of the New Compound. All around them, chimneys smoked, axes *thunked,* and dwarves bustled about to build the new town in the Garnet range. Even as the town took shape all around them, work progressed on manufacturing more of the black powder, and a new, even stronger bombardment device.

Immediately upon his arrival here, Dram had sent word to his old homeland of Kaolyn—the dwarf kingdom underneath the highest mountains of the range—and he was pleased to see that Rogard Smashfinger personally had come to talk some business.

The two mountain dwarves were old acquaintances, and Dram knew that the smith could be trusted but would demand an exorbitant price. But the steel forged in that mountain dwarf kingdom was without peer, so Dram didn't hesitate to reach down to the floor and lift up a small sack of jewels he had prepared for just this moment. He raised it to the table, upended it, and watched with satisfaction as Rogard's eyes grew wide.

"That's for the first ton, and a comparable sum will be set aside for every ton that follows. And just this season alone, I'll need at least ten tons, as soon as possible."

Rogard reached into the sack and picked up several stones for

250

inspection—a mixture of rubies, emeralds, and diamonds. He held them, one by one, up to the sun. He squinted suspiciously, muttering to himself as he appraised the stones. His tongue emerged from between his teeth as he beheld a particularly splendid emerald, and he couldn't help but lick his lips again as he scrutinized the largest stone, a diamond.

"Aye," he said grouchily. "I suppose these'll do." He scooped the gems into the sack and was about to tuck the bag into his pocket when Dram plucked it out of his hand, grinning.

"Tomorrow morning, then?" he said, chuckling. "You can take this away with you when I have the Kaolyn steel."

"All right!" Rogard huffed. He had, of course, expected nothing less from such a tough businessman as Dram. "Just let me have another look."

"Be my guest," Dram offered, watching as the master forger carefully counted out the stones and once more hefted the bag, feeling its reassuring weight.

"We have a deal, then?" Rogard said, handing the sack back to Dram.

"Let's make it official. Sally!" he called.

His wife scrambled up from the nearby stream bank. Her face was smudged, her hands and apron covered with fish scales and guts—she had been helping to clean the catch for this evening's supper.

"How about a couple of cold tankards to close this deal between old friends?" Dram asked breezily.

"Get your own damn tankards!" she snapped. "Can't you see I'm busy?"

Dram blinked in surprise then looked at Rogard sheepishly. "That's what I get for marrying a hill dwarf," he admitted with a pang in his heart, making a joke of it even as he watched her stomp back to the stream.

"Let's have a drink when I bring the steel down," Rogard said diplomatically, rising to his feet. "I'd better get moving. Tomorrow morning it is!"

✥❖✥❖✥❖✥❖✥❖✥❖✥❖✥

The steeple of the temple, a shrine dedicated to Kiri-Jolith, gave them a chance to look over much of the western half of the city. They could see violent skirmishes raging in the street below as a line of knights stood behind a makeshift barricade of wagons and upturned tables removed from a nearby inn. The men were armed with swords and shields and fought valiantly against a press of goblins that had surged up against the obstacle.

Howling and jeering, the attackers pressed between the planks, crawled under the wagons, and thrust spears and swords at the knights. But the men gave better than they got, cutting down the few gobs who pushed through the barricade, chopping at the hands and heads of those enemy warriors thronging on the other side. Their discipline was admirable and for the time being, that particular group of attackers was stymied.

Things were worse down the adjacent street, they could see, where a platoon of ogres lumbered toward the palace, chasing the last survivors of a collapsed position. One knight, on foot, stood in the path of the attackers. He cut down the first ogre with a lightning-quick slash of his two-handed sword, and crippled two more with swift stabs at their legs. Even as the brutes tumbled, bellowing in agony, he was borne down by a trio of the hulking warriors, each smashing him with a crude axe until the remains were bloody.

Before the ogres could regroup, however, three mounted knights charged in from a side street. They rode in a line abreast, blocking any further advance. The horses kicked out, driving several ogres back, and the knights bore home their attack, holding their tenuous position and slowly pushing the ogres away from the palace.

"There!" cried Sir Maxwell, examining his magical compass. "Look to the north, past the armory!"

The elemental king came into view a few blocks away, striding out from behind the tall, square fortress. The giant reached out to smash down a three-story stone building, crushing the roof with a hammer blow, then pummeling the rest of the sturdy structure into rubble. Flames surged from its eyes, and immediately the interior of the broken building erupted into a conflagration. Black smoke billowed skyward, forming another of the pyres that already burned in a dozen places around the city. Stepping through the inferno, the elemental king crossed to the next block and began smashing a warehouse.

"Ankhar won't be very far away, if the kender's report is accurate," Jaymes noted.

"It is!" protested Moptop.

"There's the half-giant!" Brianna said, pointing toward the Duke's Avenue, the wide street where goblins were hurling themselves against the barricade.

Now they could clearly see Ankhar swaggering along, several hundred yards behind the skirmishing. He was accompanied by several humans in black armor—former Dark Knights—as well as by the gray-robed Thorn Knight and the huddled, decrepit figure of the old witch-doctor. They were several blocks away from the temple, in a section of the city where all the human defenders had apparently been slain or driven out.

With his fists planted on his hips, the half-giant commander looked first toward the line of battle and the palace. Then his head quickly swiveled to the north. "He's searching for the elemental," Brianna guessed. The other men murmured agreement.

As they watched, the conjured creature left the wreckage of the burning building and once again passed behind the armory, heading toward the northwest. It was backtracking through its path of destruction, entering another quarter, a long block of tall buildings housing formerly prosperous mercantile shops. One sinuous limb tore through the front of a weaver's store and cast a rainbow array of colored woolen fabrics into the air.

Ankhar and his party started after the creature, but they halted as the half-giant indicated a large, undamaged inn on a corner of the Duke's Avenue. The watchers on the temple spire observed the bodyguards enter the stone-walled building, which was dominated by a thirty-foot tower at one corner. A moment later one of the men emerged and gestured, and the half-giant, with his wizard and shaman, followed them inside.

"Looks like he's going to set up a temporary headquarters," Jaymes said. He touched Moptop's shoulder. "Do you think you can find a way over there through the sewers?"

"Sure! I can find my way anywhere; that's why I'm called a pathfinder. We can go down through that grate that's right over there in front of the temple. And we'll have to find a place to come up over by that inn, but it shouldn't be difficult. Just got to consult my maps," he said, reaching into one of his pouches as one of the Solamnics could be heard to sigh deeply.

"Some of the grates are settled so firmly they can't be removed," Brianna cautioned.

Jaymes raised a hand to the hilt of his sword. "I can cut through steel, if need be," he assured her.

"Good luck," she said, placing a hand on his arm, squeezing him with surprising force. "And be careful."

"You too," he said, placing his own hand over hers then quickly breaking from her clasp, grabbing the kender by the shoulder, and pushing him into action.

The three Sword Knights, the Kingfisher, Moptop, and Jaymes quickly descended to the street level. Passing out through the front doors of the temple, they found the temple grate in an alley just to the side of the building. Two of the knights lifted off the heavy iron grid, exposing a shaft descending into the darkness. Rusty iron brackets set in the wall of the shaft held a ladder that looked to have been installed before the Cataclysm.

"This will do," Jaymes said, the first to sit on the edge of the hole and drop his feet toward the first rung.

"Can't I lead the way?" the kender complained plaintively, plopping down to sit beside the lord marshal. "I'm the pathfinder, remember?"

"I'll go first," Jaymes interjected, winking at the others. "The pathfinder must be protected. When we get below safely, you can advise me which way to go."

With a shrug, the kender moved his legs to the side and allowed the lord marshal to precede him into the darkness. He came swiftly behind, however, followed by Sir Maxwell and the three Knights of the Sword. The kender, as usual, had a supply of small torches and passed a pair of them to two of the knights. They were ignited by the touch of one of his matches, and when held aloft produced enough illumination to tolerably light the way. Sir Maxwell, meanwhile, cast a light spell on the blade of his dagger, and held the weapon before him to add its cool, milky illumination to their mission.

Jaymes went in the lead, holding one of his small crossbows cocked and ready. Sir Maxwell, with his lit blade, advanced beside him, followed by the kender and the other knights. The passage was roughly cylindrical, with an arched ceiling and walls, though the floor was solid and flat. Muddy puddles of water reflected the torchlight, but they were able to step around these and for the most part, keep dry.

Moptop pulled out a long sheet of parchment and scrutinized it under the torchlight. "Now, we follow this until it ends up ahead, and then we take a left," the kender said.

"I hope you know what you're doing," grumbled Sir Michael, holding the torch high with his left hand while his right rested on the hilt of his sword.

"I can attest that he has a way of finding paths," Jaymes said quietly.

They advanced in silence for perhaps a hundred paces to discover that, true to Moptop's prediction, the tunnel did end in a T-intersection. They took the left branch and continued for a similar distance, past several small tunnels shooting off in different directions. When they came to a larger juncture, with three full-size passages leading away, the kender silently pointed them to the right, and they continued on for a short distance.

Moptop gestured to Sir Michael, and the knight lowered the torch for the kender to squint at his parchment again. Looking over the pathfinder's shoulder, the knight shook his head in dismay as he saw the tangled patchwork of charcoal marks. But he bit his tongue, as Moptop curled up his parchment and tucked it back into his pouch.

"Right this way," he said in an exaggerated whisper. "Now is when we should start looking for a way up and out of here."

They found a way up in only another fifteen paces, tucked in a small alcove to the side of the tunnel, where a series of rusty rungs similar to the ones they descended led toward a metal grate overhead. No sunlight illuminated this grid, so Jaymes guessed they were either under a building or a roof's overhang or perhaps in a narrow alley. Any of the three boded well for a surreptitious exit.

The lord marshal gathered the members of the little party at the base of the ladder, speaking quietly and quickly.

"Remember, the Thorn Knight first," he said. "The giant and the witch-doctor are dangerous, but it's the magic-user who is likely the chief link to the elemental. After we take him down, make for Ankhar and the shaman. All set?"

"I'm ready," Sir Maxwell said. Most of the color had drained from his young face.

"Let's go," Sir Michael said, nodding curtly. "We're all ready."

Jaymes led the way, still holding one small crossbow while using his free hand to climb the ladder. He moved as stealthily as possible as he ascended, peering through the bars of the sewer grate, trying to get some idea of where they were going to come out above. By the time he was at the top of the ladder, he could see two walls with exterior surfaces of sooty stone, which seemed to indicate that they would be within a narrow alley. There was a thin line of smoky sky visible between two roofs that nearly overlapped each other, casting the whole area in welcoming shadows.

The grate was not so welcoming, however. Jaymes shoved at it with one hand, but it wouldn't budge. Reluctantly uncocking his crossbow and slinging it at his belt, he put both hands against the rusty bars and braced his feet on a ladder rung. He pressed with all his strength, gritting his teeth, sweat beading around his eyes, but the grate was stuck fast.

Putting his face right up to the bars, he peered to the right and left. He saw barrels stacked nearby, apparently blocking off one end of the alley. The other end opened onto a wide avenue, and as he watched, a pair of ogres lumbered past. They paid no attention to the alley, but the grate was only a couple of dozen feet away from the street.

He turned around and dropped a few rungs, nearly stepping on Moptop's fingers before turning to whisper to the kender. "Which building do you think is the inn where Ankhar went?"

"Well, let's see. . . ." The kender pulled out his scroll of parchment, allowing it to unroll downward until it dangled past his feet, swinging past the nose of the knight behind him. He looked up through the grate then back at the sheet. Finally he nodded. "That one over there—it has to be that one," he said, indicating the structure to the right side of the narrow alley.

"Fair enough," Jaymes said, trying to mute his skepticism. "We're going to have to move fast," he informed them all. "I'm going to cut through the grate with my sword, which might attract some attention. So get ready. Everybody up and out in half a breath."

"Lead on," Sir Michael said. "We'll be right behind you."

At the top of the ladder again, Jaymes cocked both crossbows and slung them at the ready. Then he twisted sideways so he could draw Giantsmiter out of its long scabbard. Balancing on his feet, with one knee propped around the back of a rusty rung, he slowly extended the tip of the sword between the bars of the sewer grate.

When he twisted the hilt in his hands, flames appeared along the steel edge, soundlessly flaring, bright blue in the shadows of the sewer shaft. He touched the blade to one rusty bar, producing a noise like the hiss of water spattering in a hot pan; the weapon quickly cut through the bar and came to the next with another loud, sibilant noise. Sparks and bits of molten metal spattered downward, some of them singeing his arms.

He ignored the pain and kept up the pressure with the sword. In a moment he had cut through all the bars at one end. Swiftly he repeated the process on the other three sides. Slicing through all but one of the metal rods, he lowered his sword and with one hand, bent down the almost-severed grate to open up a clear route to the alley.

With a glance down, confirming that his companions were poised for action, he pulled himself upward and out, quickly scrambling into a crouching position on the rough cobblestones of the alley. His eyes fixed upon the open end of the narrow passage. Fortunately, all he saw was a deserted section of the Duke's Avenue. He slipped his sword back into its scabbard and took up his twin crossbows, one in each hand.

By then Moptop and the Kingfisher had emerged, with the three Knights of the Sword coming after. Maxwell looked almost boyish in his bright tunic and leather leggings. He held his dagger at the ready while offering a hand to Sir Michael, the last of the knights to emerge.

"There's a doorway over here . . . looks like a kitchen door to the inn," Moptop said, striding over to a rickety wooden barrier. The smell of lard seemed to confirm his diagnosis.

"Keep an eye on the entrance to the alley," Jaymes ordered one of the knights. "We'll be going back down that hole in a moment."

He led the others to the kitchen door and tried the latch, finding it locked. Shrugging, he dropped his shoulder and plunged forward, breaking easily through the flimsy planking. Lunging into the empty room, he saw another door past the long cooking counter and huge iron oven. He advanced through the kitchen at a run, but the door to the main room flew open before he got there.

Jaymes found himself almost on top of one of the Dark Knight bodyguards who had accompanied Ankhar down the street. The man was clearly shocked to see an intruder in the kitchen, and he reached for his sword with lightning reflexes.

Jaymes raised one of his crossbows and shot, the powerful weapon punching the lethal bolt into the man's throat just above the rim of his breastplate.

Gagging, the knight fell back, and the lord marshal charged into the inn's great room. He spotted the half-giant at once; Ankhar was standing near the front window, where he had apparently been watching his troops pass by in the street. He spun around, mouth gaping in a tusk-baring expression of astonishment. The little hob-wench was there as well and reacted quickly, shrieking in agitation and shaking her grotesque totem at the intruders. But where was the Thorn Knight?

Jaymes caught sight of the Gray Robe on the far side of the room. The man moved with liquid grace, gliding behind a stout pillar as if he knew that he was the target of this sudden intrusion. Other Dark Knights, more of Ankhar's bodyguards, closed in, but Jaymes dashed across the room, while Sir Michael and the other knight met the guards with their steel. The lord marshal rounded the pillar and confronted the Gray Robe.

The Thorn Knight's eyes met his. The magic-user was working on some kind of spell, murmuring an arcane word, gesturing with the slender fingers of his right hand while he waved a slender stick of wood in his left.

The lord marshal started to raise his crossbow, but the mage, without hesitation, charged right toward him—and away from him at the same time. Jaymes swung a fist at the Gray Robe, and his hand passed right through the image, causing it to disappear. Suddenly there were four identical wizards, all running from behind the pillar, each going in a different direction. The lord marshal swung the weapon, with its single remaining shot, from one of the images to the next, unsure which was the real Thorn Knight.

Moptop sprinted past and flew at one of the gray-robed figures, stretching his arms wide in an attempted tackle. The kender flew right through the magical image and landed hard on his nose. At the same time, the conjured reflection of the wizard vanished from sight. But that still left three possible targets, one racing toward the front door, and two diverging into opposite ends of the great room.

Meanwhile, Ankhar had recovered his wits and entered the fray. He pulled a sword from his belt that, while it was styled like a short sword for the half-giant, boasted a blade every bit as long as Giantsmiter's.

Making a guess, Jaymes started after the Gray Robe who was heading for the door. He raised his crossbow, ready to shoot the man in the back. He barely noticed the Kingfisher, frantically chanting something and waving his hands around the room.

"There!" cried Sir Maxwell as the image in front of Jaymes disappeared.

The lord marshal spun around. The image of the Thorn Knight heading toward the back of the inn was also gone; only the one to the side of the room remained, his robe sweeping behind him as he leaped for the stairs leading to the second floor. Lunging after him, Jaymes slammed into genuine flesh, knocking the Gray Robe down.

The wizard fell into the railing, slumping backward. His lips curled into a snarl and his hands—one holding the wand, the other empty—gestured before his face.

But he wouldn't have time to finish the casting.

Jaymes had raised the crossbow and now shot his bolt right into the man's chest. The force of the strike hurled him backward, but the lord marshal was already on him as he fell. He saw the wand falling from the mage's limp fingers and dived to snatch it up. He felt it snap between his strong hand and the floor before it rolled under a nearby crate.

"He destroyed the wand!" shrieked the shaman, her tone horrified.

"No!" Ankhar bellowed.

Jaymes could see that the Thorn Knight was badly, perhaps fatally, wounded. The half giant's bellow, every bit as panicked as his mother's cry, echoed in the room. More of Ankhar's troops charged toward the front door, a press of reinforcements.

Clearly, the outnumbered attackers needed to withdraw. "We've accomplished what we wanted!" he cried, now pulling Giantsmiter from its sheath at his back. He rushed toward Sir Michael, who stood alone against a pair of Ankhar's bodyguards. Moptop, his nose bleeding, ran along beside him, leaping over the body of the slain Sword Knight who had stood at Michael's side when they entered the room.

"Where's Maxwell?" demanded Jaymes, holding his great sword with one hand and spinning on his heel.

But Ankhar had closed in on the young Kingfisher. With one great hand, he gripped the young wizard around the throat and lifted him from the floor. Maxwell's feet kicked and his arms thrashed, but he could do nothing against the hulking brute. With a deep, wet snarl, the half-giant tightened his fingers around the man's neck.

Sir Michael cut down the last of the Dark Knights with a thrust to the gut, and joined Jaymes as both turned to rush toward the enemy commander. The hobgoblin shaman shrieked something, and both warriors halted abruptly as if they had crashed against an invisible fence. The lord marshal swung his flaming sword at the barrier and felt it wavering as Maxwell's face turned blue, his flailing limbs suddenly drooping limply.

Moptop sprang across the room, jumping right at the sha-man's head. He wrapped his arms around her face, and the two of them stumbled crazily toward a large stone fireplace—the hearth, fortunately, cold. Their shouts and screams mingled chaotically as they tumbled onto the granite shelf, the kender on top of the old witch-doctor. With a shout of triumph, the kender broke free of the shaman's violent embrace.

At the same time, the door to the street burst open and a troop of ogres charged in. "Kill them!" shrieked the witch-doctor, pointing with her skull's-head rattle, and the brutes charged en masse toward the two swordsmen and the kender.

Maxwell made one last desperate gesture—a wave of his hand toward Jaymes. His mouth worked, and though no sound emerged, he clearly signaled: "Go!"

More ogres spilled through the door. The hob-wench shrieked her "Kill!" command over and over.

"You've got to flee," Michael said to Jaymes, as they edged back from the approaching ogres.

"You too," commanded the lord marshal, taking the other man by the shoulder and pulling him back. "There's nothing more we can do."

Grimacing in fury and grief, the Sword Knight acknowledged this truth. Moptop was already out the door, and they turned and followed him into the kitchen, stopping only to pull a heavy ice chest down to block their escape.

In the alley they saw that the last Sword Knight had taken up position near the street, where he stood matching swords with a burly ogre, giving ground slowly. Arrows zinged around them as some of Ankhar's archers, responding to the alarms, shot wildly into the alley. The knight groaned and fell, bleeding from a gash through his chest, but before the ogre could advance, Sir Michael charged to replace the fallen man.

"Get away from here!" the swordsman shouted over his shoulder before cutting down the ogre with a single stab. More of the brutish warriors filled the mouth of the alley.

"Go!" Michael cried before meeting the next ogre with a resounding parry. *"Est Sularus oth Mithas!"* he shouted, the ecstasy of honorable battle radiant in his voice.

Jaymes shoved Moptop toward the gaping sewer hole. With a yelp, the kender ducked out of sight, and the lord marshal tumbled after. They ran into the darkness, chased by the sounds of ringing steel from the lone knight's valiant holding action.

After no more than ten breaths, the sounds of battle suddenly ceased, but soon they were around the first corner, sprinting away through the sewers of Solanthus.

CHAPTER NINETEEN

UNLEASHED

"What happened?" Ankhar roared, seizing the chief of his bodyguard detail and shaking him by the shoulder until the man's neck broke with an audible snap. The half-giant cast the suddenly limp body aside, glaring down at his stepmother. "What happened?" he repeated, his voice, if anything, louder and angrier.

Yet Laka didn't even spare him a glance. She was busy pressing her hand to the bleeding wound on Hoarst's chest, muttering some prayer to the Prince of Lies. Abruptly, as the half-giant stared, she plucked out the bloody bolt and tossed it aside. She hoisted her death's-head talisman, held it over the Thorn Knight's pallid face, and shook it wildly. The pebbles in the skull rattled and the green stones in the eyes glowed, visible even in the daylight. Finally the hobgoblin dropped the device so the fleshless mouth of the skull met the cold, blue lips of the dying man.

Hoarst gave a hideous shriek. The green light flashed again, so brightly this time that Ankhar was forced to blink. In spite of himself, he leaned closer, watching the bleeding Thorn Knight with narrowed eyes.

Hoarst gasped and coughed, choking violently. Laka turned him onto his side, and he vomited blood onto the inn's smooth floorboards, convulsing with pain and finally curling into a ball and drawing ragged, retching breaths. The wizard's eyes were shut, his hands curled into fists and clutched against his chest, as he shivered like one in the depths of Nordmaar fever.

"Almost dead," Laka said, standing and fixing the army commander with a sharp-toothed grin. "But not quite."

"The wand!" spluttered the half-giant. "Can't you use it?"

Laka shrugged. "Dunno," she replied with a lot less concern than the army commander expected to see.

"What will we do without it?" he growled.

"You take it," she replied, handing him the slender pieces of wood she plucked from under the crate. He looked at the things, like a broken toothpick in his massive hand, and suppressed the urge to throw them to the floor. They looked so tiny, so insignificant, he couldn't believe it would make any difference if he waved them at the elemental king and tried to give it orders.

Laka dusted off the ashes that covered her all over from her tumble into the hearth. She patted her belt purse and shook her head grimly as she glared upward at her stepson.

"Wand's not the worst of it." Laka pulled a small, ruby-encrusted object from her pouch, and showed it to Ankhar. The lid of the little box had broken loose and lay separately in her weathered hand. Several of the stones were loose—tiny chips of crimson flecking her brown, parchment-like skin.

"We have no box to hold the giant when it comes for us." She made the announcement as if she were reporting a shortage of butter to spread on the army commander's ration of bread.

Ankhar looked askance at the broken box. Its magic was gone, the half-giant realized. The wand was of little use even if it were in one piece. The elemental king could no longer be imprisoned in the magic box. The thought of that horrific being stomping toward him, free of its prison and out of control, suddenly struck home. It was a very unsettling thought, indeed.

"It will come soon, won't it? And it will be seeking us—you, and me, and the Gray Robe?"

Laka snorted. "What do you think?"

Ankhar threw back his head and roared with exasperation. He beat a mighty fist against his chest then struggled to think, to regain command of, first, his own emotions, then his army, then this battle.

"Yes, I understand. The wizard who held the king at bay is wounded and possibly dying, and the box that we have held him in is broken." He growled, turning his back and stomping angrily across the inn's hall. He spun again and pointed a thick finger at his stepmother and the still-huddled form of the Thorn Knight.

"There is only one thing to do: fix it!" he roared. "Before it kills us all!"

⟨⊶⊙⊶⊙⊶⊙⊶❀⊶⊙⊶⊙⊶⊙⊶⟩

Jaymes and Moptop, a little muddy and wet from their trek through the sewers, raced into the Temple of Kiri-Jolith, where the duchess agreed to wait for them. They found her and her captains in a side vestibule, examining a map of the city that was spread over a desk.

"You're back!" Brianna cried, rushing to embrace the lord marshal. "How did you fare?"

He shrugged. "Not well. We managed to attack the wizard. He is badly injured, possibly slain, but a company of ogres charged in before we could do any more damage. We were driven back."

267

"But at least you foiled the wizard!" cried the duchess, seizing at the straw. "If he can't help the enemy any more, that's got to be good for us."

"It came at no small cost," the lord marshal admitted. "Four brave knights fell in the course of our escape." Jaymes turned to Lord Martin. "Your son's courage was pivotal to our attack . . . but I am sorry to tell you that he paid for that courage with his life."

The lord's face drained of color. He staggered almost imperceptibly. Then he stood straight, forcing the words out through his clenched jaw. "The Kingfishers hold to the same creed as the other orders: *Est Sularus oth Mithas*. I am grateful his death was not in vain."

"By all that's holy—did you just leave the dead behind? The bodies of those brave men?" demanded Lord Harbor. He faced Jaymes across the table. "Do you mean to say you just fled for your own safety? That you didn't make the wretches pay?"

"Don't talk nonsense!" snapped Brianna.

"But the honor of the knighthood—the tradition! An honorable knight does not leave his comrades' bodies in the hands of the enemy!"

"Such traditions must give way to dire necessity," the duchess said.

"Your Grace," said the lord, drawing himself up stiffly. "If it has come to the point where my advice is no longer req—"

"I require your *good* advice, my lord!" she declared. "And I shall continue to expect it. But right now we must address the emergencies at hand!"

"I intend to make the enemy pay dearly," Jaymes told the lord. "I will not forget the sacrifice of good men. But we must persist with our plan. We can't stop the elemental king, but now is our chance to strike at the army that flanks his advance."

Lord Martin cleared his throat. "The elemental has gained ground rapidly—faster than his support troops can follow," he noted. His pallor remained ashen, but his voice was firm and purposeful. "You are right; we might be able to come at them from behind and from the sides, hit them hard, while the monster is elsewhere."

"Where is the giant now?" Jaymes asked.

"It began to demolish the armory shortly after you descended into the tunnel. It has been smashing away on the walls and towers there—almost in a frenzy. It's not far from here," Brianna explained.

"I remember where the armory is," Jaymes said. "I should head there directly and have a look. If possible, I can harass and delay the creature. How many troops do you have in nearby positions?"

"Several companies have fallen back from the gate," Martin informed him. "One or more can go with you."

"Good. Get the rest of the garrison into a position for an all-out attack on the ogres and goblins."

"We'll have them ready as soon as we can," said the duchess, her cheeks flushing. "There's no time to waste." She touched his beard with her small hand, looking up at him with shining eyes. "You . . . take care. May the gods watch over you."

"All is not lost," he replied. "Keep your faith, but be ready for anything."

"Farewell, my Lord Marshal," she said, pulling her hand away with visible reluctance.

With a final wave, the lord marshal and his professional guide and pathfinder extraordinaire dashed out the door and into the smoky streets of Solanthus. Lord Martin had preceded them and was waiting with nearly a hundred swordsmen and archers in two units. Raising shields and blades, the swordsmen swung behind Jaymes and the kender, while the archers hoisted their full quivers and trotted along, bringing up the rear.

⊱⋅⋄⋅⋄⋅⋄⋅⋄⋅❀⋅⋄⋅⋄⋅⋄⋅⋄⋅⊰

The monster loomed over the wreckage of a military barracks, standing amidst the shattered stone walls. Winds whirled around its cyclone legs, raising a thick, noxious cloud of dust and casting medium-sized rocks through the air. These missiles flew randomly in all directions, crashing and skidding along the ground wherever they landed, adding to the chaos and destruction as they smashed through the wooden walls of nearby buildings.

Flames flickered around the lofty visage of its craggy face, and for a moment the monster paused, as if surveying its accomplishments thus far. The armory, once a small but sturdy castle, had been reduced to mounds of broken stone. Here and there were bonfires where the monster had aimed its fiery gaze, but the remnants of the stony structure lacked much in the way of combustibles, so there were no major conflagrations, just small blazes, smoldering piles of charred logs, and pyres of black smoke.

Jaymes and Moptop had spotted the elemental king as soon as they emerged from the temple. They cut down a side street, moving north for a couple of blocks then circling around through a narrow alley and entering the yard of a nearby stable. Lord Martin and his makeshift company trailed close behind. Now they all watched the conjured monster from behind a broken doorway and the shattered walls of the building across the street.

"What now?" asked the kender in a small voice, looking skeptically at the monster. "I hope it doesn't notice us. It's not like we can do much to stop it, can we?"

270

"I'm not at all sure what we're going to do," replied the man—a remark that caused his companion to blink in surprise or perhaps consternation. For once, however, the loquacious kender seemed at a lack for words; he merely nodded sagely.

The elemental king had wrecked much of the west side of Solanthus. Now, with the armory and adjacent barracks utterly demolished, it was faced with a choice. To the north sprawled vast neighborhoods of houses and apartments, while a turn east would take it toward the ducal palace and the heart of the Solanthian metropolis.

After a moment's respite, the hulking creature took a step through the wreckage, striding toward the stable where the lord marshal and kender crouched in concealment. But they were beneath notice and hadn't been spotted. One of its massive, swinging legs kicked through the remnant of the armory wall, coming to rest in the street. Dust billowed out and up with each step, and the smoke thickened in the force of the swirling winds. The monster took another step, and another, and soon moved away down the avenue.

"This way," Jaymes said, leading Martin and the fighting men to the west, away from the elemental, keeping the shattered wall between themselves and the hulking monster.

In moments they reached a cross street. To the right, a small company of ogres were lumbering along in the wake of the elemental. In the opposite direction, they saw the brown, shaggy figures of a dozen warg wolves, each ridden by a goblin. The unruly, snarling beasts were poking through the ruins of a house, while their riders jabbered and shrieked.

"Here's as good a chance as any," Jaymes said to the lord. "Have your archers concentrate on those wolves. I'll lead a group of swordsmen against the ogres."

"Very good," Martin replied. The bowmen, each with a sturdy longbow, nocked arrows to their strings. The soldiers with swords and shields took up their positions.

"Now!" Jaymes declared, drawing Giantsmiter and charging into the street with the swordsmen following.

Immediately the ogres barked and hooted, turning and charging the defenders in a mass. In moments the two sides were clashing. In the lead, Jaymes fought like a madman, slashing to the right and left. He dropped two ogres as the enemy clubs and blades smashed into the shields of the Solanthian footmen, and the narrow lane was filled with flailing bodies; slashing weapons; and howling, screaming combatants.

Jaymes swept another ogre off its feet, followed up by a fast stab that penetrated the brute's breastplate, chest, and heart. Breaking from the melee, he glanced over his shoulder to see the archers were firing away, arrows scything into the goblins and wargs, dropping wolves and riders at fifty paces. Within breaths, the whole detachment of cavalry was wiped out, and a moment later the last of the ogres fell, bleeding and dying.

But then, before anyone could rejoice, a huge shape loomed into sight, as the elemental king, with no apparent pattern in its random movements, came lurching back the way it had come. The men found themselves exposed in the street, and looking up, scattered.

The lord marshal froze, expecting the monster to charge and trample them all.

Instead, the gigantic being veered away to the side. Fire flashed from its eyes, and the yawning mouth opened in a surreal growl, like the moaning of a powerful wind through a desolate wood—only a hundred times as loud.

"What's it doing?" asked Martin, who ran up besides Jaymes.

"I don't know. It's as though it's been distracted," the lord marshal replied.

"Look!" cried one of the swordsmen. "The kender!"

They saw him then, standing on top of the roof of one of the few intact buildings down the street. Moptop was jeering and hooting imaginative insults, waving his arms and shouting in his high-pitched voice at the elemental king. The monster turned its immense face toward the diminutive kender, as though disbelieving. It roared and shivered.

"What makes you think you're so tough?" Moptop yodeled. "I've lit *matches* that made more fire than you! You're probably scared of little old me! Well, aren't you?"

The elemental roared again, the sound pounding against their eardrums like a hurricane wind. The creature stood in place, limbs gesticulating madly, fire blossoming from its cave-like eye sockets. The gargantuan figure twisted and flailed in obvious torment. Moptop vanished from sight as the creature took a hunkering step toward him. Once more the monster halted, roaring and bellowing; then his tormentor was back in view.

The kender had climbed up a cone-shaped pile of broken rock, scrambling over large sections of wall, pulling himself up the steep summit with one hand. At the top, he braced his feet on a pair of flat stones, stood up to his full height, and brandished his fist, pointing straight at the monstrous creature.

"I'm warning you, big ugly. Get out of here, you!" Moptop screamed, hopping up and down on the rock. "You stupid fire-face! This is your last chance to run!" He clenched both fists, shaking them in the air, and whooped and shrieked in triumph and glee. "You're nothing but a big, overgrown thunderclap— that's what you are!"

The elemental roared again, even louder than before, anguished by—as Moptop would claim for the rest of his life—the incredible humiliation resulting from the kender's taunts. The mighty creature took a step forward then another. It lumbered closer, kicking through a row of shattered houses. Violent winds gusted in its wake, and raindrops splashed all over the street, only to be instantly dried by the swirling gale.

Jaymes spotted a ladder nearby, leaning against the balcony of a two-story building. Quickly he scrambled up the rungs and onto the overhanging perch. He pushed through the door, raced down a narrow hallway, and found a stairway leading to the roof. Scrambling up, he emerged several buildings away from Moptop, but with a view of all the city.

From his high vantage, Jaymes could see a whole regiment of ogres advancing in formation down the Duke's Avenue. He could see that Moptop was still busy hollering taunts, though the lord marshal was too far away to fathom his words. Nor was it clear that the elemental king understood. But the important thing was that the monster remained focused on the diminutive taunter as it strode right into the midst of the ogre battalion.

The brutish warriors noticed too late that the monster was upon them, and they began to flee, but they couldn't get out of the way in time. Those whirlwind legs swept through the regiment, tossing dozens of ogres through the air as if they were milkweed puffballs or dandelion seeds. A few ogres tossed spears or hurled axes at their supposed ally, but these weapons had no more effect than had the blades of the city's defenders.

Not content with that initial and apparently accidental massacre, however, the elemental bent down to swipe at other ogres with its crushing arms, bashing them to the ground or sweeping them up against the walls that stood on either side of the street. Dozens of brutal, strapping warriors were squashed like bugs. Huge columns of flames erupted from the elemental's eyes, immolating other screaming ogres with infernal heat.

Jaymes looked down into the street and spotted Lord Martin.

"Get back to the duchess!" he yelled. "Tell her that the creature is moving away from here. Now's the time to attack Ankhar's warriors, while they are thoroughly disorganized!"

"I'm off!" replied the nobleman. "Good luck to you!"

Lord Martin raced away at a sprint, while the archers in the streets took shelter and directed a volley of fire at another group of Ankhar's infantry, painted goblins who had appeared in the nearby street and were moving toward the ducal palace. The attackers took shelter behind barrels and in the shells of buildings to avoid the lethal arrows.

The king roared again, exulting as he thrashed around violently. Only when all the ogres had been slain, knocked senseless, or driven away did the elemental pause. Remembering, it looked back, fiery eyes seeking the kender, who was no longer in view. Jaymes leaped from his rooftop perch onto a lower building then dropped to the ground. Once more he held the great sword high, waving it over his head as he gathered the swordsmen around him, the whole company starting forward at a trot.

Then the monster changed direction again, moving away from the site of its orgiastic violence, lumbering toward the plazas, the gap in the city wall, and the teeming army of Ankhar the Truth, the vast bulk of which was still gathered on the plains.

⊱⋅☽☀☾⋅⊰

The elemental king, a being of pure power and energy, did not have thoughts, plans, or ideas in the manner of men and other sentient, intelligent creatures. Rather, it was driven by mysterious instincts, lusts, and furies whose urges were primal, fundamental.

Now those instincts carried the creature toward those who had enslaved it, had stolen it from the realm—however hellish—that had been its lair, its kingdom, its home.

It roared and spumed like a terrible force of nature, leaving only death and destruction in its wake. Where there had been buildings, now there was only rubble. Stone walls toppled, everything made of wood burned. But the elemental king took no note of the damage, the havoc. Its fiery eyes scanned ahead, seeking its intended target.

Seeking the one who had enslaved it.

⚜

"It's moving away, Your Grace! I can't believe it, but the kender has succeeded in taunting the beast and drawing it away from the center of the city!" declared Lord Martin.

Brianna could make no reply, perhaps because the swell of her emotions so tightened her throat that she didn't trust herself to utter any words of hope. But the evidence was clear in the violent spectacle before her eyes: the fire elemental, for some reason, had turned upon its former allies, the savage warriors of Ankhar the Truth.

After decimating a whole regiment of ogre soldiers, the fiery monster had proceeded to rip the ranks of goblin archers who had been assembling on the West Gate plaza. Then the creature had turned to slice through the whole line of enemy bowmen, casting hundreds of them through the air with the gale-force winds of its cyclonic legs. Storms of lashing water gushed from the liquid arms, sweeping away entire companies, drowning those goblins too small or stunned to pull themselves free from the torrent.

The duchess looked around her. The garrison had assembled more than two hundred Knights of the Sword, all armored, mounted, and bearing heavy lances. She had ordered them to gather in the courtyard before the palace. Summoned to the ducal banner—the sigil of the Sword—they had ridden here at once and awaited her orders.

The road was wide enough for some forty riders to charge abreast, so the mounted knights had formed six lines. Nearby stood hundreds of other troops, including swordsmen and axers, companies of militia bearing spears and shields, and several companies of longbowmen. The last-named had been armed with all of the feathered missiles remaining in the city arsenal. All the defenders were eager to avenge the terrible damage that had been inflicted on their city, and their comrades, in the previous days.

After months of siege and days of disaster, they were ready to strike back. To a man, these warriors understood that the coming battle must result in victory, or the city that they loved, that had sheltered their families and property, would be forever lost.

"But, Your Grace," Harbor continued, lowering his voice and leaning closer to the slender young woman who had not yet spoken. "Surely you don't need to lead the charge. Let my veteran knights take that responsibility, while you inspire us from the rear."

"My lord," she said, her stern tone softened by the warmth in her eyes. "I have watched too much of this battle—and this war—from the window of my lofty tower. Now I must lead, and I will wield my own steel in my city's defense."

Harbor tried to plead his case further until he realized with chagrin that the duchess was staring off without listening. He settled for quietly admonishing the nearby knights to look out for Brianna, on pain of their honor and their lives.

She sat high in the saddle of her black mare. Her copper-colored hair was unbound, trailing across her shoulders; Brianna

DOUGLAS NILES

had disdained a helmet because she decided it was important that she be seen and recognized. A small shield was strapped to her left arm, and a slender-bladed sword—more of a rapier—nestled in a scabbard at her belt.

Now the duchess drew that blade with a flourish and held it over her head. Her mare shivered restlessly, and she heard the snorting and stomping of the other horses as they, too, stirred under their riders now on alert, feeling the imminence of battle.

"Warriors of Solanthus!" she cried, her voice clear and strong. "Today is the day we reclaim our city! Follow your captains! The time has come! Acquit your honor!"

She pressed her knees together, and the big horse started forward, the knights abreast to either side of her advancing slowly at first, down the Duke's Avenue. Brianna rode in the middle of the front rank, between a pair of large Sword Knights, who flanked her protectively. She didn't glance at them or behind her, but rode easily for a short distance before kicking her mare and increasing to a trot. The ranks of knights kept pace.

They came to the place in the avenue where scores of ogres lay dead, many of them mangled or crushed by the elemental king. Again Brianna spurred her mount and the mare broke into a canter with the rest of the line sweeping forward to match her speed. Surging now, the men and horses thundered toward the enemy. The columns of Solanthian infantry ran hard to keep as close as possible to the mounted knights.

But the galloping horses pulled ahead. The wind blew Brianna's coppery hair back in a shimmering plume. The noise of the pounding hooves echoed and reverberated from the surrounding buildings. Dust billowed, smoke swirled, and the noise swelled.

Brianna felt a thrill she had never known before, a sense of fate and inevitability, as if all the experiences she had undergone in her life, all of her choices—including her marriage to the duke who had proved a scoundrel—had conspired to lead her to this, the realization of her destiny.

The first rank of knights drew close to the great plaza, where thousands of Ankhar's troops had collected. These goblins and hobs, ogres and humans—including many who had recently witnessed and survived the rampage of the giant elemental—were in disorder. Units were scattered; captains tried to reassemble their troops.

And none had been posted as sentries to watch the approaches.

The smoke swirled across the avenue, parting enough for some weary goblins to catch a glimpse of the approaching army. They shrieked a warning and turned to run. Others of Ankhar's troops looked up, hastily raising arms, trying to discern the cause of the alarm. But none of the enemy units was formed or prepared to receive the charge of armored knights bearing lances.

Brianna felt a surge of transcendent emotion as the riders burst into the plaza. She had never killed in battle before, but now she felt an almost frantic urge to skewer the flesh of an enemy with her steel. A dozen goblins were scrabbling on their hands and knees right before her. They scrambled to get out of the way, but every one was pierced by a knight's lance or crushed under the hooves of a charger before they could flee.

The attacking knights spread out, the first rank riding ahead. Brianna's blade finally drank deep of blood as she slashed a burly shoulder—but the momentum of her racing horse drove the blade so deep the weapon was almost pulled from her hand.

The city's infantry spilled into the plaza. They attacked with swords and axes, pikes and spears, and they exploded from all the smaller streets and alleys connecting the plaza to the rest of the city. Trumpets blared, blown by heralds on their light, fleet horses.

The lofty giant, its head still surrounded with oily smoke from its flaming eyes, was busy stalking across the plain outside the city. With vengeful purpose, it tore through the trenches and approach routes the ogres had so carefully excavated in the ruined gatehouse, smashing down great walls of stone, filling the entrenchments with muddy water. Breaking onto the plain, the elemental king reached Ankhar's observation tower and crushed it flat with a single stomp of its massive leg. Its purposeful advance never hesitated, and soon it neared the headquarters camp of the half-giant's army.

Brianna saw Jaymes, equally purposeful amidst the chaos. He had his sword in his hands now. He and the kender fought side by side, hacking and slaying at the head of a company of Solanthian footmen. The lord marshal's eyes met the duchess's, and he raised the weapon in a salute then dropped it to cut down a roaring ogre that the humans had surrounded and trapped.

Fighting raged around other pockets of resistance across the plaza, but there was only sporadic opposition as the Solanthians swiftly cut down every invader who didn't have the sense to turn and retreat. Regardless, many managed to escape, crawling through the chaotic wreckage left in the elemental's wake, scrambling for survival in panic.

Outside the ruined city wall, a few goblins raised their bows and fired volleys of arrows at the citizen army. Their missiles soared overhead and showered down on the plaza, but the volleys were not dense enough to slow the counterattack.

Ankhar's troops were driven from the city, with all semblance of resistance shattered.

That Battle for Solanthus was won.

"Put the damned box together—now!" roared Ankhar. "Remember, old mother, *Est Sudanus oth Nikkas!* My power is my Truth!"

And the Truth, he could see with his own eyes, was that he was going to die very soon if they could not find a way to control the raging, uncontrolled elemental king.

It had burst out of the city, wiping out the tower and breastworks that had been constructed at such effort. Hundreds, perhaps thousands, of Ankhar's warriors had perished in the storm of its passage. The half-giant looked down at the little chip of wood in his hand, Hoarst's wand, which he had lashed together with a leather thong. Surely the wand was useless.

Ankhar wished most fervently that he could become a dormouse or a bat or some other creature that could hide or beat a hasty retreat. But it was not to be, for even now the elemental king advanced toward the half-giant with great, determined strides.

"It is nearly ready," said his stepmother with maddening calmness.

She knelt on the ground, carefully affixing the rubies to the outside of the tiny container. They were not attached with any adhesive; she had popped each stone into her mouth and murmured a prayer to the Prince of Lies as she held it against the flat surface. Each time she removed her hand, the stone stayed in place—until the last, when, simultaneously, four or five of the ruby chits had fallen at once.

Laka scrambled through the dust, trying to pick up the precious gems, while Ankhar growled and paced in agitation. "Hurry!" he barked, but this only caused his stepmother to halt and glare wordlessly up at him. This being the opposite of the effect he was trying to provoke, the half-giant angrily held his tongue, turning his back on the old hob-witch so he was not tempted to strike her the blow she so richly deserved.

The Thorn Knight, Hoarst, lay on the ground where Ankhar had set him down. The wizard's eyes were open, but he was pale. He had not spoken since his wounding in the sudden sneak attack. His gray robe still bore the stain of the blood, now dried, shed when the lord marshal's bolt had pierced his chest. He had borne the wound, and the retreat from the city, without complaint, but now the Gray Robe seemed near death.

Ankhar looked at the mage with faint scorn. He was furious about the surprise attack and blamed the wizard for failing to defend himself and his commander. But something in Hoarst's cold, cruel eyes prevented the half-giant from rebuking him.

The elemental king was moving ever closer. The magical creature had emerged from the rubble of the ruined West Gate, kicking through the mass of goblins there. Troops scattered in every direction, shrieking in terror. Each step taken by the king crushed more of them, while its gusting winds hurled soldier after soldier through the air. Ankhar had ordered a rank of pikemen to form up before his headquarters, hoping to buy time, but the commander could only watch in contempt as the troops dropped their unwieldy weapons and fled long before the conjured creature was upon them.

The giant elemental drew closer and closer, and for the first time in his life, Ankhar felt pure, abject terror. Every fiber of his being urged him to turn and run. With a sneer that bared both of his tusks, he took up his heavy, emerald-tipped spear, and cocked back his arm for one final throw. He would not die without at least a symbolic resistance.

Hoarst spat one word, a noise like a guttural curse, and abruptly disappeared.

Then the elemental king was there, towering overhead. Ankhar cast his spear, and the creature swatted it aside like a pesky gnat. One mighty fist smashed outward, the monster aiming directly at the half-giant. It had clearly singled out Ankhar for death.

"I cannot fix the box!" cackled Laka in frustration. She looked up, her thin lips parted in a sneering grin. "You must help! You must wield the wand!"

Ankhar looked again at the toothpick of wood, pinched between the forefinger and thumb of his right hand. Shaking to his toes, he lifted the little thing and pointed it at the approaching monster.

And, before the killing blow could land, the king of the elementals turned and strode away.

⊱⋅⊰⋅⊱⋅⊰⋅♦⋅⊱⋅⊰⋅⊱⋅⊰

The elemental king felt the repulsion effect of the magic wand as a despised presence that, however intangible, could not be defeated. It flailed and roared but almost immediately redirected its frustration toward other targets it could hate. There were many creatures moving across the plains, thousands of mortals that were not protected by the unseen talisman. A mighty foot kicked through a column of Dark Knights, scattering riders and steeds high into the air. Screaming and thrashing, the doomed creatures tumbled back to earth, their broken bodies strewn, shattered upon the ground.

A group of hobgoblin archers took flight at the monster's approach, and the king sent a tornado tearing through their ranks. Roaring with fresh freedom, the monster kicked through the rear ranks of the army. It felt unconstrained, released.

And the whole vast Plain of Solamnia was open before it.

⊱⋅⊰⋅⊱⋅⊰⋅♦⋅⊱⋅⊰⋅⊱⋅⊰

The kender looked up at Jaymes, and even in the shadows of late afternoon, the lord marshal noted the rarity of tears in his eyes. Smoke swirled around them, but the worst of the battle was over, the noise muted. Soldiers moved about, counting the dead.

"She said I was a good pathfinder," Moptop said plaintively.

He held the duchess Brianna's head in his lap. An arrow jutted grotesquely from her neck. There was blood everywhere. "I should have looked out for her better!"

Jaymes knelt and reached to her neck, feeling for a pulse, even though the effects of that arrow were obvious and telling.

The Duchess of Solanthus was dead.

CHAPTER TWENTY

MISSIONS URGENT

The body of the duchess was laid in state in the great hall of the ducal palace. Though Ankhar's troops had been completely driven from the city, the shocked and shaken people of Solanthus couldn't celebrate a victory. The troops of the garrison returned to their walls, and labored to build a defensive position across the bloody battleground of the West Gate. The rest of the populace gathered, quietly grieving, around the looming bulk of the Cleft Spires and across the plaza, the ducal palace.

Within that lofty structure, Lords Harbor and Martin took the lead in walking slowly, reverently, past the casket, while the other captains, nobles, and guildmasters of the city assembled in the anteroom. One by one, the others filed past to pay their last respects.

Duchess Brianna looked beautiful and at peace. Coils of copper hair surrounded her face and concealed the gruesome wound caused by the arrow that had taken her life. Her slender hands were folded on her stomach, her eyes closed as though she slumbered.

The penultimate person to go through that line was the professional guide and pathfinder extraordinaire who had cradled

Duchess Brianna's head as she breathed her last. The kender paused at the casket, standing on tiptoes so he could lean closer to the body. Moptop sniffled loudly, the tears flowing from his eyes unchecked.

"You didn't deserve to get killed like that," he said, gently touching her cold cheek. "You ought to have seen the battle won, and the fire giant chasing after Ankhar and everything. You would have been real happy about it. I . . . I'm sorry you didn't," he said.

The last person in the funeral line was Lord Marshal Jaymes Markham, commander of the Army of Solamnia. He, too, paused for a moment to look down at the still, beautiful features of the dead duchess. If her death caused him any heartache, any fury, or sense of injustice, he carefully concealed such emotions. He touched the fingers of her right hand then strode away as the priests of Kiri-Jolith came forward to close the casket and prepare for the funeral. She would be borne through the city to give the people a chance to say farewell and would be interred in the nobles' vault beneath the northernmost of the Cleft Spires.

Jaymes made his way through the throng of officers to the two lords, who were standing on the front steps of the temple. The plaza was filled with people and was silent except for the sound of muffled sobbing.

"I need to leave the city," Jaymes said to the two lords. "I intend to return, as soon as possible, with the army."

"What if the elemental returns?" asked Harbor guardedly. "How will we stand against it without you?"

"We couldn't stand against it this time," Jaymes replied. "Perhaps you should pray to whichever gods you hold holy that it finds another target for its wrath. If it returns here again, there may be nothing we can do to stop it."

"Surely Ankhar will send the elemental again," said Lord

Martin. He stared at the enemy army still massed beyond the city wall, tears in his eyes.

"We can only hope not," Jaymes said. "It seems to me our attack against the Thorn Knight has weakened his hold upon the monster, somehow. For that, we have your son—and his noble sacrifice—to thank."

"How long will you be gone?" asked Harbor.

The lord marshal shrugged. "Ankhar's army has suffered terrible losses—it will be days, at the least, before it can recover enough to make any kind of attack. By then my army should be across the Vingaard in force. If Ankhar stays put, we'll be ready to hit him from the rear and—with fortune—break his army for once and for all."

"Very well—but make haste!" said the nobleman, descendent of a long line of noblemen.

Jaymes merely stared at him coldly for a long time until Lord Harbor finally harrumphed, mumbled something, turned, and walked away.

"We're grateful that you came," Sir Martin said. "The cost has been high, but without you the battle surely would have been lost, with the effects catastrophic."

"Your son was a very brave man, a credit to the Kingfishers," Jaymes said. "I will see that word of his valor is carried to Sancrist, to the Whitestone Council and the Grand Master."

"Thank you, my Lord Marshal." For just a moment, Martin's voice broke. Then he stood firm, at attention, with his hand on the hilt of his sword.

"Est Sularus oth Mithas," he said.

✦◦◦◦◦◦◦◦◦❀◦◦◦◦◦◦◦✦

Generals Markus, Dayr, and Rankin rode together near the head of their massive combined army. They were making good progress, the enemy troops having fallen back all across the plains as soon as the river crossing was consolidated. Solanthus lay no more than forty miles ahead, and they were driving their troops at double time in their urge to close upon the city, break the siege, and learn what had become of the lord marshal.

Their eyes were fixed upon the horizon, seeking their first sign of the enemy or the besieged city. What they saw instead was a horror, a monstrous figure of fire and earth, wind and water, which strode across the plains like a rampaging storm. It howled down upon their vanguard, scattering the light cavalry that was screening the advance.

The generals ordered their troops to stand firm, but the hulking elemental king came on like a whirlwind, mowing through the lines. Men screamed and died, hurled through the air like chaff and smashed to the ground like children's toys. Hundreds died, and many more fled in terror when it became apparent they could do nothing to impede the monster. The great herds of horses and cattle that accompanied the army broke away from their drovers and fled in panic, thousands of animals stampeding across the plains.

Many survived only because the horrific monster swooped down on them, tore through the lines, and moved on. It did not so much as glance over its shoulder as it stormed on, taking no more note of its pathetic victims than a tornado would notice the shattered and broken farms left damaged and ruined in its wake.

⋘⋙⋘⋙⋘⋙

"Really?" Moptop's eyes were wide. "You want *me* to go?"

"There's no one else who would even have a chance," Jaymes affirmed with a straight face. "This task calls for a professional guide and pathfinder extraordinaire."

288

"Well, sure, if you want me to, I'll go." The kender nodded his head, his topknot bobbing enthusiastically. He and Jaymes were speaking together in the shadow of the Cleft Spires, even as the funeral for the duchess was proceeding through the city's great central square. The lord marshal had brought Moptop here with a whispered word then leaned down and spoken conspiratorially to the kender.

"You know, I think she would have wanted me to go, too," Moptop said seriously, looking out across the plaza at Duchess Brianna's funeral procession, with the hearse pulled by a dozen black horses. The vast sea of people had parted, almost magically, to open a path for the hearse. The crowd watched, mostly in silence, though there were enough murmured prayers that the whole throng seemed to be softly chanting.

"I'm sure she would have."

"But . . . I just remembered something! When we came out of the Cleft Spires, the wall turned real solid and rocky behind us, remember? I don't think I can get back through that way. Too solid and rocky." The kender gazed apprehensively at the tall pillars and their impermeable surface of flat, hard stone.

"No, I doubt that you can."

"Then how do you think I should go about it?" Moptop asked, his voice wavering. "Considering, I have to go . . . I know she would want me to, and everything. But—*how?*"

"As I said, you're the very best professional guide and pathfinder extraordinaire," Jaymes said. He touched the little fellow's shoulder and gave him an encouraging squeeze. "I'm thinking you'll have to discover a new path."

<hr />

A palace servant ushered Jaymes back to the guest chamber, which he had never slept in, and when he entered, alone, he closed the door behind himself and locked it

After a quick look around the room, he pulled the curtains away from the wall, checked inside the two large wardrobes, and went to the panel concealing the secret passage connecting this room to the sleeping chamber of the duchess. The door opened soundlessly. He took an oil lamp from a nearby table, lit it, and entered the narrow, straight corridor. The door slid shut behind him, and he made his way quickly.

When he reached the other end of the corridor, he placed his ear to the panel and listened for a moment, hearing nothing. Carefully he opened the secret door and stepped into the sleeping chamber of Duchess Brianna. He halted just inside, extinguished the lamp, and set it down. The drapes were open on the large windows, revealing a view to the west and a spectacular sunset over the area that had, hours earlier, been a bloody battleground.

The room was very much as he had left it that very morning. The bed had been made, the two wine glasses and empty decanter removed, but there was no obvious sign that the person who had lived here would not be returning at any moment. He hesitated, looking at the bed and the gauzy dressing gown draped casually over a nearby chair.

After a moment Jaymes crossed the room to the elegant, mirrored dressing table. He almost flinched at the sight of himself in that reflecting glass: he was dirty, his beard was plastered to his chin, and one eye was nearly swollen shut from a blow he'd taken during the fighting. His hands were filthy, too, and he hesitated again before touching the pearl handle on one of the lady's dresser drawers.

But finally he took the delicate handle, so clearly designed for a lady's slender fingers, and pulled open the drawer. Within lay a collection of gloves, in pairs, ranging from white and elegant to shiny black leather. Each pair was folded neatly, all of them nestled in rows. He lifted out a pair made of white silk, raised them to his face, and gently inhaled.

There was a hint of perfume, or perhaps it was only soap. It was a sweet and alluring scent, and the knuckles of his fingers whitened as he clenched the white silk gloves very tightly. Gently he folded them and tucked them into an interior fold of his smoke-stained, sooty tunic. He carefully closed the drawer and picked up the lamp. Without bothering to light it, he passed through the secret door and retraced his steps through the passage to his own room.

Now there was nothing left for him to do in Solanthus. He adjusted his kit and made certain that he had the helm of mind reading, his crossbows, and his great sword all carefully stowed. When he was ready, he touched the ring of teleportation on his left hand, turning the circlet on his finger as Coryn had shown him. He pictured the lord mayor's palace in Palanthas, and particularly those rooms that belonged to the Princess Selinda.

Then he enabled the magic. A soft puff of air blew into the room, coming under the door, filling the empty place from where the lord marshal had just disappeared.

⟨∞⊙∞⊙∞⊙ 🌼 ⊙∞⊙∞⊙∞⟩

"You!" Jaymes barked in surprise.

He stood in the magical laboratory of Coryn the White's house, right outside the alcove where she kept her porcelain bowl. His eyes narrowed as the wizard approached.

"You brought me here?" he accused.

"Instead of the chambers of that silly wench you've bewitched?" she asked. She picked up a rag and dipped it in a bucket of water that just happened to be resting on her bench then tossed the cloth at him. "Here," she said. "Clean yourself up, and then we have to talk."

Angrily he took the cloth and wiped it across his face, wincing as it came into contact with his swollen eye. He dipped it in water again and spent a few moments cleaning up, washing his hands, even wiping the dust from his leather breastplate. Finally he knelt down to apply a quick polish to his boots. By the time he was completed, his anger had abated and been replaced with a curiosity as to why he had been brought here.

"Why this concern with my appearance?" he asked, tossing the grimy cloth into the bucket. "Are you afraid I'll frighten the princess when she sees me?" he added coldly.

The remark obviously stung Coryn. She blinked, almost as if to control unbidden tears, but her jawline tightened and she met his gaze with her own angry eyes. "That wouldn't be likely," she said. "The potion, from all reports, has worked as well as you could have hoped. She spends every day pining for you, going to the top of the Golden Spire and looking up the Vingaard road—waiting for you to come riding back to her!"

"Well, that's all to the good. Don't pretend you don't remember why I needed that potion. The future of Solamnia may well depend on its success."

"The future . . . *your* future!" Her voice broke. "My future—" She stopped abruptly and collected herself with a visible effort. When she spoke again, her tone was flat. "I know, more than anyone, what sacrifices must be made for the future of Solamnia. But you need to understand what's been going on in the city while you have been gone."

"Very well. Do you mind if we sit down?"

Coryn wordlessly led him to a small couch positioned near the wide veranda outside of her laboratory. The view was spectacular: the sun was setting over the Bay of Branchala, outlining the splendid manors of Nobles Hill as they spilled down the slope and into the city itself. Several ships were in full sail—the tide must have been going out—and those sails billowed rapturously, as stark white as gull's wings, catching the gentle offshore breezes, and riding wind and water toward the north.

Closer than the waterfront stood the old city wall, which surrounded a cluster of houses, temples, and guildhalls. The Tower of High Sorcery—Fistandantilus's, then Raistlin's, then Dalamar's Tower—once loomed on a great smear of broken ground there. The tower was gone now, destroyed thought most people. Coryn knew differently.

Even after all these years, no one dared to use that land, despite its prime location in the center of the most vibrant city on Ansalon. Doubtless, no one ever would, so long as stories of the black-robed magic-users were still recounted in the annals of the world.

The most dramatic feature, from the vantage of Coryn's house, was the great, glass-walled enclosure of the lord mayor's palace, dominated by the lofty needle known as the Golden Spire. The great house rested on a hilltop on the opposite side of the valley from Nobles Hill but was clearly visible from here, as from nearly every place in Palanthas.

"The lord mayor does like to be noticed," Jaymes said, his glance appreciating the sweep of the elegant mansion, the windows that gleamed like mirrors in the setting sun, the glass-enclosed circular chamber at the top of the spire.

"Perhaps you care to know that he has taken notice of you, once again," the white wizard said.

He merely looked at her, waiting for an explanation.

"Du Chagne made a speech at the Nobles Ball. He didn't exactly call for your replacement but criticized the conduct of the war. He implied that the campaign to free Solanthus is taking too long because you have other priorities. He publicly speculated about your Compound, asking if anyone present knew what secret business was going on there."

"None of them did, I trust?"

"No. But they don't know who to be more afraid of—you or du Chagne. Everyone knows you destroyed the Kings Bridge two years ago not with magic, but with some new technology."

"A destruction that, incidentally, made possible the survival of the Solamnic Army," he said icily.

She shrugged. "They think their way of life is threatened by you."

Jaymes chuckled, cold and not amused. "Well, I *am* a threat to their way of life," he noted. "You and I both know that the old order, their corruption and the venality, has bled the very life out of Solamnia. These greedy bastards who think only of their own aggrandizement would destroy this land just so they could feast upon its corpse!"

"Well said," Coryn noted, smiling in spite of herself. "But it's no less than you predicted; du Chagne seeks to undermine you, turn the people against you.

"The solution to that is twofold, the way I see it. My army needs to win this war, and I need to set about concluding my business with the princess of Palanthas."

"Then," Coryn said, once again serious. "I suggest you get started with the princess."

⊰•❧•⊱

The three armies of Solamnia made camp after the passing of the elemental king. Clerist knights and other clerics tended to the wounded, with guards alert on the perimeter, cavalry units patrolling ahead and behind the vast formation. Terrified troops were rounded up and rallied, and the herd of cattle and spare horses that had stampeded in the face of the attack was gathered and returned to the large, military corrals.

The three generals, grim faced and shaken, met around the fire of the command camp in the center of the larger body. Each man stared wordlessly into the flames, wrapped in his own thoughts, haunted by memories of the horrible attack by the monster.

Where had it come from? Where was it headed? Would the monster be coming back? How could they ever stand against a creature like that?

And, finally, where was the lord marshal, on whom they all depended for counsel, command, and inspiration?

"We have to consider that our lord marshal might already be dead," Dayr finally said, voicing the common thought they dreaded to hear aloud. "No one could fight it and live."

"Aye," Rankin agreed. He looked at his fellow generals, all former rivals back in the time when they had been captains of the ducal lords. The one thing that united them was the leadership of Jaymes. "And what does this mean for us, for the knighthood, and indeed for our world?"

"Enough children's chatter!" Markus barked. "If he was dead, Sir Templar or one of them spell-users would have perceived that awful truth and told us. I believe he's alive, and he's still trying to win this fight. Monster or no monster, he'd want us to follow his orders."

"You're right, Sir Rose," Dayr said, nodding thoughtfully. Rankin, too, concurred.

"That means that, tomorrow, even if we must leave our wounded behind, we will resume the march to Solanthus and be there ready when the lord marshal shows himself again."

⊀⊙⊛⊷⊙⊛⊷⊙⊛✦⊙⊛⊷⊙⊛⊷⊙⊛⊁

DOUGLAS NILES

The mood in Palanthas was dramatically different from
Jaymes's last visit. He borrowed a horse from Coryn's stable and
rode down the winding roadway from Nobles Hill. At the city
gates, the troops of the guard stood at attention as he passed.

As he rode the wide streets, people came out onto balconies
to watch him or looked up from their market stalls. The citizens'
expressions were not hostile, but there was a wariness that was
a change from the welcome and approval he had experienced
before.

Word of his passage seemed to spread quickly, as more and
more people gathered. By the time he had ridden out the other side
of the city and started on the climb up to du Chagne's residence,
a crowd had collected along both sides of the road.

"When you going to finish this thing?" one old man demanded.
"This war against brute savages? It's been going on for too
long!"

"My son been carrying a spear for you for four years!" said
an old farmwife. "I want him back home!"

The warrior shrugged his cape off of his shoulders and let
the proud hilt of Giantsmiter jut into view over his head. He
had commanded the army for only the previous two years, yet
he ignored the muttered taunts and insults and took little note
of the rabble.

Riding steadily, he approached the manor, and the front gates
flew open. A young woman sprinted out to greet him. Selinda
raced down the cobblestone road, her arms flung wide. When
she reached him, he leaned down and scooped her up.

She was still hugging him, sobbing quietly, as he continued
into her father's courtyard, and the massive vallenwood gates
swung heavily shut behind him.

"I've come home," was all he said to her.

CHAPTER TWENTY-ONE

ENSNARED

'How many of your ogres fell?" Ankhar the Truth asked Bloodgutter of Lemish. The half-giant had witnessed the carnage at the edge of the city and was prepared for the worst. Though the elemental king had disappeared over the horizon some hours before, he was still trembling at the memory of the rampage and at his utter inability to control his "ally."

"Too many," grunted the captain. "I have maybe five hundreds left but lost even more than that. The monster crushed and burned them—even drownded some!" Bloodgutter looked accusingly at his commander. The half-giant glowered back, making clear than no further comment from the ogre chief was necessary or desired.

"Even against that, not one ogre ran away," the captain declared proudly.

Ankhar finally grunted an acknowledgement, and the ogre captain stomped away. The army commander had already heard from Spleenripper, who had lost thousands of his infantry, and Eaglebeak, whose archers, likewise, had been reduced to less than half of their original number by the violence of the elemental king and the sharp, savage counterattack of the city garrison.

On the bright side, Captain Blackgaard's mercenaries and Rib Chewer's warg riders reported only light losses from their resistance to the river crossing of the three great wings of the Solamnic Army. The knights in that battle had suffered heavy losses, especially when they had been showered with arrows while still in their boats. Others had ridden futilely to their deaths against Blackgaard's well-disciplined pikemen.

Furthermore, both captains had handled their highly mobile forces with skill, falling back to the siege lines while delaying the approach of the three wings of the knightly armies. They had forced the knights to deploy for battle repeatedly then skillfully withdrew their units before the enemy could strike. When the elemental king had come striding toward them, Blackgaard had swiftly wheeled his force out of the monster's path and watched as it savaged the army of Solamnia. His final sighting of the creature had it moving southward, toward the foothills of the Garnet range.

Now Blackgaard and Rib Chewer joined Ankhar, while the Solamnics had regrouped, continuing eastward. The vanguard of the knightly army lay just over the horizon. It was clear to Ankhar that he had decisions to make, but his thoughts were in a muddle. His recent setbacks argued against another attempt to conquer the city, and the humans in the city had quickly repaired the breach in their defenses after driving the invaders out.

The elemental king remained missing, and he could hope and pray it would continue to inflict damage and spread terror among the lands of the humans. Hoarst was slowly recovering from his nearly fatal wounds, but the Thorn Knight, as yet, was unable to attempt to create another wand of control. Without such a device, Ankhar was not about to make any rash predictions about the conjured creature.

As usual, he turned to the counsel of his stepmother. She listened sagely as he discussed the losses his army had suffered and pondered his next course of action.

"The Prince of Lies, as always, knows the Truth!" declared the old hobgoblin. She picked up her skull rattle and shook it at him. Immediately he felt a swelling of his power and his determination as the blessing of the dark god was bestowed.

"Battles will be lost, and battles be won," she intoned. "In the shadows of mountains, my victorious son!"

"Aye," he said. "Sage advice, as usual. We need to move away from here, to use the mountains as shelter. The Solamnics will come for us, and there we will meet them."

In the back of his mind, he suspected the elemental king, too, might have gone into the mountains. If it emerged, he could at least try to recapture it with the ruby box the old crone had repaired. Then if only the Thorn Knight would recover his senses.

"There you will destroy them, my son!" cackled Laka gleefully.

Ankhar nodded and touched his mother tenderly on her frail, bony shoulder. *"Est Sudanus oth Nikkas,"* he said, satisfied that he had made the right decision.

<hr />

"Were you thinking about me, while you were off in Solanthus, battling that terrible monster?" asked Selinda.

The princess of Palanthas was alone with her beloved, having sent the efficient—but overly intrusive—servants away with the last of the dessert dishes. She had ordered up a magnificent torte, with iced cream and red berries that had been shipped from far down the coast and transported in cases filled with ice. The palace chef had outdone himself, creating a sweet, chilled pastry that had been beautiful to behold and sumptuous to consume.

Unhappily, her guest had only picked at the delicacy, and eventually the cream, the berries, and the torte had all melted together to form an unappetizing sludge on his plate. One of the servant girls had eventually carried it away, looking almost tearfully at the culinary magnificence wasted.

But of course, the lord marshal was tired, drained by the perils he had faced over the past few weeks. It was, the princess knew, nothing short of a miracle he was even alive. He hadn't told her much about the monstrous elemental being, but even his scant description sent a chill of terror down her spine. She clutched his hand until her knuckles turned white, as if the pressure of her grasp would be enough to ward off any future dangers.

She was terribly worried about him. The stories she had been hearing from her servants lately were quite distressing. The people were complaining that the war was taking too long, that the army cost too much money! Didn't they understand how important this war was? And how difficult? To Selinda such complaints were heartbreaking, and she had wasted no time in speaking up for this great man whenever someone dared to criticize him within her hearing. So vehement was her defense that it had not taken very long before people stopped voicing these thoughts in Selinda's presence.

"But the battle in the city . . . you drove Ankhar's army out of Solanthus?"

"Yes—a costly battle, but a key victory. Now the three wings of the Army of Solamnia are closing in on the city. They might even be within sight of the walls by now."

"Shouldn't you tell people, then?" she asked. "I'm sure there would be rejoicing. Everyone would be happy about that."

"Whether the people of Palanthas are happy is not my concern," he said with a shrug. His eyes met hers as he reached into a pocket of his tunic. "I have a gift for you. From Solanthus."

She was thrilled. "But . . . how in all Krynn did you—?"

"Here," he said, reaching into a fold of his tunic.

He pulled out a small bundle of white gauze and handed it to Selinda. She carefully unfolded the material to find a pair of elegant gloves with lace extending far up the wearer's forearms. She gasped with delight and pulled first one, then the other onto her hands.

"They're beautiful!" she cried. She leaped to her feet, dashed around the small table, and embraced him. "I love them!"

"Good. I was thinking of you while I was there and wanted to bring you something so that you would know that." He stood, gently easing out of her hug, just as someone knocked on the door and quickly opened it.

"Marie!" snapped Selinda, looking around in dismay to see her maid's head poking through the widening aperture.

"Begging your ladyship's pardon," the girl said. She was wide eyed as she curtsied. "It's the lord inquisitor. He wishes to see you—claims it's very important! He's here, right outside—"

The servant was interrupted as the dour, hawk-faced cleric pushed past her. "My dear princess," he declared haughtily. "The hour is nigh upon midnight! I beg of you to consider your reputation, your standing in this fair city. You cannot allow this man to remain here! I fear considerable damage has already been done to your prestige. If you won't send him away for your own sake, think about your father!" The inquisitor turned stiffly to regard the lord marshal. "I beg you, my lord, leave immediately."

Jaymes stared at the priest with an expression of wry amusement on his face. Selinda, however, glared at him in fury. "How dare you intrude here? Does my father know?"

"It is your father, dear child, who sent me," Frost replied mildly.

"Where is he? I'm going to speak to him immediately!"

"You will find him in his private drawing room, I believe. I suggest you go there at once."

Selinda didn't even take time to throw on a shawl. She rushed toward the door, pushed past the cleric, and started through the palace hall. She didn't glance back, didn't notice Jaymes Markham and Inquisitor Frost eyeing each other very carefully indeed.

"Good evening, my lord," said the cleric . . . eventually. He bowed stiffly.

"Actually, let us walk together," the lord marshal said, brushing past the inquisitor then turning to beckon him with a wave. "It's time we *all* went and had a talk with the lord regent."

⊱⚬⊰⚬⊱⚬⊰⚬⊰⚬⊰⚬⊱⚬⊰⚬⊱

"Father, you had no business sending the inquisitor to my apartments!" Selinda declared hotly as soon as she had entered the drawing room, trailed by one of the two guards.

"I'm sorry, Excellency!" the guard apologized. "I told her you couldn't be—"

"That's all right, Roland. You may go now. Good evening, my dear," said du Chagne coolly, rising from his chair beside the dark hearth. "I can see that you're upset, but surely you will understand that it was for your own good."

"I see nothing of the sort!" she retorted. "We were having a pleasant dinner, and poor Jaymes is terribly weary from the war, from his travels. We were doing nothing wrong!"

"Of course not, child. I trust you implicitly. But you know how people talk!"

"Let them talk," she replied, drawing herself to her full height—she was an inch taller than her father. "I'll have

302

something to say to them when the time is right, but for now I will say it to you in private."

"Yes?" the regent said warily.

"I intend to marry that man," she announced. "And there is nothing you can do to stop me!"

Her father took the news surprisingly well, she thought. He merely gave her a sharp look and sat down in his chair again. Father and daughter both turned to the door as it opened abruptly, allowing Jaymes and the lord inquisitor to enter the room.

"What are *you* doing here?" du Chagne demanded of the lord marshal.

"Time is short; I need to return to the front. This is no time to stand on ceremony. We might as well get some matters settled right now," Jaymes replied evenly.

"What matters are those?"

"Your daughter and I intend to be married."

"She was just now telling me something about that," du Chagne replied dryly.

"Did she tell you that the ceremony is going to take place tomorrow?"

"Tomorrow? Impossible!" This, at last, brought the lord regent to his feet, his face purpling. As for the lord inquisitor, he looked stunned and at a loss for words.

"Tomorrow!" cried Selinda, astonished and as pleased as her father was shocked. She threw her arms around Jaymes's neck and hugged him close. "Yes—it must be so!"

"There's no way the arrangements can be made so quickly," the lord inquisitor interposed, forcing himself to sound reasonable. "There are auguries to be made; an auspicious date must be determined. And of course, this is a matter of high statecraft and diplomacy—surely you'll want to have representatives from the other Solamnic realms, at least? And Sancrist? The Grand Master himself will certainly wish to be present!"

"There's no time for that, for any of that," Jaymes responded curtly. "The campaign is at a crucial stage, and I must return to my army at once."

"Why not get married when matters in the field have been resolved?" Inquisitor Frost asked after a long pause, finally finding his voice.

"Because this marriage is a key step in the ultimate victory of my army," Jaymes replied firmly.

"I should think you'd have more important things to do than to argue this matter while your troops are still on the battlefield and the enemy is ringed around Solanthus!" Lord Regent du Chagne declared. "Ankhar remains a formidable opponent."

Jaymes shrugged. "I have his measure. He's formidable, indeed, but so am I. This fight won't take much longer. But I am here to make two demands of you."

"Demands?" The lord regent's eyebrows rose in an expression of disdain. "Aren't you busy enough, fighting a battle for the future of Solamnia? What else do you want besides the hand of my daughter? I suppose you'd like a dowry, a gift of gold as well!"

"I am not interested in your gold. But I am risking my army on the field of battle. Indeed, I am risking my life. I am fairly confident that my passing would not be terribly mourned by your lordship."

Du Chagne gestured impatiently for Jaymes to get to the point.

"Two things: One, your daughter *will* marry me tomorrow—you see yourself that she wants it to be so and has agreed. The wedding will take place immediately . . . before I return to the plains."

THE CROWN AND THE SWORD

Du Chagne's jaw tightened, but he said merely, "And the other demand?"

"Lord Frankish commanded the Palanthian Legion. You will recall, the general challenged me, and he paid for that mistake with his life. I believe his legion is currently without a commanding officer. I claim the legion in lieu of a dowry. There is no one more deserving of that post, no one more appropriate to command your private army."

The lord regent appeared to consider the stakes very carefully before he spoke tersely. "Very well. You shall have the legion. Now get out of here, and let me speak to my daughter and my high priest. There is much that we have to arrange."

Jaymes was already heading toward the door.

CHAPTER TWENTY-TWO

ACQUISITIONS

The lord marshal visited the Crier's Guild before dawn on the following day. With the expenditure of a single sparkling stone, he contracted two dozen heralds, and by sunrise these men and women were abroad in the city, announcing the news of the royal wedding that very evening. This development stunned and excited the people of Palanthas.

By the time Jaymes returned to the lord regent's palace at noon, riding the white gelding that Donny had tended for him, the population was joyously thronging in the street. Their displeasure with the progress of the war had been forgotten; they cheered and hailed him as he passed, and lined the roadway leading down from the palace, eagerly anticipating the wedding procession they expected to witness later in the day.

Within the palace, the lord marshal went immediately to Bakkard du Chagne.

The marshal was received by the regent in the palace drawing room. Du Chagne sat sullenly and listened to the lord marshal outline his intentions.

"I will take command of the legion immediately," Jaymes informed du Chagne. "I intend to use an honor guard from the legion for the wedding. Immediately following the ceremony, the entire force will march with me to the plains, where I will launch the final phase of the war."

"So you really intend to go through with this sham of a marriage? This mockery?" said du Chagne, finally finding his voice.

"Your daughter seems to be happy; I should think that would please you. She has chosen a setting for the event and has asked a priestess, a friend of hers, to preside over the vows. And yes, of course I intend to be there and as you put it, go through with it."

"And what of me? My station—my house—my *gold?* I suppose you intend to claim everything eventually?" The lord regent patted at the sheen of sweat on his balding head with a handkerchief. "I've suspected it all along: you intend to ruin me!"

"Whether you are ruined or not is of little concern to me. But you should understand that you have brought all this upon yourself," said the marshal with a shrug. "It was foolish to put Lord Frankish in a position where I had no choice but to kill him. It was he who challenged me, but I am certain you were behind his foolhardy attempt on my life."

"But I have granted you command of his legion!" du Chagne retorted. "As for my daughter, I don't know what kind of hex you've placed upon her, but—"

Jaymes reached out his fist and pounded it on the desk, causing the regent to recoil with a squeal. The marshal's eyes narrowed to slits, and he seemed to be controlling his temper only with visible effort. His hands were shaking as he drew himself up to his full height, glaring down at the pudgy man who was the father of his bride.

"Matters between your daughter and myself are not your concern," he said sharply. "You will do well to remember that in the future. I told you that your welfare or ruin is no concern of mine, but if you try to block my plans, if you try to obstruct me. . . ." He laughed once, a bark of contempt. "Well, you saw what happened to your assassin . . . and what happened to your three dukes when they tried to challenge me. Next time, my steel will be seeking your own heart. Consider yourself warned, dear father-in-law."

Chuckling, the lord marshal walked around the large office, stopping to admire the view from the windows. Du Chagne stared at him but said nothing, nor did he attempt to rise from his chair. The first rays of the sun spilled from beneath a layer of golden clouds, casting the entire valley—the city and the bay—in a shimmering, almost ethereal glow.

The scene of transcendent beauty went unnoticed by du Chagne.

"As for this"—Jaymes gestured, encompassing the palace, the city, all the view in sight—"you can keep it. I have no interest in your station nor, believe or not, your gold. Except, of course, what may be necessary to fund military operations. That bill you will continue to pay."

The lord regent merely glowered. There was nothing, really, that he could say. Jaymes walked to the door, turned the handle, and glanced back at du Chagne.

"The wedding will occur this evening. For reasons that I don't fully understand, Selinda wants you to be present. So can I expect you on your best behavior?"

For several breaths the regent's jaw worked, but his mouth couldn't seem to form words. Finally, he nodded curtly. "Yes," he said. "I'll be there."

Generals Dayr, Markus, and Rankin led their separate columns eastward across the Plains of Solamnia, moving as swiftly as their exhausted troops could march and their weary knights could ride. The outposts of Ankhar's army had no choice but to fall back before them, for without the river as a defensive barrier, they were too widely scattered to oppose. If these units—mainly goblin riders and human mercenaries—had not retreated, the mobile columns of knights would have isolated and destroyed them.

However, each of the three army wings had been brutalized by the costly river crossing; then the combined force had been shocked and battered by the passage of the monstrous elemental being. Even though the Solamnic troops had not directly confronted the creature, it had inflicted a thousand casualties in a matter of moments.

Now hundreds of wounded were being tended by clerics in a great hospital camp set up on the west bank of the river. Many supplies had been expended or lost in the crossing or burned by the elemental. Food, spare weapons, and medical resources were in short supply.

General Dayr's Crown Army had been reduced to less than half its starting strength. The shower of arrows had killed many men in their boats, and countless others had drowned when the frail little crafts had capsized. In the immediate aftermath of the battle, the Crowns had been forced to lick their wounds on the west bank and were able to cross at a ford only when the goblin cavalry had withdrawn to avoid being outflanked.

The Sword Army of General Rankin had not lost quite as many of its rank and file, but his elite knights had been shattered in the charges against Blackgaard's pikemen. Their courage had been epic, but their tactics disastrous. The steady lines of the defenders, their tight discipline, enabled the long weapons to gut hundreds of horses and pierce the flesh of nearly as many riders. The pathetic remnant of Sword Knights accompanying the columns of infantry eastward effectively numbered only a few hundred now.

General Markus and the Army of the Rose had fared a little better than their northern counterparts, but even that force had been considerably reduced. In addition to the casualties suffered in the crossing, Markus had been forced to detach a sizable contingent to screen the army from the prospect of attack from the Garnet Mountains.

That range was Ankhar's home territory, and he had used the forested slopes and rocky valleys before to launch his actions. So Markus had sent companies of swordsmen and archers, positioning them to the south, where they were responsible for keeping an eye on the many routes out of the mountains. The elemental king had last been seen striding into the heights, and they were also scouting for any sign of the monster.

All three wings of the great army inched steadily eastward, however, driving Ankhar's cavalry and mercenaries steadily before them. By the time they drew near to the city of Solanthus, scouts reported that the enemy was withdrawing from his siege lines. First reports indicated the horde was falling back to the east or southeast, possibly toward the savage realm of Lemish—known to be a stronghold of the ogre race. But details were sketchy, and the mountains also promised concealment, shelter, and a place to regroup.

Finally, the Solamnic Army stopped within sight of the Cleft Spires of Solanthus. The soldiers could clearly see the great swath of destruction where the mighty West Gate lay in ruins. Beyond stood the towers of the city. A fortified line of trenches and wooden breastworks faced them, but already it was clear that those enemy positions had been abandoned.

The three generals, Dayr, Markus, and Rankin, met face to face to debate their next move.

"Any word from the lord marshal?" asked Markus, as soon as he and the other two generals had dismounted.

"None," Dayr replied. Rankin said the same. When the captain of the Freemen, Jaymes's personal bodyguard, arrived a moment later, Markus put the question to Captain Powell.

"I'm sorry, General. But we have had no word since the White Witch sent him into the city—and that, I fear, was many days ago."

"Do you think he's still in there somewhere?" Markus asked, indicating the looming bulk of Solanthus. "Could some trap await us inside the city?"

"No, it seems like Ankhar is falling back," Rankin guessed. "There ought to be nothing to prevent him from coming out to us now. It's strange, this long absence and silence."

While the three generals were discussing their options, two noblemen rode out of the city to greet them. Lords Harbor and Martin welcomed the troops of the liberating army and sadly informed the generals that the Duchess Brianna had fallen heroically in the ultimate battle just at the moment of victory.

They recounted the tale of the city's battle with the elemental, and Jaymes's role in that clash. But when asked about the lord marshal's whereabouts, the two noblemen could only shrug and report that he had disappeared from within the ducal palace. No one had seen him depart the building, and several days of vigorous searching had turned up no clues.

"However, we have to believe that he left the city safely as mysteriously as he arrived," Martin reported. "Probably by magic. The kender who came with him also disappeared, at more or less the same time. Believe me, we would know if the kender was still about."

Mystified, the three generals and two nobles retired to the headquarters of the encampment, where they might, with more comfort, mull over a plan of action.

"Ankhar's army is only a dozen miles to the east," Martin explained after they had all settled with tea and a ration of biscuits. "We've had scouts following him, and it doesn't seem like he's in a great hurry to flee. Can't you strike him there soon?"

All three generals shook their heads, though it was Markus who offered the explanation. "Our men are exhausted, and we are all woefully under strength. This army needs rest, replenishment, and reinforcements—if any can be found. It would be rash to the point of recklessness to charge into battle now, even if we could catch up to the fiend."

"But he's right there, within your grasp!" insisted Lord Harbor, gesturing vaguely toward the east. "Surely this is an opportunity we can't afford to pass up?"

"What about your own garrison?" asked General Rankin sharply. "Do you have perhaps a thousand knights ready to ride? Can you contribute five times that many footmen to our strength? Or two regiments of archers, with twenty arrows for every man?"

"Of course not!" the lord retorted. "We have barely survived this siege with a skeleton garrison. We have perhaps three hundred horses, woefully underfed. And our footmen are half starved. But we drove the enemy away—we have already given our full measure!"

"What my colleague means," Lord Martin suggested diplomatically, "is that we have also suffered and are diminished. It seems obvious that, even if we combined all our forces, we don't have enough troops to confront the enemy—not at the present time, at least."

Sir Templar arrived to find the two groups huddled around

the campfire, their command counsel rapidly deteriorating into sighs and long, gloomy silences.

"Sirs," he reported breathlessly. "I have received word from one of my fellow clerics, in Palanthas."

"Do you mean that inquisitor fellow?" asked Dayr suspiciously. "I don't trust anything he has to tell us!"

"No, not him." The young Clerist knight, who had proved his worth to the generals beyond any doubt when he screened the bridge attack over the Vingaard, spoke frankly. "In point of fact, I share your suspicions about the inquisitor, especially where this army is concerned. But I received an ethereal missive from a priestess, Melissa du Juliette. And she is a woman, a cleric, I trust implicitly."

"And what did this priestess have to say?" asked Markus impatiently.

"The lord marshal is in Palanthas!" The words, the momentous news, seemed to burst excitedly from the Clerist. "He's been there twice in the last month, apparently, most recently appearing there several days ago. Evidently he travels by magic—perhaps the White Witch teleports him. The first time he was there, he fought a duel with Lord Frankish over the Princess Selinda—it was Frankish who issued the challenge—and the lord marshal won, I'm pleased to report. Frankish himself was slain. Today the lord marshal is marrying the princess—it was she who was the cause of the duel. and finally, Lord Marshal Jaymes has taken command of the Palanthian Legion and will be marching at its head on the morrow, hastening here to join us at the front! With him are marching a thousand knights, and six or eight thousand infantry!"

"Well," General Dayr said, with the first smile that had graced his visage since the successful crossing of the Vingaard. "That rather changes things, I should say."

Selinda disdained the great temple in the center of Palanthas, and instead had selected a modest chapel of Kiri-Jolith for her wedding site. The whole city was celebrating the holiday, but there would be less than a hundred people who could actually crowd into the small building. Of these guests, virtually all were friends of the bride from the court or diplomats who represented places from across Ansalon.

The presiding cleric, Melissa du Juliette, a young priestess of Kiri-Jolith, was not the most experienced nor best-known member of the clergy. But she had been a young maid at the regent's court when Lady du Chagne was alive, and there she had befriended and mentored the young princess. Now Selinda remembered her wisdom, affection, and kindness and asked Melissa to preside over the marriage ceremony. Melissa had warned Selinda that she would offend a number of the temple's hierarchy by selecting the young priestess to perform the ceremony, but the princess had shrugged away her concern.

"I have offended them already," Selinda said coolly. "Jaymes is not a nobleman, and this match is unthinkable to the hidebound who consider themselves the adjudicators of what is right and proper. But I love him . . . and I believe he is the greatest man of the age."

"Marrying for love is good," Melissa replied diplomatically. "Though your courtship did happen so quickly. Are you sure you don't want to wait for a little time to pass?"

"No—we must marry now. We are both in a hurry. And he has a war to win!"

"This immediate wedding—was it his idea?" asked the priestess.

"I can't even recall," the princess declared. "No—he proposed to me, of course, but I insisted we marry at once, before he returns to the front. Oh, Melissa, I'm so happy!"

"I'm glad," the cleric said, tenderly touching the younger woman on the cheek.

So the nuptials were arranged and commenced before sunset on that very day. The lord regent was present, looking splendid in a gold frock coat and powdered wig. He escorted his daughter down the aisle in the center of the great church, bowing—ever so slightly—as Lord Marshal Jaymes Markham stepped forward. The princess gave her father a peck on the cheek then took the arm of the man she was marrying.

If anyone noticed that neither Lord Inquisitor Frost nor the Kingfisher, Sir Moorvan, was in attendance, they did not remark on the fact. There were whispered comments, however, about the absence of Coryn the White—who was known to be in the city. She was a famous ally of the regent's, a friend of the bride, and a steadfast companion of the groom's, so where was she? Inevitably her absence provoked speculation. Was she jealous of the princess? Did she, in fact, love Jaymes Markham, as many gossiped? Or did she have secret reasons for objecting to the match?

The celebration was heightened when good news arrived from the battlefield. Carrier pigeons brought the first reports, but overnight several couriers arrived from the plains, riding their staggering horses through the city gates. Their dispatches were posted throughout the city, announcing the relief of Solanthus, the general retreat of Ankhar's army, and the continued advance of the Army of Solamnia. Even without its famous commander, the steadfast Knights of the Rose, Crown, and Sword were liberating conquered lands and rekindling the legendary glories of their historic orders.

Everyone agreed the bridal couple made a splendid match—boding well for the future of the Solamnic nation. To the common people it mattered little that Jaymes Markham was not of the nobility. His martial air inspired awe and boosted by the good news from the front, fresh admiration. As for Selinda, she embodied the city's legacy, symbolized by the lofty rank of lord regent held by her father, the highest ranking possible in the Solamnic territories, considering the kingship no longer existed.

When at last Jaymes and Selinda made their appearance outside the chapel, the citizens in the square cheered lustily. Selinda was radiant in a gown of white silk, embellished with gauze, accented with strands of pearls at her throat and wrapped around both wrists. Her golden hair, coiffed magnificently atop her head, sparkled with an array of diamond combs. Her happiness was plain to all, as she did not wear a veil.

The lord marshal, somewhat to the surprise of the few who knew him, was also resplendent. He wore a red coat, white trousers, and tall black horseman's boots that had been shined to a fault. A black, knee-length cape accented his wedding garb. Jaymes wore a ceremonial sword—which the most astute recognized as the blade with which he had killed Lord Frankish in the duel—in a jeweled scabbard at his belt.

They stood at the plaza, accepting the accolades of the throng, for nearly half an hour, until people pressed so close that the honor guard of Rose Knights from the Palanthian Legion was forced back almost to the door of the little church. Before the couple turned to reenter the chapel, Jaymes leaned over and spoke briefly to the captain of the honor guard.

"Have the legion assemble outside the city tonight, in bivouac," he said. "We march for the plains at first light."

"As you command, my Lord Marshal," replied the captain, awed and overwhelmed by his new leader. He and his men had been forced to cool their heels in the city for the past two years, while their counterparts in the three armies had been waging a glorious campaign for Solamnia. Now they would see action at last!

By the time the doors closed behind Jaymes and Selinda, the captain was already gathering his lieutenants, issuing orders, and ensuring the lord marshal's command would be immediately obeyed.

〜◦◎◦◦◦◦◦◦◎◎◦◦◦◦◦◦〜

The lights winked out in the great manor on Nobles Hill, except for the pale glow that emanated from the central alcove in the wizard's laboratory. The image in the bowl had just been displaying the plaza, with its cheering throng and the newlywed couple, and now it returned to the interior view of the chapel of Kiri-Jolith, following through the door as Jaymes and Selinda passed inside, away from the adoring crowd.

The white wizard was very still as she watched the image, her hands tightening into white-knuckled fists that gripped each side of the porcelain bowl. Coryn watched as the couple passed into a darkened hallway, toward a side door that would emerge onto a quiet street where a carriage awaited, the conveyance that would take them up the hill to the regent's palace for their wedding night.

Before they reached the door, the white wizard saw, Selinda paused and pulled on Jaymes's arm to stop him. She looked up at him, her eyes, her whole face, radiating a transcendent happiness. With a sly smile—a smile Coryn had seen many times, very near to her own mouth—the lord marshal leaned down and kissed his bride. He gathered her into his strong arms in an embrace. The princess pulled him even closer, her arms reaching around his neck, pulling him down as they pressed their lips together.

Coryn splashed the wine with her fist, scattering the liquid around the room. Then she put her face into her hands and cried.

The next morning Jaymes rode out before dawn. The legion camp was already astir, as Captains Weaver and Roman had anticipated their new commander's arrival.

"Tell me your numbers," the lord marshal said as he dismounted, accepting a cup of steaming tea hurriedly brought by a captain's aide.

"We have a little more than a thousand Knights of the Rose," reported Weaver, "two thousand pikes, an equal number of longbows, and better than three thousand militia swordsmen, in companies of three hundred men apiece."

"Good," said the lord marshal. "Weaver, I hereby promote you to general. Captain Roman, you will be second in command. The legion will now be known as the Army of Palanthas, and we will be marching over the High Clerist's Pass to the Vingaard and beyond."

"Yes, my lord! Thank you!" declared the two officers.

"Now, let's get these troops on the way. We have a war to win."

CHAPTER TWENTY-THREE

CONCENTRATIONS

"Do you think it has a chance of working this time?" Sulfie asked, eyeing the bombard weapon skeptically. The weapon was a massive tube, half again as long as the previous versions and somewhat thicker. It was angled slightly upward, the muzzle facing in the general direction of a small lake in the valley below. "Even with all the extra steel holding the boards together, I'm not sure it will be enough."

"All we can do is ram a ball down the barrel and see what happens," the mountain dwarf replied philosophically. "But if *this* one doesn't work, I'm not sure we're ever going to be able to get something we can use."

The bombard was set up on a low ridge beside the New Compound. The target range was downstream of the town and industrial complex, a shallow body of water marked by lily pads and few floating geese who were—they hoped—about to be startled out of their reverie. The already thriving town snaked along the valley floor below them, a swath of wooden buildings, smoking foundries, and storage yards that was already larger than the original Compound in the Vingaard range.

In a matter of only three weeks, the whole place had sprung into existence, transforming a pastoral wilderness into a smoking, churning manufacturing center. Houses for the workers were still going up, a dozen of them every day, but the production facilities were going strong. Charcoal was being rendered in long fire sheds, and great mixing chambers measured and prepared the charcoal, sulfur, and saltpeter in proper proportions to create the black powder.

One reason for the increased size of the installation was the enthusiastic participation of the dwarves of Kaolyn. No doubt inspired by the new market for their steel, that alloy of legendary strength and flexibility, the dwarf king himself had taken an interest in Dram's endeavors. He had sent several master smiths and stone carvers, as well as miners and forgers, to work in the New Compound—for very good wages, of course.

Soon after the manufacturing was under way, Dram had received word from the Solamnic Armies. The lord marshal was marching overland from Palanthas, leading a large reinforcement of fresh troops, the Palanthian Legion, to join the forces in the field. The mountain dwarf knew that battle was imminent, and any help from the New Compound was urgent.

Rogard Smashfinger, the emissary of the king of Kaolyn, had climbed the ridge to join Dram and Sulfie and a host of hill dwarf laborers, for the experimental firing. Now they stood about, impatient and agitated, waiting for this crucial test. "If this doesn't work," Dram had confided, "we'll be looking at next year before we can make another try."

The tube itself was considerably modified from the barrel that had exploded in the Vingaards, regretfully claiming the life of Sulfie's brother, Salty Pete. There were twice as many steel bands around this device, and the ironwood logs were fitted together with tongue-in-groove carvings that ensured even more of the pressure from the blast would be contained. Furthermore, Dram had assigned the Kaolyn stone carvers to carve boulders in perfect spheres, in the exact dimensions of the weapon's bore. He had already assembled dozens of potential missiles and now only awaited the successful test of the actual weapon.

The fuses, too, had been radically improved. After much experimentation, using the usual trial-and-error method, they had learned that by soaking the twine in a salty brine before infusing it with powder, they could regulate more carefully the flammability of the long strings. No longer did they find, by accident, that an occasional fuse would burn furiously fast or refuse to ignite at all. Now the crucial igniting component of the bombard had been standardized so that every one of the fuses burned predictably.

The black powder itself still possessed the potential for unpredictability. But now all the grains of the ingredients had been ground to standard specifications, and the mixing process had become more efficient and tightly controlled. With careful inspection of the raw materials, still more inconsistencies had been weeded out of the process.

Finally all preparations were complete. The barrel was propped on a heavy wagon, the wheels braced and staked, the end of the weapon elevated to almost a forty-five degree angle.

"Isn't Sally coming to see the demonstration?" Sulfie asked, looking down the path to the town. They could see the whole mile of the route, and there was no one visible wending their way up to the ridge. "Do you want to wait until she shows up?"

"She's not coming," Dram declared. He scowled momentarily then shrugged. "I'm ready to make the test. Let's get going."

As before, a cask of powder was rammed down until it was lodged in the very base of the barrel, rigged to ignite via a fuse that extended out the back. When the explosive keg was settled into place, Dram signaled to one of the stone carvers. That dwarf, standing in the bed of a wagon, raised a stone ball that weighed more than a hundred pounds up to the mouth of the barrel, placed it inside, and let it roll down until they heard it thump solidly against the keg of black powder. Quickly the loader climbed down and raced to join the other observers to the rear, and off to the side, of the experimental bombard.

"Fire the fuse!" Dram called.

One hill dwarf remained alongside the weapon, and he quickly touched off the flame then sprinted away. He and the other observers put their hands over their ears, watching as the string was rapidly consumed by the smoking, sputtering flame. The fire burned up to the place where the fuse disappeared into the bore of the weapon then disappeared.

Dram held his breath subconsciously. So much work had gone into this moment—so much planning, sacrifice, and energy—and he really didn't know if it was going to work. Again he felt that shiver of trepidation: if this one failed. . . .

He shook his head, refusing to consider that prospect.

The answer came in a tremendous eruption of smoke and fire, a blast that emerged from the mouth of the bombard and billowed a hundred feet through the air, churning and sparking like a nightmare of heat and fire. The smoke cloud was so thick they couldn't see through it; the billowing murk expanded and boiled all around them.

At first Dram wondered what had happened to the ball—in previous experiments he had always been able to see it fly from the muzzle—but then he looked across the valley and picked it out. Already a mile away, it had soared hundreds of feet into the air. With a sense of awe, the mountain dwarf watched it arc downward and fall away, finally splashing into the placid lake, creating a gout of white water. The startled geese flapped their wings and honking, took to the air.

Dram whooped, a cheer that was echoed by all the workers on the hilltop.

"Never had a test with even a quarter of that distance before!" he proclaimed proudly. "That thing must have flown a mile and a half!"

"Do you think it will work again?" asked Rogard.

Dram shrugged. "Only one way to tell," he replied.

This had been the crux of previous problems. None of their trial barrels had survived more than four or five firings before the bombard itself had been blasted apart, either completely shattered or, at the very least, too cracked and crumbling for further use. But they'd find out soon enough. Already the gunners advanced with the mops and were swabbing out the barrel, making sure that no sparks lingered before they rolled down the keg for the next test. Swiftly another ball was loaded, a second fuse rigged.

"Shot number two—fire away!" Dram called.

Again the bombard blasted, tossing the second ball right after the first, the same arc and distance, into the far pond.

Now the team of loaders found their rhythm. The loading and firing procedure was repeated, and the barrel spewed its fire for a third time. The workers had come out of the buildings down in the New Compound, and the loggers gathered at the edge of the woods. All eyes were on the ridgetop as the bombard shot this ball toward the lake, where it landed very close to the place where the first two shots had struck.

Again and again the procedure was repeated, until ten shots in succession followed the same pattern. Each ball of stone reached the lake. However, on the last few shots, each fell a few paces shorter than on the prior explosions. With these later blasts, smoke began to emerge from the joints where the ironwood logs were connected, and the steel straps holding the barrel together were growing noticeably more loosened.

"We're starting to forfeit a little pressure," Dram said critically, eying the wooden planks and steel rings holding the contraption together. "But that's nothing we can't solve by tightening these clamps a little. I do believe we're almost there."

He lifted his gaze to the north, where the city of Solanthus was just barely visible on the horizon. It was too far away to see the army camp, but he knew where the Solamnics were gathered and approximately where Ankhar had retreated.

"Jaymes, my old friend," he said softly. "I think I have a present for you."

⋉⊙⋖⊙⋐⊙⊙⊛⊙⊙⋐⊙⋗⊙⋗

Ankhar approached the gray tent, the only such shelter in the whole vast encampment of his army. As the commander, he was entitled to go anywhere he wanted in that camp, but for some reason he hesitated outside this tent. He cleared his throat gruffly and was rewarded by a faint voice beckoning him from within.

"Come!" croaked the Thorn Knight.

The half-giant ducked and pulled back the flap, squinting against the darkness within. The tent was larger than most, but Ankhar still had to duck down pretty low in order to get inside. He moved inside and hunkered down on his haunches, studying the pale face of the Gray Robe.

"How is pain?" he asked.

Hoarst moved a hand to his chest, where the lord marshal's bolt had pierced him—had actually punctured his heart. He would have died if it weren't for Laka's healing magic.

324

"Severe," he said. "I can hardly draw a breath."

"I am sorry," the half-giant acknowledged. He extended a cup that he had carefully carried in his big hands to the Thorn Knight. "Laka says you must drink."

The human didn't ask any questions. He merely reached out a hand, took the vessel, and tipped it to his lips. The vile stink of the liquid filled the tent—like a skunk had been startled nearby—but Hoarst didn't hesitate to drink the strong tea down in several bitter, galling sips. He coughed violently, and Ankhar helpfully removed the cup so the Thorn Knight wouldn't drop it.

"Did that help?" the half-giant asked when the man's coughing had eased and he was again able to draw a breath.

"Surprisingly enough, it did," Hoarst admitted, pushing himself to a sitting position. He inhaled and exhaled, clearly relishing the deep lungful of air. "I can breathe again!"

"Good. I need you to get up and go to work now."

Hoarst propped himself up with both hands. "It must be important," he grunted. "But I'm not sure I can walk."

"You don't need to walk—you need to carve," the half-giant said. When the man raised his eyebrows in mute question, Ankhar continued. "The army of the knights is reinforced. They are moving from Solanthus now, coming toward us. We must fight them here, in the shadow of the mountains. The king is up there, in mountains someplace. I wish to get him back. But to unleash king against humans, I must have another wand."

Hoarst nodded, understanding. "All right, I can make another one if you bring me the material."

"What do you need?"

"The branch of a mature willow tree. The tree must be large—larger, for example, than I could wrap my arms around and touch my hands together on the opposite side. The limb must

325

be one that hangs down far enough so that the tip is brushing the water. You must bring me the whole branch, even though I'll only use the very tip. And after you cut off the limb, the tree itself must be cut down and burned in a very hot fire."

Ankhar nodded, committing these curious instructions to memory. "You rest," he said, "and I will return."

It was harder to find a willow tree than he had expected, but after dispatching dozens of human horsemen—the scouts of Blackgaard's light cavalry—he learned of the whereabouts of such a tree in a valley not terribly far away. Not trusting anyone else to the task, he and Laka traveled there with several ogres who were skilled in the use of axes. With Laka's guidance, the half-giant selected a proper branch and hacked it off with a few blows of his knife. Then he instructed the ogres to chop down the tree and burn it on a large bonfire, fueled by dozens of brittle, dead pine trunks that stood nearby.

He returned with the limb to the camp on the following day to find the wizard had, once again, lapsed into uncomfortable, restless sleep. Ankhar waited impatiently while Laka brewed another cup of the vile, but restorative, tea. He watched her mix ingredients that looked like bark and berries with some unidentifiable components that might have been dried animal parts, pulling all the varied elements from different pouches and pockets on her person.

While he was pacing about the fire, Ankhar was approached by Rib Chewer. "The army of the knights is coming this way still," Rib Chewer reported.

"How far away now?"

"Less than ten miles, by my best mark," the goblin—whose idea of distances was imprecise at best—replied.

"They are getting close, then. We must make ready to face them very soon," the half-giant concluded.

Finally the tea was ready, and the army commander took it in to the magic-user. Once again Hoarst sat up on his cot, breathing easily for a few hours because of the potion. He instructed Ankhar to trim the leaves from the willow branch then told the army commander to leave him alone while he went to work with his tiny, razor-sharp knife.

The half-giant paced back to the fire, where his stepmother sat on her haunches, staring into the flames.

"Can you make another brew of that terrible tea?" he asked. "In case the Gray Robe cannot finish before the effects wear off?"

"I can make another batch, and still another and another," Laka replied with a shrug. "But it is a dangerous blessing—for though it makes him well for a few hours, if he drinks enough of it, the stuff will build up in his system."

"And then what?" Ankhar asked.

"Then it will kill him," she replied, reaching for her mortar and pestle and starting to grind up another batch of herbs.

⊰∘⊱∘⊰∘⊱◍⊰∘⊱∘⊰∘⊱

"I was beginning to think you'd forgotten me," Jaymes Markham said as he greeted Dram Feldspar.

"You ain't that lucky," said the dwarf, who was feeling his usual disgust with traveling by horseback. He was dusty and saddle sore. Still, he clasped his old companion's hand in a firm grip as he slid down from the saddle and stretched the kinks out of his muscles. "Got anything cold to drink around here?" he wondered.

"I've been chilling a cask in the stream over there ever since I heard you were on the way," Jaymes replied. He dispatched a pair of men to fetch the barrel while he turned his attention to the wagons that were still rumbling into the camp—the wagons that Dram Feldspar had brought down from the New Compound.

"Six of them, eh?" the lord marshal remarked, impressed.

There were an even half dozen bombards, one each on the leading wagons of the train, their muzzles extending out the back of the bed. Each bombard wagon was hauled by eight oxen. The following wagons were smaller and varied in type and cargo. Many of them were filled with kegs containing the black powder. Others were piled with rocks, each stone carved to an identical smooth, perfectly round sphere. Jaymes took in the whole train with his hands on his hips, nodding in satisfaction.

"We got a range of more than a mile in our tests," Dram finished explaining an hour later as he pulled on a cold beer. He was unmistakably proud.

And with good reason, Jaymes acknowledged.

"Ankhar's army is over the next ridge, with his left flank anchored on the mountains. Our numbers are about equal to his, so up until now it's been a standoff," the lord marshal said to his mountain dwarf companion as he poured them each a fresh tankard.

"Old friend," he said, raising his glass in a toast, "I think you've just changed the odds in our favor."

⊱･◌⊰⊱◌⊰･◌⊱❦⊰◌･⊰⊱◌⊰

It was the goblin warg rider Rib Chewer who at last brought Ankhar the news he had been waiting to hear—and dreading he would never receive.

"The fire-monster has crossed over the mountains," reported Rib Chewer. "He moves down through these valleys, coming toward your army."

"How far away?"

"Less than one day's march, for sure."

"Excellent," growled Ankhar. He immediately went to fetch his mother, who emerged from her tent, clutching the small, ruby encrusted box that she had repaired. With Rib Chewer on foot leading the way, the army commander and his stepmother proceeded up the nearest valley leading between the foothills. Ahead of them loomed the tall, snowy crest of the Garnet Mountains.

By the time the half-giant and his mother, who despite her frail appearance could scramble overland with remarkable speed, had hiked ten miles from the army camp, Ankhar detected the smell of smoke. They came across a low ridge to see an entire forest smoldering, blackened trunks still casting up clouds of smoke. Only the moist ground and verdancy of the forest had prevented a major conflagration from erupting.

And there, looming against the backdrop of the blackened landscape, rose the elemental king. His cavernous eyes, flaring like the coals of the Abyss, burned brightly as the half-giant boldly stepped within view of the monster. Ankhar raised his emerald-tipped spear, waving the weapon over his head in a taunt.

The elemental king roared, the sound so ferocious it was like a physical assault. Ankhar roared back challengingly, and the conjured creature charged him.

The ground shuddered underfoot as the great creature advanced upon the half-giant. Whirlwinds swirled around its massive legs, tearing up trees and sending great spumes of water into the air as it cut across the mountain stream. It roared closer, rearing high, the sound of its cries echoing back from the ridges, filling the valley with noise . . .

Until Laka opened her small, ruby-encrusted box.

CHAPTER TWENTY-FOUR

THUNDER ON THE MOUNTAIN

The battlefield lay where the Garnet Mountains flowed down onto the plains, some fifty miles east and south of Solanthus. The few villages in the area had been long abandoned. Finally the maneuvering was done, the units in place for a decisive showdown. Morale was high on both sides, and with the two-year siege behind them, the Solamnics and Ankhar's army were equal in one respect: they were ready for the matter to be resolved.

Horses kicked and whinnied with eagerness, the drooling warg wolves snarled, and men, goblins, ogres, and dwarves sharpened their blades and through narrowed eyes, studied the enemy's positions. All the warriors on both sides sensed there would be no more marching, no more feints and impasses and skirmishes. A great battle was nigh.

The two armies formed opposite each other alongside the northeast fringe of the Garnet Mountains. Ankhar's army, facing north and west, held its left flank anchored on the precipitous slopes of a rocky ridge. Jaymes, in turn, maintained his front toward the south and east, and by the use of light cavalry and skirmishers, intended to keep his right flank flexible enough to respond to any threat that might materialize in the high country.

The Palanthian Legion had swelled the ranks of the Solamnic force to an unprecedented number. The three knightly armies were well rested. Nearly two months had elapsed since the crossing of the Vingaard, and the time had been put to good use. Many of the wounded had recovered and been brought forward to rejoin the army. Stocks of arrows and replacement weapons had been expanded by the diligent work of the armorers until all units were fully equipped. One enterprising quartermaster had sent away as far as Kalaman to purchase a herd of more than six hundred good, strong horses.

Bloodgutter, meanwhile, had sent urgent messages to the wilds of Lemish, promising booty, land, and slaves to new volunteers. As a result, Ankhar was able to welcome reinforcements totaling hundreds of ogres and thousands of goblins.

The first day on the field, the armies watched each other warily, jockeying with slight changes in position, skirmishing with scouts and light cavalry although neither commander made a move to open up major hostilities. The lancers on their fleet horses brawled with Rib Chewer's goblins on their warg wolves for much of the afternoon, the fracas fading away with the daylight. No great change resulted, but riders on both sides returned to their camps boasting of enemies slain and new glories attained.

On Ankhar's part, he was content to wait and see what his opponent tried to do while, at the same time, waiting for even more reinforcements to come up from the south. They continued to arrive—a hundred and fifty hobgoblins from near the Lords of Doom, several wandering tribes of gobs marching out of the Garnet range. Most important to the half-giant, he was secure in the knowledge that the king of the elementals was once more his prisoner, his slave to command. That imposing monster, for now, remained trapped in Laka's ruby box. But when the time was ready—and that time would be very, very soon—the king would be released to once more walk upon the world, to wage war, and to destroy.

⊰⊙⊱⊙⊱⊙⊱⊙⊛⊙⊱⊙⊱⊙⊱⊙⊰

Jaymes, to Ankhar, was making a show of useless busy work: His troops were deployed. They dug ditches and erected barriers of sharpened stakes. But the half-giant didn't realize the real purpose was to distract him from activity on the western slope of a low ridge overlooking the field, a slope concealed by its crest from enemy observation.

It took the better part of two days for a team of Kaolyn Axers to chop through the pine forest on that concealed slope and clear a road up to the flat ridge that rose to the extreme right of the Solamnic Army's position. The work was grueling, but Jaymes had chosen this ridge as the best firing position for the bombards, and his troops knew better than to question their commander's judgment.

So the dwarves had chopped down hundreds of trees, while a whole regiment of militiamen—armed with picks and shovels instead of swords—followed along, digging and ditching and leveling out the path so the huge freight wagons could be hauled up into the foothills. Planks and logs were laid to smooth out the roughest parts of the road, while sturdy retaining walls were constructed on the steepest stretches, ensuring even a steady rainfall would not be enough to wash out the newly created road—a road created for a single, critical purpose.

General Weaver pleaded for his Rose Knights from the Army

332

of Palanthas to have the honor of striking the first blow in the morrow's battle, and the army commander agreed.

"Thank you, my lord—and I want you to know that this request comes not just from me, but from every one of my men. Too long we have waited in our city while the war raged across the mountains. We are eager to make our own contribution to the cause of Solamnia."

"That's a pretty speech," Jaymes remarked. "I have no doubt that your men will fight as well as you talk."

"I want you to know, sir," said Weaver, "that we knights of Palanthas have chafed for a long time under the command of the lord regent. He might hold his title by birthright, but to us he does not embody the tenets of the knighthood. You, on the other hand, are a warrior that any man would feel honored to serve. Your example makes us believe that, perhaps, there's hope we will once again have a nation to call our own."

Then the general drew himself up to his full height and clapped a fist to his chest. "My lord," he declared, mustache quivering, *"Est Sularus oth Mithas!"*

At the eleventh hour, the army was further augmented by a regiment of heavy infantry dispatched from Kaolyn. Wearing black plate mail armor, carrying an assortment of axes and wicked-looking battle hammers, the fighters marched into the camp singing a battle song and were cheerfully welcomed by the Solamnics and all of their allies.

"I think old King Metast wants to protect his source of income," Dram noted with a chuckle. He had told Jaymes about the transaction for Kaolyn steel, of course.

"We can use their steel, and we can use their numbers," the lord marshal noted with pleasure.

At last, the road up the back of the ridge was completed, and the heavy wagons were hauled to the crest—though, for the time being, they parked just below the summit on the west side to avoid being seen from the enemy lines. The real battle would begin in the morning.

The long night passed quietly. Those who knew how to write penned missives for home and helped their less literate comrades to compose brief notes as well.

Jaymes himself walked calmly among the men of all four wings of his armies, speaking to knights and militia volunteers, lords and squires. He praised the work of the Rose Knights, congratulated the men of Solanthus and the Sword Army on their accomplishment in liberating that long-besieged city, encouraged General Dayr and the battered warriors of the Crown Army. The Freemen, his personal bodyguards, walked beside him and remained vigilant while the commander relaxed, joked, and shared a drink or a piece of bread with the men as he passed among them.

The lord marshal himself made sure to get an unusual amount of rest, turning in before midnight and ordering that he not be disturbed until two hours before dawn. He pulled a thin blanket over himself, stretched out on his cot, and fell asleep immediately. His dreams were comforting, as he was visited by images of Coryn and oddly enough, Moptop Bristlebrow. Curiously, his new wife was as absent from his dreams as she was from his waking thoughts.

When an orderly came to wake him at the designated time, Jaymes emerged from his tent refreshed. He broke his fast with a few pieces of bread and cheese and mounted his horse, riding among the camps, observing—and being observed—as the units assembled.

By dawn, the knights—more than two thousand five hundred of them—had saddled their horses and formed up with lances and armor polished to a splendid shine, horses groomed and combed. Men led their horses by their long bridles, remaining dismounted until the moment of truth, when they took their places in the forefront of the army. The Palanthians under General Weaver formed a long front rank, while the Crown, Sword, and Rose contingents waited in three massive columns behind their comrades from the gleaming city on the bay. The Palanthian knights would strike in their long line, while the following columns maneuvered to seek gaps of opportunity in the enemy formations.

"My Lord Marshal!"

Jaymes looked up to see one of the Solanthian lords—Lord Martin—approaching on horseback. The nobleman's expression was grim but excited. "I have another company of militia from the city . . . just reached camp last night. A thousand swords."

The lord marshal nodded approvingly. "We'll hold them in reserve for now. But have them ready."

"Aye, aye, sir. And good luck, my lord," said Martin before riding back to his own company—heavy infantry from the city, armed with halberds.

Jaymes mounted his horse, the steadfast roan mare that had carried him for so many miles across the plain. Captain Powell and the Freemen, armed and alert, arrayed their mounts in a casual circle around the lord marshal. The army commander was about to ride out with his staff when there came a stir of excitement from the men nearby.

"It's the White Witch!" one exclaimed before glancing in chagrin at the lord marshal—who was known to disapprove of that appellation for the Lady Coryn.

But Jaymes Markham was not paying any attention to the man. Instead, he was staring at the place where his men milled away from a swirling puff of sparkling air, clear proof of magic. The lord marshal dismounted as Coryn stepped forward from the shimmering air, the nearby soldiers scrambling to get out of her way. She walked up to him with a pensive look in her eyes but with the hint of a smile playing about her lips.

He took her by the arms and looked at her closely. "I'm glad you've come," he said. "I didn't expect it—didn't dare hope for it. But I'm glad you're here."

"I helped you start this war," she said simply. "The least I can do is be here to finish it."

⊰◦❈◦⊱

"They're going to come at me with a whole army of Salamis on horseback, eh?" Ankhar said with a chuckle. He was addressing Captain Blackgaard, who sat astride his black stallion next to his army commander. "Perhaps they forgot what your pikes did to them on the bank of the Vingaard, eh?"

Blackgaard narrowed his eyes, studying the long line of armored riders, their lance tips raised so they sparkled in the new sunlight of the day. "I am not so sure about that, my lord. The Solamnics are stubborn, to a fault, but they are not fools. I doubt they will ever forget the crossing of the Vingaard River. However, I agree, we need to deploy our pikes in the front line."

The human captain gave the necessary orders, and his crack troops with their long weapons moved out in front of Ankhar's army. They deployed in their three-rank formation, standing at rest—the butts of their pikes resting on the ground for the time being—while they awaited developments. They would be able to raise their weapons to form their impenetrable line on a moment's notice, far more rapidly than the knights could cover the half mile or so of distance to confront them, even with their fastest charge.

While waiting for the knights to make the first move, Ankhar turned to his stepmother, who as usual was close by his side.

336

"Did you brew your tea for the Gray Robe?"

"Yes," she replied. "He has drunk it and is making his way here."

"You said that potion will kill him. He will not die today, will he?"

Laka cackled. "It should have killed him already. I begin to think that the Thorn Knight has magic even mightier than my own. But no, my son, I do not think it will kill him—at least not today."

"And the wand? You have it?"

She pulled back her cape, showing him the slender piece of wood tucked securely into her belt. "He says that it is better than the first one. And I will be ready when the time comes." She opened her pouch and showed him the ruby box. The half-giant blinked, still surprised—despite his experience with the device—that such a small container could hold a force so terrible and awe inspiring.

"My lord!" called Blackgaard, drawing Ankhar's attention back to the enemy. "It seems the knights have begun to move."

"Aye, indeed," grunted the half-giant. The vast ranks of armored riders had mounted now and were riding forward, their pace a measured walk. "And your pikes?"

"See, there," said the human captain with a nod. Indeed, the men with their long pole arms were taking up positions, hoisting the long shafts into a bristling, deadly fence. Three deep, they knelt, crouched, or stood, holding firm to the steel pikes with razor-sharp tips.

"Good. Let the knights impale themselves," Ankhar said with a belly-deep chuckle. He tried to suppress a small sense of disquiet, but the feeling wouldn't quite go away: Why would the humans cling to a tactic that was so obviously bound to fail?

"How about the back ranks?" he asked Eaglebeak and Spleenripper, who were standing nearby.

"The archers are ready, lord."

"So, too, my footmen."

"And I have a thousand ogres, ready to advance when the enemy breaks," Bloodgutter pledged, lumbering up to the command conference.

To the rear, Rib Chewer's lupine cavalry milled. Already mounted, the gobs clutched their reins and tried to hold their eager, hungry mounts under control. The half-giant knew that they would be slavering for blood by the time he gave the order.

Surprisingly, Ankhar heard something like thunder booming from the direction of the Garnet Mountains. A deep rumble shook the air, a powerful sound he felt in the pit of his stomach as much as he heard it in his ears. He looked up toward the foothills with their snowy summits—the white peaks brilliantly outlined in the morning sun—beyond. However, there was not even a suggestion of a rain cloud in the pristine sky.

Peering more closely, he saw something resembling a gray fog swirling around one of the near ridgetops—but that seemed more like the smoke from a grass fire than any gathering of moisture in the sky. The vapors billowed and churned along the crest. Definitely not a storm cloud, Ankhar told himself. When he looked to the sky again, puzzled, Ankhar could still not determine any suggestion of threatening weather.

"Strange," he murmured. "How can there be thunder without any clouds?"

<hr/>

"I think we're going to fall just a bit short," Dram remarked, speaking almost conversationally to Sulfie. They peered through the thick smoke of the muzzle blast, watching the six balls from the first bombard volley soar through the air—they were still visible, though dwindling into the distance—plunging down toward the plain. His target was the long, unbroken formation of pikemen. The pikes extended for more than a mile, screening the entire front of Ankhar's horde. Let's see how those well-disciplined soldiers face up to a rain of unforgiving stone balls, Dram thought grimly.

True to his prediction, the six spheres all thudded to the ground several hundred yards short of the enemy line. Several of them simply sank into the soft dirt and vanished, but three or four others bounced and rolled. Momentum carried them along with irresistible force, and they bowled through the line of pikemen like balls striking down ninepins. Even from a mile away, the dwarf and the gnome could see the shock effect of the missiles as the line of pikes wavered and a number of men were taken down.

The Solamnic Knights still advanced slowly, lances and pennants aloft, armor gleaming in the sunlight. The great formation looked more like a parade than a charge, horses still proceeding at a walk nearly half a mile before the enemy lines. The Palanthian Legion was in the lead of the broad line, and the three columns of Sword, Rose, and Crown knights maintained a steady interval between each wing as they came behind.

"Raise the elevation just a quarter turn," the dwarf ordered, and his gunners complied by adjusting the massive screws set under the muzzles. The hill dwarves cranked the simple machines, and the barrels were raised almost imperceptibly.

Even as the aim was being adjusted, other gunners swarmed over the wagons, swabbing out the barrels and loading in new casks of powder. Six of the burliest dwarves acted as the ball handlers, and each of these now lifted his heavy missile over his head and dropped it into the gaping black mouth of the bombard.

"All right," Dram said with relish. "Let's try this again."

CHAPTER TWENTY-FIVE

SOUND OF THE GUNS

S ix perfect spheres of stone, each weighing well more than
one hundred pounds, soared lazily through the air. From a
distance they looked harmless, like a spray of pebbles tossed by a
child. But as they neared, they grew in apparent size even as their
flight remained deceptively lyrical. Ultimately the rocks crashed
only a few dozen paces before the line of Blackgaard's pikemen,
striking with enough force to send tremors through the ground.

One of the balls landed in a low, wet swale and simply
vanished into the mud with an audible plop. The other five
missiles struck harder patches, and they bounced and tumbled
irresistibly forward. Momentum carried them onward, not at all
lazily now, thumping and pounding the ground as they rolled.
In scant moments they tore through the tightly packed ranks of
human flesh and wooden shafts. Pikes splintered and snapped,
bones shattered, and flesh was crushed by the irresistible mix
of mass and momentum.

Wherever they hit that line, the heavy balls simply burst
through, following the trajectory imposed when they blasted out
of the muzzles of the bombards a mile away on their mountain

ridge. They came up against no obstacle that could obstruct them or even seriously impede their progress. Any stick or body in the way of the flying boulders was simply borne along as the balls blasted through the line and tumbled across the grass to settle at the rear. Thus, human heads, torsos, arms, legs, and sometimes complete bodies, were blasted away, swept like grains of sand propelled by a broom, leaving a gory wake of body parts in the path of each of the five balls. The unbroken line of leveled pikes wavered as five distinct gaps were instantly carved in the previously unbroken formation.

Most of the spherical missiles rolled far enough to end up between the large, dense blocks of Ankhar's troops, assembled a hundred paces or more behind the pikes. One rolled in a seemingly gentle fashion up to a column of goblins. A gob raised a foot in a casual attempt to bring the ball to a stop as it approached, only to have both of his legs torn away by the shot's weight and thrust. By the time the stone ball came to rest, in the middle of the column, a dozen more goblins were down with broken legs or crushed feet.

Now another boom sounded from the ridgetop. Smoke tinged with angry yellow flame billowed from the six barrels, and six more balls exploded on their trajectory toward the distant line. There were slight variables between the paths of the two volleys—the kegs of black powder did not possess identical explosive force, and furthermore the heavy wagons had been jolted back by the recoil of the first round. When the hill dwarf gunners rolled them back into firing position, the barrels were not aimed exactly as before.

The result was the shots of the second volley landed in slightly different places. Two were lost to soft ground, but the four that rumbled onward tore through the shaken line of pikemen in different areas. Before the men and their startled officers could even grasp what was happening to them, four additional holes had been punched through the line—the line that depended on unbroken integrity for its battlefield effectiveness.

Now the horses of the Solamnic Knights picked up the pace of their advance. They trotted, the thunder of many thousands of hooves reverberating across the distance between the two armies. The gap was narrowing so the armored lancers were only a quarter mile away from the pikes. Still, they came in a measured, far from hasty charge.

The thunder of the hoofbeats was nearly drowned out by the stunning explosive noise when the next volley blasted from the bombards. Officers in the line of pikemen had recovered their wits and were frantically ordering their men to fill in the gaps in the line. These efforts met with some success until the next, stronger volley ripped through.

One of the shots took off the head of a veteran sergeant major just as he was trying to rearrange his men into some semblance of order. The corpse of the grizzled warrior fell, blood spouting from its neck, and a hundred men who had witnessed the decapitating blow dropped their pikes and fled to the rear. They left a wide gap in the center, and the men of the neighboring companies nervously shifted their eyes among that breach, the approaching horsemen, and the imagined safety far behind them.

The guns belched again, their position clearly marked by the cloud of smoke that blossomed across the ridgetop. More balls ripped through the line, even as another volley boomed forth. Now the gray, churning smoke all but enveloped the ride and nothing else could be seen, except for the repeated flashes that burst through the cloud, bright as the fires of the Abyss.

Then the battle began in earnest as the captains of the knights raised their lances, shouted their battle cries, and all their armored warriors spurred their heavy warhorses into a gallop.

"What are they doing to us?" demanded Ankhar, watching in horror as dozens more of his pikemen were punched out of the line by a strange new power he still could not comprehend. He glared up at the smoke-shrouded ridge, certain that the explosive noises up there and the lethal destruction in front of him were related somehow. But aside from the flashes of flame, he could make out nothing within that murk.

And he couldn't understand what was happening!

"Some kind of projectile weapon," Hoarst speculated, his tone surprisingly dispassionate as he came up beside the army commander, giving Ankhar a start. "It's launching those stones like it was a giant sling . . . or a tremendously powerful catapult. They're flying a mile or more before they come down."

"Is it magic?" demanded the half-giant. "Can you fight it with spells?"

Maddeningly, the Thorn Knight merely shrugged. "I don't see how—not from here in any event. However, I came to speak with you about another important matter—the wand."

"What?" Ankhar was so distracted that he had to think for a moment to realize what the Thorn Knight was talking about. "Yes, my mother tells me it has been finished."

"Yes. I should be able to use it to command the elemental king . . . even better than before. We will have the monster to lead us in battle again."

"But I must have an army left for that to happen!" roared the half-giant. "Look at the line! You must go up there and try to destroy those . . . things!" ordered Ankhar until he was distracted by an even more immediate threat. "Damn them! Look, the knights!"

The armored knights were bearing down on his army now at breakneck speed, riding shoulder to shoulder, heavy lances leveled. The pike line was a shambles. Many men had fallen, but even more of the troops had panicked and run. Huge gaps had opened up and the galloping knights poured through these openings. Once through, they curled around to the right and left, stabbing with lances, hacking with swords, and the footmen could not possibly wield their cumbersome weapons fast enough to defend themselves.

The principle behind the pike formation was the uniform presentation of a line of the weapons. Once the line was ruptured, however, the individual pikeman was almost helpless against an enemy on horseback—a soldier wielding a twenty-foot shaft of wood with a steel blade on the end could do very little against a close, mobile opponent. And even if a lone man tried to hold a horse at bay with a pike, the knight could easily bash the tip of the ungainly weapon to one side or the other then ride in for the kill.

And kill the Solamnics did, along the whole breadth of the once-formidable line. The horsemen trampled the pikemen. When they were too close to use their lances, the knights drew massive swords and cleaved the helpless pikemen. The horses kicked and reared, stomping on the men of the infantry, further smashing the crumbled line.

At the same time, the thunderous assault continued and adjusted to the shifting battle. Now the balls flew over the heads of the knights and pikemen, thumping to the ground and rolling through the rear formations of Ankhar's army. These were spread out enough so that many shots fell between the units, but whenever a tumbling ball crashed into a tightly packed column of warriors, it inflicted terrible carnage. Ankhar was shocked to see an ogre blasted in two by a hit in his belly, and he could only gape in horror as the same ball rolled on to knock down a dozen more of the brutish warriors.

"Rib Chewer!" cried the half-giant, summoning his goblin warg rider. He pointed at the melee, where the last of the pikemen were frantically trying to form squares or circles to hold the swarming knights at bay. It already seemed a losing cause.

"Attack the knights! Break up that charge!" ordered the army commander. "We need time!"

"Yes, lord!" cried the venerable captain. He raced away atop his wolf, howling for the attention of his men.

Soon a tide of savage cavalry was loping toward the front of the half-giant's army.

Once more the terrible weapons on the ridgetop roared, fire flashing through the clouds of smoke. Ankhar remembered his command to the Thorn Knight and turned to repeat the order. But Hoarst had disappeared.

⊱⊰⊱⊰⊱⊰❀⊱⊰⊱⊰⊱⊰

Dram was pacing up and down behind the line of bombards, encouraging his gunners and occasionally running forward far enough to watch the shots land. As he scurried back to the ammunition wagons, amidst the swirling smoke a flash of white caught his eye, and he veered toward the familiar, alabaster figure.

"Lady Coryn!" he exclaimed, recognizing the white-robed wizard as she materialized to the rear of the cannons. She was holding her hands to her ears, and her face—like Dram's and everyone else's—was streaked with soot and sweat. Her robe, somehow, remained as white as a blanket of new-fallen snow. "What are you doing up here?"

"Looking for trouble," she replied after lowering her hands. "I have a feeling you've attracted Ankhar's undivided attention."

The mountain dwarf grinned. "Yeah, they're doing the job, aren't they," he said proudly, standing beside her as he watched the nearest bombards—the only two he could see because of the thick smoke—get loaded for their next shot.

"Very impressive," Coryn said.

Dram had good cause to be pleased. The tubes were all holding up well. His armorers periodically tightened the clamps on the steel straps holding them together, and none had shown signs of failure. If anything, the steady firing was turning out to be harder on the wagons supporting the bombards than on the weapons themselves.

"Cover your ears!" he warned, doing the same as the fuses were ignited.

Moments later the massive weapons belched their lethal balls into the sky. At the same time, the heavy wagons jerked backward, as they had with each shot, rolling several dozen feet before stopping against the heavy chains that anchored them. Dozens of hill dwarves swarmed around each wagon, turning the great wheels by hand, laboriously pushing them forward into firing position.

"Chief!" It was Sulfie, dashing through the smoke, looking for Dram.

"Over here!" he bellowed.

The diminutive gnome came trotting up to him, out of breath. She was covered from head to foot in soot and grime, looking as if she had tumbled into a coal pit. But her eyes were bright with excitement, and she flashed incongruously white teeth as she smiled momentarily.

"Hello, Lady," she said to Coryn. "Welcome to the battery!"

"Hi, Sulfie. You and your brothers have made quite a contribution," the white wizard replied.

"Yes," the gnome said, her expression showing melancholy for a moment. "I wish Carbo and Pete could be here to see this."

But then she remembered her news and frowned seriously. "We lost a wheel on Number Two!" she reported. "Broke it on the recoil."

"Damn!" snapped the dwarf. Dram nodded to Coryn. "I'd better go have a look, see if we can get it up and firing again."

"Good luck," she said. "I've got things to do. See you later . . . maybe."

The dwarf nodded and took off at a jog. For the first time, he became conscious of his own fatigue—he was sweating like a blacksmith on a summer day—and when he reached the disabled bombard, he had to stop and lean against the frame for a few moments just to catch his breath. The smoke clogged his lungs, and he felt grit on his tongue and in his nostrils.

He saw immediately that the rear axle of the heavy wagon had snapped in two, leaving the bed sagging to the ground and the barrel canted upward toward the sky. "I've got some spare axles," he told the crew captain. "You work on getting this thing jacked up, and I'll send a replacement up from the supply park."

Although he was reluctant to leave the scene, he didn't trust anyone else to make sure the proper piece was sent forward, so he departed at a trot. The replacement wagons, as well as spare powder and ammunition, were parked beside the newly made road, several hundred yards down the back side of the ridge, since there hadn't been enough room for all of them on the summit. It would take only a few moments, he hoped, to bring the spare part forward.

He moved quickly and after a moment had moved from the stinking, stinging cloud into a mountainside meadow of bright flowers, a splashing brook, and—most amazingly—fresh air. But he couldn't pause to enjoy it, and moments later he was huffing and puffing around the last switchback. He located the wagon with the spare axles in a flash, and he quickly got the attention of several teamsters.

"Get this up to the ridge," he ordered. "Take it right to Number Two."

"Gotcha, Chief," replied the wagon drivers—humans who had been farming on the Vingaard Plain, but they had signed up to make good money working at the Compound. They quickly headed for the pasture to collect a team of draft horses.

Satisfied, Dram turned back up the hill. He could only move at a walk, and beside the brook he decided to stop, kneel down, and take a refreshing drink of cool water.

It was a drink that would save his life.

⊱⊰⊱⊰⊱⊰●⊱⊰⊱⊰⊱⊰

Coryn felt a tingling sense of alarm. Something was terribly wrong, and that something involved magic. She spoke a word and immediately disappeared from sight. Cloaked by invisibility, she strode behind the thundering bombards, peering through the smoke with her magical acuity. She didn't know the nature of the threat, but every one of her senses told her to beware.

She enchanted herself with spells allowing her to detect magic and also to see invisible objects or beings. She knew the damage these great weapons were doing to the enemy army, and she did not think that Ankhar or his Thorn Knight would allow this assault to proceed unchallenged. But what could they do? How would they strike?

A breeze came up, incongruous and even refreshing; the gentle wind served to clear some of the smoke away, though each new volley spewed fresh, stinking, sulfur-tainted fog into the air. But for a moment she could see all the bombards at once as the five active weapons were rolled into place for another shot. She could see, too, a team of hill dwarves frantically working

349

the screw of a huge mechanical jack, lifting up the bed of the disabled bombard.

The white wizard saw someone coming directly toward her—it was the little gnome, Sulfie—and Coryn nimbly moved her invisible form out of her path. Sulfie was hurrying to one of the massive ammunition wagons, where casks of the black powder were stored, to be brought forward as needed to the bombards. Coryn watched her go then stiffened.

Something else was moving toward that wagon!

Her magical sense was tingling, though she couldn't make out the details. It was a shapeless thing, like a blob in the air—not exactly invisible. Abruptly that cloud took shape, and she saw the Gray Robe of a Thorn Knight appearing. He had traveled up here under the concealment of magic, rendering himself by potion or spell into a gaseous cloud of ephemeral vapor that cloaked him until he arrived at the site of the thundering battery.

The Gray Robe's hand was already raised, and he cast a single, lethal spell before Coryn could react. A tiny pebble of light appeared at his fingertips, a little marble-sized glob of fire that drifted, unerringly, toward the powder wagon and its great stack of casks. Sulfie was up on that wagon, barking orders to several hill dwarves as they manhandled the large kegs of black powder.

"No!" cried the White Robe. She raised her own hand, her lips shaping a spell that would strike the Thorn Knight down—but in that same instant the man disappeared, teleporting himself away from there.

In the next breath, his fireball spell exploded.

Jaymes was watching the progress of the battle with satisfaction. He sat astride his roan with several signalmen; the Freemen of his bodyguard were also mounted and arrayed protectively around him. They were atop a low elevation that gave him a good vantage over the field. He could observe the battery in action, and he also had a good view of the charge of the knights. Coryn had left his side to go keep an eye on the cannons, while General Weaver charged ahead with the heavy cavalry. Generals Dayr, Rankin, and Markus were at the heads of their respective armies, awaiting orders.

The effectiveness of the bombards had exceeded the lord marshal's wildest expectations, and the charging knights had wasted no time in utterly destroying the line of pikes. Now the knights were checked momentarily, as they swirled through a melee with Ankhar's wolf-mounted goblins. But the heavy horses showed no fear of the snapping, lupine jaws, and the countercharge failed to deter the mounted men.

Jaymes gestured to three signalmen, who snapped to attention.

"Raise the banners for the Sword, the Rose, the Crown," he said. "Signal a general advance."

The men dutifully hoisted their pennants, the battle flags snapping and blowing as the breeze grew stronger. They dipped their poles forward and repeated the signal. Jaymes was satisfied to see the three great columns respond immediately, thousands of infantry starting toward Ankhar's army at a steady march.

A clap of thunderous noise suddenly overwhelmed all the chaos of the battle. It was louder by far than any volley of the guns or, for that matter, anything Jaymes had ever heard. The lord marshal twisted in his saddle and looked toward the ridge.

He saw the aftermath of a tremendous explosion, a vast column of smoke churning into the sky. Several wagon wheels spun out of the murk, and one of the massive barrels tumbled into view, rolling down the ridge like a runaway log. Other things were flying through the air, too, and he grimaced with the realization that they were bodies, dozens of gunners, teamsters, and others caught up in the blast like rag dolls.

He knew that Dram and Sulfie had been up there. His next thought was that Coryn had been going to that place as well.

⚬⚬⚬⚬⚬⚬⚬⚬⚬⚬⚬⚬

"He did it!" cried Ankhar, pumping his fists in the air. He watched in exultation as the ridgetop exploded and all the enemy's terrible weapons erupted with all the violence of a volcano. Fire spewed into the air in great, roiling balls, and smoke billowed and surged upward so quickly that, in moments, the pillar of darkness extended more than a mile into the sky.

Ankhar blinked in surprise as Hoarst materialized before him. "Well done!" he roared, only with difficulty resisting the urge to embrace the man.

"Yes—the weapons are destroyed, and those who wield them have been killed," Hoarst reported. He staggered slightly, and the half-giant reached out a hand to support him. "Is that enough to win the battle?" Hoarst asked, his voice a hacking croak.

"No," Ankhar conceded. He gestured to his stepmother, who crouched on her haunches nearby, as he addressed the wizard. "But it was a tremendous blow, and now we are ready for the next step. Make ready your wand."

"I am ready."

"Laka will release the king. You will drive it forward."

"I will give the device to you," the Thorn Knight objected. "You should carry the wand yourself, my lord."

"Me?" Ankhar responded, shocked.

"You can do it exceedingly well, I am sure," Hoarst replied, coughing spasmodically for a moment. He wheezed, recovered his breath, and looked at his skeptical commander. "There is no magic use required. Simply brandish the device. The repulsion spell is inherent and will drive the elemental king away when you confront him."

"And you?" growled the half-giant, squinting at his Thorn Knight suspiciously. "What will you do?"

"I will seek out the enemy commander, the lord marshal. It may be that I can strike him down with my magic—as he tried to strike me down with an arrow to the heart."

Ankhar pondered this for a moment then threw his head back and laughed, a great bray of sound. "Very well. I will hold the wand, and you will seek the enemy commander. And we will let the king do the wholesale killing!"

Hoarst removed the slender stick of wood and handed it to Ankhar, watching closely as Laka opened the lid of the ruby-covered box. Instantly the twin specks of fire emerged, swirling upward, glowing brightly against the backdrop of a sunny sky. The shaman cackled with glee as a great spume of black smoke billowed upward, following the twin sparks into the sky. That was when the massive torso took shape, blocking out the light of the sun. The limbs of tornado and cyclone stretched outward and down. Sound wailed, a shrill keening of wind and water, and a deeper, more visceral power.

And once again, the king of the elementals took shape upon the surface of Krynn.

CHAPTER TWENTY-SIX

TRIUMPH AND DESTRUCTION

J aymes saw the black vapors coalesce into the familiar humanoid shape, towering high above the raging battlefield. The lofty, clifflike face solidified, its cavernous sockets glowing with the fires of the Abyss. Those burning eyes swept across the field, flaring in anticipation of the killing to come. The sound of a whirlwind filled the air, a roar that kicked up dust and debris around the conjured giant's lower extremities.

It was ghastly, terrifying. The monster, so long vanished, had returned in the service of the enemy commander, of that much Jaymes was certain. How Ankhar had regained control of the creature, or where it had been in the meantime, Jaymes did not know.

He did know that all of his plans for this battle would have to change. The huge column of black smoke that was conspicuous on the ridgetop marked the vulnerable spot where Coryn, Dram, and Sulfie had been directing the battery. And now this monster from the depths of the world, unassailable and incomprehensible, flicked his eyes in that direction.

The lord marshal had spurred his horse toward the front as soon as he discerned the looming shape. Now he rode directly toward the conjured monster, Giantsmiter in his hand, a look of cool detachment—utterly concealing his acute sense of despair—upon his face. He let his men see him ride past, their lusty cheers doing nothing to improve his confidence.

The struggle now raged along the front for a mile or more, the two armies entangled along that whole distance. The armored riders of the Solamnic Army, led by the Rose Knights of Palanthas, had formed close ranks to meet the charge of the wolf-riding goblin cavalry. In a bloody clash, the savage riders and their lupine mounts fell steadily back. Many riders and mounts fell on both sides. Wolves snarled and bit at the hamstrings of the knights' warhorses, and the horses kicked and stomped their tormentors. Goblins and knights clashed desperately with clanging swords.

Meanwhile, the infantry of all three wings of Jaymes's army drove into Ankhar's force, pressing the hobgoblins and ogres hard. Arrows from archers on both sides plummeted into the melee, striking indiscriminately. Here a company of ogres pushed ahead, stretching the Solamnic lines; there, the Kaolyn Axers plunged through many lines of hobgoblins, gleefully hacking at their ancestral foes. The result, everywhere, was a great mass of fighting warriors with little organization or apparent pattern.

As yet, the elemental king hadn't moved, and most of the men of Jaymes's army—engaged in fighting enemies only a few feet in front of their faces—had not taken stock of the great figure behind them. Here and there Jaymes heard a groan of dismay or a cry of abject terror, and as these sounds grew more numerous, he knew it was only a matter of moments before the morale of his troops was shaken by the monster in their midst.

The cold hilt of the sword in his hand was not comforting—it could do little against the looming, otherworldly presence. His loyal Freemen, the two dozens knights of no sign who had sworn loyalty to him personally and now rode alongside him, did not show any hesitation to accompany their commander on his steadfast advance. Captain Powell had his own broadsword bared and held the blade across his lap, ready for use.

But Jaymes had no plan. He skirted the pockets of furious battle as much as possible, fixing his attention on the solidifying figure of the elemental. Now he could see the lashing tendrils of its liquid limbs, and he knew it was preparing for an attack. On the far side of the action, the lord marshal reined in, watching and waiting for the being to move.

"What can we do, my lord?" Powell asked, reining in close, his low voice urgent. "We Freemen are yours to command."

"I know," replied the lord marshal. "I wish I had an order for you. I fear that our only course will be to harry and flee, but that idea galls me more than I can say."

Something glimmered off to the side, barely a dozen yards away. It was the Thorn Knight in the gray robe, blinking instantaneously into view. Jaymes saw that the man's hands were gesturing, his eyes flashing hatred as his gaze focused on the lord marshal.

"Beware of sorcery!" cried Powell, wheeling his horse around and raising his sword. But he was on the wrong side of Jaymes and could only attempt to shoulder his commander out of the way as he spurred his mount into a charge toward the Thorn Knight.

"Kill the Gray Robe!" shouted another of the Freemen, spotting the enemy magic-user. He and a companion spurred their horses toward the man, who took little notice of them as they galloped threateningly toward him.

Instead, the Thorn Knight stared at Jaymes for the length of a breath then gestured and shouted a guttural sound. Jaymes's roan whinnied and reared, and something solid struck the lord marshal in the solar plexus, knocking him from the saddle. The wind was driven from his lungs as he slammed to the ground.

The pair of Freemen reached the Gray Robe but, with a final gesture, the Thorn Knight disappeared a moment before they could cut him down.

Gasping for air, Jaymes sat up painfully as he tried to catch his breath. The roan was nearby, looking at him with upraised ears, nickering curiously. Sergeant Ian of the Freemen reached him, helping Jaymes to rise unsteadily to his feet and brushing the commander's tunic.

Only then did Jaymes see the other knight, who was wearing the white tunic of his personal bodyguard. The Freeman was obviously dead, still and blue, his eyes locked open in an expression of . . . what? Not horror or fear, as the lord marshal would have expected. Instead, the knight's dead face was frozen into a leer of great, almost inexpressible joy.

"He was killed by death magic," Captain Powell suggested, dismounting and looking ruefully at the dead Freeman. "This was Sir Benedict. He tackled you, drove you from the saddle before the wizard's spell could reach you. It was he who took the blow."

"Taking the magic on himself instead," Jaymes realized, shaken. "A very brave man."

He wanted to say more, much more, but now the elemental king started to move.

⊱•⊰•⊱◉⊰•⊱•⊰

Hoarst teleported back to the half-giant, who stood with his emerald-tipped spear planted beside him and the upraised wand in his meaty fist. Ankhar had been glaring in awe and consternation at the fully materialized elemental king and started slightly as the Thorn Knight appeared.

"Oh, there you are! Did you kill him?" he asked.

"I'm not sure," Hoarst replied in his usual unflappable way. "I used a powerful spell, but he is very well guarded. It may be that the lord marshal survived."

"No matter," barked the half-giant. "I am ready to send the king against the knights!"

Ankhar swept the wand through a half circle, gesturing toward the elemental, forcing it to recoil, to lumber away from them. "See how it obeys my will!" he crowed exuberantly. "Go! Kill! Attack at once!"

The force of the magic caused the elemental king to roar and immediately turn away. It lumbered toward the enemy army, kicking through any soldiers hapless enough to find themselves in its path. The battlefield dissolved in terror as the troops of both armies scrambled madly to get out of the way, men slashing at men who stood in their path, ogres doing the same to other ogres. The panic was general and all consuming.

One cyclonic limb kicked through a group of dwarf axe men, sweeping dozens of them hundreds of feet through the air. A fear-maddened ogre was plucked from the ground by a pinch of vaporous fingers, lifted high above the ground, then dropped, screaming, into a knot of his fear-crazed fellows. Almost as if it were dancing with joy, the huge monster swept from one leg back to the other, spinning faster and faster until the twin tornadoes of its lower limbs melded into one screamingly powerful storm.

As many goblins and ogres as humans died in this violent vortex, and the line of battle was cleaved in two by the massive monster's passage. All combatants fled, their petty quarrels forgotten in the face of certain extinction. Horses and wolves raced away at full speed, ignoring the commands of riders who tried to steer them. Back and forth along the front, the monstrous being wreaked its doom until a cloud of dust—shot through with lightning and stinging droplets of water—obscured much of the chaos on the ground.

Ankhar stood watching, his jaw slackened by awe, as the beast killed and destroyed and rampaged. Only after several moments did he remember the slender talisman in his hand. Finally he lifted the wand, waving it broadly before him and striding purposefully forward. The force of the magic device repelled the king of the elementals, and with a screeching roar—a sound unlike anything in nature—it began to move away.

Hoarst and Ankhar continued to advance, the half-giant still wielding his wand. The monster continued to move, and in moments it was wading into the bulk of the Solamnic Army, those units that had been held in reserve behind the front and had been observing, frozen and horrified, the irresistible onslaught of the elemental king.

Those valiant warriors—knowing they could do nothing against the monstrous presence—turned their backs and ran or put spurs to their steeds and galloped from the fight.

×‹∘◉‹∘◉‹∘◉‹∘◉∘›◉∘›◉∘›◉∘›×

Dram picked himself up. His ears were ringing; he was covered with soot. The clear stream he had been drinking from was now a muddy sludge, and the green meadow had blackened around him. He looked up the hill and saw that all the trees had been flattened by some terrible force, the ridgetop itself swept clear of everything.

Groggily and in growing terror, he scrambled up the hill. He had to climb over the charred trunks of trees that had been knocked over to completely block the roadway that had been utterly clear when he descended a few moments earlier. Now the ridgetop was a hellish landscape, scoured clean of wagons, bombards, supplies—everything was simply gone.

He saw bodies scattered around, blackened and broken. Sulfie was there, charred and lifeless; only her diminutive size allowed him to recognize her. Gently he rolled her over, his tears falling on the tiny, blackened corpse.

"You deserved better, little gnome," Dram said quietly. He thought of Jaymes, then, and it was not a friendly thought: his companion had used the three gnomes, taken their knowledge for his own purposes. One by one they had fallen in a cause that was not their own. As for Jaymes Markham, would he even take note of the sacrifices made in his name?

Dram knew that he wouldn't.

There was a spot of whiteness in all the smoldering ruin. The Lady Coryn lay huddled in a ball, her white robe, somehow, still curiously unsullied. Dram knelt beside her, touched her, and gasped with surprise when the white wizard moaned.

Somehow she was still alive. Her eyebrows had been burned away, her face and hands were burned red, but her flesh, wherever her robe had covered it, seemed all right.

"Coryn—what happened?" Dram asked frantically. Her only reply was a low moan. He knelt, touched her hand, and her eyes flashed open. The cowl of her robe fell back, revealing that her black hair had not been burned. Somehow, the dwarf realized, she had cloaked herself in just enough protection to save her life in the midst of the blast.

Again she moaned, looking at Dram, her tongue appearing between cracked and blistered lips.

"Water! I've got to get you water!" he jumped up, looking around. There had been water wagons to the rear of each bombard, but those—like everything else on this ridgetop—had been blasted to oblivion.

Weeping in frustration, he ran all the way back to the stream. He filled the small waterskin he carried with him and ran back to the wizard. Dram brought it up to Coryn's lips, giving her a few drops.

"Here," he said. "Drink a little. Everything's going to be all right."

But the smoke had cleared enough for him to look at the battlefield, and even as he spoke them, he knew the words were a lie.

><

The four wings of the Army of Solamnia had fallen back before the irresistible monster. They had scattered from the field, troops simply trying to survive. The Army of the Rose was retreating to the north, while the Crowns and Swords were fleeing westward. There was little sense of formation or purpose—the men were terrified and wanted only to get away. The horsemen moved fastest, while the more heavily armed footmen threw away armor, equipment, even weapons in their haste. All of the army's supply wagons were abandoned, and the wounded were left to fend for themselves.

The Palanthians, on the south flank of the original position, were forced to withdraw into a valley of the Garnets, moving to higher ground, and it was this wing that the elemental king pursued. Jaymes rode past the creature as it swept through a rank of crossbowmen, the cyclonic winds of its lower limbs tossing the armored humans around like chaff in a strong wind. It seemed to be loping along with these troops, crossing over a ridge and crushing a wide path through a forest of pines then settling back to the valley floor.

The lord marshal rode just ahead of the looming horror, sweeping into the valley where the legion had fled. He found General Weaver trying to organize a line of defense.

"Stand, you wretches!" the officer ordered his terrified troops, who retained enough discipline that many of them actually obeyed the order. They fired arrows at the elemental, but those arrows vanished, without effect, against the massive torso. A small band of knights charged with lances, but the elemental's winds tossed them back.

"General!" shouted Jaymes, riding up to Weaver's prancing stallion. "You'll have to fall back; your men can't fight this thing!"

"Run? By Joli, I cannot, sir!" he protested. "By the Oath and the Measure, we must make our stand here!"

"General!" barked Jaymes. "That's an order—withdraw! Lead your men up into the mountains. Break them into small groups—see that as many survive as possible!"

His sorrowful eyes showing his frustration, the Rose Knight obeyed his lord marshal, pulling his men back from the elemental and urging them higher into the mountain range. They scrambled over the rocky ground, some of them splashing up the streambed, others sprinting through the woods as fast. As if toying with them, the elemental king hesitated, pausing at the mouth of the valley. The grim, lofty face scanned its helpless targets.

The men kept fleeing, completely abandoning all discipline, but the legion's flight was thwarted a half mile away. The retreating troops rushed around a bend in the narrow valley and halted in consternation and panic. A sheer cliff rose directly before them, blocking any further progress into the mountains. Then the elemental king, his pursuit at an almost leisurely pace, came into view, striding resolutely forward.

Jaymes turned to General Weaver.

"We'll stand here, my lord!" declared the general. *"Est Sularus oth Mithas!"*

"Yes," agreed the lord marshal bitterly. There was no way out of this place, and it seemed certain many thousands of brave men would pay for that reality with their lives.

"Hey, Jaymes! Sir Lord Marshal! It's me; I'm back!"

Jaymes whirled in his saddle, his jaw dropping in amazement as Moptop Bristlebrow came scrambling right out of a nearby rock pile to stand on a boulder at the foot of the cliff. The kender waved cheerfully then looked around at the soldiers he had startled with his sudden appearance. "You guys are a little jumpy, aren't you?" he asked.

It was then that the elemental king uttered a thunderous roar that rolled up the valley, echoing between the cliffs and resounding through the air.

Moptop hopped down off the rock and sauntered toward Jaymes. He waved nonchalantly at the monster looming into the air barely a mile away.

"Oh, him again," he said. "I guess I got here just in time."

CHAPTER TWENTY-SEVEN

THE MARCH
OF THE ADAMITES

For several breaths Jaymes Markham was utterly speechless. He simply stared at Moptop, stunned by the kender's appearance on the battlefield. The pathfinder's air of utter nonchalance was incongruous against the backdrop of death and mayhem, and it took the lord marshal an act of will to shake his head and convince himself that he was not imagining the bizarre scene as the kender ambled cheerfully down from the rocks toward the army commander.

A glance over his shoulder showed Jaymes that the monster was pressing the advance, as if it sensed the helplessness of the trapped humans. Another bellow exploded from the elemental king, this one a thunderous convulsion that shook the ground and caused a small rockslide in the valley. The noise finally startled his tongue into action.

"Moptop! What in the name of all the gods are you doing here? Where did you come from?" the lord marshal demanded when he finally regained the power of speech.

The kender grinned happily. "Well, I found another path. But it's not like it looks—I mean, I didn't just magically walk through the rocks, like we did at the Cleft Spires. I went back underground like you asked me to, and I had to look around for a really long time. But I found my way back out again!" He chucked a thumb over his shoulder, indicating the tumble of large rocks at the base of the cliff. "See, there's a cave down here, and I came out of the hole."

"Of course." The lord marshal thought quickly. He looked up and saw the looming form of the elemental king, its black shape etched against the sky and two fiery eyes fixed upon the milling soldiers of the Palanthian Legion trapped here in this valley. They were hard up against the cliff. There were several thousand men in here, many hundreds of them on horseback. Brave and willing to fight to the last man, they were nevertheless incapable of battling the looming monster. Their only hope of survival was escape.

Looking at the sheer cliff, the rock wall looming a hundred feet in the air, capped by a cruel overhang that would have prevented even a skilled climber from attaining the top, Jaymes could see there would be no further retreat on the ground. Even though the kender claimed to have found a cave at the base of that precipitous barrier somewhere within the great pile of large boulders, Jaymes couldn't spy any opening.

"You say there's a cave in there. Is it large enough for these men to escape into it?" Even as he asked the question, he felt the looming presence of the giant elemental and knew it was a futile hope.

Moptop confirmed that knowledge with his first words. "Not really—it's pretty small and narrow. If they left these horses outside, they could go in there one at a time, I guess, if the cave wasn't filled with adamites. But they pretty much block the whole thing up."

"Adamites?" Jaymes felt a flickering of hope. "So you found them? And they came with you?"

"Yes—and you were right! They all followed me right along, the whole army of them, after I told them what you told me to say. They're lined up down there right now. Here they come!"

The lord marshal saw the proof emerging into view even as the kender spoke. Grayish white, the color of naked rock, the first of the stony warriors came out of the hidden cave to appear between a pair of large, square boulders. The stone-skinned warrior slid nimbly down the shelf to stand at attention on the floor of the valley. Another warrior came behind the first, and still another followed, both of them dropping to the ground to flank the first of the statuelike warriors.

The file of adamites emerged from the cave in eerie silence, their heads capped by the antique, bristling helmets, each bearing a small round shield in its left hand and the stout, sturdy spear in its right. But they came quickly; in no time at all, there were more than a dozen standing there, and this rank took a step forward as still more emerged to fill out a second rank just behind the first. The second group marched to the side to take up a position beside the first, extending the front to some twenty-five warriors—and twenty-five sharp, sturdy spears—while more and more and more of them continued to climb out from the narrow cavern.

"My lord!" cried General Weaver, approaching with his sword in his hand. He glared worriedly at the adamites as the first rank took another few steps away from the cliff wall to make room for yet more of their comrades. "Are we being attacked from behind, as well?"

"No, General," Jaymes replied, holding up his hand to dissuade nearby knights who had turned about to face these new arrivals, their weapons at the ready. "If I have guessed correctly, we've just been reinforced."

"What in the name of the gods *are* they?" Weaver said.

"I don't know if we can call them allies, but I do believe they're the sworn enemies of *that* thing," the marshal replied, pointing up at the elemental as the monster took another step closer. One of the cyclone legs kicked into a formation of legionnaires, knocking the men of Palanthas down like stacks of straw. Horses neighed shrilly, rearing and bucking. A volley of arrows flew from a company of archers, vanishing without effect against the great swath of the elemental king's belly.

The human troops closer to the adamites backed away to make room for the great, swelling block of troops, already numbering several hundred. Swordsmen muttered curses and exclamations, and archers raised their bows—holding their arrows—as more and more of these lifelike, but clearly stone, beings sprouted from the narrow cave. The adamites marched quickly, forming up in single-file ranks in an ever-expanding front around the concealed aperture at the foot of the cliff. There were hundreds of them now gathered and more still marching out of the tunnel. The front was a hundred paces long by now, and every yard of it was preceded by the wicked, spade-shaped spear points.

"They hate that elemental," Moptop explained, looking curiously up at the looming monster. "I think they want to catch it and take it back where it belongs."

Already the adamites were marching forward, ignoring the human warriors who scrambled and stumbled to get out of the way. The spears never wavered; the line did not bend, even as the magical warriors flowed around trees and rocks, splashed through the shallow stream that meandered through the valley floor. Moving away from the cliff, spears held level at shoulder height, they tromped steadily toward the massive elemental king.

"How will they . . . oh, never mind," Jaymes said. Spinning around, he barked at General Weaver. "Open your line all the way! Let them through without trouble!" he ordered.

The soldiers of the Palanthian Legion pulled back hastily, more than willing to allow these weirdly unnatural warriors to pass without hindrance. The adamites continued their advance in a tightly packed formation bristling with spears, their feet stepping in cadence as they marched smoothly past the Palanthian troops and on toward the horrific giant. Marching with steady, exacting precision, their feet crunched over the ground in an increasingly audible rhythm.

Stony spears extended, the adamites, numbering at least a thousand strong by this time, stretched across the valley floor. Lines from the rear marched to the sides, faced front again, and expanded the ranks with perfect discipline and formation. They continued to march forward, long spears extended, closing rapidly on the king of the elementals.

As yet that awe-inspiring monster showed no fear of the new arrivals. Instead, the twin cyclones of its great legs kicked faster, and the monster waded heavily into the first rank of the adamites, uttering another bellow with enough force to break three or four shelves of rock loose from the overhanging wall of cliff.

✕◦❀◦◦❀◦◦❀◦ ⬤ ◦❀◦◦❀◦◦❀◦✕

"It will crush them there; they can retreat no farther!" gloated Ankhar the half-giant as he and Hoarst hurried around the shoulder of the valley wall. The army commander gazed almost rapturously at the gigantic being as it closed on the trapped Solamnic army. The sheer wall with its lofty overhang formed the perfect trap. The milling humans, trapped against the steep, precipitous barrier, had lost all formation, showed none of the cohesion and discipline he had come to expect from the knights.

"The whole army will die here!" he crowed.

The half-giant and the Thorn Knight had hastened after the monster as it pursued the fleeing Solamnics, the pair moving far ahead of most of the army. Most of Ankhar's troops were behind them, still reeling from the chaos of the battle, though several hundred of his goblin warg-riders had formed up and escorted the pair in their pursuit. Ankhar had insisted upon rushing ahead of the bulk of his troops, leaving even Laka, so he could see all that was going to transpire and revel in his ultimate triumph.

"Hurry up!" he exhorted the wizard. "We will be witness to a great victory!"

Only then did Ankhar notice that Hoarst, his face oddly impassive, wasn't looking at the monster. His staring eyes were directed elsewhere.

"What are those things?" asked the Thorn Knight, his voice unusually urgent and concerned.

"What things? What are you talking about?"

Hoarst seemed agitated, and this irritated Ankhar. Why could he not just relish this great moment, this historic success? But the human, ignoring his commander's frown of displeasure, turned and rushed to climb some rocks that had tumbled to the foot of the nearby valley wall.

"Get up here; we can see better from a higher vantage," urged the Thorn Knight in a peremptory tone.

Ankhar scowled but followed the irritating man up the loose shelf of rocks. He stumbled and scuffed his hands trying to find solid purchase, and he wrenched his knee when one of the rocks yielded to his weight to tumble loosely down to the ground. Cursing, the half-giant hoisted himself to the ledge where Hoarst stood then turned around to look.

He could clearly see the mass of enemy troops, fractured lines and broken companies huddled against the cliff that barred their progress up the valley. Some of the riders had dismounted and were holding their panic-stricken horses by the reins. It was clear they could find no escape, no route out of the valley save the one they had taken in retreat, and that path was now held by the massive presence of the king of the elementals.

But there was another source of movement down in the valley, something Ankhar had to squint to see. It was like the rocky floor of the valley was slinking forward like a living carpet, a flood of ghostly gray stone spreading out to confront the king of the elementals, to block its path toward its human quarry. Squinting, the half-giant made out an array of spear tips—many hundreds of them—and, with a start, realized these new stone-colored arrivals bore the shapes of men.

"What are they?" he demanded, annoyed by the postponement of slaughter, though still not overly worried about the outcome of the fight.

"I don't know," the Thorn Knight replied curtly.

"Strange warriors . . . and look, they attack the king," the half giant grunted, amused. This would be good entertainment. He would watch these mysterious newcomers die.

"Whatever they are, they don't lack for courage," the man noted.

"Let them die bravely instead of cravenly, then," snorted Ankhar. But his bravado had an element of bluster to it. After all, what *were* those things?

He began to feel a little sick to his stomach.

The bizarre newcomers looked somewhat like humans but seemed to be made of stone. and as Ankhar watched with fascination, they swarmed up to the elemental king, surrounding it, thrusting at it with their long spears. The monster advanced right into the midst of that rank, swinging the great columns of its legs, stomping mightily right on top of the stony spear-carriers.

Surprisingly, the new attackers showed an equal enthusiasm for the fray. Holding their spears pointed upward, they marched fearlessly right under the crushing force of the king's striding legs. The monster pounded downward, burying dozens of the warriors under each foot. But when it tried to move on, the thing lurched unsteadily and remained locked in place.

"Like it stepped into a pit of tar," Hoarst remarked. "It seems to be stuck."

"No! They will be crushed!" Ankhar insisted, his expectations overruling the evidence of his eyes.

For, indeed, it seemed like the elemental king was anchored fast. It roared the mightiest bellow yet—even the *echoes* hurt Ankhar's ears—but it could not lift either foot off of the ground. Bending at the waist, the gigantic being swept a granite fist across the front of the spear-wielders. But instead of smashing them to the ground, it collected them, like a shaggy dog collects burrs. Each warrior met the elemental's blow with an upraised spear, and the weapon drove into the monstrous fist and remained embedded there. The stony warrior, in turn, held unfailingly to the spear, so when the king raised his fist again, he had a score or more of the gray-colored warriors dangling from the limb.

And the following ranks of the bizarre attackers continued to advance and fight similarly. All around the king circled a ring of these stone beings, and the later ranks climbed over their fellows—who remained stuck fast to the monster's feet—to thrust and plunge their own spears into its ankles, its calves. In moments the being was skirted all about, and the things continued to climb, to stab, to cling.

Strangely, these newcomers did not seem to be dying, though the elemental king struggled to kick with its massive legs and continued to smash downward with clublike arms. The massive torso twisted back and forth, flexed and leaned, and quivered violently. Yet the burrlike warriors remained fixed to the huge shape, every place they touched it, and still more of them climbed up, stabbed, and held on. Another great forearm smashed to the ground, but when the king raised the limb, nearly a hundred of the stone warriors dangled from it, like a strangely decorative fringe.

The stone warriors continued to attack, to stab with their spears, and to lodge their weapons in the monsters. The king roared and thrashed but didn't seem capable of destroying the attackers. Ankhar blinked, growling deep within his chest. So strange and unexpected! What in the world was happening? Even when the monster lashed out, each of the stone warriors struck by an elemental limb seemed to grab onto it, until the lower extremities of the monstrous being were wrapped in a skirt of stone ornaments.

The stone warriors rattled and clattered as the huge being shook, banging together and swinging about, but still none of them broke free. Instead, more came on, climbing, stabbing, clinging.

And the weight was clearly dragging the monster down.

Thrashing desperately, the king of the elementals seemed to shrink, its lower limbs slipping into the ground. The attackers affixed to the feet and lower legs disappeared, vanishing through the bedrock of the valley floor, and the king sank with them.

More and more of the spear-carrying warriors closed in, climbing on top of each other, swarming like ants higher and higher up onto the shoulders of the massive being, even as the king continued to shrink down closer to the ground. Almost waist deep now, the monster fought desperately with its arms, twisting its torso. But each blow only attached more of the mysterious spearmen to the creature's immortal form. Spears stabbed into the great vault of the king's chest, while more of the enterprising stone warriors—moving nimbly, despite their stiff facades—scrambled onto the creature's collar, nape, and neck.

The attackers scrambled and stabbed, and finally they completely covered the elemental king. Ankhar could see no sign of the fiery eyes, the craggy shoulders, the stormy arms and legs. His great monster was just a huge, shaggy pile of stone creatures that coated the being, inexorably dragging it under. Still fighting, thrashing, convulsing, the massive form continued to sink under the ground.

Now it was chest deep in the solid bedrock of the valley and sinking deeper still. It roared once more, but even that was a hollow sound, coming as though from very far away and sounding more like hellish pain than fury. Even as the king howled, the stone attackers climbed into its gaping mouth, stabbing with those spears, dragging it down, down. Now only its shoulders and head remained above the ground, and even those moved sluggishly, totally overwhelmed by the stony weight of the spear-carrying attackers.

Within a few moments, the elemental king had sunk out of sight, bearing with it the heavy weight of the mysterious stone warriors. Still they piled on, spears pointing down into the ground now, the attackers stabbing, following the force of their thrusts into the ground, and descending from sight.

They continued until, at last, there were none of them remaining on the surface of the world.

Only then did Ankhar glance elsewhere, taking note of the human warriors, suddenly rallying under the command of their lord marshal and a general wearing the sigil of the Rose. The few goblins on their wolves who had followed closely behind

Ankhar were being cut down by companies of mounted knights, the men refreshed and heartened by the defeat of their monstrous foe. Trumpets sounded, and the whole of the Palanthian Legion started forward, pushing the scattered remnants of Ankhar's horde before them.

"I think," Hoarst said with a low, rueful sigh as he started to climb down from the shelf of rock, "that we had better get back to the army."

<hr/>

The Palanthian Legion led the counterattack, emerging from the mountain valley with a vengeance, sweeping into the scattered companies of Ankhar's horde. Jaymes and his Freemen rode with General Weaver at the forefront of the charge, though the army commander immediately dispatched messengers from his bodyguard to his other retreating troops.

Within an hour the men of the Rose, Crown, and Sword were streaming back to the field from the west and north. Word of the elemental king's defeat infused them with new energy, fueling the strength of a fresh charge. The barbarians and monsters of the half-giant's horde, recognizing imminent disaster, began a flight to the south and east.

It became obvious that the shattered enemy army would continue routing all the way to Lemish. Exhausted and drained, the humans of the Solamnic Army finally abandoned the pursuit as night cloaked the battlefield in darkness. Too much had happened during this momentous day for any soldier to keep fighting. The enemy was clearly defeated, broken, and demoralized.

Annihilation would have to wait for another campaign.

CHAPTER TWENTY-EIGHT

END OF THE BEGINNING

"The adamites' sole purpose was to guard the elemental king, to prevent it from journeying to the upper world and wreaking the kind of destruction of which it was capable. They must have been stationed there many centuries ago—perhaps even during the Age of Dreams."

Jaymes was explaining the situation to Lord Martin as the two of them rode to Solanthus, accompanying the withdrawing army of Solamnia. Thousands of troops marched with them, before and behind, all proceeding in a massive column. The joy of a great victory propelled them, but it was tempered by the memory of the many grievous losses, men and women slain, cities sacked and burned, during the three years of Ankhar's war.

"We must offer a prayer of gratitude for whichever of our ancestors, or our ancestors' gods, had the foresight to assign them to that ageless duty," remarked the nobleman of Solanthus. "Without them, our cause surely would have failed."

"Not just our cause," Jaymes noted. "Imagine if that creature was free to roam the surface of the world. No city could stand against it. Even the greatest dragons might have had no choice but to flee or die."

The army was marching westward, finally, away from the battlefield and the Garnet foothills. Of course, scouts and outriders were closely watching the area around the great force, and the men still carried their weapons at the ready. But all reports indicated the enemy was thoroughly broken, scattering to the southeast, and even the lord marshal allowed himself to relax a little.

The two men rode their horses at a slow walk, following behind an enclosed wagon that served as an ambulance, softly furnished to carry Coryn as comfortably as possible. The Clerist knight, Sir Templar, rode inside the wagon with the wizard, using his healing magic to ease her pain and recuperation. The lord marshal intended to accompany the wagon all the way to Palanthas, but Solanthus was the first stop on the long ride.

Generals Weaver, Dayr, and Markus were riding with their own troops, elsewhere in the great column. General Rankin had fallen in the Battle of the Foothills, as it was being called, and his body was carried in another wagon not too far away. He would be returned to Solanthus for a state funeral. Captain Powell and the Freemen were riding in a loose formation around the lord marshal, near enough to be summoned if necessary. One other rider, the slight figure of Moptop Bristlebrow astride a small pony, trailed very closely behind Martin and Jaymes.

"So you dispatched the kender to search for these adamites, to lure them up to the surface?" Martin said, shaking his head in astonishment. "How did he know where to find them? Or where to bring them to the battlefield?"

Now it was Jaymes's turn to shake his head wonderingly. "All I can say is he calls himself a professional guide and pathfinder extraordinaire, and if anyone ever earned his title, it's Moptop

Bristlebrow. He must have a very benevolent god looking out for his welfare. I've never met anyone who can find his way like he can, and yesterday he found a path that saved a whole army."

Yet Moptop, listening in as he rode beside the two humans, was unusually subdued and self-effacing. "I thought this whole war thing would be a grand adventure," he said with a heavy sigh. "But there's too many people who get hurt. The city got all broken up, and I can't stand seeing all those horses get killed."

"Aye, my friend," said Jaymes, clapping him on the shoulder. "Far too many people get hurt."

"We're going back to Solanthus, but it makes me so sad to think of that place without the duchess. She led those people through that long siege, and she won't be there now. Not ever again!" the kender declared, sniffling noisily.

"Aye," Lord Martin agreed. "But she held us together, kept the city alive, during those years of the siege. You may rest assured, my friend, that her memory will live as long as there are people in Solanthus strong enough to draw a breath."

"That's something, I guess," he admitted. "But I still miss her."

"Indeed." Martin nodded solemnly. "As do we all."

The princess of Palanthas looked out of the window from her chambers high up in one of the towers of her father's palace. Her eyes were drawn to the east, where the crest of the Vingaard range was outlined in the purplish rays of the setting sun. She held a piece of paper in her hand, a few sentences quickly scribed and messengered to the city in a courier's pouch. That same pouch, carried by a fleet rider, had brought news of the great victory.

All the city was celebrating Ankhar's defeat. His army had been banished to Lemish, said the report, and the threat to the lands of the knighthood was quelled for the foreseeable future.

The other note that had been delivered to her was a personal missive from the lord marshal himself:

I have won the field. My army has triumphed, and I returning to Palanthas. I am coming home to you, my bride.

The missive had provoked a strange reaction—not the delirious joy she would have expected, nor even a tremulous sense of relief, the weight of concern for her husband's fate lifted by the good news.

Instead, she felt confused and frightened.

She remembered her tears, her almost uncontrollable hysteria when Jaymes had departed for the war the morning after the wedding. She had locked herself in her rooms for days, seeing no one but her faithful maid, Marie, and her trusted counselor, the priestess Melissa du Juliette. The cleric had remained at her side, caring for her tirelessly, speaking softly, soothing the grieving young woman, until at last Selinda began to feel more like her old, confident self.

Emerging at last from her self-imposed seclusion, she had found a palace, a city, a people she barely recognized. It was this altered awareness that finally brought home to her that, though her surroundings remained the same, she herself had undergone some deep, fundamental transformation. It was a frightening and disorienting awareness, so she had tried hard to figure out what had happened to change her so.

At first she had prayed to every goddess she knew, hoping that the seed of her wedding night's passion would take root within her womb and begin to grow into the baby she desperately desired.

Within a few weeks, however, she had learned she was not yet pregnant, and with that realization had come a new sense of wonder, and mystery, and another dawning realization.

Did she desire a child?

No, not yet, she had decided, and with that decision had come more questions. Why had she fallen so giddily for this man she had known for years and had previously regarded with a certain wary respect. What had happened to her? What had changed her?

And what would her future hold?

⊱•⊰⊱•⊰❀⊱•⊰⊱•⊰

"You fool!" shouted Ankhar, raising his fist over his stepmother's wrinkled face. "You pledged me an undefeatable ally, and he was defeated at the very moment of my triumph!"

"He was as mighty as they come!" shrieked Laka, not the least bit cowed. "You are the fool, to let him be trapped in the mountains! You should have driven him across the plains with the wand!"

"Bah! He was killed by that army of stone! Who were they? Where did they come from all of a sudden?"

Laka only glared at him. The half-giant's hand trembled, but he could not bring himself to smash it downward. Instead, he whirled about and spotted the Thorn Knight watching him through narrowed eyes.

They were in a bivouac of the retreating army, a sprawling encampment near the marshes that marked the border between Solamnia and Lemish. That land, dark and mysterious and peopled with monsters and goblins and other wretched beings, lay like a shroud on the southern horizon. For miles around the trio, the remnants of the half-giant's horde were scattered in tents and bedrolls on the wet, miserable ground. Mosquitoes and other insects whined around their ears. All of the half-giant's captains had found compelling reasons to avoid their commander on this dark and ill-omened night.

"Why could you not foresee the danger?" Ankhar asked the wizard, his voice a low growl.

"Who could have?" Hoarst replied, not illogically. "Those stone soldiers are unknown in all the history of the world."

"Fool!" the half-giant cursed, still trembling. Impulsively he slapped with his great hand, a blow that would have snapped the wizard's neck had it landed where he aimed, right on the smug, almost contemptuous face.

However, the Thorn Knight was no longer there; he had blinked himself magically out of sight a fraction of a breath before the powerful blow landed. Ankhar swung through a wide arc, striking only the air, staggering off balance to keep from falling.

"Where did he go?" he demanded of the old hob-wench.

Laka shrugged in that maddening way of hers. "Away," she replied. "Perhaps he will return when you have calmed down."

The half-giant forced himself to draw a breath. He squinted, remembering. "You said that potion, the tea he drank to gain strength, would kill him eventually!"

"It should have," the shaman replied with a shrug. "But he has a well of strength I did not perceive. It seems my potion not only healed him for a time, but ended up by making him stronger."

"He is a dangerous man."

"A powerful enemy, to be sure. But also a powerful ally."

"Will he really come back?" Ankhar asked, discouraged. It occurred to him, a trifle belatedly, how much he had come to rely upon the Thorn Knight. Hoarst's spells, and his knowledge, had been key elements in the army commander's success, and he knew that he wouldn't fare nearly as well without his magic.

The half-giant slumped to the ground, ignoring the swampy wetness that instantly soaked through his breeches. Laka came over to him, placing a clawlike hand upon his beefy forearm.

"If he has reason to come back, he will," she said. "You have made him a very rich man, and he will remember that. For now, you must rest. Tomorrow we march into Lemish. There, my son, you will be master of all—King Ankhar!"

"King of Lemish? Lord of a swamp and a forest? Master of a few crude villages? What good is that?" he demanded.

"It is a new start," she said. "A place for you to begin afresh, grow strong again, my bold son. For I had another dream, just this night."

"A dream? Of what?"

"A dream that you will return to Solamnia. Your army will be mightier than ever, and the humans of the world will bow down to you and beg for mercy."

"A prophecy," Ankhar said. He leaned back, stretching out on the ground, suddenly conscious of the weariness that seeped through every fiber of his bones. "I like this prophecy," he remarked. "Tell me more."

But by the time Laka began to speak, he was already snoring.

⊱❖⊰

The great column of the Solamnic forces dispersed as it marched. A large contingent, representing all four armies, stayed in the vicinity of Solanthus, there to keep a wary eye on the border with Lemish, and to watch for any reappearance of Ankhar's vanished—and vanquished—horde. General Rankin of the Sword Army, former captain of Solanthus, would be laid to rest in a great funeral in the city, but the lord marshal offered his regrets and explained that he would hurry on to Palanthas with Coryn the White.

Detachments of the Rose Army headed south and west for Caergoth, while many of the Crown Knights made for the site of ruined Thelgaard, where rebuilding was already under way. The Kaolyn Axers turned their faces toward the high Garnet Mountains and the undermountain kingdom.

Many men of the Vingaard plains simply bade farewell and returned to their homes and farms. Dram, with the very few survivors of his original company—the hill dwarves who had garrisoned the supply park, mostly—would ride to the New Compound.

"It will take some time to settle the affairs of all those dwarves who died with the battery," Dram explained to Jaymes, his expression stern, his eyes cold and unclouded by tears. "That's the most important thing. It will be next year before we're ready to start working again."

"I understand," said the lord marshal. If he was anxious to accelerate the work on the compound, and to have a new battery of bombards to replace those lost on the ridge, he knew his able assistant too well to press the point.

"Good luck," was all he said as his oldest and most loyal follower rode toward the mountains on his sturdy pony. Dram didn't look back.

The Palanthian Legion led the way back to that glorious city. Jaymes Markham, accompanied by his Freemen, rode in the wake of the legion, marking slow progress as they escorted the wagon in which Coryn was resting and recovering. It took three weeks for the force to make its way across the plains, over the High Clerist's Pass, and down into the city.

They approached the high walls at a steady marc. the great victory on the field, not in a triumphal proce. troops were met at the gate by a great crowd, but the ople sensed their lord's somber mood and refrained from cheers and applause. Instead they watched solemnly as, flanked by his two dozen Freemen, Jaymes Markham broke away from the great column of the Palanthian legion, following the enclosed ambulance through the city and up the inclined road leading onto Nobles Hill.

Finally, the white wizard was brought to her own home, and a young priestess of the city—as close a friend of Coryn's as of the princess—arrived to see to her convalescence.

"The Lady Coryn is resting comfortably now," reported that priestess, Melissa du Juliette, to Jaymes Markham as he paced in the anteroom of her manor. "The journey was hard on her, but Sir Templar's magic did its job, keeping her alive. I anticipate she will make a slow but full recovery. Her robe protected her from the worst—and I think she cast some sort of defensive spell at the very last moment, before the blast surrounded her."

"Thank you," Jaymes said. "Will you stay her with her?"

"Of course. I presume you are headed to the palace . . . to call upon your wife? I think she would like to talk to you."

The question was a pointed one, and the lord marshal flushed. "Of course," he replied. "I know she will want to see me."

Melissa du Juliette looked at him coldly. "I said nothing about her wanting to see you. I said she wanted to talk to you."

With that, she pushed shut the door to Coryn's bedroom and left Jaymes Markham no choice but to walk away.

∗ ∗ ∗

"My Lord Marshal, it is a pleasure to see you, to welcome you back to Palanthas!" The Lord Regent Bakkard du Chagne himself bustled through the anteroom of the palace, rushing up to Jaymes and shaking his hand heartily.

"Allow me to add my congratulations to his lordship's," added the Clerist Inquisitor Frost, close behind. "These creatures everyone is talking about—so they came and dragged away the elemental king! Simply splendid! The gods favored you on that day, my lord."

"If there is anything we can do to help, now that the enemy is defeated," Sir Moorvan of the Kingfishers chimed in. "Please, let us know."

"Who told you the war was over?" Jaymes asked. "Ankhar and most of his troops got away. They have fallen back into Lemish, but unless we root them out of there, they will most certainly be back. There will be a pause in the fighting; that is all."

"Then, my Lord Marshal," said Bakkard du Chagne. "Hadn't you better get back to the field?"

"Not for a while," Jaymes replied. "Now, if you will excuse me, I must go to my wife."

He made his way through the dark halls of the palace and climbed the stairs to the lofty room where the Princess Selinda had moved her chambers, following the wedding. He was out of breath when he got there and somewhat surprised—even a little irritated—she had not yet materialized to greet him.

He went to the chambers and as the master of his own rooms, opened the door without knocking. He found Selinda in the next room, the dining room, but she did not rush ardently into his arms as he expected.

Instead, she regarded him ambiguously across the long table and finally came around somewhat closer but halted a few steps away.

"So the war is won?" she asked. "Can this be true?"

"It is won, at least for a time," he said. "Ankhar
but I have the knights pursuing what's left of his arn
where he goes and what should be done next. It will take a. other
campaign, probably, to expunge them for good."

"What happened?" Selinda asked.

"Well, we were able to drive them back from Solanthus—"

"Not that . . . not 'what happened in the war?'" she retorted
harshly. She looked at him fiercely, and for the first time he
saw the anger and anguish in her eyes. "I mean . . . with your
courtship . . . me losing my head, like a silly schoolgirl . . .
everything happening just the way you wanted it to—just when
you wanted it to happen!"

"I . . . I . . ." he began.

"You know I mean—" She drew a deep breath, but her cold
stare did not waver. "What treachery, what trick did you play?
What did you *do* to *me*?"

A NEW TRILOGY FROM MARGARET WEIS & TRACY HICKMAN

THE DARK CHRONICLES
Dragons of the Dwarven Depths
Volume One

Tanis, Tasslehoff, Riverwind and Raistlin
are trapped as refugees in Thorbardin, as the
draconian army closes in on the dwarven
kingdom. To save his homeland, Flint begins a
search for the Hammer of Kharas.

Available July 2006

For more information visit **www.wizards.com**

THE YEAR OF ROGUE DRAGONS
BY RICHARD LEE BYERS

Dragons across Faerûn begin to slip into madness, bringing all of the
world to the edge of cataclysm. The Year of Rogue Dragons has come.

THE RAGE
Renegade dragon hunter Dorn has devoted his entire life to killing
dragons. As every dragon across Faerûn begins to slip into madness,
civilization's only hope may lie in the last alliance Dorn and his
fellow hunters would ever accept.

THE RITE
Rampaging dragons appear in more places every day. But all the
dragons have to do to avoid the madness is trade their
immortal souls for an eternity of undeath.

THE RUIN
May 2006

For more information visit **www.wizards.com**

THE FIRST INTO BATTLE,

THEY HOLD THE LINE, THEY ARE...

THE FIGHTERS

MASTER OF CHAINS

Once he was a hero, but that was before he was nearly killed and
sold into slavery. Now he has nothing but hate and the chains of
his bondage: the only weapons he has with which to escape.

GHOSTWALKER

His first memories were of death. His second, of those who killed him.
Now he walks with specters, consumed by revenge.

SON OF THUNDER

Forgotten in a valley of the High Forest dwell the thunderbeasts,
kept secret by ancient and powerful magic. When the Zhentarim find
out about this magic, a young barbarian must defend his reptilian
brethren from those who would seize their power.

BLADESINGER

Corruption grips the heart of Rashemen in the one place they thought
it could not take root: the council of wise women who guide the people.
A half-elf bladesinger traveling north with his companions is the people's
only hope, but first, he must convince them to accept his help.

For more information visit **www.wizards.com**

HOUSE OF SERPENTS TRILOGY
By The New York Times best-selling author
Lisa Smedman

VENOM'S TASTE
The Pox, a human cult whose members worship the goddess of
plague and disease, begins to work the deadly will of Sibyls' Chosen.
As humans throughout the city begin to transform into the freakish
tainted ones, it's up to a yuan-ti halfbood to stop them all.

VIPER'S KISS
A mind-mage of growing power begins a secret journey to Sespeth.
There he meets a yuan-ti halfblood who has her eyes set on the scion
of house Extaminos – said to hold the fabled Circled Serpent.

VANITY'S BROOD
The merging of human and serpent may be the most dangerous
betrayal of nature the Realms has ever seen. But it could also be the
only thing that can bring a human slave and his yuan-ti mistress
together against a common foe.

www.wizards.com

ENTER THE NEW WORLD OF

EBERRON

THE DREAMING DARK TRILOGY

By Keith Baker

A hundred years of war...

Kingdoms lie shattered, armies are broken, and an entire
country has been laid to waste. Now an uneasy
peace settles on the land.

Into Sharn come four battle-hardened soldiers. Tired of
blood, weary of killing, they only want a place to call home.

The shadowed City of Towers has other plans...

THE CITY OF TOWERS
Volume One

THE SHATTERED LAND
Volume Two

THE GATES OF NIGHT
Volume Three
DECEMBER 2006

For more information visit **www.wizards.com**

ENTER THE NEW WORLD OF

THE WAR~TORN

After a hundred years of fighting the war is now over, and the people
of Eberron pray it will be the Last War. An uneasy peace settles
over the continent of Khorvaire.

But what of the soldiers, warriors, nobles, spies, healers, clerics, and
wizards whose lives were forever changed by the decades of war? What
does a world without war hold for those who have known nothing
but violence? What fate lies for these, the war-torn?

THE CRIMSON TALISMAN

BOOK 1

Adrian Cole

Erethindel, the fabled Crimson Talisman. Long sought by
the forces of darkness. Long guarded in secret by one family. Now the
secret has been revealed, and only one young man can keep it safe.

THE ORB OF XORIAT

BOOK 2

Edward Bolme

The last time Xoriat, the Realm of Madness, touched the world, years of
warfare and death erupted. A new portal to the Realm of Madness has
been found — a fabled orb, long thought lost. Now it has been stolen.

IN THE CLAWS OF THE TIGER

BOOK 3

James Wyatt

BLOOD AND HONOR

BOOK 4

Graeme Davis

For more information visit **www.wizards.com**

CHALLENGE MONSTERS

BE THE HERO

BATTLE YOUR FRIENDS

If you like adventures and challenges
you'll love the D&D® Miniatures Game.

Play out furious battles with your friends
or collect and trade the figures.

Ask for the D&D Miniatures Entry Pack
at your favorite book or game store and get ready to battle!

For more information visit **www.wizards.com**

R.A. Salvatore
Road of the Patriarch
The Sellswords, Book III

Jarlaxle and Entreri have found a home in the
monster-haunted steppes of the Bloodstone Lands,
and have even managed to make a few new friends.
But in a place as cruel as this, none of those friends are
naive enough to trust a drow mercenary and a shadowy
assassin to be anything but what they are: as dangerous
as the monsters they hunt.

October 2006

Servant of the Shard
The Sellswords, Book I

Powerful assassin Artemis Entreri tightens his grip on the streets
of Calimport, driven by the power of his hidden drow supporters.
His sponsor Jarlaxle grows more ambitious, and Entreri struggles to
remain cautious and in control. The power of the Crystal Shard grows
greater than them both, threatening to draw them into a vast web of
treachery from which there will be no escape.

Promise of the Witch-King
The Sellswords, Book II

Entreri and Jarlaxle might be strangers in the rugged, unforgiving
mountains of the Bloodstone Lands, but they have been in difficult places
before. Caught between the ghost of a power-mad lich, and the righteous
fury of an oath-bound knight, they have never felt more at home.

Now Available

For more information visit **www.wizards.com**

THE NEW ADVENTURES

A Practical Guide to Dragons
By Sindri Suncatcher

Sindri Suncatcher—wizard's apprentice—opens up
his personal notebooks to share his knowledge of these
awe-inspiring creatures, from the life cycle of a kind copper
dragon to the best way to counteract a red dragon's fiery
breath. This lavishly illustrated guide showcases the wide
array of fantastic dragons encountered on the world of Krynn.

The perfect companion to the Dragonlance: The New
Adventures series, for both loyal fans and new readers alike.

Sindri Suncatcher is a three-and-a-half foot tall kender,
who enjoys storytelling, collecting magical tokens, and
fighting dragons. He lives in Solamnia and is currently
studying magic under the auspices of the black-robed
wizard Maddoc. You can catch Sindri in the midst of
his latest adventure in *The Wayward Wizard*.

For more information visit www.mirrorstonebooks.com

For ages ten and up.